Archie
FRESHMAN YEAR®
BOOK TWO

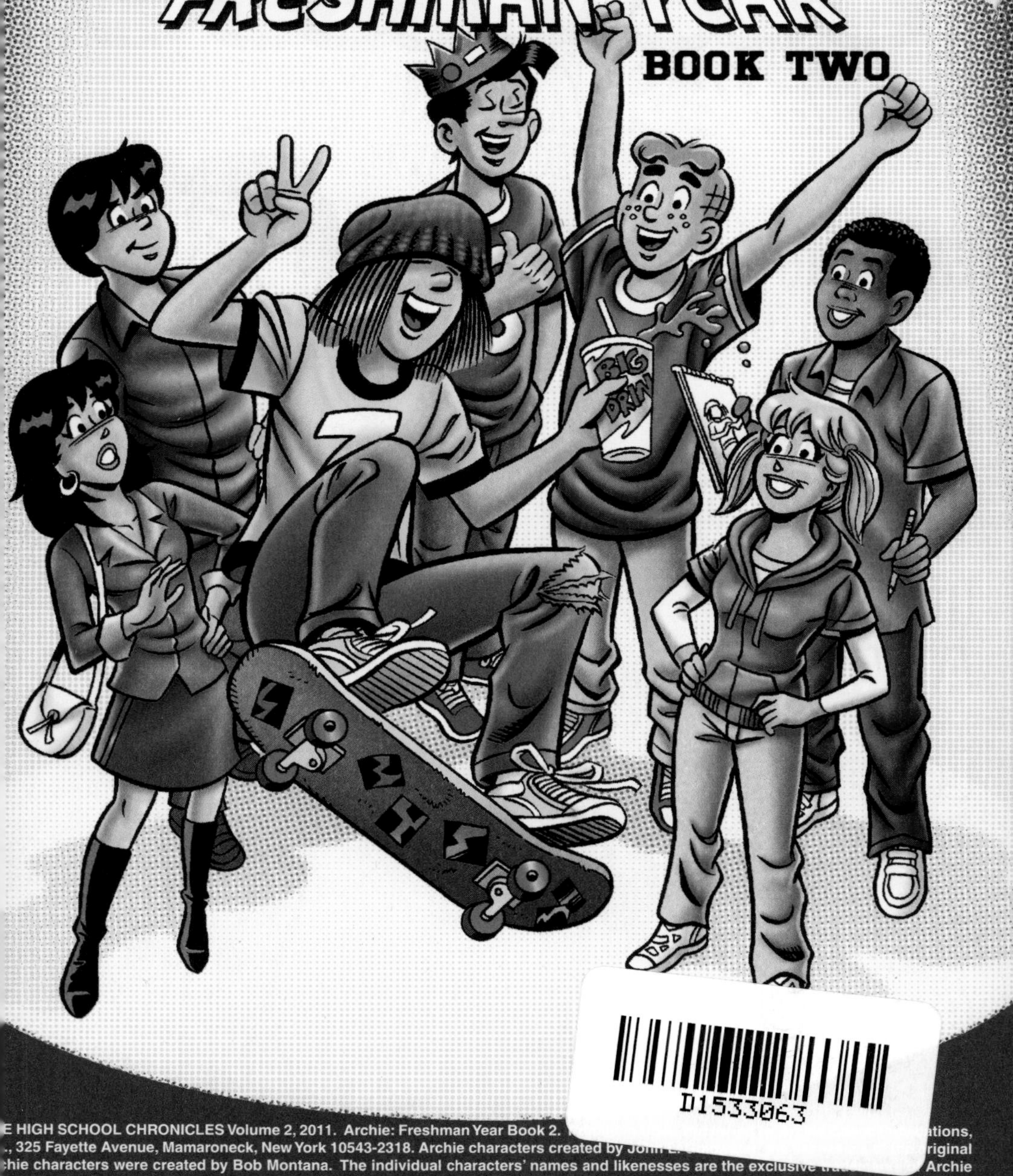

E HIGH SCHOOL CHRONICLES Volume 2, 2011. Archie: Freshman Year Book 2. ations,
., 325 Fayette Avenue, Mamaroneck, New York 10543-2318. Archie characters created by John riginal
hie characters were created by Bob Montana. The individual characters' names and likenesses are the exclusive Archie
mic Publications, Inc. All stories previously published and copyrighted by Archie Comic Publications, Inc. (or its predecessors) in
gazine form in 2010. This compilation copyright © 2011 Archie Comic Publications, Inc. All rights reserved. Nothing may be reprinted in
ole or part without written permission from Archie Comic Publications, Inc. ISBN: 978-1-879794-71-9

Archie

FRESHMAN YEAR

BOOK TWO

Written by
Batton Lash

Penciled by
Bill Galvan

Inked by
Al Milgrom

Lettered by
Jack Morelli

Colored by
Glenn Whitmore

Co-CEO: Jon Goldwater, Co-CEO: Nancy Silberkleit, President: Mike Pellerito,
Co-President/Editor-In-Chief: Victor Gorelick, Director of Circulation: Bill Horan,
Executive Director of Publishing/Operations: Harold Buchholz,
Executive Director of Publicity & Marketing: Alex Segura,
Project Coordinator: Joe Morciglio, Production Manager: Stephen Oswald,
Production: Paul Kaminski, Tito Peña, Jon Gray, Pat Woodruff & Duncan McLachlan

THE MISSING CHAPTERS: PART 1

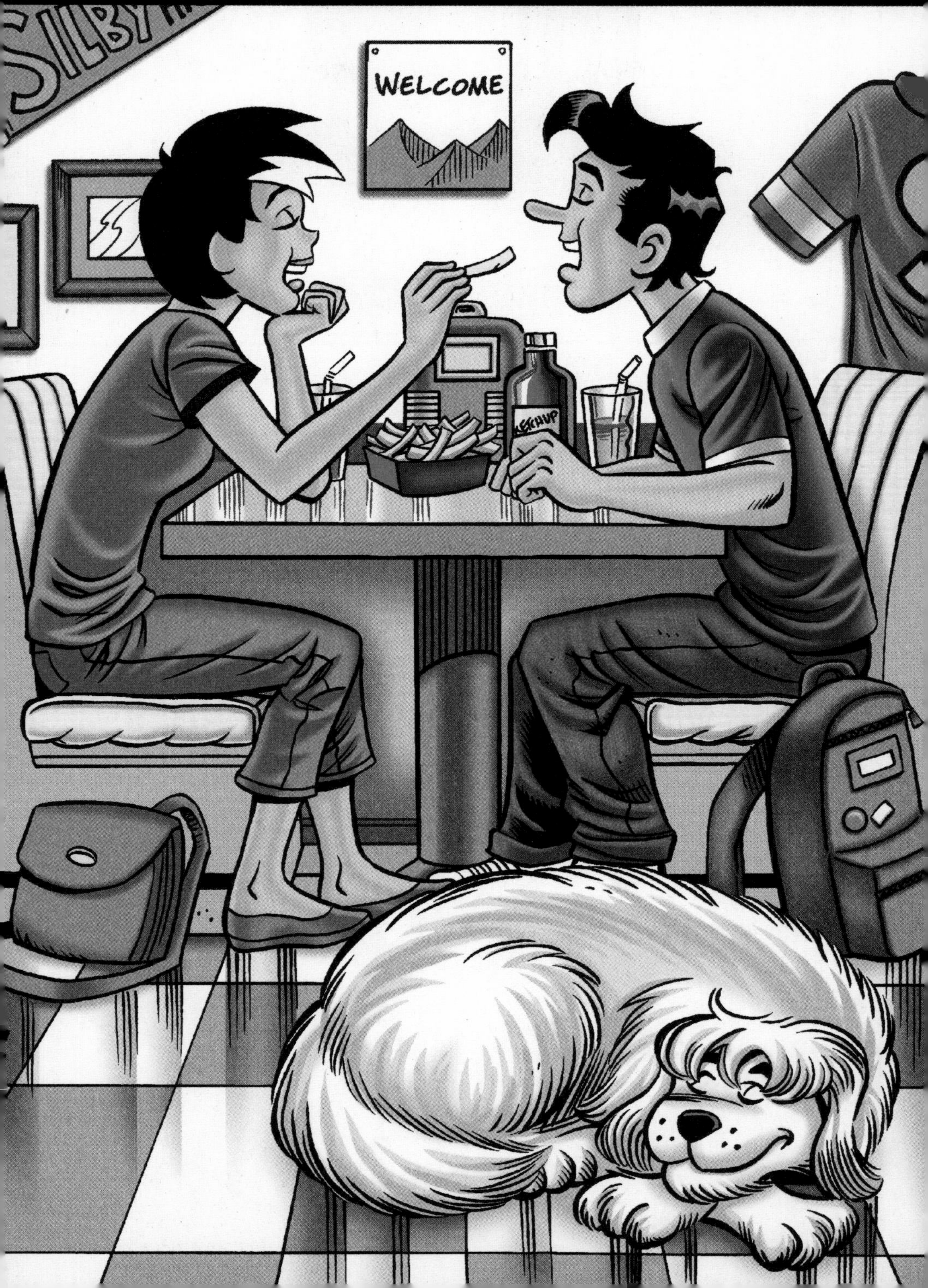
WELCOME
KETCHUP

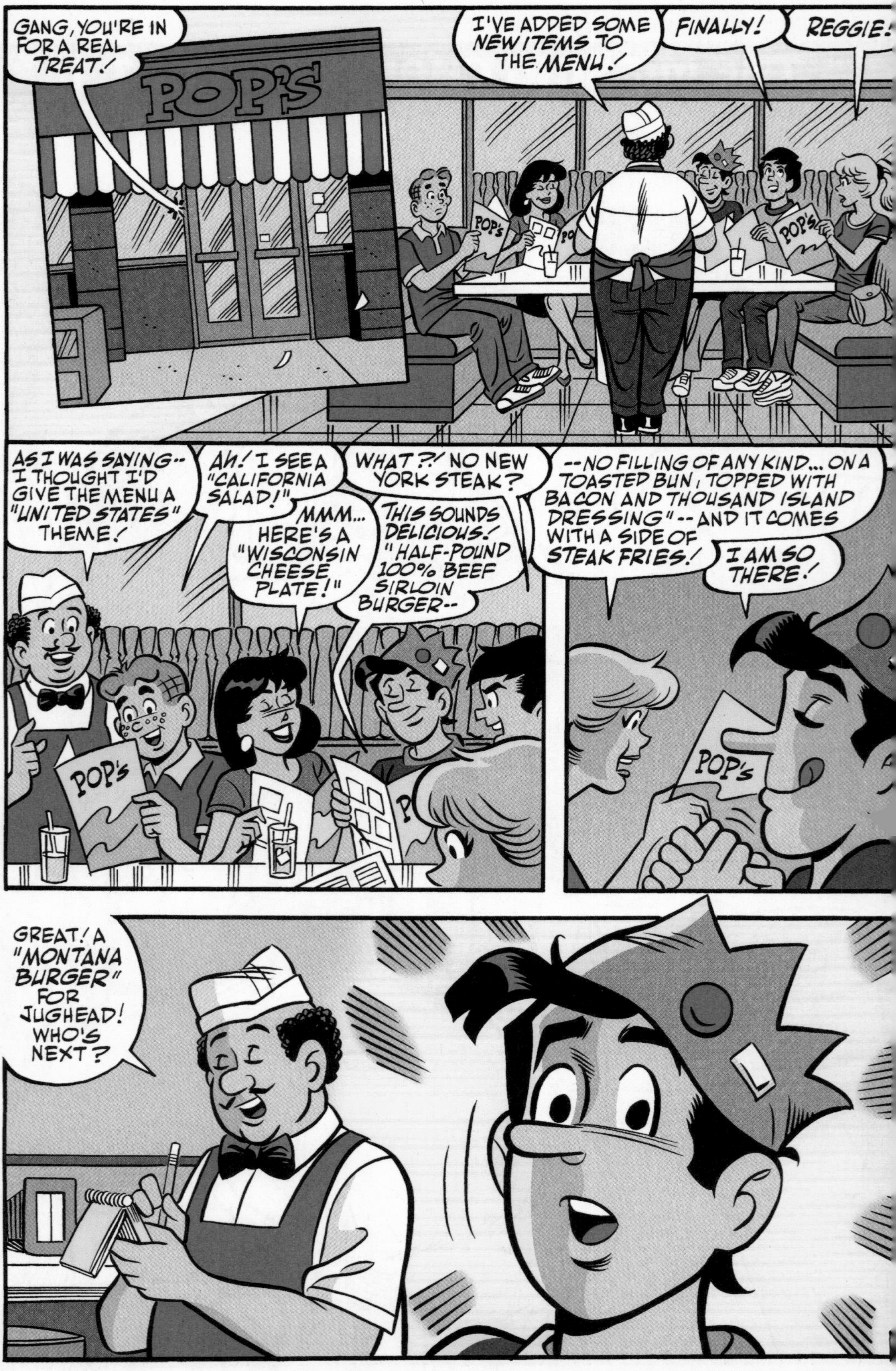
GANG, YOU'RE IN FOR A REAL TREAT!
POP'S
I'VE ADDED SOME NEW ITEMS TO THE MENU!
FINALLY!
REGGIE!
AS I WAS SAYING-- I THOUGHT I'D GIVE THE MENU A "UNITED STATES" THEME!
AH! I SEE A "CALIFORNIA SALAD!"
MMM... HERE'S A "WISCONSIN CHEESE PLATE!"
WHAT?! NO NEW YORK STEAK?
THIS SOUNDS DELICIOUS! "HALF-POUND 100% BEEF SIRLOIN BURGER--
--NO FILLING OF ANY KIND... ON A TOASTED BUN, TOPPED WITH BACON AND THOUSAND ISLAND DRESSING" -- AND IT COMES WITH A SIDE OF STEAK FRIES!
I AM SO THERE!
GREAT! A "MONTANA BURGER" FOR JUGHEAD! WHO'S NEXT?

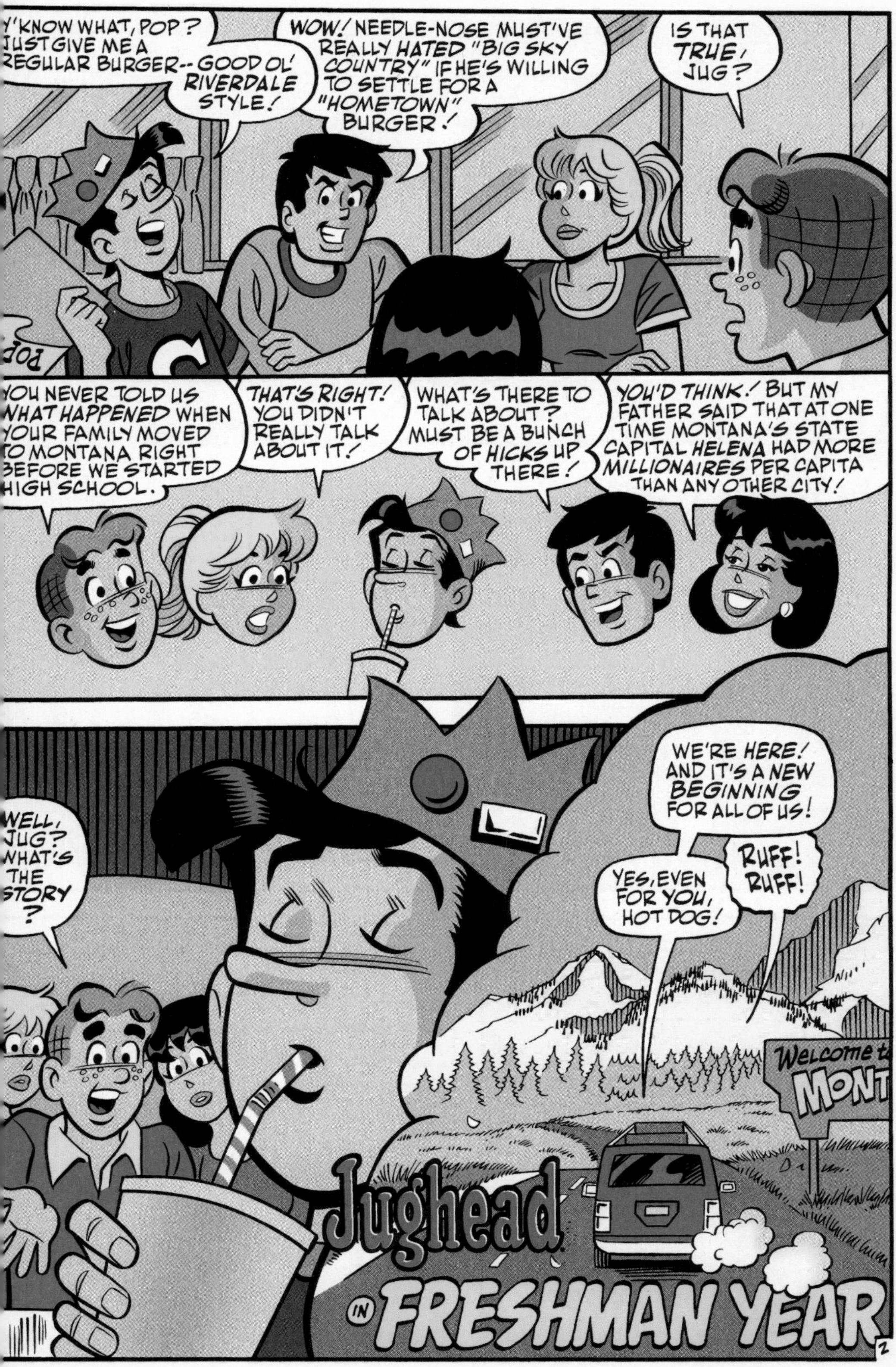
Y'KNOW WHAT, POP? JUST GIVE ME A REGULAR BURGER-- GOOD OL' RIVERDALE STYLE!
WOW! NEEDLE-NOSE MUST'VE REALLY HATED "BIG SKY COUNTRY" IF HE'S WILLING TO SETTLE FOR A "HOMETOWN" BURGER!
IS THAT TRUE, JUG?
POP
YOU NEVER TOLD US WHAT HAPPENED WHEN YOUR FAMILY MOVED TO MONTANA RIGHT BEFORE WE STARTED HIGH SCHOOL.
THAT'S RIGHT! YOU DIDN'T REALLY TALK ABOUT IT!
WHAT'S THERE TO TALK ABOUT? MUST BE A BUNCH OF HICKS UP THERE!
YOU'D THINK! BUT MY FATHER SAID THAT AT ONE TIME MONTANA'S STATE CAPITAL HELENA HAD MORE MILLIONAIRES PER CAPITA THAN ANY OTHER CITY!
WELL, JUG? WHAT'S THE STORY?
WE'RE HERE! AND IT'S A NEW BEGINNING FOR ALL OF US!
YES, EVEN FOR YOU, HOT DOG!
RUFF! RUFF!
Welcome t
MONT
Jughead
IN
FRESHMAN YEAR

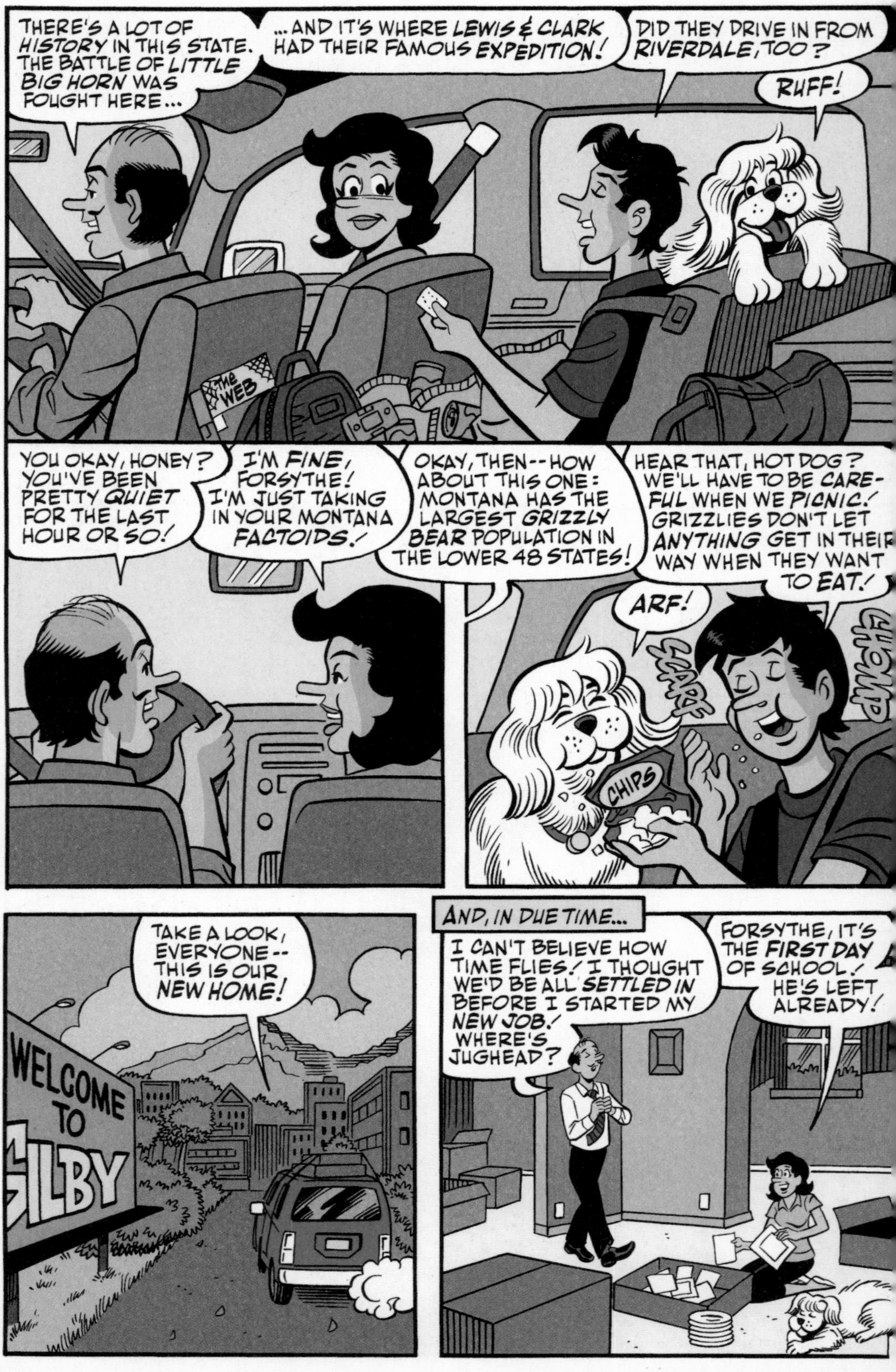
THERE'S A LOT OF HISTORY IN THIS STATE. THE BATTLE OF LITTLE BIG HORN WAS FOUGHT HERE...
...AND IT'S WHERE LEWIS & CLARK HAD THEIR FAMOUS EXPEDITION!
DID THEY DRIVE IN FROM RIVERDALE, TOO?
RUFF!
THE WEB
YOU OKAY, HONEY? YOU'VE BEEN PRETTY QUIET FOR THE LAST HOUR OR SO!
I'M FINE, FORSYTHE! I'M JUST TAKING IN YOUR MONTANA FACTOIDS!
OKAY, THEN--HOW ABOUT THIS ONE: MONTANA HAS THE LARGEST GRIZZLY BEAR POPULATION IN THE LOWER 48 STATES!
HEAR THAT, HOT DOG? WE'LL HAVE TO BE CAREFUL WHEN WE PICNIC! GRIZZLIES DON'T LET ANYTHING GET IN THEIR WAY WHEN THEY WANT TO EAT!
ARF!
SCARF
CHOMP
CHIPS
TAKE A LOOK, EVERYONE--THIS IS OUR NEW HOME!
WELCOME TO GILBY
AND, IN DUE TIME...
I CAN'T BELIEVE HOW TIME FLIES! I THOUGHT WE'D BE ALL SETTLED IN BEFORE I STARTED MY NEW JOB! WHERE'S JUGHEAD?
FORSYTHE, IT'S THE FIRST DAY OF SCHOOL! HE'S LEFT ALREADY!

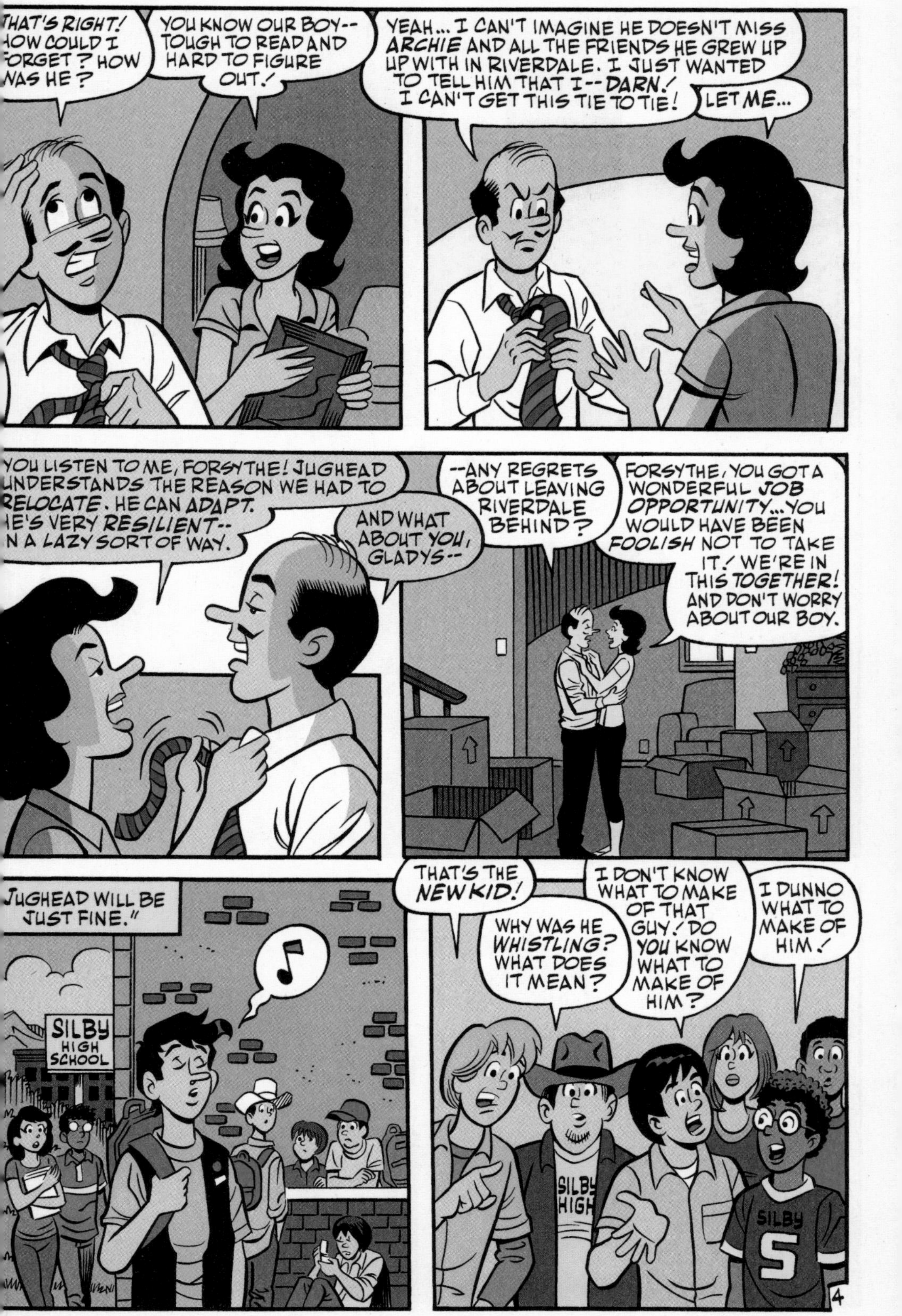
THAT'S RIGHT! HOW COULD I FORGET? HOW WAS HE?
YOU KNOW OUR BOY-- TOUGH TO READ AND HARD TO FIGURE OUT!
YEAH... I CAN'T IMAGINE HE DOESN'T MISS ARCHIE AND ALL THE FRIENDS HE GREW UP UP WITH IN RIVERDALE. I JUST WANTED TO TELL HIM THAT I-- DARN! I CAN'T GET THIS TIE TO TIE!
LET ME...
YOU LISTEN TO ME, FORSYTHE! JUGHEAD UNDERSTANDS THE REASON WE HAD TO RELOCATE. HE CAN ADAPT. HE'S VERY RESILIENT-- IN A LAZY SORT OF WAY.
AND WHAT ABOUT YOU, GLADYS--
--ANY REGRETS ABOUT LEAVING RIVERDALE BEHIND?
FORSYTHE, YOU GOT A WONDERFUL JOB OPPORTUNITY... YOU WOULD HAVE BEEN FOOLISH NOT TO TAKE IT! WE'RE IN THIS TOGETHER! AND DON'T WORRY ABOUT OUR BOY.
JUGHEAD WILL BE JUST FINE."
SILBY HIGH SCHOOL
THAT'S THE NEW KID!
WHY WAS HE WHISTLING? WHAT DOES IT MEAN?
I DON'T KNOW WHAT TO MAKE OF THAT GUY! DO YOU KNOW WHAT TO MAKE OF HIM?
I DUNNO WHAT TO MAKE OF HIM!
SILBY HIGH
SILBY 5
4

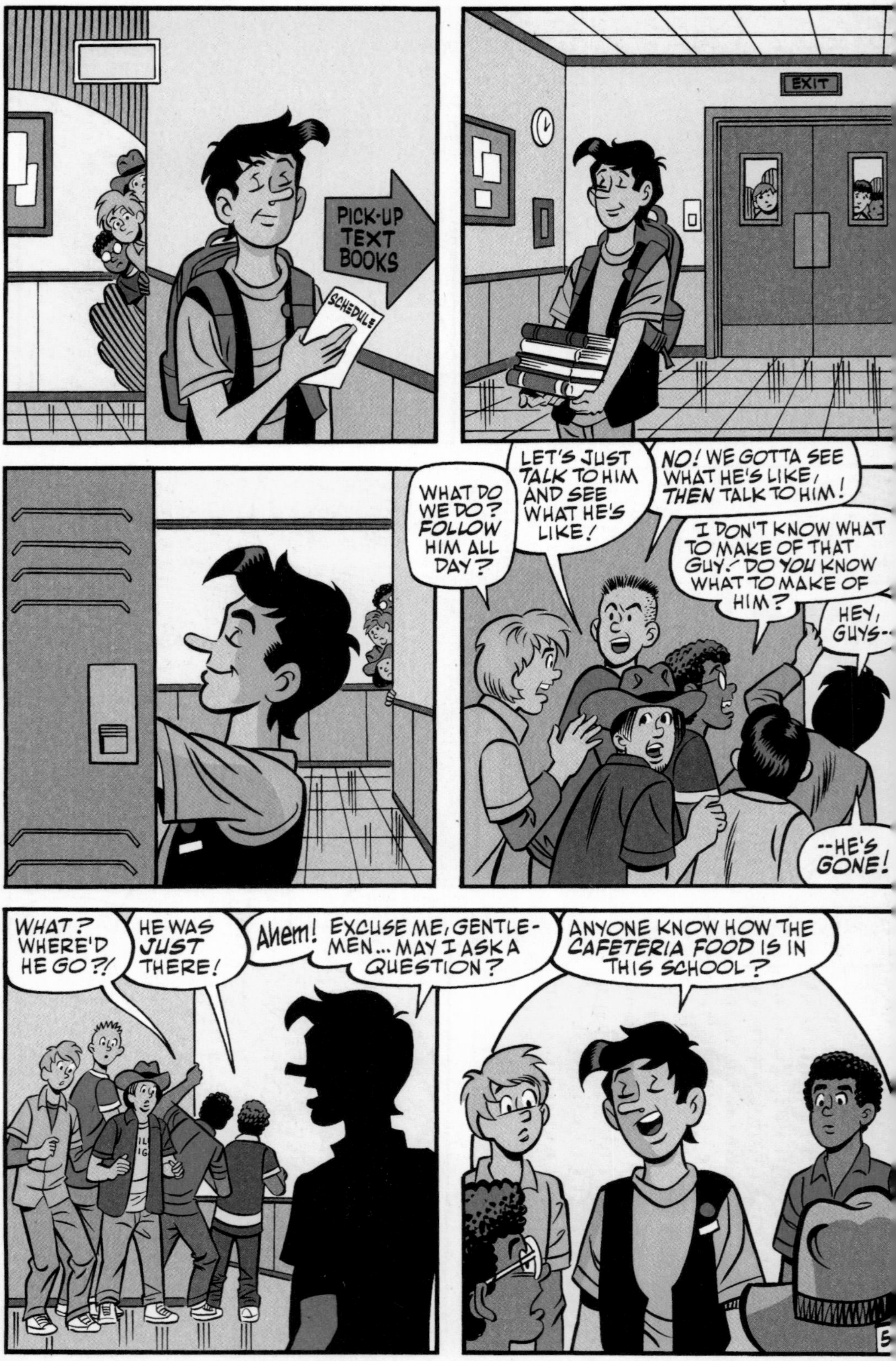
PICK-UP TEXT BOOKS
SCHEDULE
EXIT
WHAT DO WE DO? FOLLOW HIM ALL DAY?
LET'S JUST TALK TO HIM AND SEE WHAT HE'S LIKE!
NO! WE GOTTA SEE WHAT HE'S LIKE, THEN TALK TO HIM!
I DON'T KNOW WHAT TO MAKE OF THAT GUY. DO YOU KNOW WHAT TO MAKE OF HIM?
HEY, GUYS--
--HE'S GONE!
WHAT? WHERE'D HE GO?!
HE WAS JUST THERE!
Ahem! EXCUSE ME, GENTLEMEN... MAY I ASK A QUESTION?
ANYONE KNOW HOW THE CAFETERIA FOOD IS IN THIS SCHOOL?
5

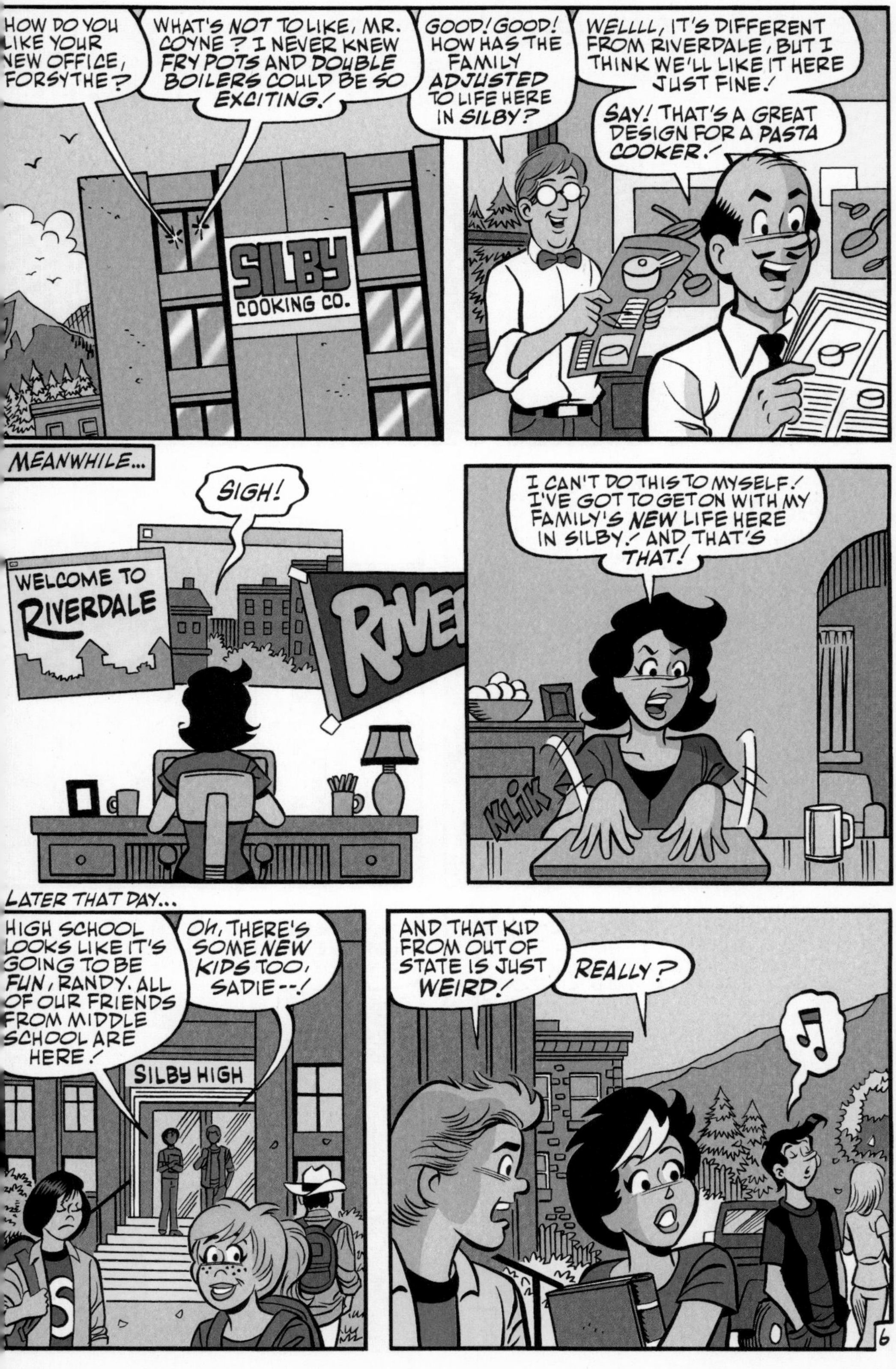
HOW DO YOU LIKE YOUR NEW OFFICE, FORSYTHE?
WHAT'S NOT TO LIKE, MR. COYNE? I NEVER KNEW FRY POTS AND DOUBLE BOILERS COULD BE SO EXCITING!
SILBY COOKING CO.
GOOD! GOOD! HOW HAS THE FAMILY ADJUSTED TO LIFE HERE IN SILBY?
WELLLL, IT'S DIFFERENT FROM RIVERDALE, BUT I THINK WE'LL LIKE IT HERE JUST FINE!
SAY! THAT'S A GREAT DESIGN FOR A PASTA COOKER!
MEANWHILE...
SIGH!
WELCOME TO RIVERDALE
RIVER
I CAN'T DO THIS TO MYSELF! I'VE GOT TO GET ON WITH MY FAMILY'S NEW LIFE HERE IN SILBY! AND THAT'S THAT!
KLIK
LATER THAT DAY...
HIGH SCHOOL LOOKS LIKE IT'S GOING TO BE FUN, RANDY. ALL OF OUR FRIENDS FROM MIDDLE SCHOOL ARE HERE!
Oh, THERE'S SOME NEW KIDS TOO, SADIE--!
SILBY HIGH
AND THAT KID FROM OUT OF STATE IS JUST WEIRD!
REALLY?

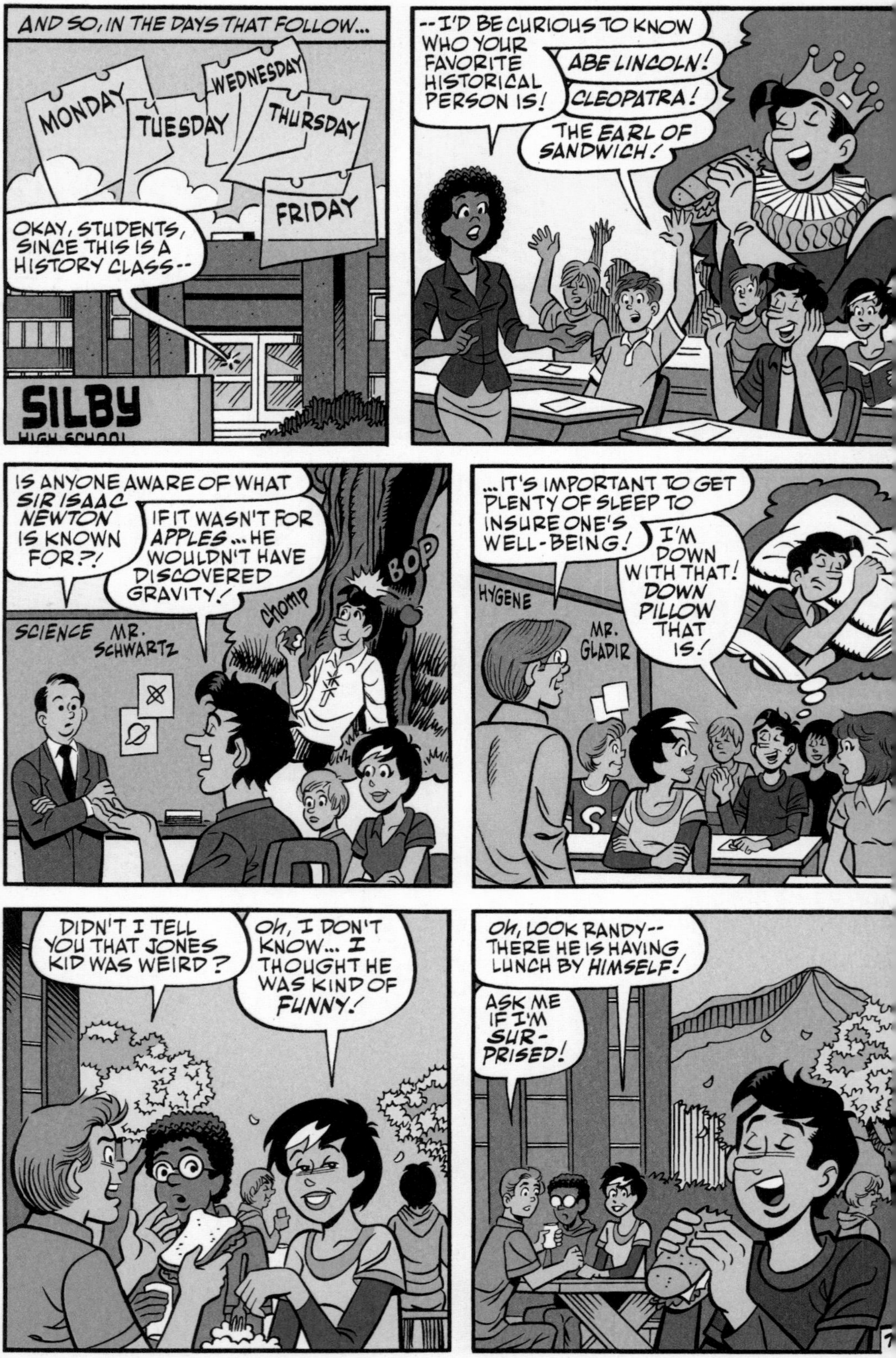
AND SO, IN THE DAYS THAT FOLLOW...
MONDAY
TUESDAY
WEDNESDAY
THURSDAY
FRIDAY
OKAY, STUDENTS, SINCE THIS IS A HISTORY CLASS--
SILBY
--I'D BE CURIOUS TO KNOW WHO YOUR FAVORITE HISTORICAL PERSON IS!
ABE LINCOLN!
CLEOPATRA!
THE EARL OF SANDWICH!
IS ANYONE AWARE OF WHAT SIR ISAAC NEWTON IS KNOWN FOR?!
IF IT WASN'T FOR APPLES... HE WOULDN'T HAVE DISCOVERED GRAVITY!
BOP
CHOMP
SCIENCE MR. SCHWARTZ
...IT'S IMPORTANT TO GET PLENTY OF SLEEP TO INSURE ONE'S WELL-BEING!
I'M DOWN WITH THAT! DOWN PILLOW THAT IS!
HYGENE
MR. GLADIR
DIDN'T I TELL YOU THAT JONES KID WAS WEIRD?
Oh, I DON'T KNOW... I THOUGHT HE WAS KIND OF FUNNY!
Oh, LOOK RANDY-- THERE HE IS HAVING LUNCH BY HIMSELF!
ASK ME IF I'M SUR-PRISED!

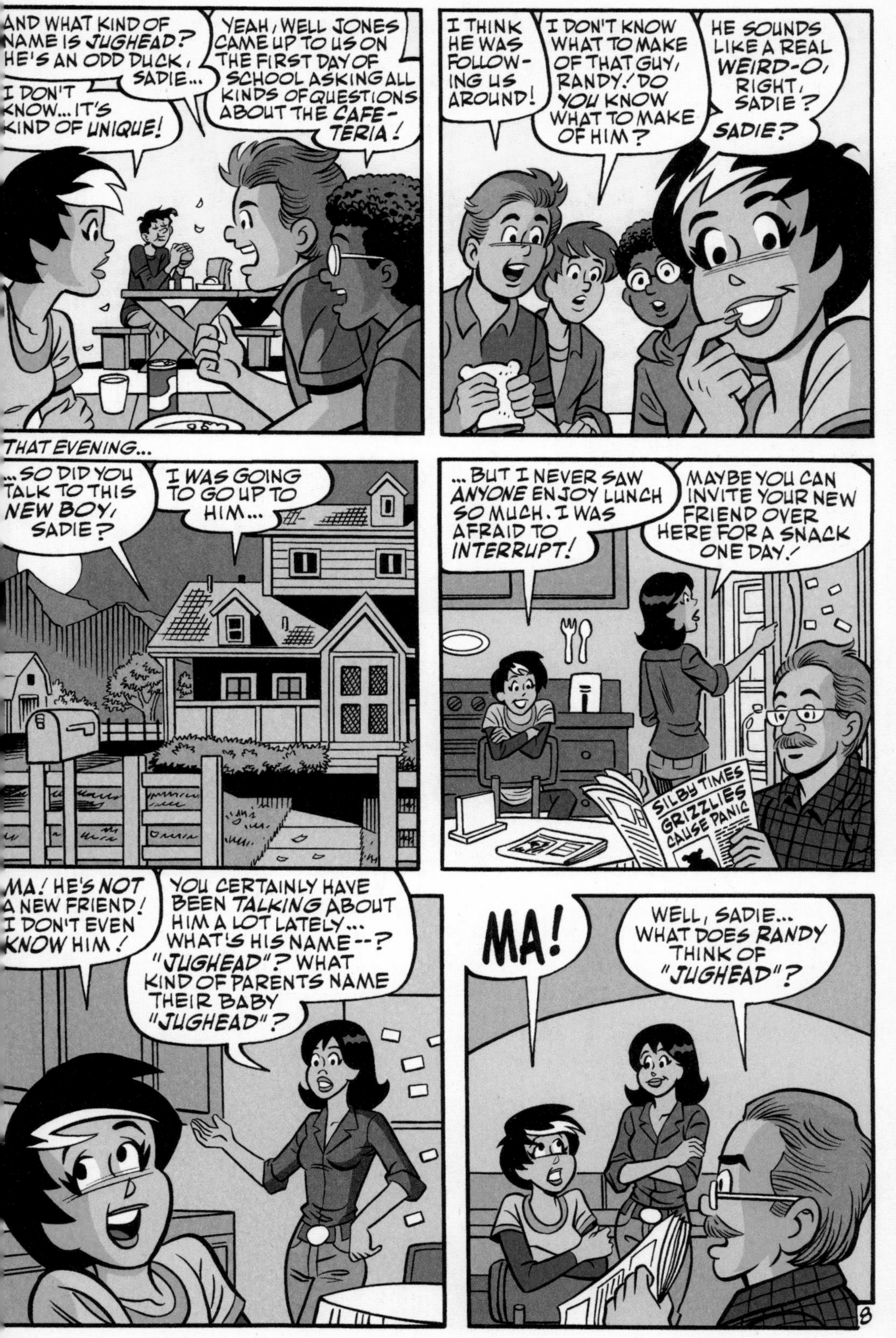
AND WHAT KIND OF NAME IS JUGHEAD? HE'S AN ODD DUCK, SADIE...
I DON'T KNOW... IT'S KIND OF UNIQUE!
YEAH, WELL JONES CAME UP TO US ON THE FIRST DAY OF SCHOOL ASKING ALL KINDS OF QUESTIONS ABOUT THE CAFE-TERIA!
I THINK HE WAS FOLLOW-ING US AROUND!
I DON'T KNOW WHAT TO MAKE OF THAT GUY, RANDY! DO YOU KNOW WHAT TO MAKE OF HIM?
HE SOUNDS LIKE A REAL WEIRD-O, RIGHT, SADIE?
SADIE?
THAT EVENING...
...SO DID YOU TALK TO THIS NEW BOY, SADIE?
I WAS GOING TO GO UP TO HIM...
...BUT I NEVER SAW ANYONE ENJOY LUNCH SO MUCH. I WAS AFRAID TO INTERRUPT!
MAYBE YOU CAN INVITE YOUR NEW FRIEND OVER HERE FOR A SNACK ONE DAY!
SILBY TIMES
GRIZZLIES CAUSE PANIC
MA! HE'S NOT A NEW FRIEND! I DON'T EVEN KNOW HIM!
YOU CERTAINLY HAVE BEEN TALKING ABOUT HIM A LOT LATELY... WHAT'S HIS NAME--? "JUGHEAD"? WHAT KIND OF PARENTS NAME THEIR BABY "JUGHEAD"?
MA!
WELL, SADIE... WHAT DOES RANDY THINK OF "JUGHEAD"?

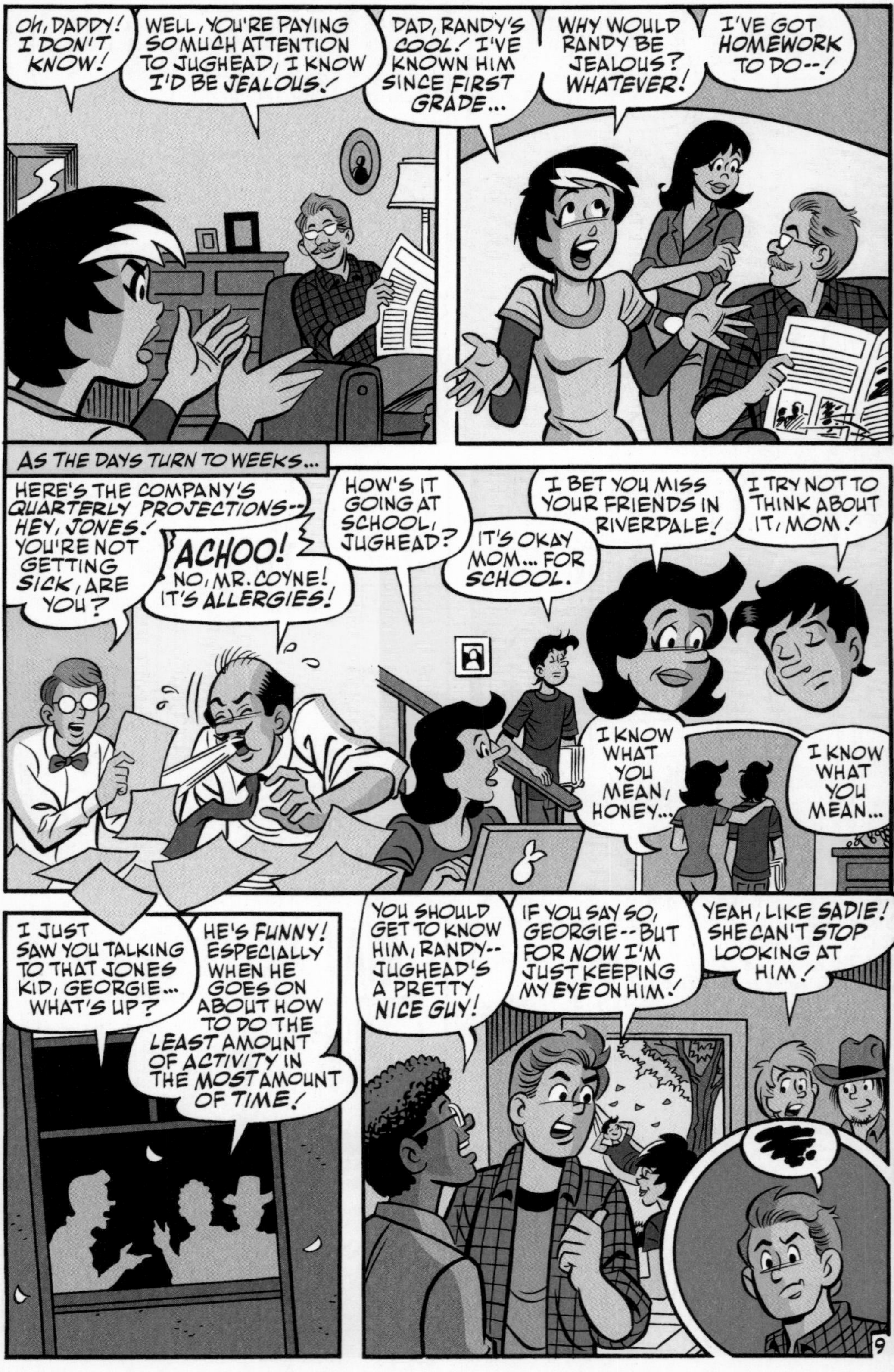
OH, DADDY! I DON'T KNOW!
WELL, YOU'RE PAYING SO MUCH ATTENTION TO JUGHEAD, I KNOW I'D BE JEALOUS!
DAD, RANDY'S COOL! I'VE KNOWN HIM SINCE FIRST GRADE...
WHY WOULD RANDY BE JEALOUS? WHATEVER!
I'VE GOT HOMEWORK TO DO--!
AS THE DAYS TURN TO WEEKS...
HERE'S THE COMPANY'S QUARTERLY PROJECTIONS-- HEY, JONES! YOU'RE NOT GETTING SICK, ARE YOU?
ACHOO! NO, MR. COYNE! IT'S ALLERGIES!
HOW'S IT GOING AT SCHOOL, JUGHEAD?
IT'S OKAY MOM... FOR SCHOOL.
I BET YOU MISS YOUR FRIENDS IN RIVERDALE!
I TRY NOT TO THINK ABOUT IT, MOM!
I KNOW WHAT YOU MEAN, HONEY...
I KNOW WHAT YOU MEAN...
I JUST SAW YOU TALKING TO THAT JONES KID, GEORGIE... WHAT'S UP?
HE'S FUNNY! ESPECIALLY WHEN HE GOES ON ABOUT HOW TO DO THE LEAST AMOUNT OF ACTIVITY IN THE MOST AMOUNT OF TIME!
YOU SHOULD GET TO KNOW HIM, RANDY-- JUGHEAD'S A PRETTY NICE GUY!
IF YOU SAY SO, GEORGIE-- BUT FOR NOW I'M JUST KEEPING MY EYE ON HIM!
YEAH, LIKE SADIE! SHE CAN'T STOP LOOKING AT HIM!

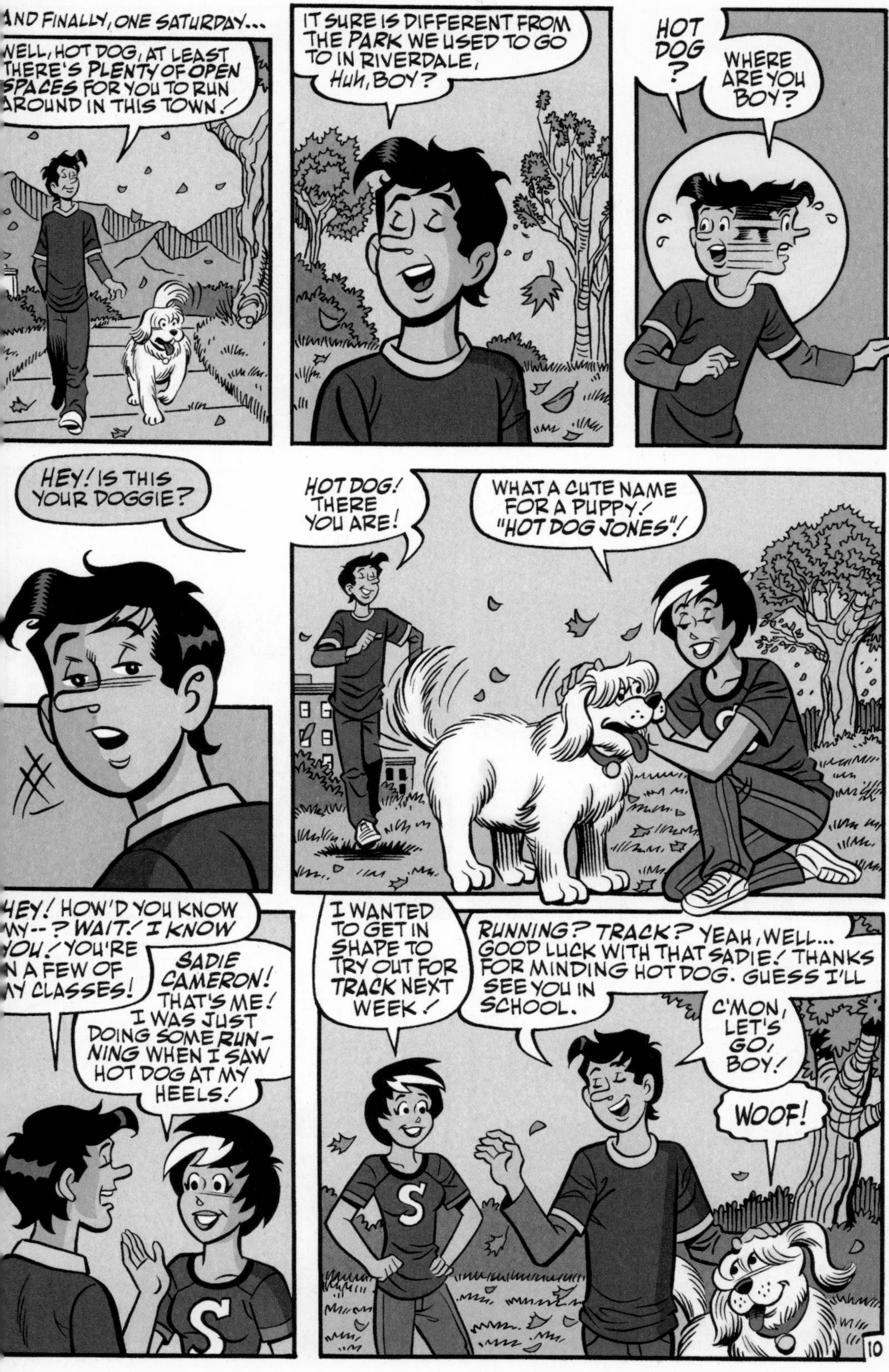

AND FINALLY, ONE SATURDAY...
WELL, HOT DOG, AT LEAST THERE'S PLENTY OF OPEN SPACES FOR YOU TO RUN AROUND IN THIS TOWN!
IT SURE IS DIFFERENT FROM THE PARK WE USED TO GO TO IN RIVERDALE, HUH, BOY?
HOT DOG?
WHERE ARE YOU BOY?
HEY! IS THIS YOUR DOGGIE?
HOT DOG! THERE YOU ARE!
WHAT A CUTE NAME FOR A PUPPY! "HOT DOG JONES"!
HEY! HOW'D YOU KNOW MY--? WAIT! I KNOW YOU! YOU'RE IN A FEW OF MY CLASSES!
SADIE CAMERON! THAT'S ME! I WAS JUST DOING SOME RUNNING WHEN I SAW HOT DOG AT MY HEELS!
I WANTED TO GET IN SHAPE TO TRY OUT FOR TRACK NEXT WEEK!
RUNNING? TRACK? YEAH, WELL... GOOD LUCK WITH THAT SADIE! THANKS FOR MINDING HOT DOG. GUESS I'LL SEE YOU IN SCHOOL.
C'MON, LET'S GO, BOY!
WOOF!

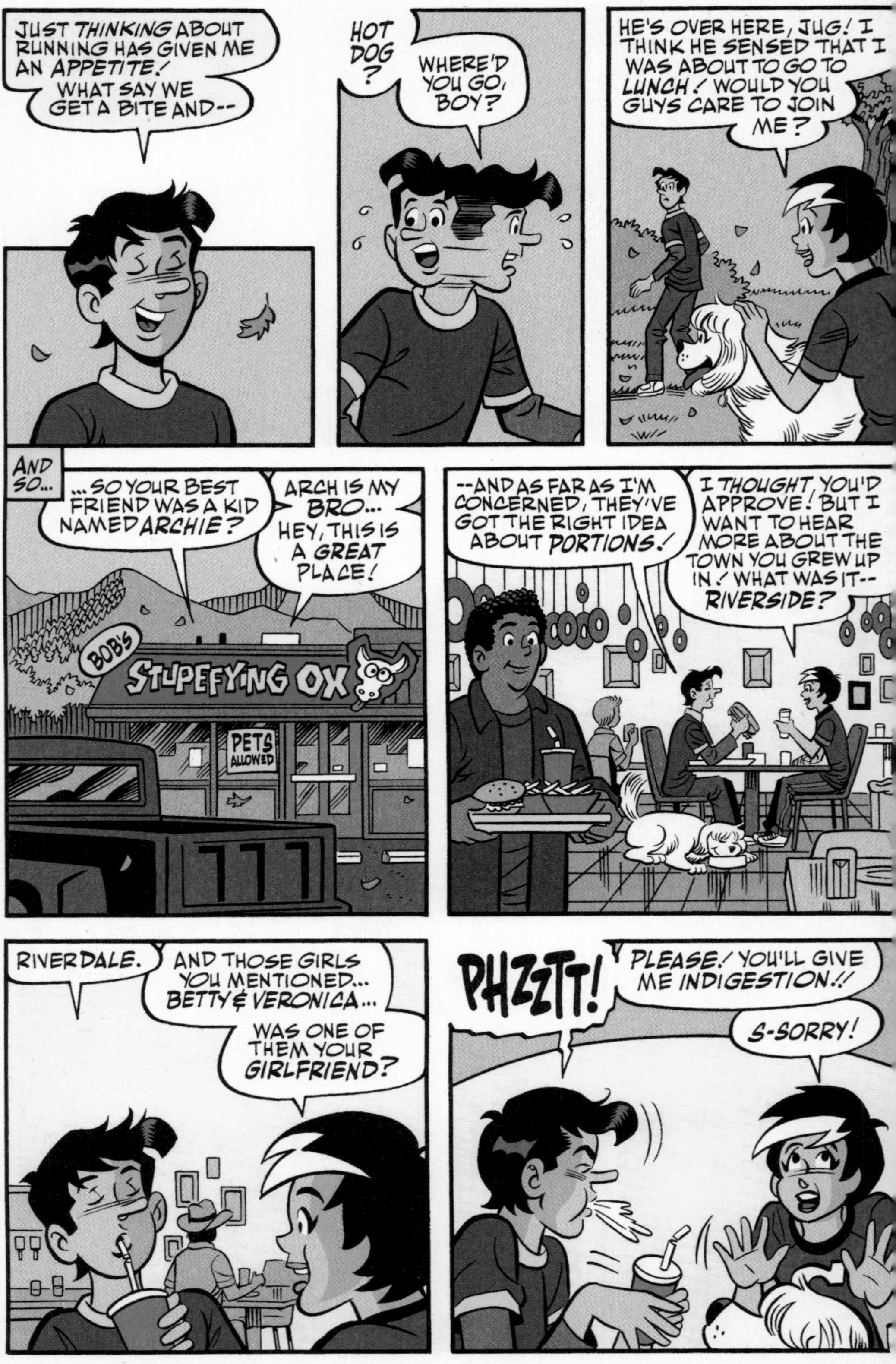
JUST THINKING ABOUT RUNNING HAS GIVEN ME AN APPETITE!
WHAT SAY WE GET A BITE AND--
HOT DOG?
WHERE'D YOU GO, BOY?
HE'S OVER HERE, JUG! I THINK HE SENSED THAT I WAS ABOUT TO GO TO LUNCH! WOULD YOU GUYS CARE TO JOIN ME?
AND SO...
...SO YOUR BEST FRIEND WAS A KID NAMED ARCHIE?
ARCH IS MY BRO...
HEY, THIS IS A GREAT PLACE!
BOB'S
STUPEFYING OX
PETS ALLOWED
--AND AS FAR AS I'M CONCERNED, THEY'VE GOT THE RIGHT IDEA ABOUT PORTIONS!
I THOUGHT YOU'D APPROVE! BUT I WANT TO HEAR MORE ABOUT THE TOWN YOU GREW UP IN! WHAT WAS IT-- RIVERSIDE?
RIVERDALE.
AND THOSE GIRLS YOU MENTIONED... BETTY & VERONICA...
WAS ONE OF THEM YOUR GIRLFRIEND?
PHZZTT!
PLEASE! YOU'LL GIVE ME INDIGESTION!!
S-SORRY!

Panel 1: DON'T GET ME WRONG-- BETTY AND VERONICA ARE GREAT GALS. BUT THEY'RE FRIENDS... AND ONLY FRIENDS!

OKAY, BUT STILL-- YOU *GREW UP* WITH THEM! ARCHIE, TOO! YOU MUST *MISS* THEM ALL!

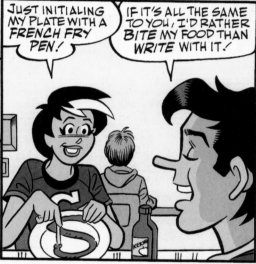

Panel 2: YEAH, WELL I CAN'T THINK *TOO MUCH* OF THE *PAST*...

...NOT WHILE I'M SPENDING ALL MY TIME IN THE *PRESENT!*

Panel 3: I *ADMIRE* THAT ATTITUDE, JUG... BUT *GEE!* I CAN'T *IMAGINE* MOVING AWAY FROM SILBY... I'D MISS TOO MUCH! THERE'S A *LOT* OF KIDS IN SCHOOL I'VE KNOWN FOR AS *LONG* AS I CAN REMEMBER! LIKE RANDY STONE! DID YOU EVER MEET HIM?-- HE'S IN SOME OF YOUR CLASSES!

OH, YEAH-- I KNOW *WHO* HE IS, BUT WE HAVEN'T-- *HEY!* WHAT DO YOU THINK YOU'RE DOING?

Panel 4: JUST INITIALING MY PLATE WITH A *FRENCH FRY PEN!*

IF IT'S ALL THE SAME TO YOU, I'D RATHER *BITE* MY FOOD THAN *WRITE* WITH IT!

Panel 5: THEN *HERE*-- I'LL SHARE MY "*PEN*" WITH YOU!

MMM... THE "*PEN*" IS TASTIER THAN THE SWORD!

Panel 6: HOLD ON--YOU'VE GOT "*INK*" ALL OVER YOUR FACE!

I DON'T KNOW WHAT TO MAKE OF THAT GUY! DO *YOU* KNOW WHAT TO MAKE OF HIM?

NO... BUT I *DO* KNOW *RANDY* AIN'T GONNA LIKE THIS!

12

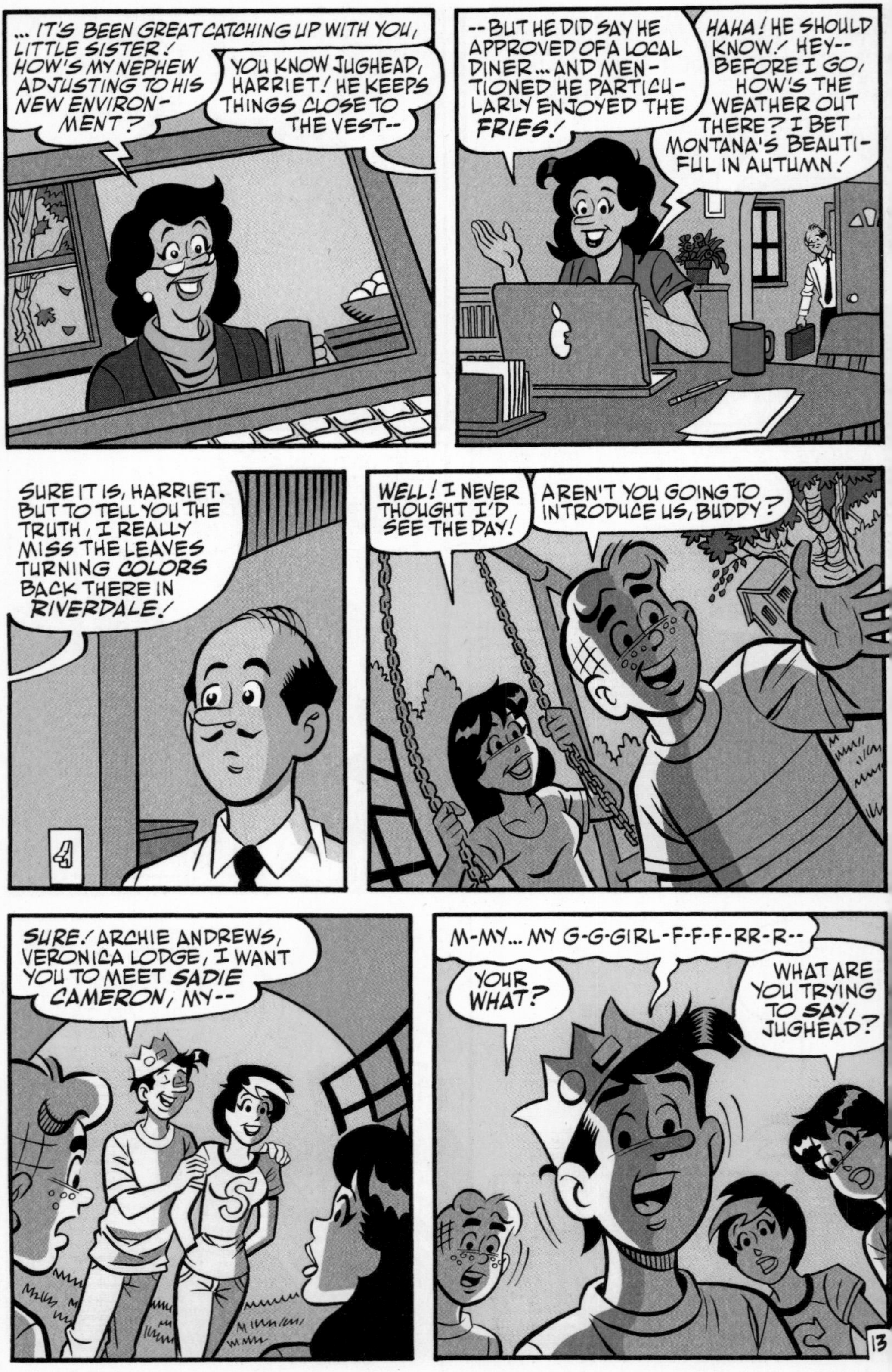
... IT'S BEEN GREAT CATCHING UP WITH YOU, LITTLE SISTER! HOW'S MY NEPHEW ADJUSTING TO HIS NEW ENVIRONMENT?
YOU KNOW JUGHEAD, HARRIET! HE KEEPS THINGS CLOSE TO THE VEST--
--BUT HE DID SAY HE APPROVED OF A LOCAL DINER... AND MENTIONED HE PARTICULARLY ENJOYED THE FRIES!
HAHA! HE SHOULD KNOW! HEY-- BEFORE I GO, HOW'S THE WEATHER OUT THERE? I BET MONTANA'S BEAUTIFUL IN AUTUMN!
SURE IT IS, HARRIET. BUT TO TELL YOU THE TRUTH, I REALLY MISS THE LEAVES TURNING COLORS BACK THERE IN RIVERDALE!
WELL! I NEVER THOUGHT I'D SEE THE DAY!
AREN'T YOU GOING TO INTRODUCE US, BUDDY?
SURE! ARCHIE ANDREWS, VERONICA LODGE, I WANT YOU TO MEET SADIE CAMERON, MY--
M-MY... MY G-G-GIRL-F-F-F-RR-R--
YOUR WHAT?
WHAT ARE YOU TRYING TO SAY, JUGHEAD?

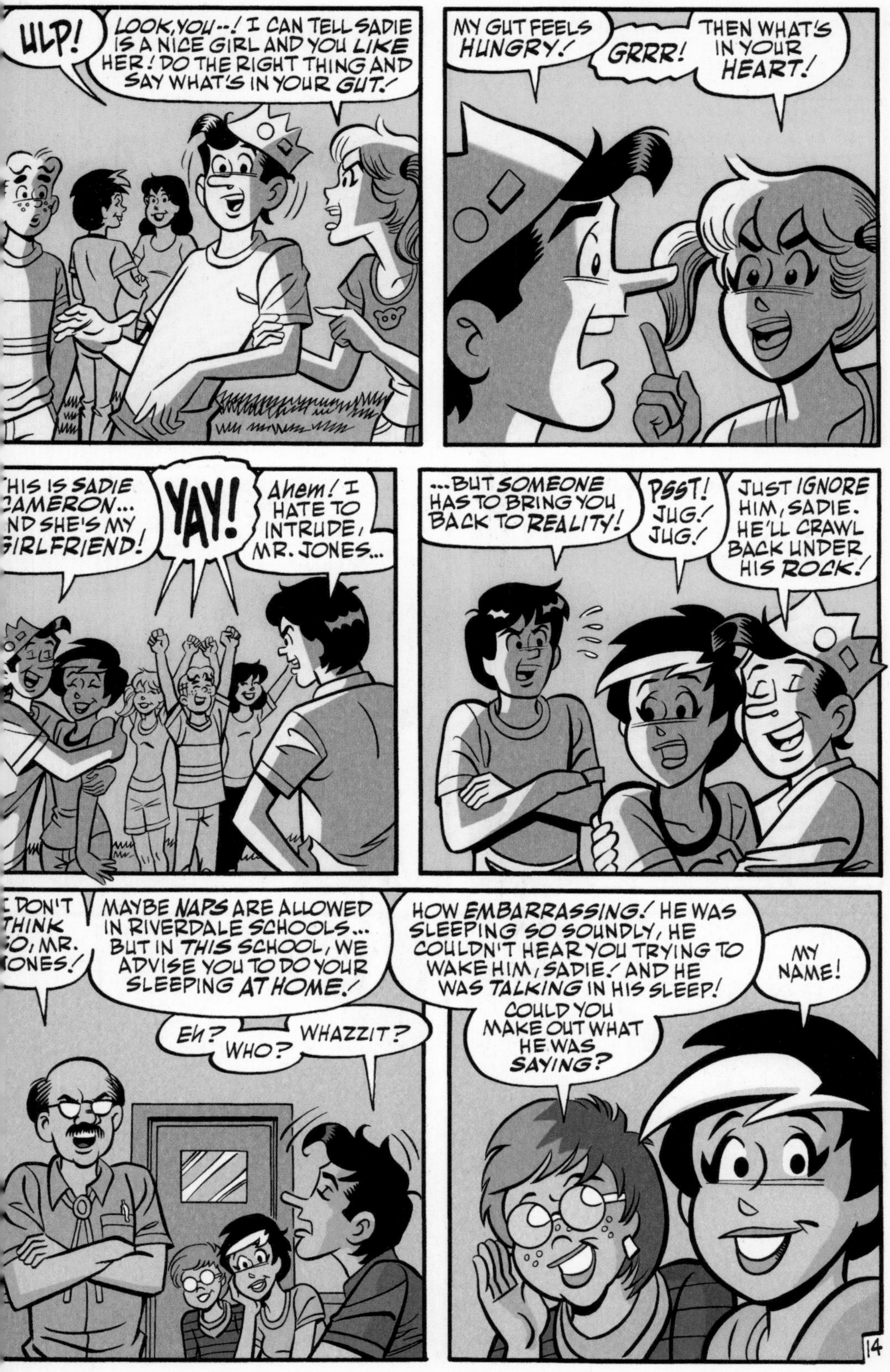

ULP!
LOOK, YOU--! I CAN TELL SADIE IS A NICE GIRL AND YOU LIKE HER! DO THE RIGHT THING AND SAY WHAT'S IN YOUR GUT!
MY GUT FEELS HUNGRY!
GRRR!
THEN WHAT'S IN YOUR HEART!
THIS IS SADIE CAMERON... ND SHE'S MY GIRLFRIEND!
YAY!
Ahem! I HATE TO INTRUDE, MR. JONES...
...BUT SOMEONE HAS TO BRING YOU BACK TO REALITY!
PSST! JUG! JUG!
JUST IGNORE HIM, SADIE. HE'LL CRAWL BACK UNDER HIS ROCK!
DON'T THINK SO, MR. JONES!
MAYBE NAPS ARE ALLOWED IN RIVERDALE SCHOOLS... BUT IN THIS SCHOOL, WE ADVISE YOU TO DO YOUR SLEEPING AT HOME!
EH? WHO? WHAZZIT?
HOW EMBARRASSING! HE WAS SLEEPING SO SOUNDLY, HE COULDN'T HEAR YOU TRYING TO WAKE HIM, SADIE! AND HE WAS TALKING IN HIS SLEEP!
COULD YOU MAKE OUT WHAT HE WAS SAYING?
MY NAME!
14

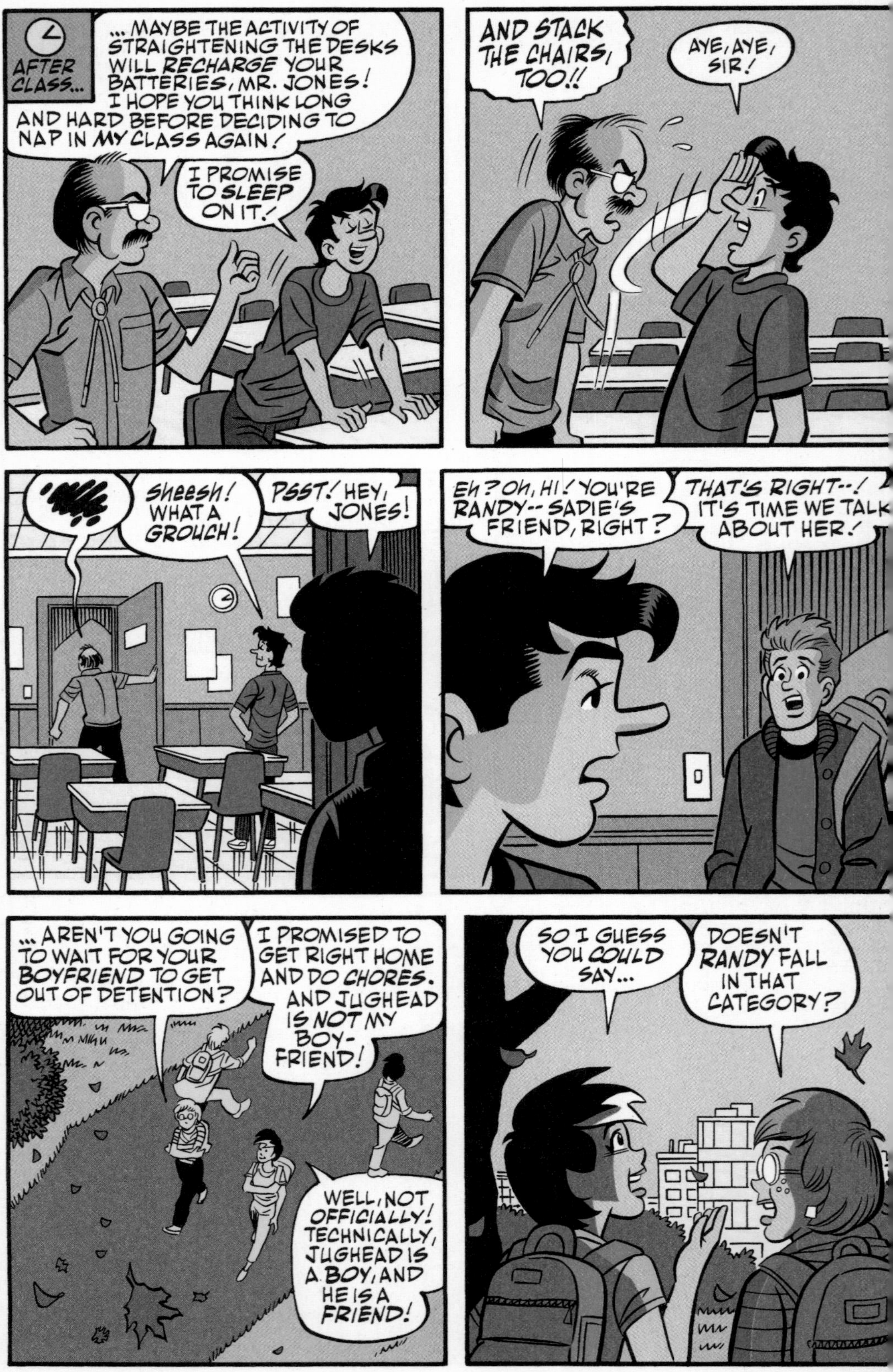
AFTER CLASS...
... MAYBE THE ACTIVITY OF STRAIGHTENING THE DESKS WILL RECHARGE YOUR BATTERIES, MR. JONES! I HOPE YOU THINK LONG AND HARD BEFORE DECIDING TO NAP IN MY CLASS AGAIN!
I PROMISE TO SLEEP ON IT!
AND STACK THE CHAIRS, TOO!!
AYE, AYE, SIR!
SHEESH! WHAT A GROUCH!
PSST! HEY, JONES!
EH? OH, HI! YOU'RE RANDY-- SADIE'S FRIEND, RIGHT?
THAT'S RIGHT--! IT'S TIME WE TALK ABOUT HER!
... AREN'T YOU GOING TO WAIT FOR YOUR BOYFRIEND TO GET OUT OF DETENTION?
I PROMISED TO GET RIGHT HOME AND DO CHORES. AND JUGHEAD IS NOT MY BOY-FRIEND!
WELL, NOT OFFICIALLY! TECHNICALLY, JUGHEAD IS A BOY, AND HE IS A FRIEND!
SO I GUESS YOU COULD SAY...
DOESN'T RANDY FALL IN THAT CATEGORY?

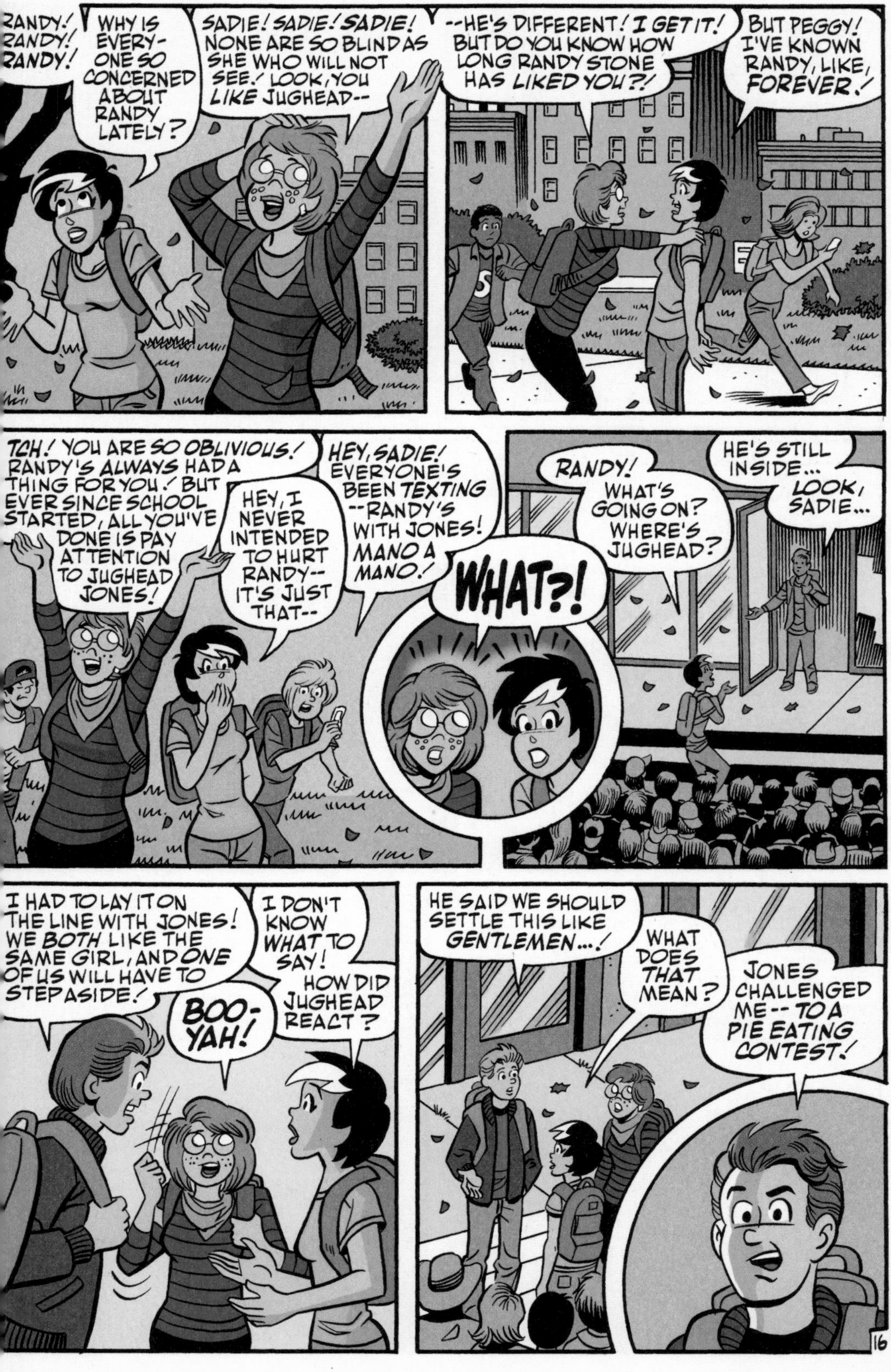
RANDY! RANDY! RANDY!
WHY IS EVERY-ONE SO CONCERNED ABOUT RANDY LATELY?
SADIE! SADIE! SADIE! NONE ARE SO BLIND AS SHE WHO WILL NOT SEE! LOOK, YOU LIKE JUGHEAD--
--HE'S DIFFERENT! I GET IT! BUT DO YOU KNOW HOW LONG RANDY STONE HAS LIKED YOU?!
BUT PEGGY! I'VE KNOWN RANDY, LIKE, FOREVER!
TCH! YOU ARE SO OBLIVIOUS! RANDY'S ALWAYS HAD A THING FOR YOU! BUT EVER SINCE SCHOOL STARTED, ALL YOU'VE DONE IS PAY ATTENTION TO JUGHEAD JONES!
HEY, I NEVER INTENDED TO HURT RANDY-- IT'S JUST THAT--
HEY, SADIE! EVERYONE'S BEEN TEXTING --RANDY'S WITH JONES! MANO A MANO!
WHAT?!
RANDY! WHAT'S GOING ON? WHERE'S JUGHEAD?
HE'S STILL INSIDE... LOOK, SADIE...
I HAD TO LAY IT ON THE LINE WITH JONES! WE BOTH LIKE THE SAME GIRL, AND ONE OF US WILL HAVE TO STEP ASIDE!
BOO-YAH!
I DON'T KNOW WHAT TO SAY! HOW DID JUGHEAD REACT?
HE SAID WE SHOULD SETTLE THIS LIKE GENTLEMEN...!
WHAT DOES THAT MEAN?
JONES CHALLENGED ME-- TO A PIE EATING CONTEST!

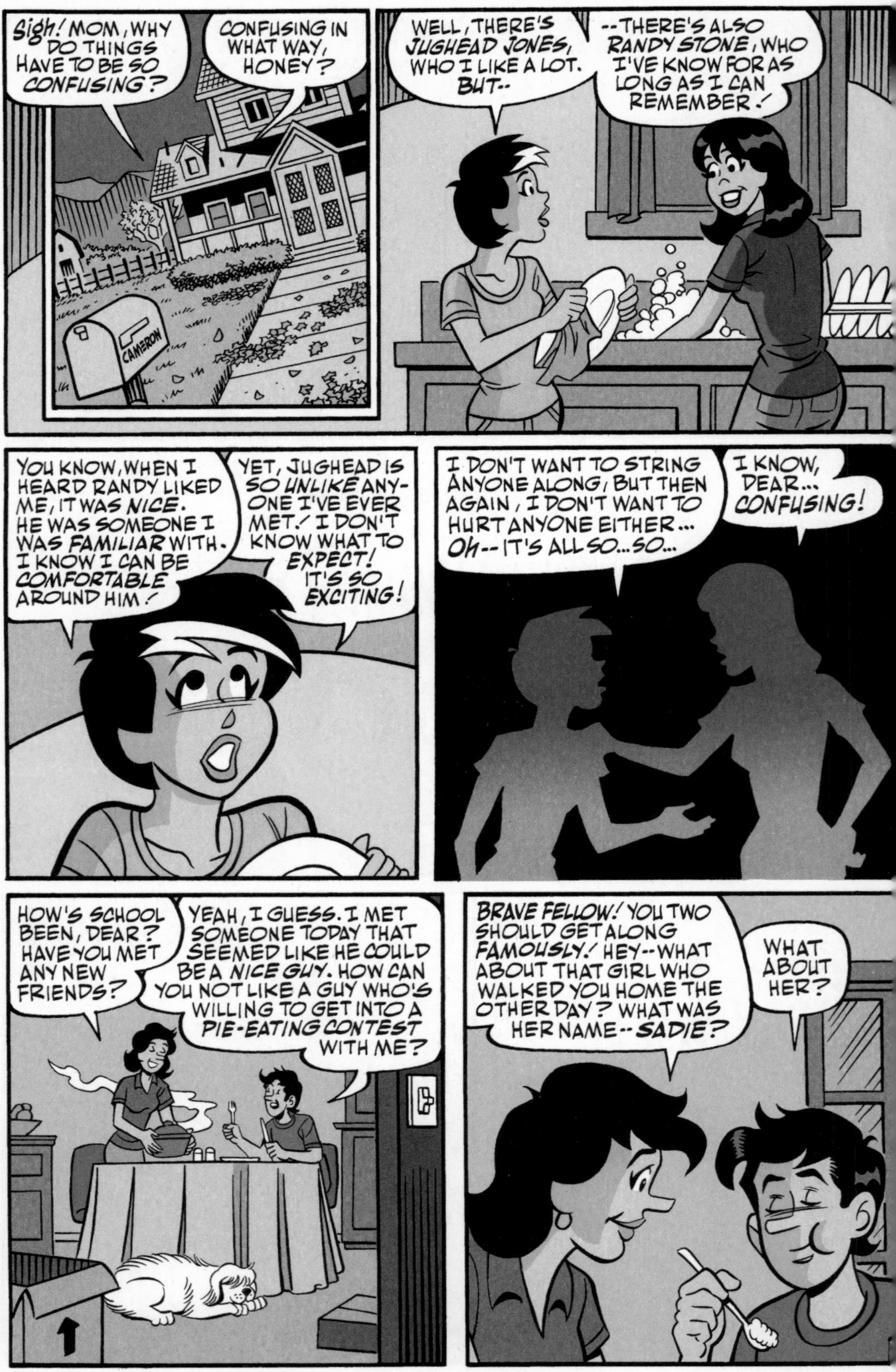

Sigh! MOM, WHY DO THINGS HAVE TO BE SO CONFUSING?
CONFUSING IN WHAT WAY, HONEY?
CAMERON
WELL, THERE'S JUGHEAD JONES, WHO I LIKE A LOT. BUT--
--THERE'S ALSO RANDY STONE, WHO I'VE KNOW FOR AS LONG AS I CAN REMEMBER!
YOU KNOW, WHEN I HEARD RANDY LIKED ME, IT WAS NICE. HE WAS SOMEONE I WAS FAMILIAR WITH. I KNOW I CAN BE COMFORTABLE AROUND HIM!
YET, JUGHEAD IS SO UNLIKE ANYONE I'VE EVER MET! I DON'T KNOW WHAT TO EXPECT! IT'S SO EXCITING!
I DON'T WANT TO STRING ANYONE ALONG, BUT THEN AGAIN, I DON'T WANT TO HURT ANYONE EITHER... Oh-- IT'S ALL SO...SO...
I KNOW, DEAR... CONFUSING!
HOW'S SCHOOL BEEN, DEAR? HAVE YOU MET ANY NEW FRIENDS?
YEAH, I GUESS. I MET SOMEONE TODAY THAT SEEMED LIKE HE COULD BE A NICE GUY. HOW CAN YOU NOT LIKE A GUY WHO'S WILLING TO GET INTO A PIE-EATING CONTEST WITH ME?
BRAVE FELLOW! YOU TWO SHOULD GET ALONG FAMOUSLY! HEY--WHAT ABOUT THAT GIRL WHO WALKED YOU HOME THE OTHER DAY? WHAT WAS HER NAME--SADIE?
WHAT ABOUT HER?

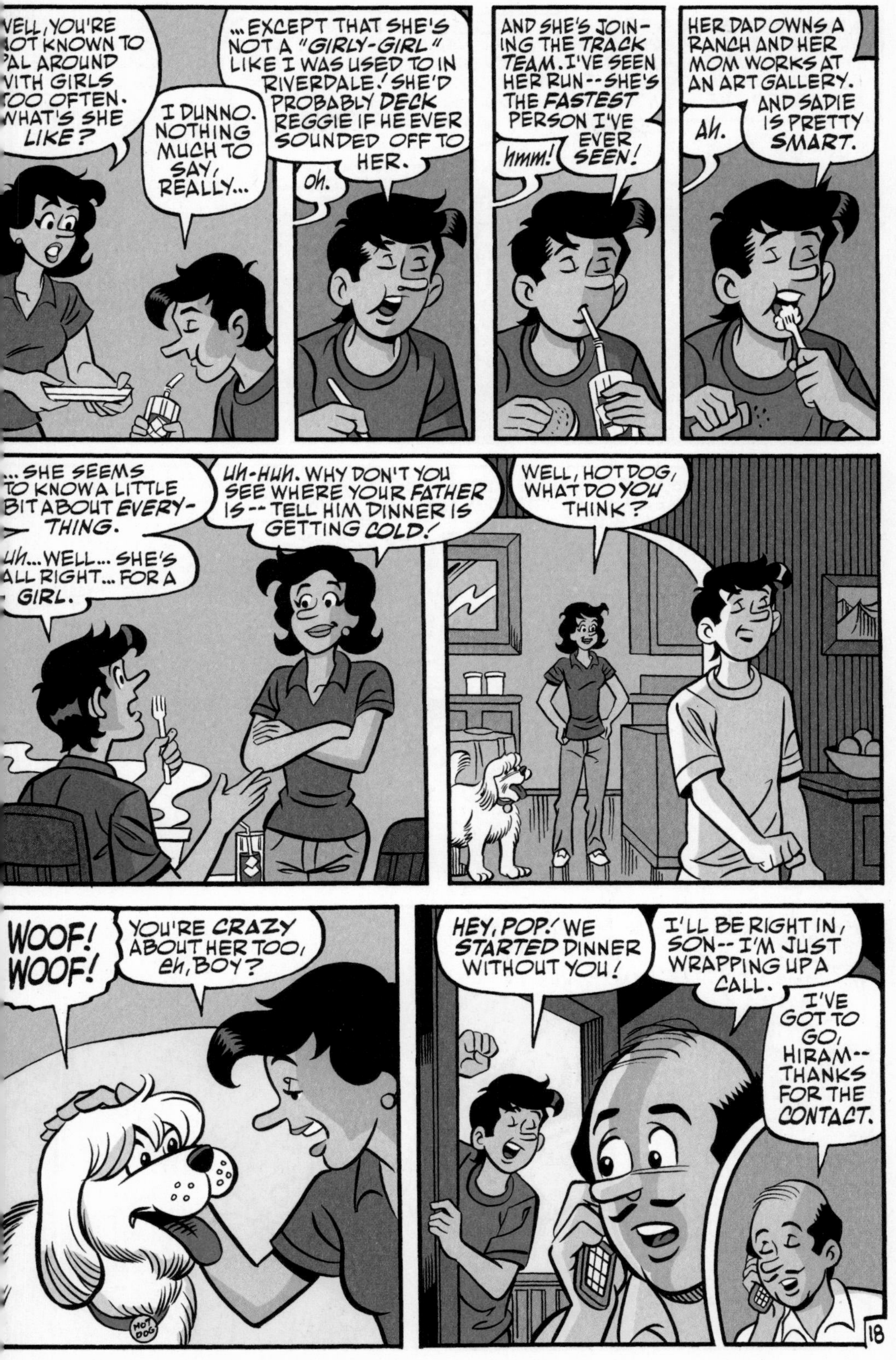
WELL, YOU'RE NOT KNOWN TO PAL AROUND WITH GIRLS TOO OFTEN. WHAT'S SHE LIKE?
I DUNNO. NOTHING MUCH TO SAY, REALLY...
...EXCEPT THAT SHE'S NOT A "GIRLY-GIRL" LIKE I WAS USED TO IN RIVERDALE! SHE'D PROBABLY DECK REGGIE IF HE EVER SOUNDED OFF TO HER.
OH.
AND SHE'S JOINING THE TRACK TEAM. I'VE SEEN HER RUN-- SHE'S THE FASTEST PERSON I'VE EVER SEEN!
HMM!
HER DAD OWNS A RANCH AND HER MOM WORKS AT AN ART GALLERY.
AH.
AND SADIE IS PRETTY SMART.
...SHE SEEMS TO KNOW A LITTLE BIT ABOUT EVERYTHING.
UH... WELL... SHE'S ALL RIGHT... FOR A GIRL.
UH-HUH. WHY DON'T YOU SEE WHERE YOUR FATHER IS -- TELL HIM DINNER IS GETTING COLD!
WELL, HOT DOG, WHAT DO YOU THINK?
WOOF! WOOF!
YOU'RE CRAZY ABOUT HER TOO, EH, BOY?
HOT DOG
HEY, POP! WE STARTED DINNER WITHOUT YOU!
I'LL BE RIGHT IN, SON-- I'M JUST WRAPPING UP A CALL.
I'VE GOT TO GO, HIRAM-- THANKS FOR THE CONTACT.

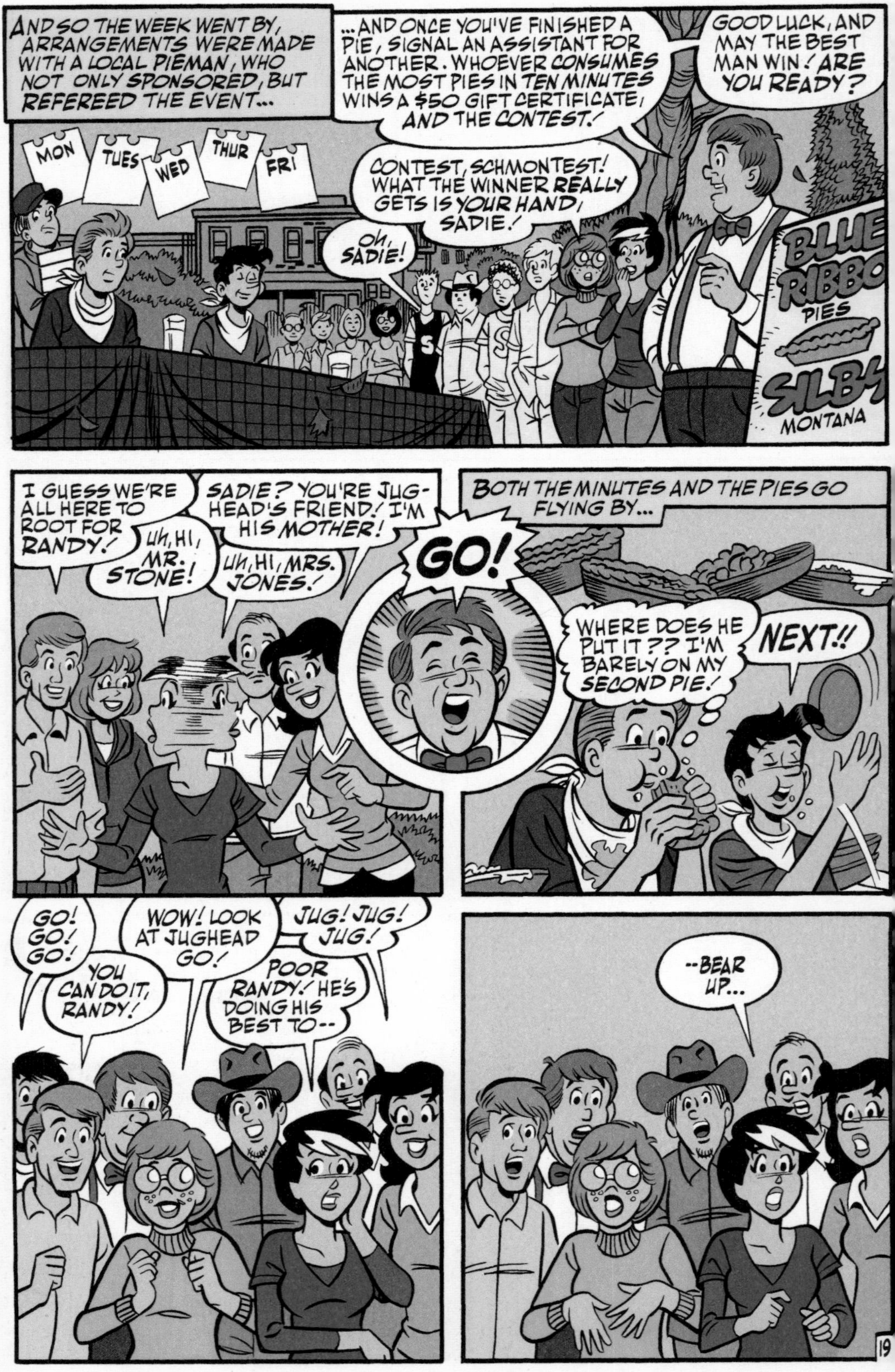
AND SO THE WEEK WENT BY, ARRANGEMENTS WERE MADE WITH A LOCAL PIEMAN, WHO NOT ONLY SPONSORED, BUT REFEREED THE EVENT...
...AND ONCE YOU'VE FINISHED A PIE, SIGNAL AN ASSISTANT FOR ANOTHER. WHOEVER CONSUMES THE MOST PIES IN TEN MINUTES WINS A $50 GIFT CERTIFICATE, AND THE CONTEST!
GOOD LUCK, AND MAY THE BEST MAN WIN! ARE YOU READY?
MON
TUES
WED
THUR
FRI
CONTEST, SCHMONTEST! WHAT THE WINNER REALLY GETS IS YOUR HAND, SADIE!
OH, SADIE!
BLUE RIBBO
PIES
SILBY
MONTANA
I GUESS WE'RE ALL HERE TO ROOT FOR RANDY!
UH, HI, MR. STONE!
SADIE? YOU'RE JUGHEAD'S FRIEND! I'M HIS MOTHER!
UH, HI, MRS. JONES!
GO!
BOTH THE MINUTES AND THE PIES GO FLYING BY...
WHERE DOES HE PUT IT?? I'M BARELY ON MY SECOND PIE!
NEXT!!
GO! GO! GO!
YOU CAN DO IT, RANDY!
WOW! LOOK AT JUGHEAD GO!
JUG! JUG! JUG!
POOR RANDY! HE'S DOING HIS BEST TO--
--BEAR UP...

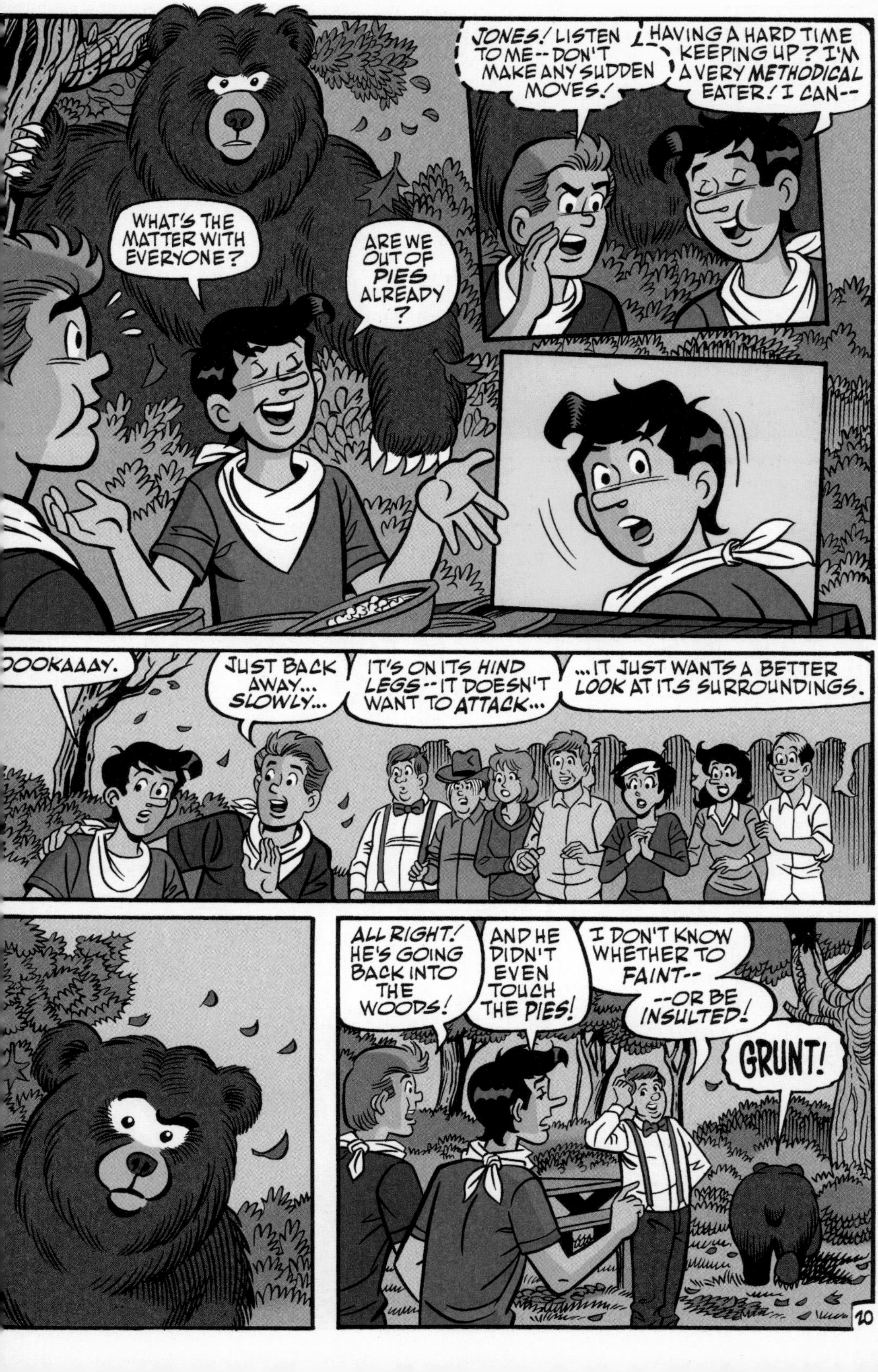
WHAT'S THE MATTER WITH EVERYONE?
ARE WE OUT OF PIES ALREADY?
JONES! LISTEN TO ME-- DON'T MAKE ANY SUDDEN MOVES!
HAVING A HARD TIME KEEPING UP? I'M A VERY METHODICAL EATER! I CAN--
OOOKAAAY.
JUST BACK AWAY... SLOWLY...
IT'S ON ITS HIND LEGS-- IT DOESN'T WANT TO ATTACK...
...IT JUST WANTS A BETTER LOOK AT ITS SURROUNDINGS.
ALL RIGHT! HE'S GOING BACK INTO THE WOODS!
AND HE DIDN'T EVEN TOUCH THE PIES!
I DON'T KNOW WHETHER TO FAINT--
--OR BE INSULTED!
GRUNT!

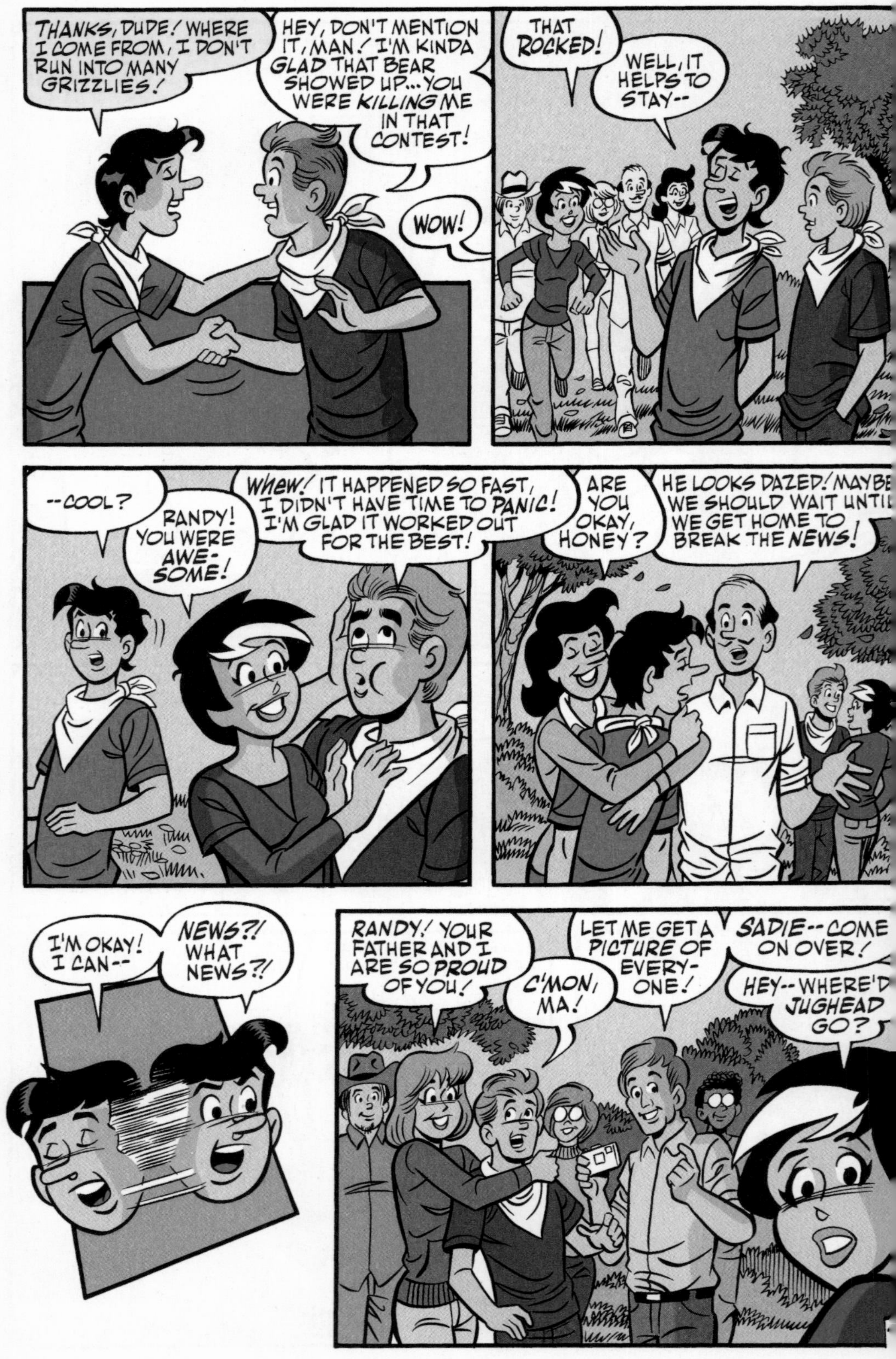
THANKS, DUDE! WHERE I COME FROM, I DON'T RUN INTO MANY GRIZZLIES!
HEY, DON'T MENTION IT, MAN! I'M KINDA GLAD THAT BEAR SHOWED UP...YOU WERE KILLING ME IN THAT CONTEST!
WOW!
THAT ROCKED!
WELL, IT HELPS TO STAY--
--COOL?
RANDY! YOU WERE AWE-SOME!
WHEW! IT HAPPENED SO FAST, I DIDN'T HAVE TIME TO PANIC! I'M GLAD IT WORKED OUT FOR THE BEST!
ARE YOU OKAY, HONEY?
HE LOOKS DAZED! MAYBE WE SHOULD WAIT UNTIL WE GET HOME TO BREAK THE NEWS!
I'M OKAY! I CAN--
NEWS?! WHAT NEWS?!
RANDY! YOUR FATHER AND I ARE SO PROUD OF YOU!
C'MON, MA!
LET ME GET A PICTURE OF EVERY-ONE!
SADIE--COME ON OVER!
HEY--WHERE'D JUGHEAD GO?

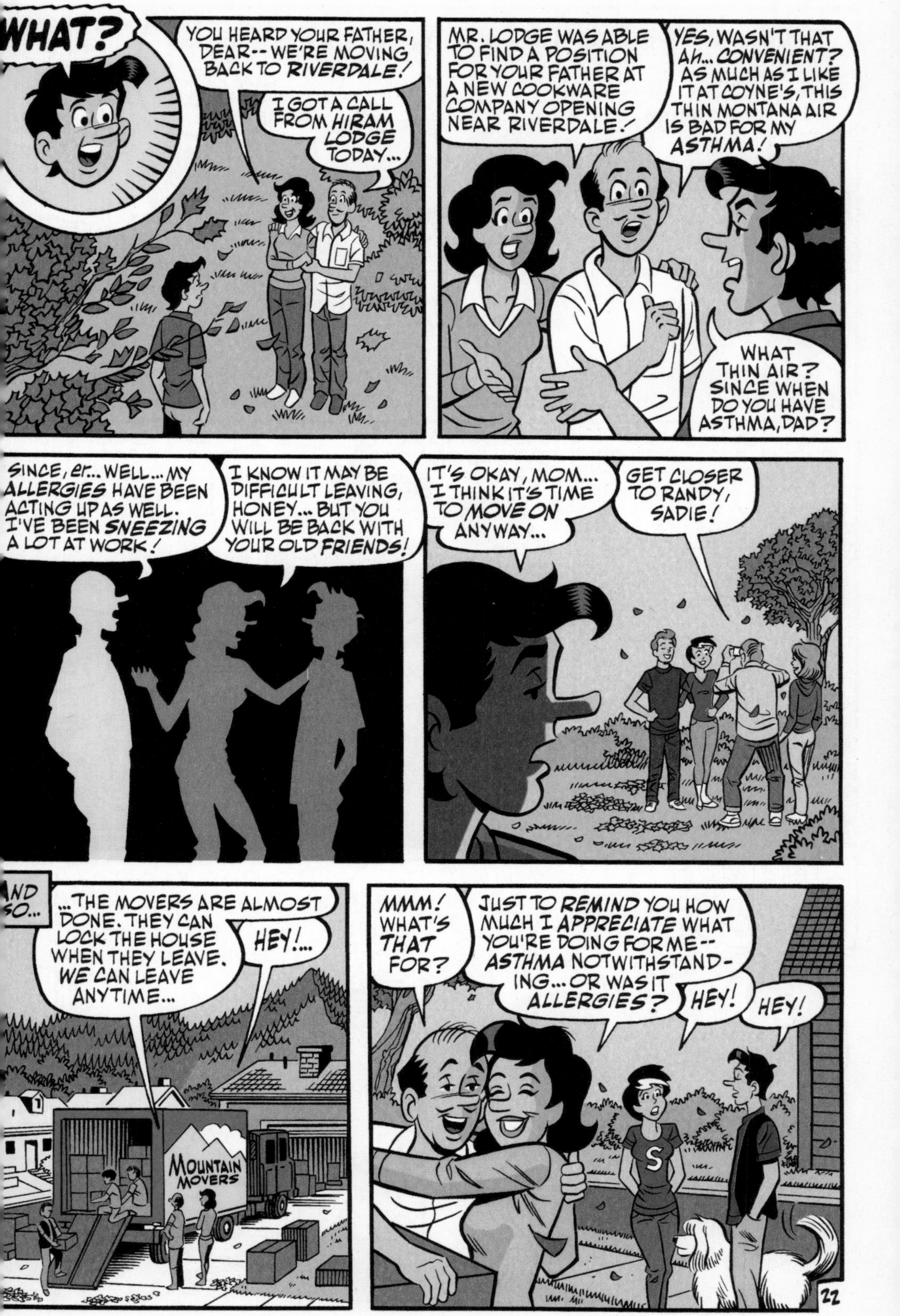
WHAT?
YOU HEARD YOUR FATHER, DEAR-- WE'RE MOVING BACK TO RIVERDALE!
I GOT A CALL FROM HIRAM LODGE TODAY...
MR. LODGE WAS ABLE TO FIND A POSITION FOR YOUR FATHER AT A NEW COOKWARE COMPANY OPENING NEAR RIVERDALE!
YES, WASN'T THAT Ah... CONVENIENT? AS MUCH AS I LIKE IT AT COYNE'S, THIS THIN MONTANA AIR IS BAD FOR MY ASTHMA!
WHAT THIN AIR? SINCE WHEN DO YOU HAVE ASTHMA, DAD?
SINCE, er... WELL... MY ALLERGIES HAVE BEEN ACTING UP AS WELL. I'VE BEEN SNEEZING A LOT AT WORK!
I KNOW IT MAY BE DIFFICULT LEAVING, HONEY... BUT YOU WILL BE BACK WITH YOUR OLD FRIENDS!
IT'S OKAY, MOM... I THINK IT'S TIME TO MOVE ON ANYWAY...
GET CLOSER TO RANDY, SADIE!
AND SO...
...THE MOVERS ARE ALMOST DONE. THEY CAN LOCK THE HOUSE WHEN THEY LEAVE. WE CAN LEAVE ANYTIME...
HEY!...
MOUNTAIN MOVERS
MMM! WHAT'S THAT FOR?
JUST TO REMIND YOU HOW MUCH I APPRECIATE WHAT YOU'RE DOING FOR ME-- ASTHMA NOTWITHSTANDING... OR WAS IT ALLERGIES?
HEY!
HEY!
22

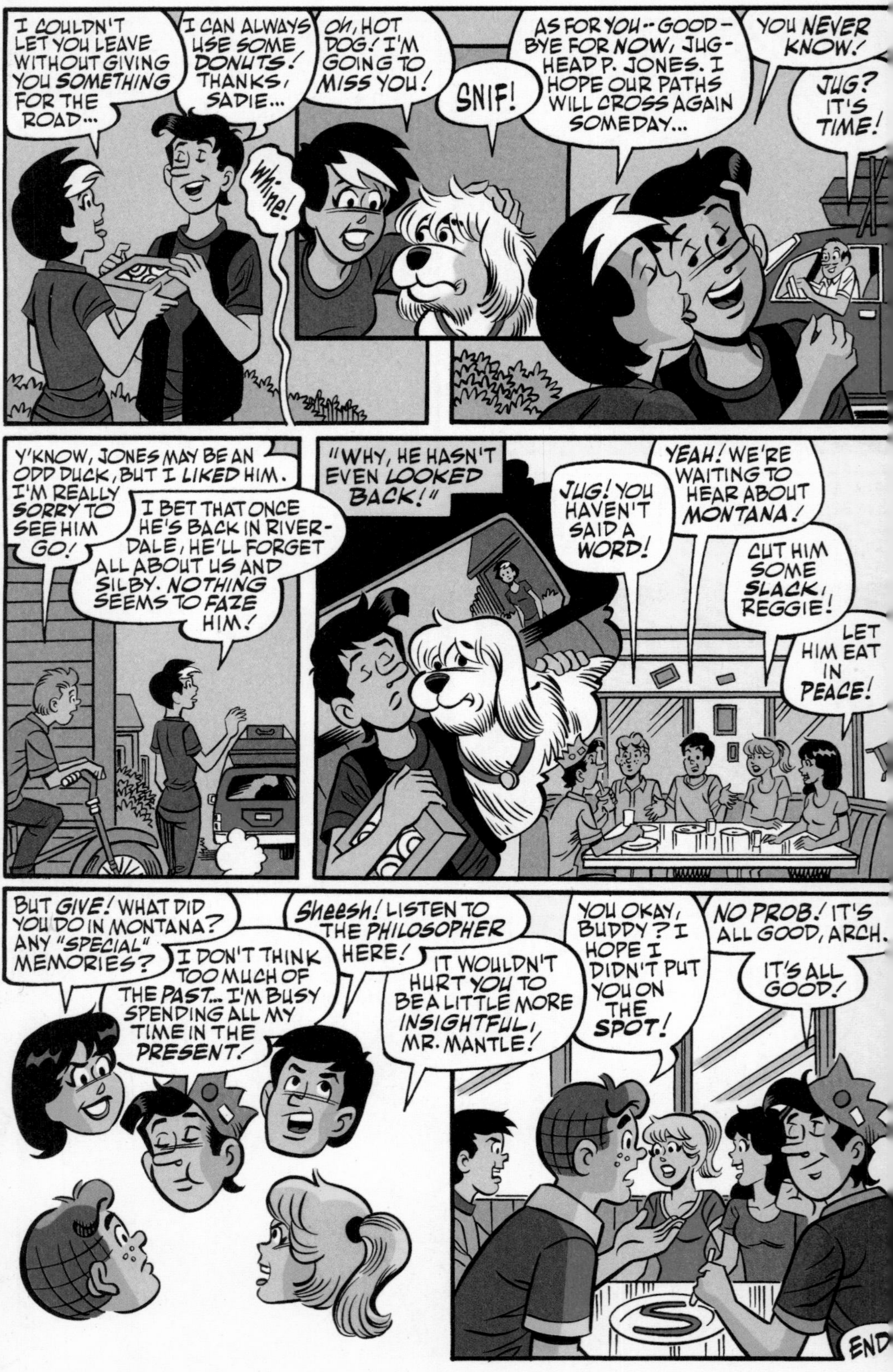
I COULDN'T LET YOU LEAVE WITHOUT GIVING YOU SOMETHING FOR THE ROAD...
I CAN ALWAYS USE SOME DONUTS! THANKS, SADIE...
Whine!
Oh, HOT DOG! I'M GOING TO MISS YOU!
SNIF!
AS FOR YOU -- GOOD-BYE FOR NOW, JUGHEAD P. JONES. I HOPE OUR PATHS WILL CROSS AGAIN SOMEDAY...
YOU NEVER KNOW!
JUG? IT'S TIME!
Y'KNOW, JONES MAY BE AN ODD DUCK, BUT I LIKED HIM. I'M REALLY SORRY TO SEE HIM GO!
I BET THAT ONCE HE'S BACK IN RIVERDALE, HE'LL FORGET ALL ABOUT US AND SILBY. NOTHING SEEMS TO FAZE HIM!
"WHY, HE HASN'T EVEN LOOKED BACK!"
JUG! YOU HAVEN'T SAID A WORD!
YEAH! WE'RE WAITING TO HEAR ABOUT MONTANA!
CUT HIM SOME SLACK, REGGIE!
LET HIM EAT IN PEACE!
BUT GIVE! WHAT DID YOU DO IN MONTANA? ANY "SPECIAL" MEMORIES?
I DON'T THINK TOO MUCH OF THE PAST... I'M BUSY SPENDING ALL MY TIME IN THE PRESENT!
Sheesh! LISTEN TO THE PHILOSOPHER HERE!
IT WOULDN'T HURT YOU TO BE A LITTLE MORE INSIGHTFUL, MR. MANTLE!
YOU OKAY, BUDDY? I HOPE I DIDN'T PUT YOU ON THE SPOT!
NO PROB! IT'S ALL GOOD, ARCH.
IT'S ALL GOOD!
END

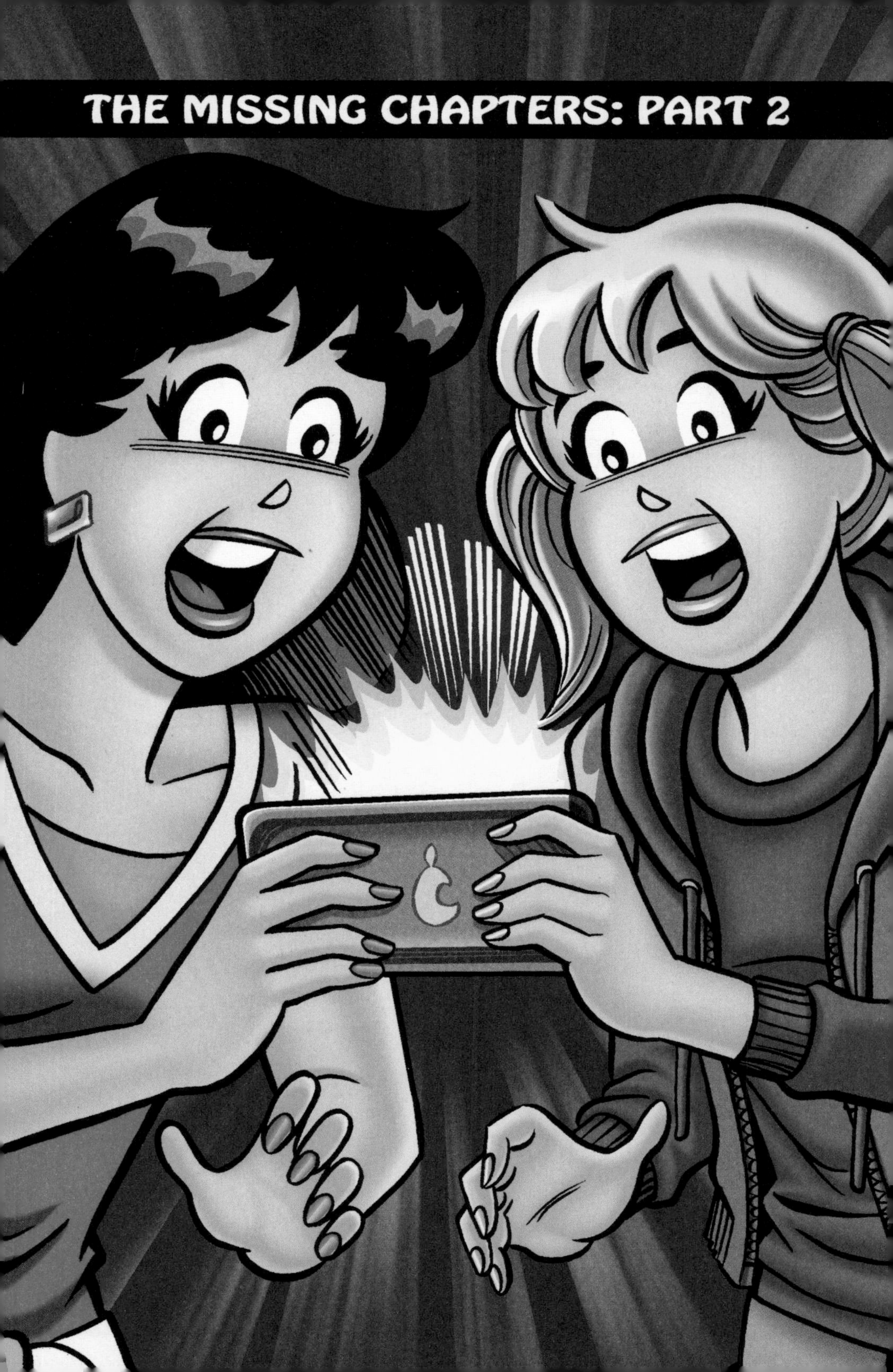
THE MISSING CHAPTERS: PART 2

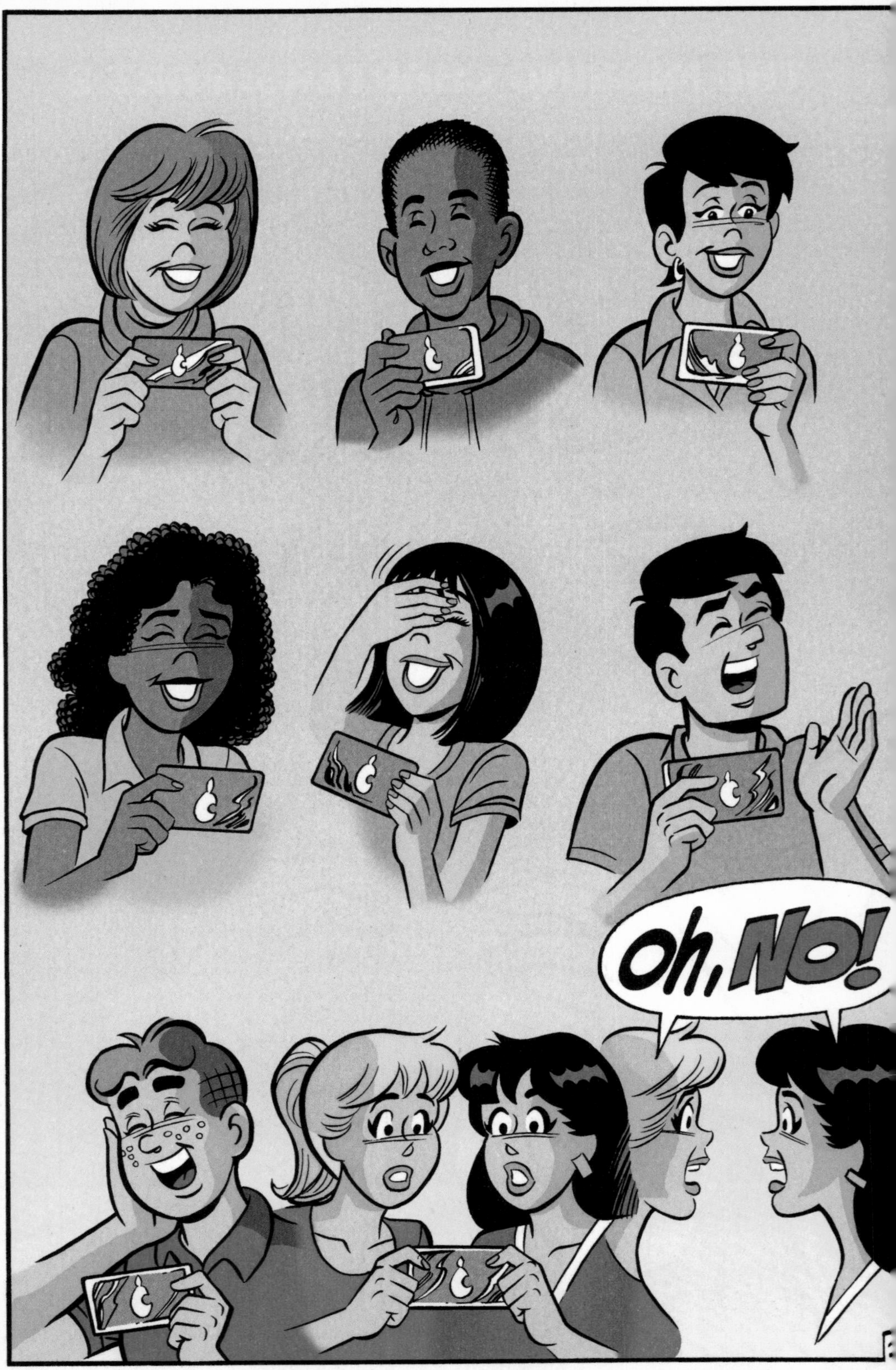
Oh, NO!

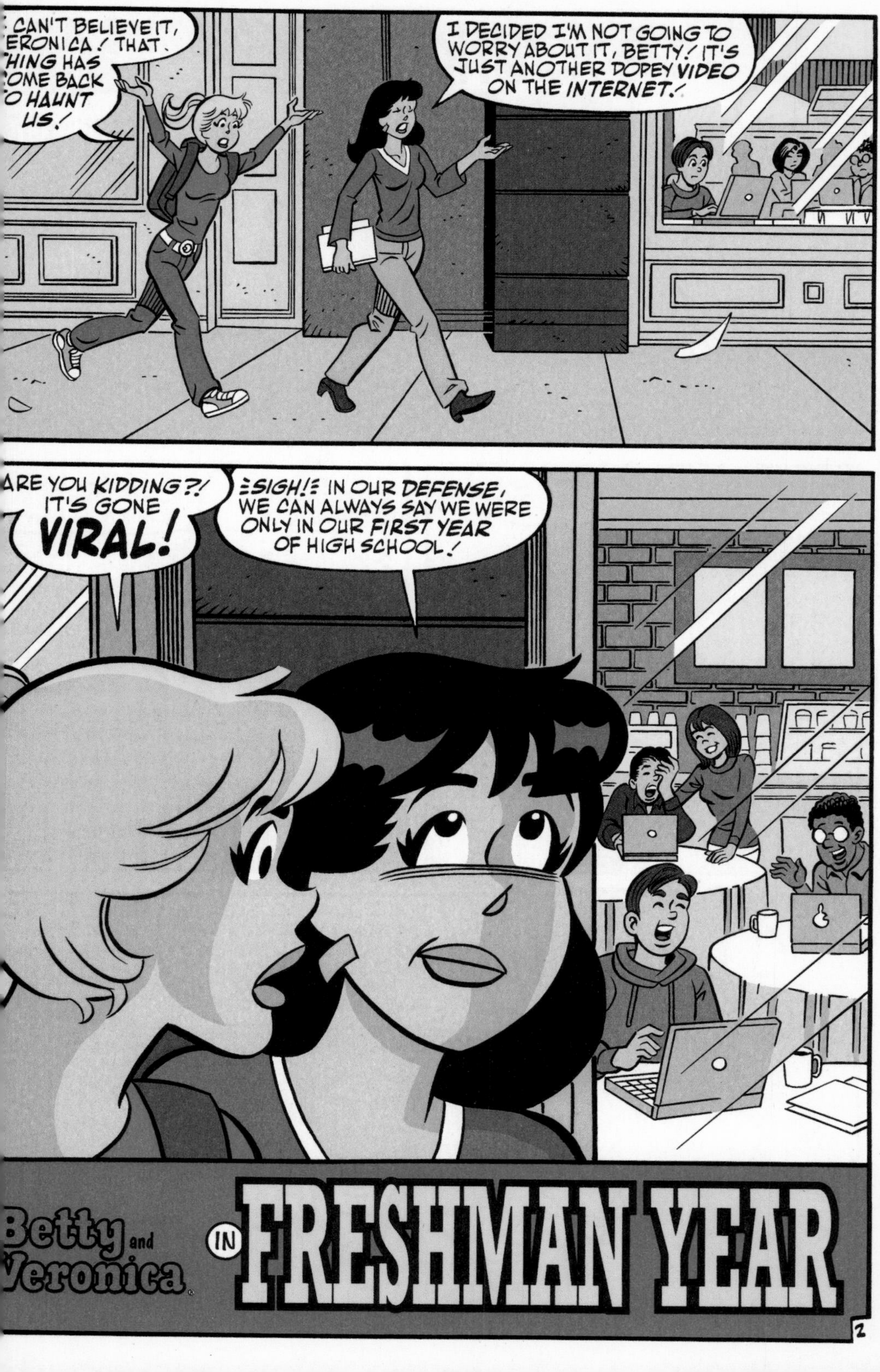

CAN'T BELIEVE IT, VERONICA! THAT THING HAS COME BACK TO HAUNT US!
I DECIDED I'M NOT GOING TO WORRY ABOUT IT, BETTY! IT'S JUST ANOTHER DOPEY VIDEO ON THE INTERNET!
ARE YOU KIDDING?! IT'S GONE VIRAL!
SIGH! IN OUR DEFENSE, WE CAN ALWAYS SAY WE WERE ONLY IN OUR FIRST YEAR OF HIGH SCHOOL!
Betty and Veronica IN FRESHMAN YEAR

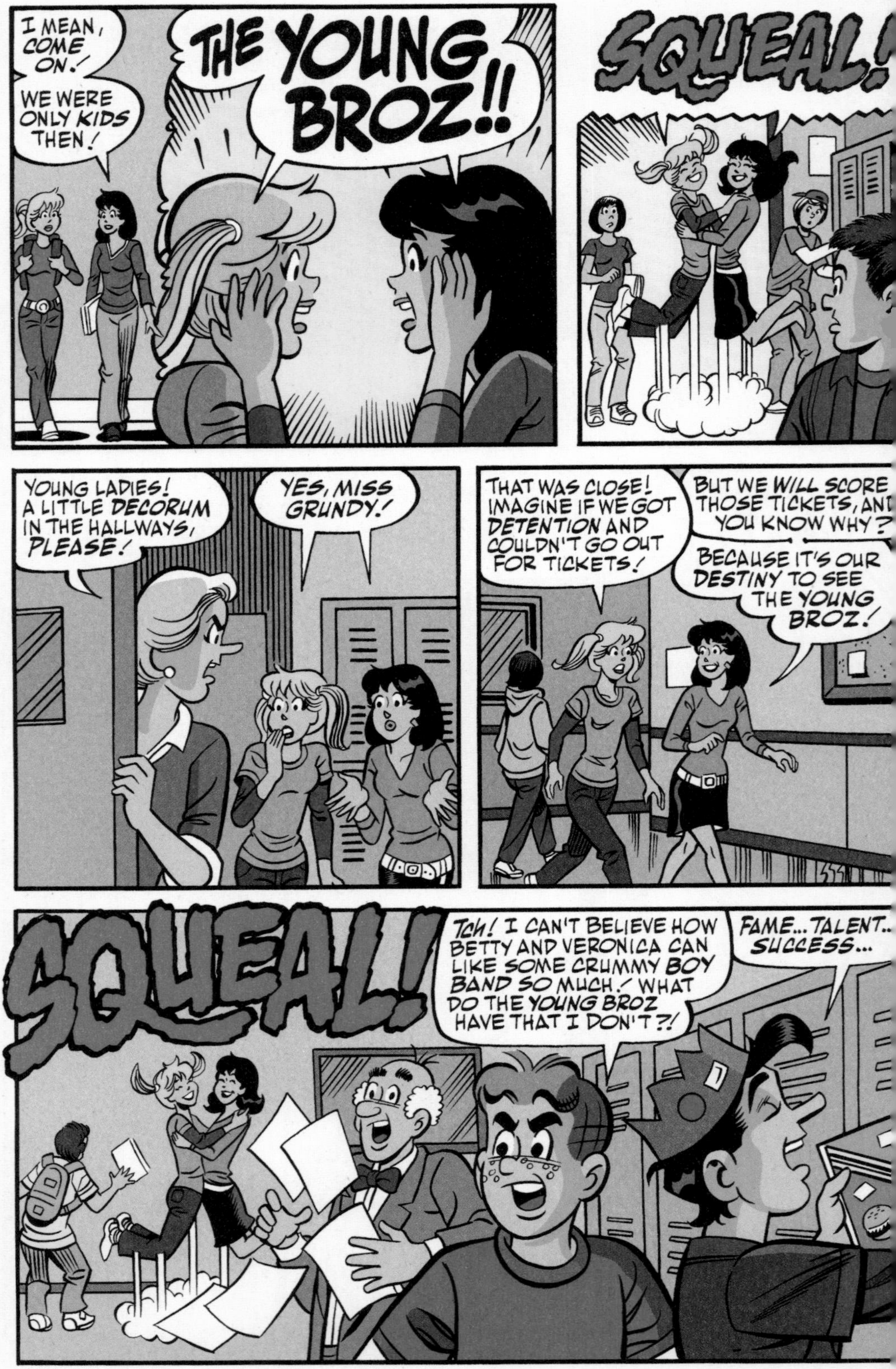
I MEAN, COME ON.!
WE WERE ONLY KIDS THEN!
THE YOUNG BROZ!!
SQUEAL!
YOUNG LADIES! A LITTLE DECORUM IN THE HALLWAYS, PLEASE!
YES, MISS GRUNDY!
THAT WAS CLOSE! IMAGINE IF WE GOT DETENTION AND COULDN'T GO OUT FOR TICKETS!
BUT WE WILL SCORE THOSE TICKETS, AND YOU KNOW WHY?
BECAUSE IT'S OUR DESTINY TO SEE THE YOUNG BROZ!
SQUEAL!
Tch! I CAN'T BELIEVE HOW BETTY AND VERONICA CAN LIKE SOME CRUMMY BOY BAND SO MUCH! WHAT DO THE YOUNG BROZ HAVE THAT I DON'T?!
FAME... TALENT... SUCCESS...

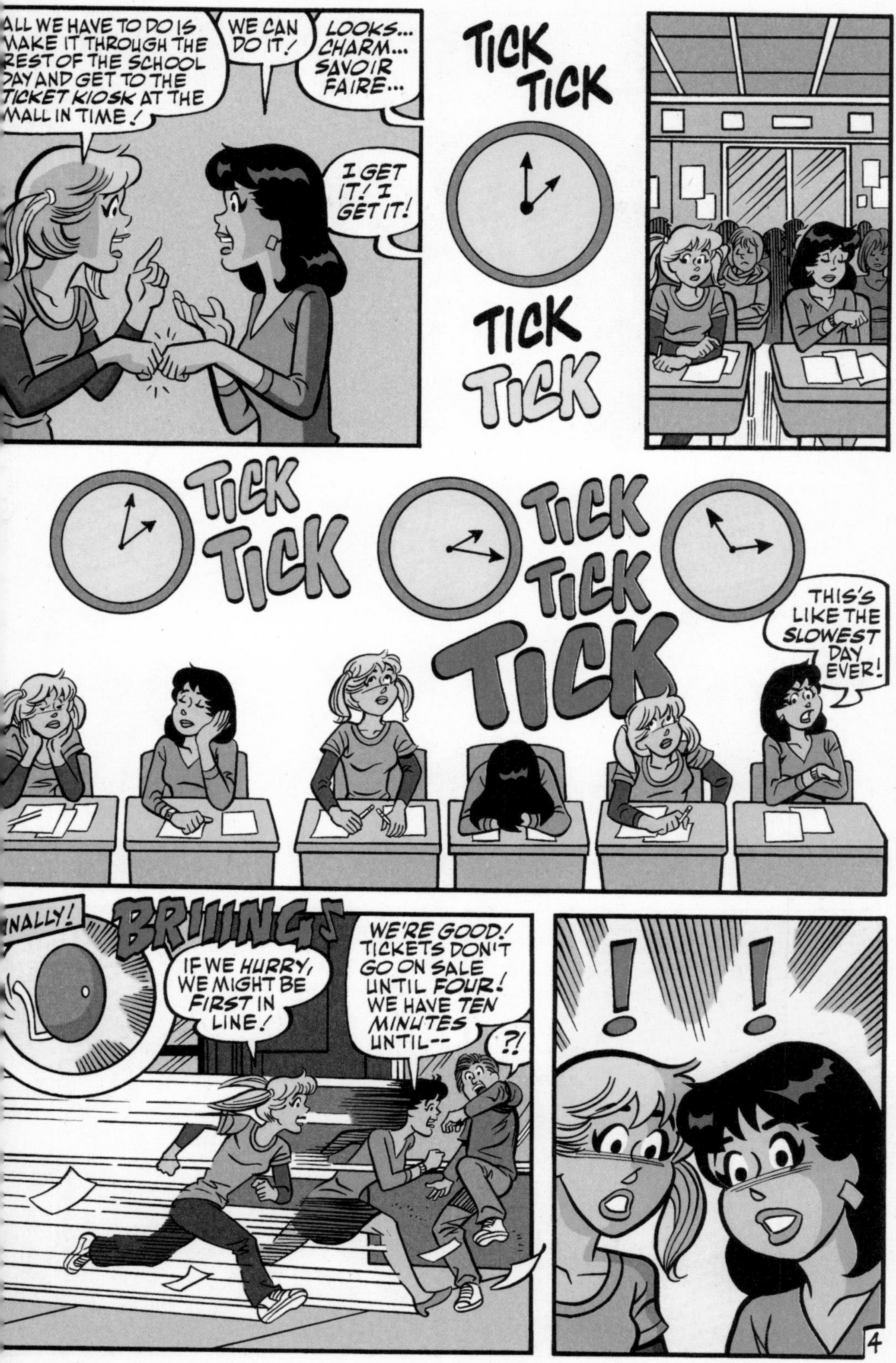
ALL WE HAVE TO DO IS MAKE IT THROUGH THE REST OF THE SCHOOL DAY AND GET TO THE TICKET KIOSK AT THE MALL IN TIME!
WE CAN DO IT!
LOOKS... CHARM... SAVOIR FAIRE...
I GET IT! I GET IT!
TICK TICK
TICK TICK
TICK TICK
TICK TICK TICK
THIS'S LIKE THE SLOWEST DAY EVER!
NALLY!
BRIIINGG
IF WE HURRY, WE MIGHT BE FIRST IN LINE!
WE'RE GOOD! TICKETS DON'T GO ON SALE UNTIL FOUR! WE HAVE TEN MINUTES UNTIL--
?!
! !

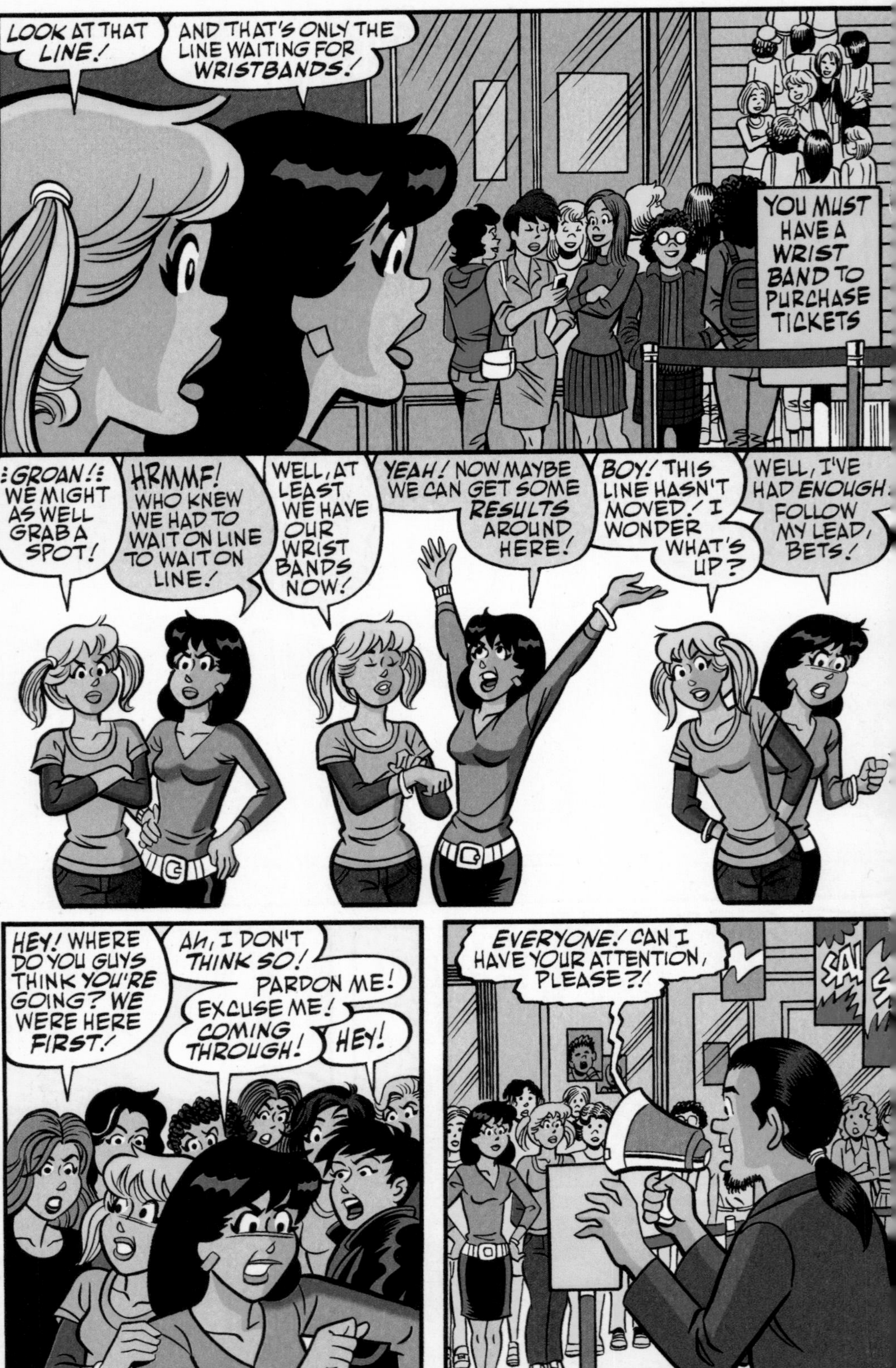
LOOK AT THAT LINE!
AND THAT'S ONLY THE LINE WAITING FOR WRISTBANDS!
YOU MUST HAVE A WRIST BAND TO PURCHASE TICKETS
:GROAN!: WE MIGHT AS WELL GRAB A SPOT!
HRMMF! WHO KNEW WE HAD TO WAIT ON LINE TO WAIT ON LINE!
WELL, AT LEAST WE HAVE OUR WRIST BANDS NOW!
YEAH! NOW MAYBE WE CAN GET SOME RESULTS AROUND HERE!
BOY! THIS LINE HASN'T MOVED! I WONDER WHAT'S UP?
WELL, I'VE HAD ENOUGH. FOLLOW MY LEAD, BETS!
HEY! WHERE DO YOU GUYS THINK YOU'RE GOING? WE WERE HERE FIRST!
Ah, I DON'T THINK SO!
PARDON ME! EXCUSE ME! COMING THROUGH!
HEY!
EVERYONE! CAN I HAVE YOUR ATTENTION, PLEASE?!

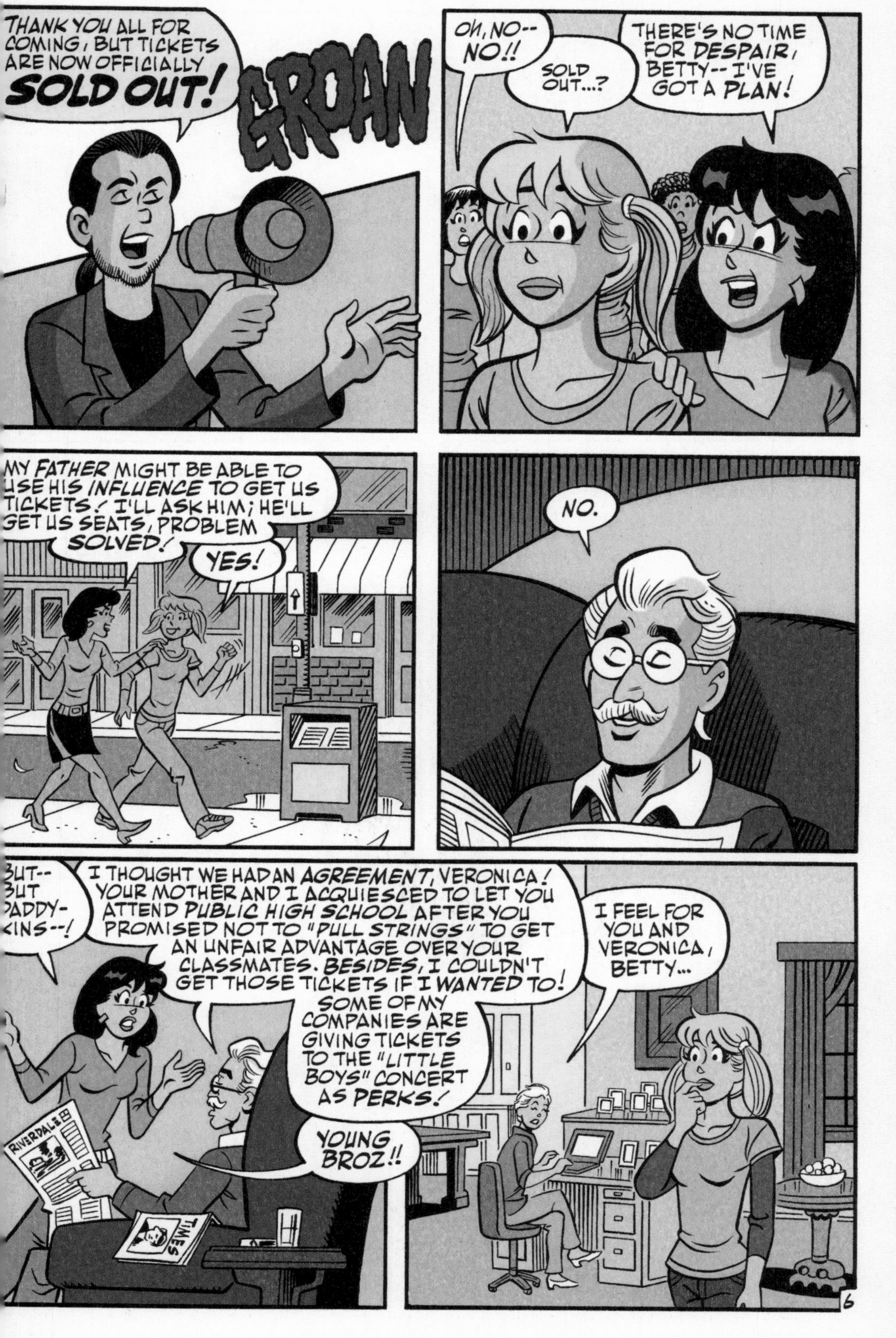
THANK YOU ALL FOR COMING, BUT TICKETS ARE NOW OFFICIALLY SOLD OUT!
GROAN
OH, NO-- NO!!
SOLD OUT...?
THERE'S NO TIME FOR DESPAIR, BETTY-- I'VE GOT A PLAN!
MY FATHER MIGHT BE ABLE TO USE HIS INFLUENCE TO GET US TICKETS! I'LL ASK HIM; HE'LL GET US SEATS, PROBLEM SOLVED!
YES!
NO.
BUT-- BUT DADDY-KINS--!
I THOUGHT WE HAD AN AGREEMENT, VERONICA! YOUR MOTHER AND I ACQUIESCED TO LET YOU ATTEND PUBLIC HIGH SCHOOL AFTER YOU PROMISED NOT TO "PULL STRINGS" TO GET AN UNFAIR ADVANTAGE OVER YOUR CLASSMATES. BESIDES, I COULDN'T GET THOSE TICKETS IF I WANTED TO!
SOME OF MY COMPANIES ARE GIVING TICKETS TO THE "LITTLE BOYS" CONCERT AS PERKS!
YOUNG BROZ!!
RIVERDALE
TIMES
I FEEL FOR YOU AND VERONICA, BETTY...

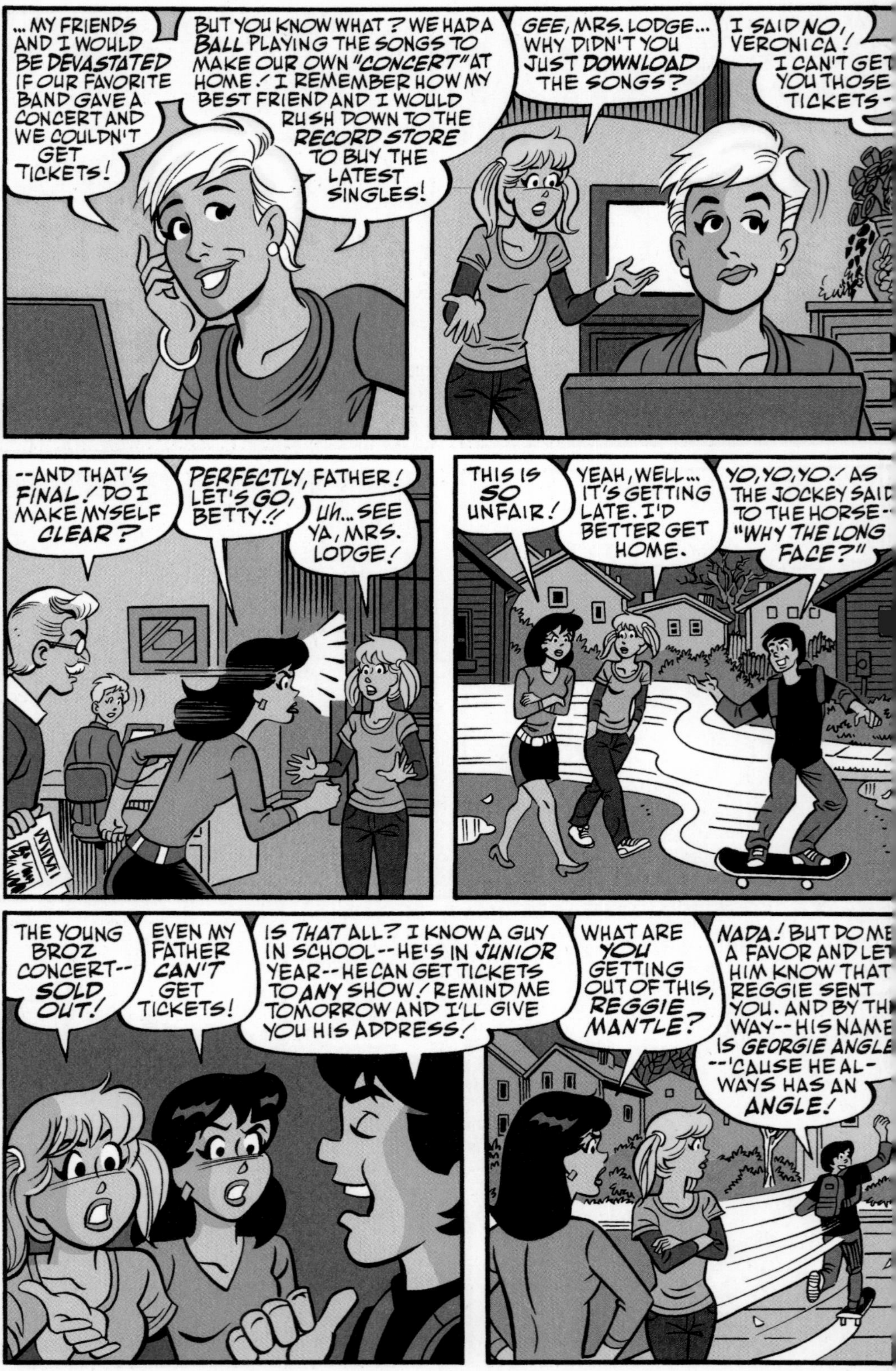

... MY FRIENDS AND I WOULD BE DEVASTATED IF OUR FAVORITE BAND GAVE A CONCERT AND WE COULDN'T GET TICKETS!
BUT YOU KNOW WHAT? WE HAD A BALL PLAYING THE SONGS TO MAKE OUR OWN "CONCERT" AT HOME! I REMEMBER HOW MY BEST FRIEND AND I WOULD RUSH DOWN TO THE RECORD STORE TO BUY THE LATEST SINGLES!
GEE, MRS. LODGE... WHY DIDN'T YOU JUST DOWNLOAD THE SONGS?
I SAID NO, VERONICA! I CAN'T GET YOU THOSE TICKETS--
--AND THAT'S FINAL! DO I MAKE MYSELF CLEAR?
PERFECTLY, FATHER! LET'S GO, BETTY!!
UH... SEE YA, MRS. LODGE!
THIS IS SO UNFAIR!
YEAH, WELL... IT'S GETTING LATE. I'D BETTER GET HOME.
YO, YO, YO! AS THE JOCKEY SAID TO THE HORSE-- "WHY THE LONG FACE?"
THE YOUNG BROZ CONCERT-- SOLD OUT!
EVEN MY FATHER CAN'T GET TICKETS!
IS THAT ALL? I KNOW A GUY IN SCHOOL--HE'S IN JUNIOR YEAR--HE CAN GET TICKETS TO ANY SHOW! REMIND ME TOMORROW AND I'LL GIVE YOU HIS ADDRESS!
WHAT ARE YOU GETTING OUT OF THIS, REGGIE MANTLE?
NADA! BUT DO ME A FAVOR AND LET HIM KNOW THAT REGGIE SENT YOU. AND BY THE WAY--HIS NAME IS GEORGIE ANGLE --'CAUSE HE ALWAYS HAS AN ANGLE!

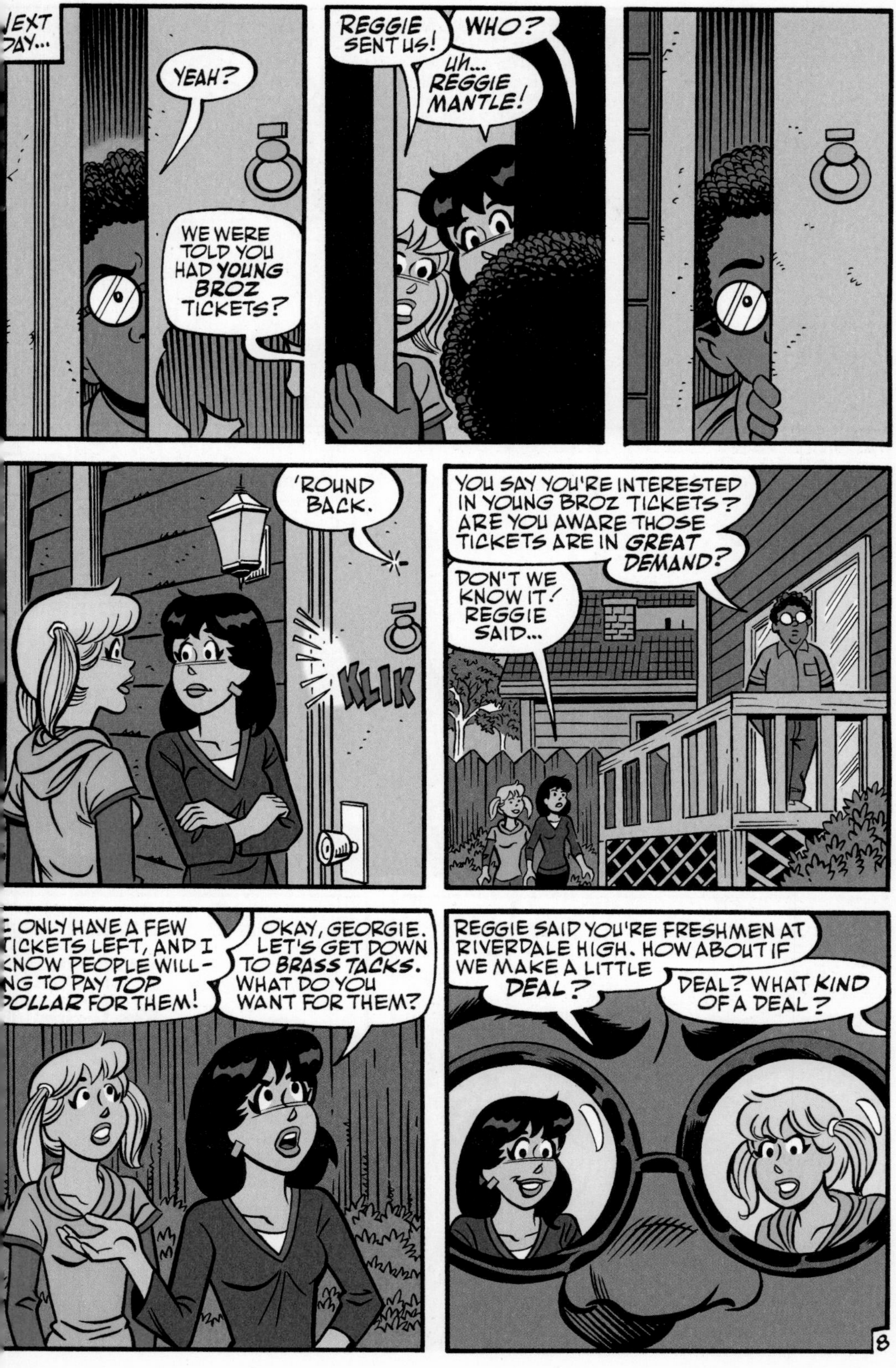

NEXT DAY...
YEAH?
WE WERE TOLD YOU HAD YOUNG BROZ TICKETS?
REGGIE SENT US!
WHO?
uh... REGGIE MANTLE!
'ROUND BACK.
KLIK
YOU SAY YOU'RE INTERESTED IN YOUNG BROZ TICKETS? ARE YOU AWARE THOSE TICKETS ARE IN GREAT DEMAND?
DON'T WE KNOW IT! REGGIE SAID...
E ONLY HAVE A FEW TICKETS LEFT, AND I KNOW PEOPLE WILL-NG TO PAY TOP DOLLAR FOR THEM!
OKAY, GEORGIE. LET'S GET DOWN TO BRASS TACKS. WHAT DO YOU WANT FOR THEM?
REGGIE SAID YOU'RE FRESHMEN AT RIVERDALE HIGH. HOW ABOUT IF WE MAKE A LITTLE DEAL?
DEAL? WHAT KIND OF A DEAL?

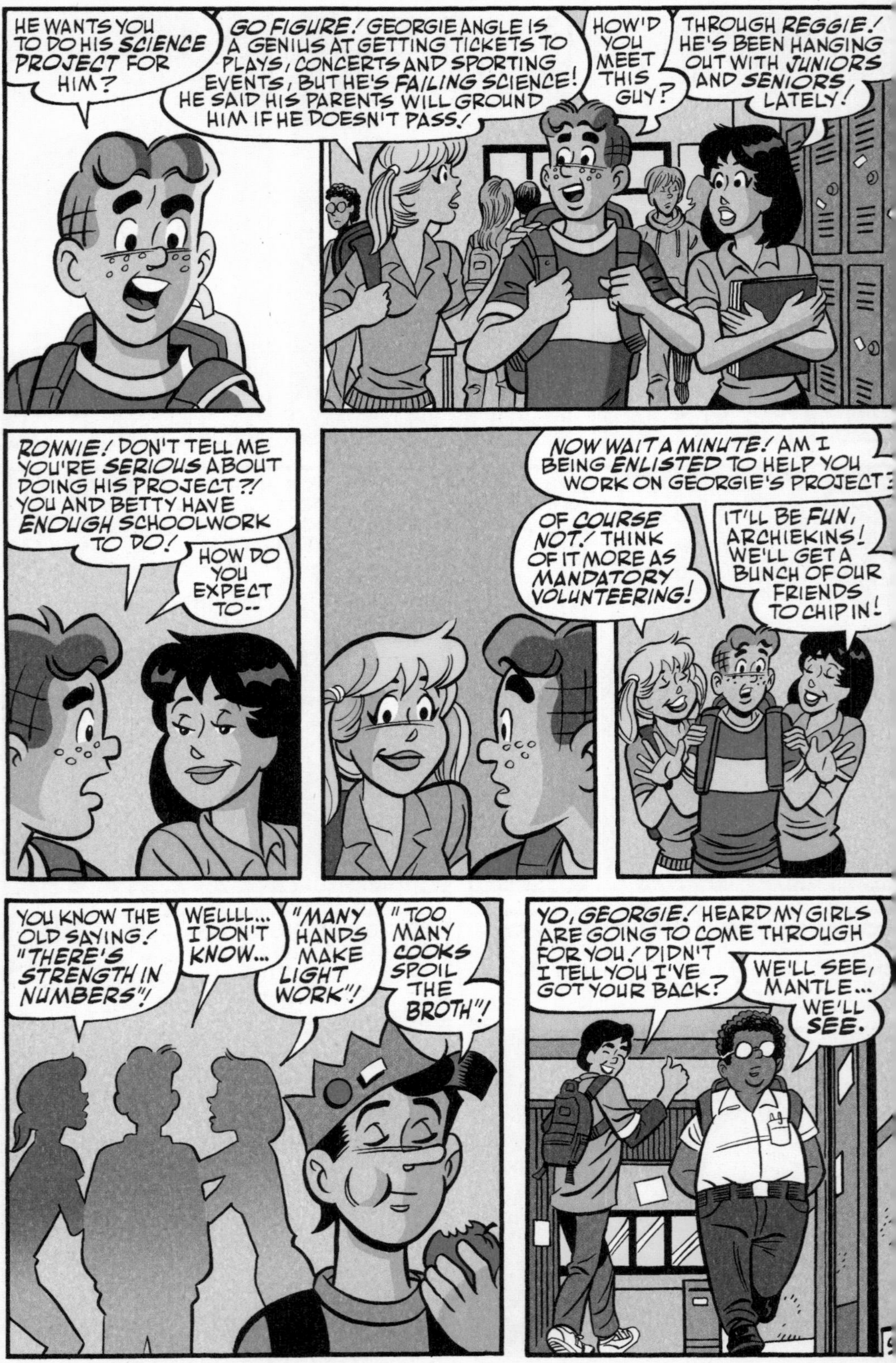
HE WANTS YOU TO DO HIS SCIENCE PROJECT FOR HIM?
GO FIGURE! GEORGIE ANGLE IS A GENIUS AT GETTING TICKETS TO PLAYS, CONCERTS AND SPORTING EVENTS, BUT HE'S FAILING SCIENCE! HE SAID HIS PARENTS WILL GROUND HIM IF HE DOESN'T PASS!
HOW'D YOU MEET THIS GUY?
THROUGH REGGIE! HE'S BEEN HANGING OUT WITH JUNIORS AND SENIORS LATELY!
RONNIE! DON'T TELL ME YOU'RE SERIOUS ABOUT DOING HIS PROJECT?! YOU AND BETTY HAVE ENOUGH SCHOOLWORK TO DO!
HOW DO YOU EXPECT TO--
NOW WAIT A MINUTE! AM I BEING ENLISTED TO HELP YOU WORK ON GEORGIE'S PROJECT?
OF COURSE NOT! THINK OF IT MORE AS MANDATORY VOLUNTEERING!
IT'LL BE FUN, ARCHIEKINS! WE'LL GET A BUNCH OF OUR FRIENDS TO CHIP IN!
YOU KNOW THE OLD SAYING! "THERE'S STRENGTH IN NUMBERS"!
WELLLL... I DON'T KNOW...
"MANY HANDS MAKE LIGHT WORK"!
"TOO MANY COOKS SPOIL THE BROTH"!
YO, GEORGIE! HEARD MY GIRLS ARE GOING TO COME THROUGH FOR YOU! DIDN'T I TELL YOU I'VE GOT YOUR BACK?
WE'LL SEE, MANTLE... WE'LL SEE.

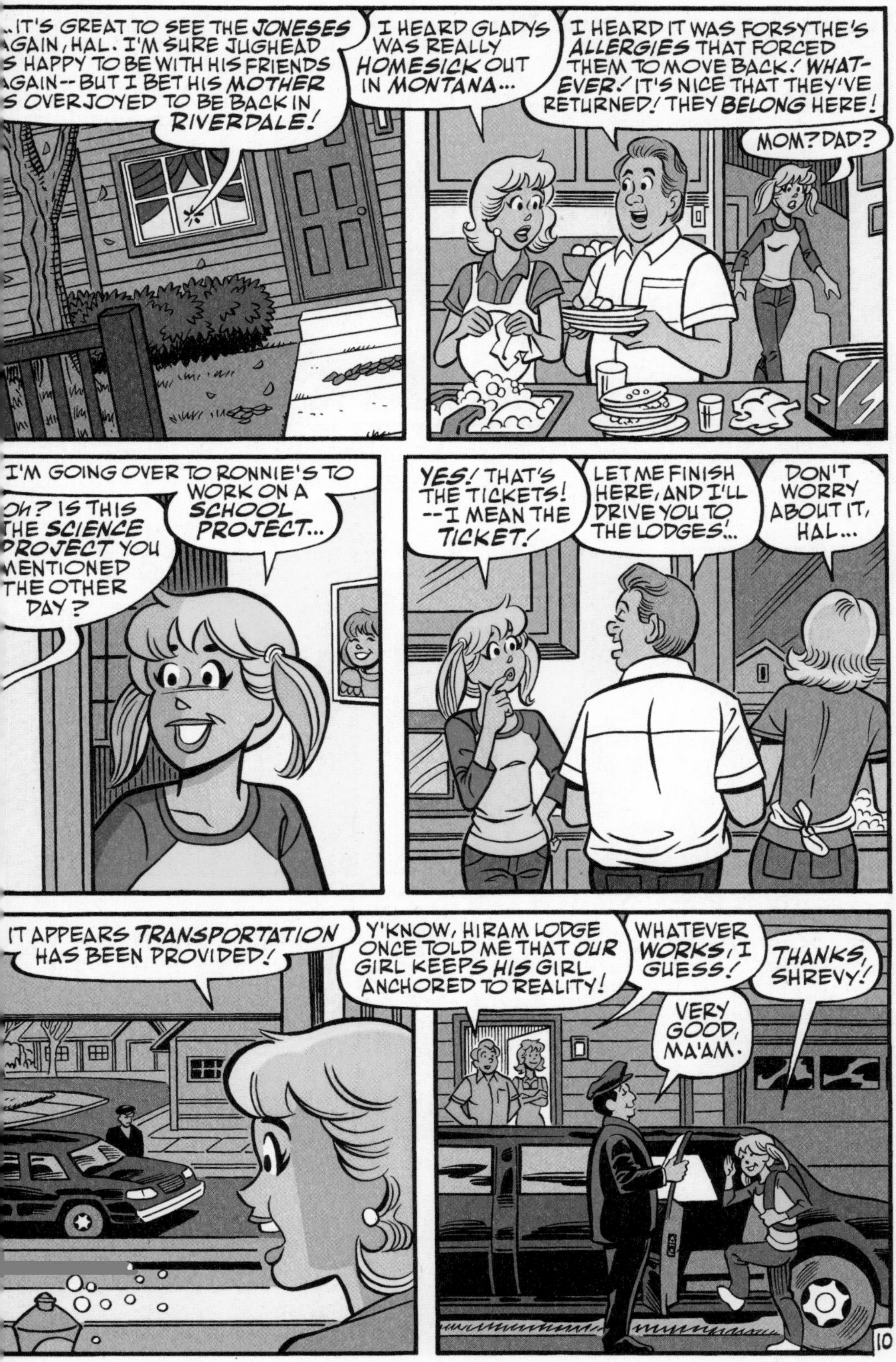
..IT'S GREAT TO SEE THE JONESES AGAIN, HAL. I'M SURE JUGHEAD IS HAPPY TO BE WITH HIS FRIENDS AGAIN -- BUT I BET HIS MOTHER IS OVERJOYED TO BE BACK IN RIVERDALE!
I HEARD GLADYS WAS REALLY HOMESICK OUT IN MONTANA...
I HEARD IT WAS FORSYTHE'S ALLERGIES THAT FORCED THEM TO MOVE BACK! WHAT-EVER! IT'S NICE THAT THEY'VE RETURNED! THEY BELONG HERE!
MOM? DAD?
I'M GOING OVER TO RONNIE'S TO WORK ON A SCHOOL PROJECT...
OH? IS THIS THE SCIENCE PROJECT YOU MENTIONED THE OTHER DAY?
YES! THAT'S THE TICKETS! --I MEAN THE TICKET!
LET ME FINISH HERE, AND I'LL DRIVE YOU TO THE LODGES!...
DON'T WORRY ABOUT IT, HAL...
IT APPEARS TRANSPORTATION HAS BEEN PROVIDED!
Y'KNOW, HIRAM LODGE ONCE TOLD ME THAT OUR GIRL KEEPS HIS GIRL ANCHORED TO REALITY!
WHATEVER WORKS, I GUESS!
VERY GOOD, MA'AM.
THANKS, SHREVY!

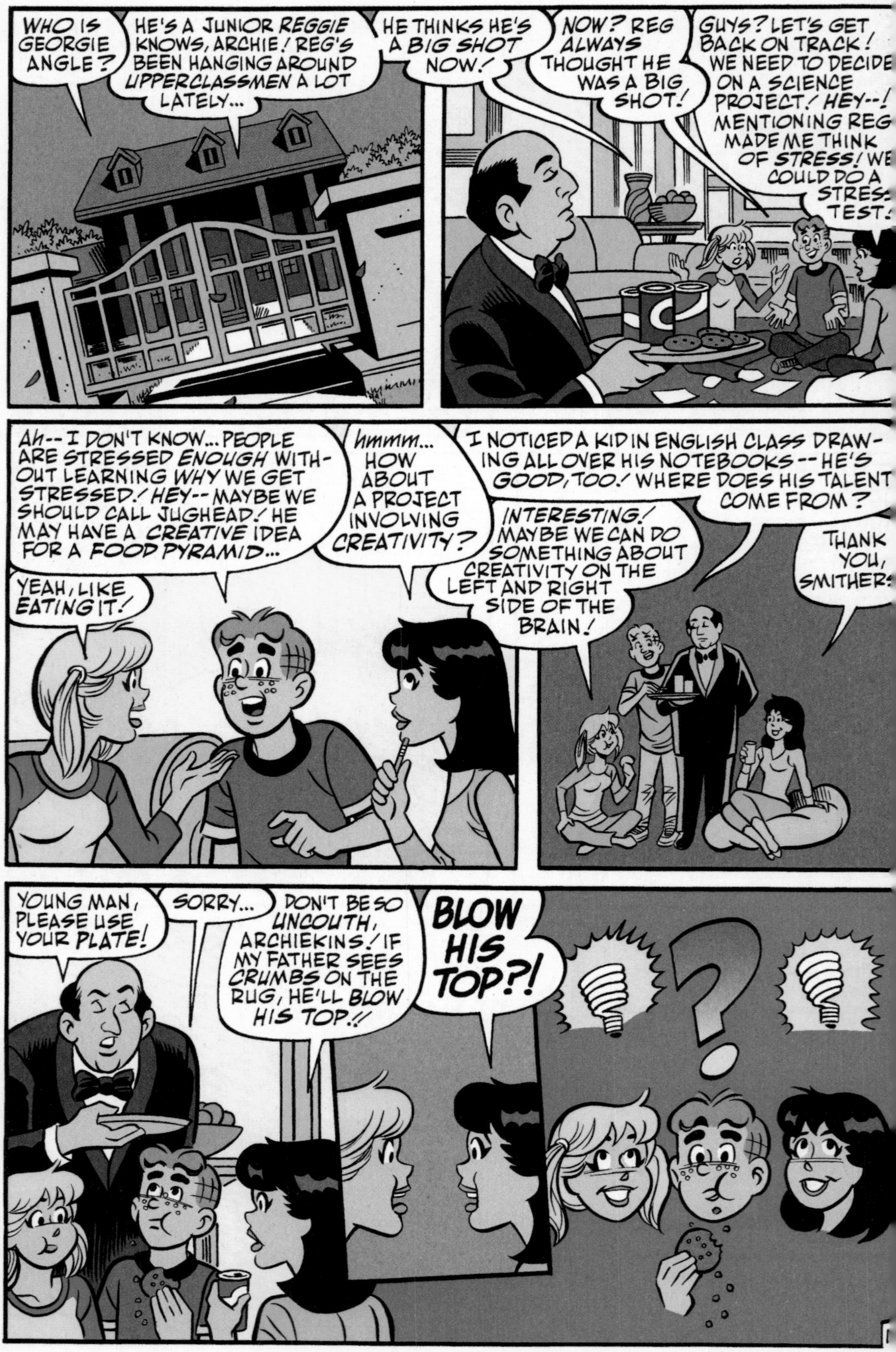
WHO IS GEORGIE ANGLE?
HE'S A JUNIOR REGGIE KNOWS, ARCHIE! REG'S BEEN HANGING AROUND UPPERCLASSMEN A LOT LATELY...
HE THINKS HE'S A BIG SHOT NOW!
NOW? REG ALWAYS THOUGHT HE WAS A BIG SHOT!
GUYS? LET'S GET BACK ON TRACK! WE NEED TO DECIDE ON A SCIENCE PROJECT! HEY--! MENTIONING REG MADE ME THINK OF STRESS! WE COULD DO A STRESS TEST!
Ah-- I DON'T KNOW... PEOPLE ARE STRESSED ENOUGH WITHOUT LEARNING WHY WE GET STRESSED! HEY-- MAYBE WE SHOULD CALL JUGHEAD! HE MAY HAVE A CREATIVE IDEA FOR A FOOD PYRAMID...
YEAH, LIKE EATING IT!
hmmm... HOW ABOUT A PROJECT INVOLVING CREATIVITY?
I NOTICED A KID IN ENGLISH CLASS DRAWING ALL OVER HIS NOTEBOOKS -- HE'S GOOD, TOO! WHERE DOES HIS TALENT COME FROM?
INTERESTING! MAYBE WE CAN DO SOMETHING ABOUT CREATIVITY ON THE LEFT AND RIGHT SIDE OF THE BRAIN!
THANK YOU, SMITHERS
YOUNG MAN, PLEASE USE YOUR PLATE!
SORRY...
DON'T BE SO UNCOUTH, ARCHIEKINS! IF MY FATHER SEES CRUMBS ON THE RUG, HE'LL BLOW HIS TOP!!
BLOW HIS TOP?!

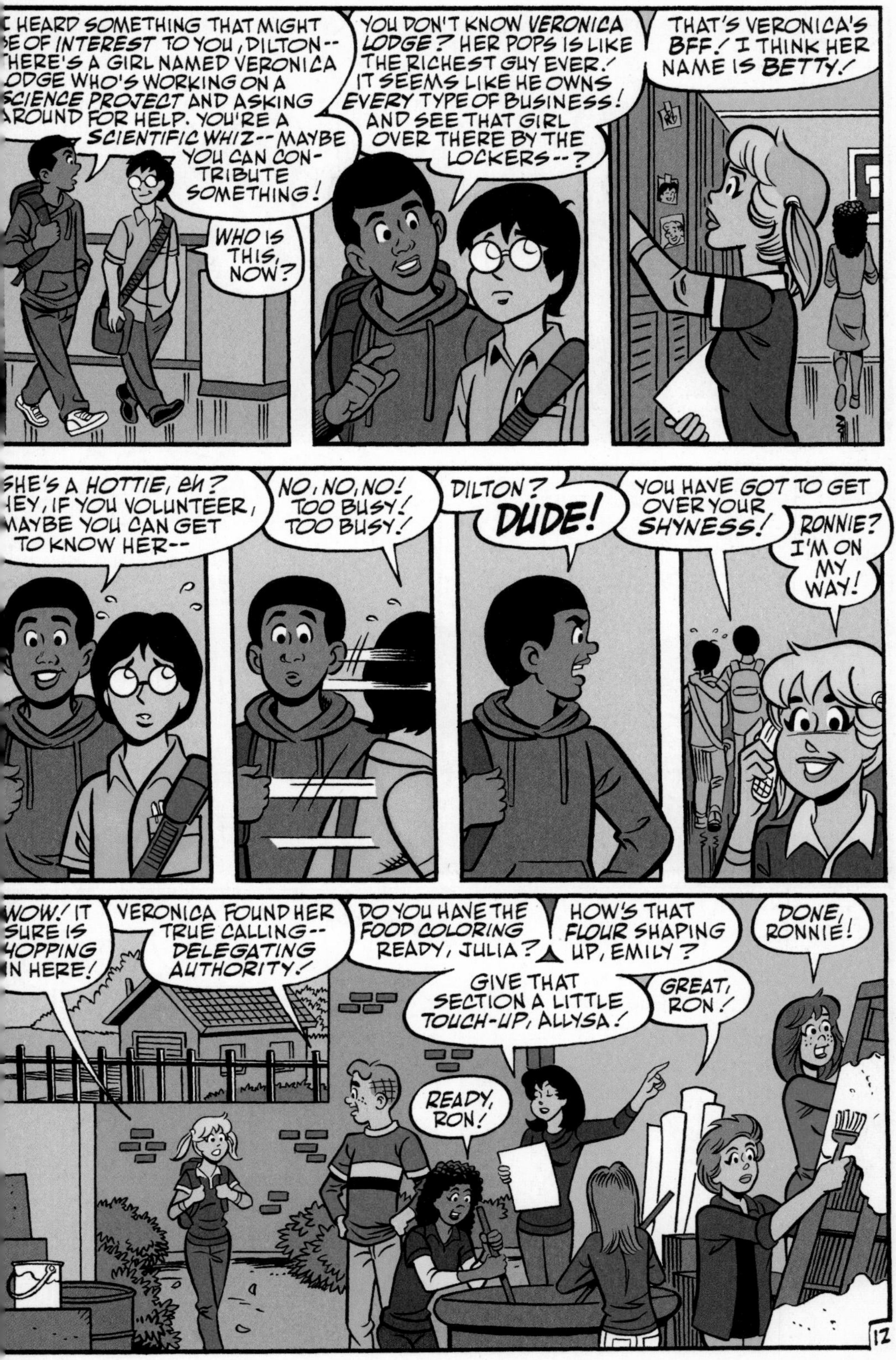
I HEARD SOMETHING THAT MIGHT BE OF INTEREST TO YOU, DILTON-- THERE'S A GIRL NAMED VERONICA LODGE WHO'S WORKING ON A SCIENCE PROJECT AND ASKING AROUND FOR HELP. YOU'RE A SCIENTIFIC WHIZ--MAYBE YOU CAN CONTRIBUTE SOMETHING!
WHO IS THIS, NOW?
YOU DON'T KNOW VERONICA LODGE? HER POPS IS LIKE THE RICHEST GUY EVER! IT SEEMS LIKE HE OWNS EVERY TYPE OF BUSINESS! AND SEE THAT GIRL OVER THERE BY THE LOCKERS--?
THAT'S VERONICA'S BFF! I THINK HER NAME IS BETTY!
SHE'S A HOTTIE, eh? HEY, IF YOU VOLUNTEER, MAYBE YOU CAN GET TO KNOW HER--
NO, NO, NO! TOO BUSY! TOO BUSY!
DILTON? DUDE!
YOU HAVE GOT TO GET OVER YOUR SHYNESS!
RONNIE? I'M ON MY WAY!
WOW! IT SURE IS HOPPING IN HERE!
VERONICA FOUND HER TRUE CALLING-- DELEGATING AUTHORITY!
DO YOU HAVE THE FOOD COLORING READY, JULIA?
HOW'S THAT FLOUR SHAPING UP, EMILY?
DONE, RONNIE!
GIVE THAT SECTION A LITTLE TOUCH-UP, ALLYSA!
GREAT, RON!
READY, RON!

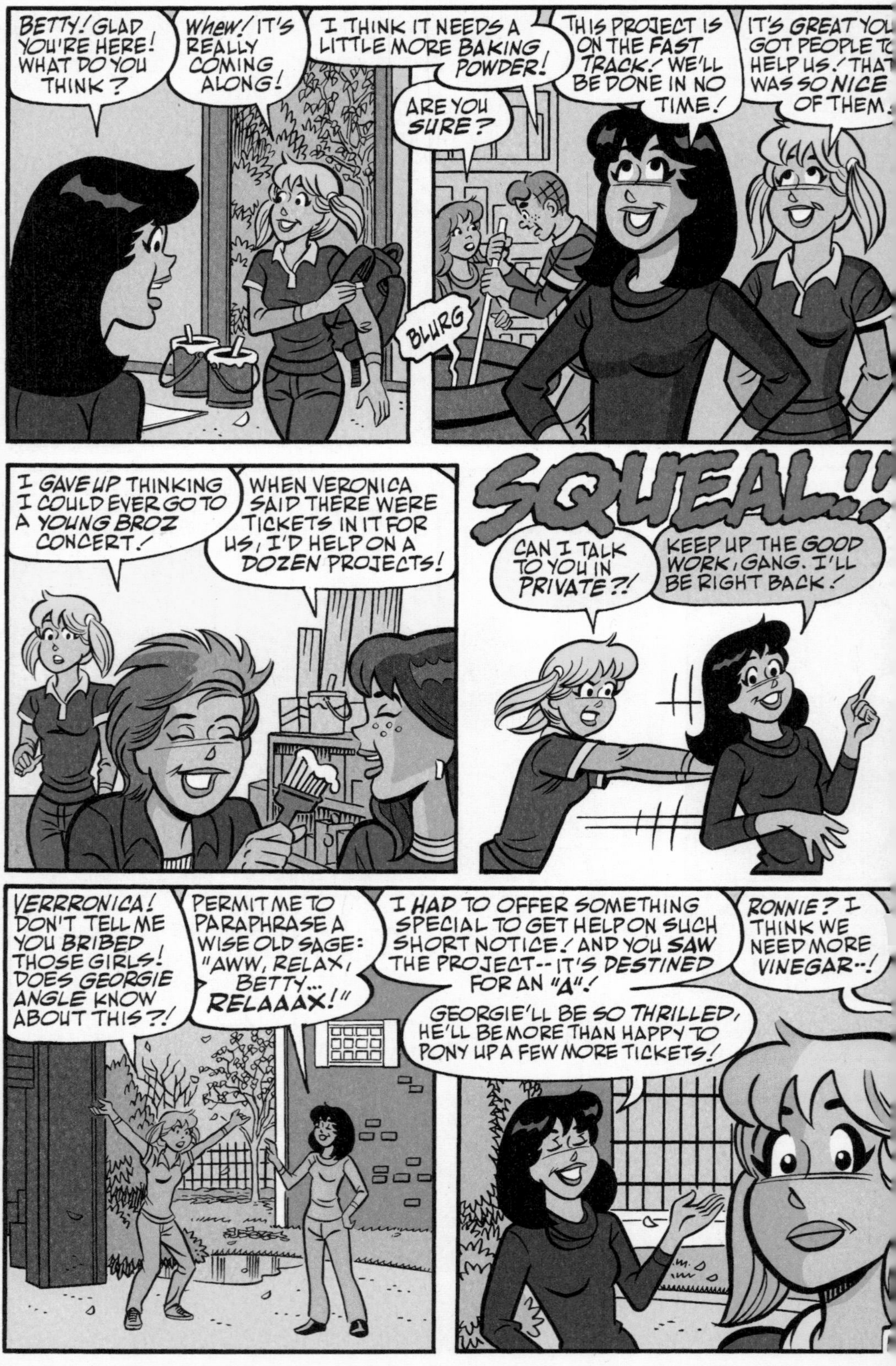
BETTY! GLAD YOU'RE HERE! WHAT DO YOU THINK?
Whew! IT'S REALLY COMING ALONG!
I THINK IT NEEDS A LITTLE MORE BAKING POWDER!
ARE YOU SURE?
BLURG
THIS PROJECT IS ON THE FAST TRACK! WE'LL BE DONE IN NO TIME!
IT'S GREAT YOU GOT PEOPLE TO HELP US! THAT WAS SO NICE OF THEM!
I GAVE UP THINKING I COULD EVER GO TO A YOUNG BROZ CONCERT!
WHEN VERONICA SAID THERE WERE TICKETS IN IT FOR US, I'D HELP ON A DOZEN PROJECTS!
SQUEAL..!!
CAN I TALK TO YOU IN PRIVATE?!
KEEP UP THE GOOD WORK, GANG. I'LL BE RIGHT BACK!
VERRRONICA! DON'T TELL ME YOU BRIBED THOSE GIRLS! DOES GEORGIE ANGLE KNOW ABOUT THIS?!
PERMIT ME TO PARAPHRASE A WISE OLD SAGE: "AWW, RELAX, BETTY... RELAAAX!"
I HAD TO OFFER SOMETHING SPECIAL TO GET HELP ON SUCH SHORT NOTICE! AND YOU SAW THE PROJECT-- IT'S DESTINED FOR AN "A"!
GEORGIE'LL BE SO THRILLED, HE'LL BE MORE THAN HAPPY TO PONY UP A FEW MORE TICKETS!
RONNIE? I THINK WE NEED MORE VINEGAR--!

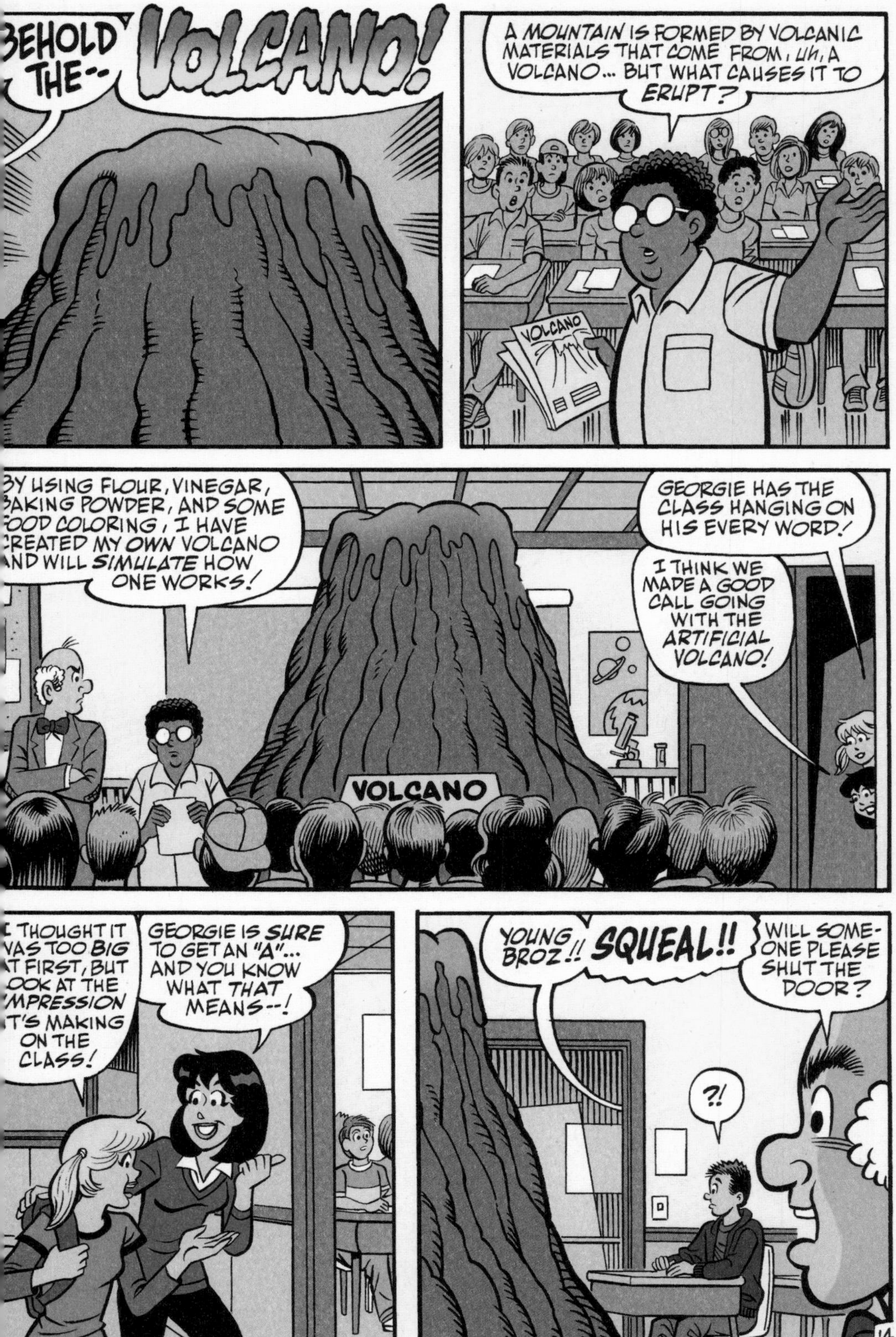

BEHOLD THE-- VOLCANO!
A MOUNTAIN IS FORMED BY VOLCANIC MATERIALS THAT COME FROM, UH, A VOLCANO... BUT WHAT CAUSES IT TO ERUPT?
VOLCANO
BY USING FLOUR, VINEGAR, BAKING POWDER, AND SOME FOOD COLORING, I HAVE CREATED MY OWN VOLCANO AND WILL SIMULATE HOW ONE WORKS!
GEORGIE HAS THE CLASS HANGING ON HIS EVERY WORD!
I THINK WE MADE A GOOD CALL GOING WITH THE ARTIFICIAL VOLCANO!
VOLCANO
I THOUGHT IT WAS TOO BIG AT FIRST, BUT LOOK AT THE IMPRESSION IT'S MAKING ON THE CLASS!
GEORGIE IS SURE TO GET AN "A"... AND YOU KNOW WHAT THAT MEANS--!
YOUNG BROZ!!
SQUEAL!!
WILL SOME-ONE PLEASE SHUT THE DOOR?
?!

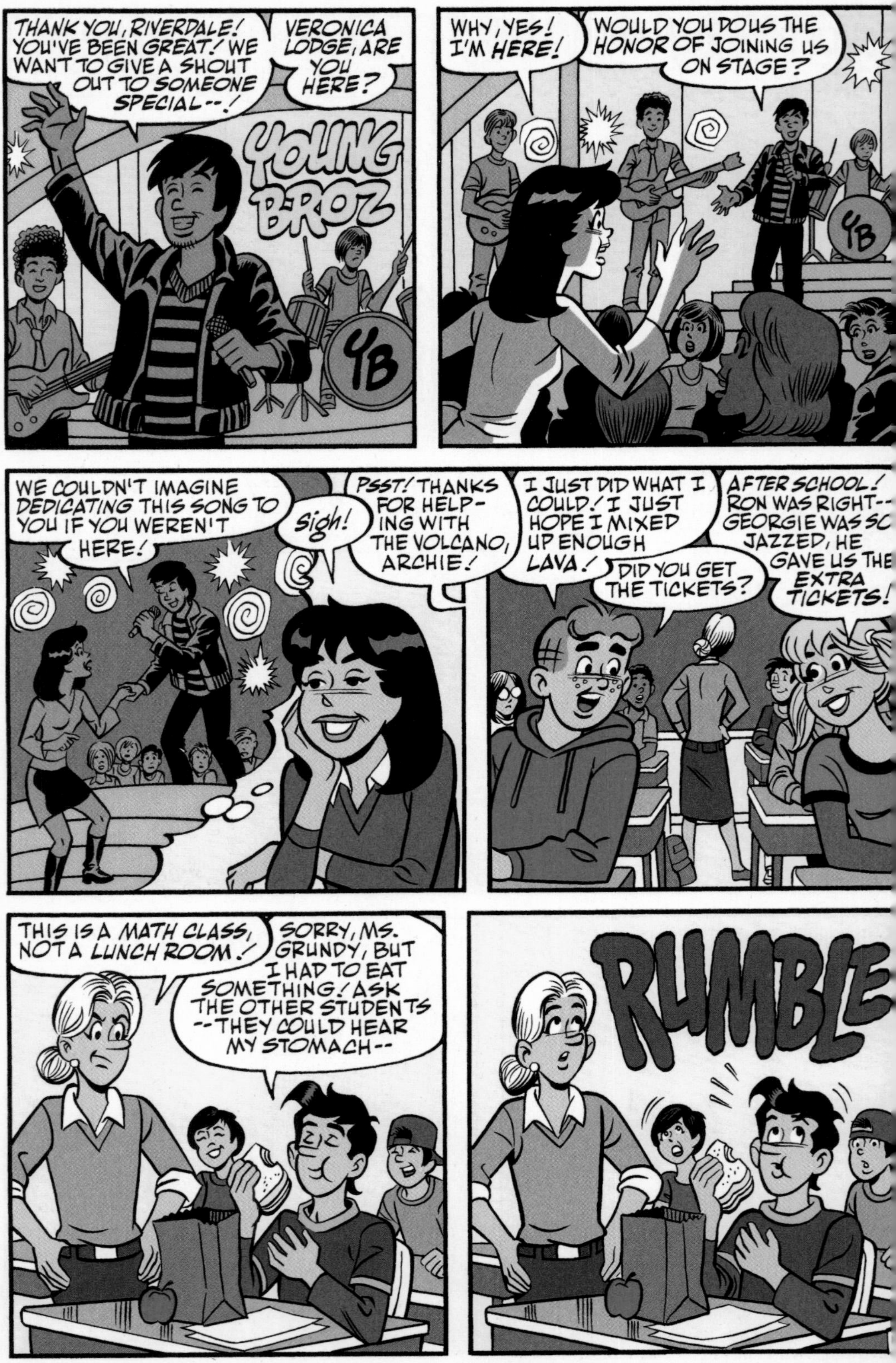
THANK YOU, RIVERDALE! YOU'VE BEEN GREAT! WE WANT TO GIVE A SHOUT OUT TO SOMEONE SPECIAL--!
VERONICA LODGE, ARE YOU HERE?
YOUNG BROZ
YB
WHY, YES! I'M HERE!
WOULD YOU DO US THE HONOR OF JOINING US ON STAGE?
YB
WE COULDN'T IMAGINE DEDICATING THIS SONG TO YOU IF YOU WEREN'T HERE!
Sigh!
PSST! THANKS FOR HELP-ING WITH THE VOLCANO, ARCHIE!
I JUST DID WHAT I COULD! I JUST HOPE I MIXED UP ENOUGH LAVA!
DID YOU GET THE TICKETS?
AFTER SCHOOL! RON WAS RIGHT-- GEORGIE WAS SO JAZZED, HE GAVE US THE EXTRA TICKETS!
THIS IS A MATH CLASS, NOT A LUNCH ROOM!
SORRY, MS. GRUNDY, BUT I HAD TO EAT SOMETHING! ASK THE OTHER STUDENTS --THEY COULD HEAR MY STOMACH--
RUMBLE

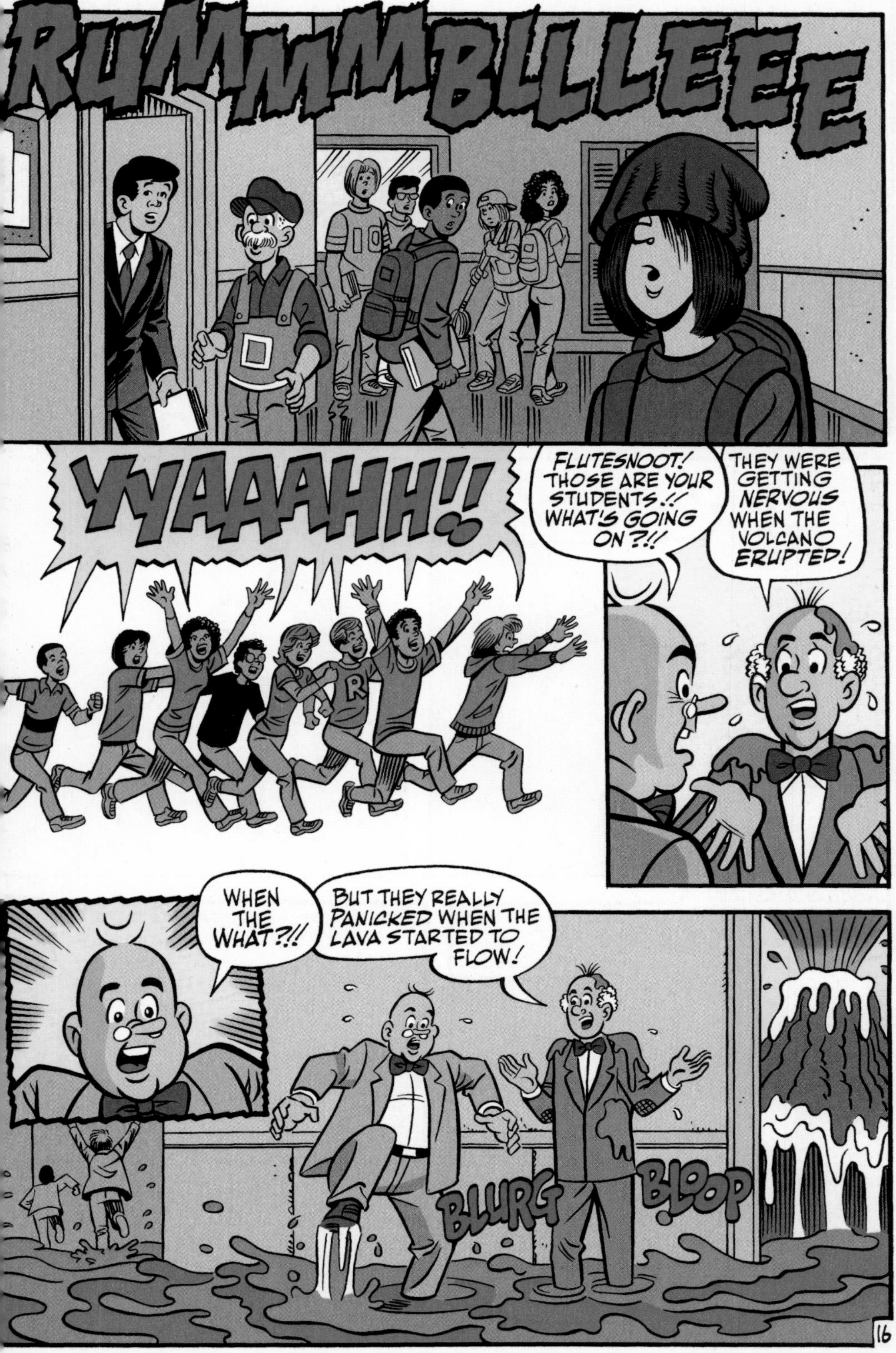
RUMMMBLLLEEE
YYAAAHH!!
FLUTESNOOT! THOSE ARE YOUR STUDENTS.!! WHAT'S GOING ON?!!
THEY WERE GETTING NERVOUS WHEN THE VOLCANO ERUPTED!
WHEN THE WHAT?!!
BUT THEY REALLY PANICKED WHEN THE LAVA STARTED TO FLOW!
BLURG
BLOOP

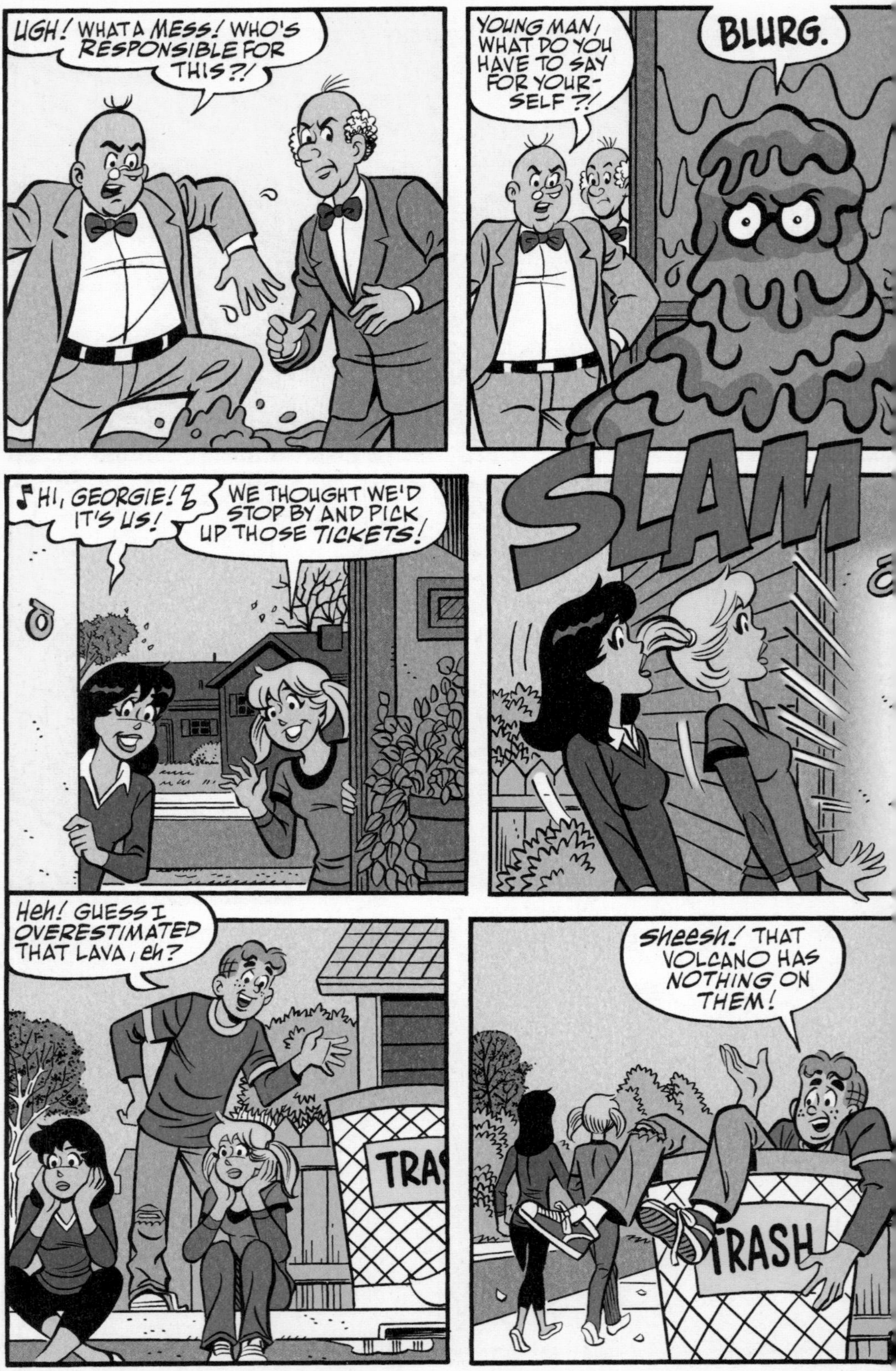
UGH! WHAT A MESS! WHO'S RESPONSIBLE FOR THIS?!
YOUNG MAN, WHAT DO YOU HAVE TO SAY FOR YOURSELF?!
BLURG.
SLAM
HI, GEORGIE! IT'S US!
WE THOUGHT WE'D STOP BY AND PICK UP THOSE TICKETS!
Heh! GUESS I OVERESTIMATED THAT LAVA, eh?
TRASH
Sheesh! THAT VOLCANO HAS NOTHING ON THEM!
TRASH

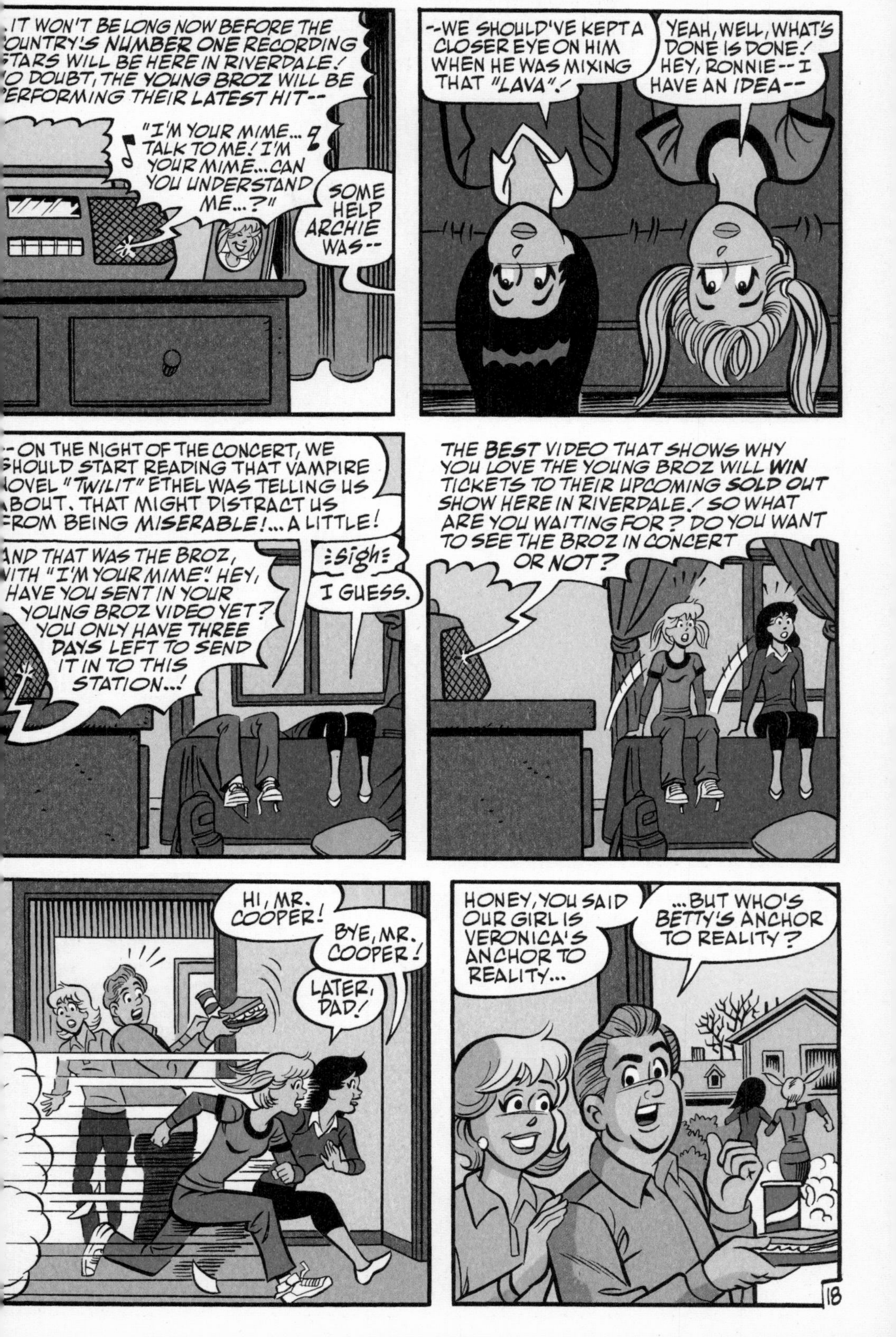
IT WON'T BE LONG NOW BEFORE THE COUNTRY'S NUMBER ONE RECORDING STARS WILL BE HERE IN RIVERDALE! NO DOUBT, THE YOUNG BROZ WILL BE PERFORMING THEIR LATEST HIT--
"I'M YOUR MIME... TALK TO ME! I'M YOUR MIME...CAN YOU UNDERSTAND ME...?"
SOME HELP ARCHIE WAS--
--WE SHOULD'VE KEPT A CLOSER EYE ON HIM WHEN HE WAS MIXING THAT "LAVA"!
YEAH, WELL, WHAT'S DONE IS DONE! HEY, RONNIE-- I HAVE AN IDEA--
--ON THE NIGHT OF THE CONCERT, WE SHOULD START READING THAT VAMPIRE NOVEL "TWILIT" ETHEL WAS TELLING US ABOUT. THAT MIGHT DISTRACT US FROM BEING MISERABLE!... A LITTLE!
AND THAT WAS THE BROZ, WITH "I'M YOUR MIME"! HEY, HAVE YOU SENT IN YOUR YOUNG BROZ VIDEO YET? YOU ONLY HAVE THREE DAYS LEFT TO SEND IT IN TO THIS STATION...!
sigh
I GUESS.
THE BEST VIDEO THAT SHOWS WHY YOU LOVE THE YOUNG BROZ WILL WIN TICKETS TO THEIR UPCOMING SOLD OUT SHOW HERE IN RIVERDALE! SO WHAT ARE YOU WAITING FOR? DO YOU WANT TO SEE THE BROZ IN CONCERT OR NOT?
HI, MR. COOPER!
BYE, MR. COOPER!
LATER, DAD!
HONEY, YOU SAID OUR GIRL IS VERONICA'S ANCHOR TO REALITY...
...BUT WHO'S BETTY'S ANCHOR TO REALITY?
18

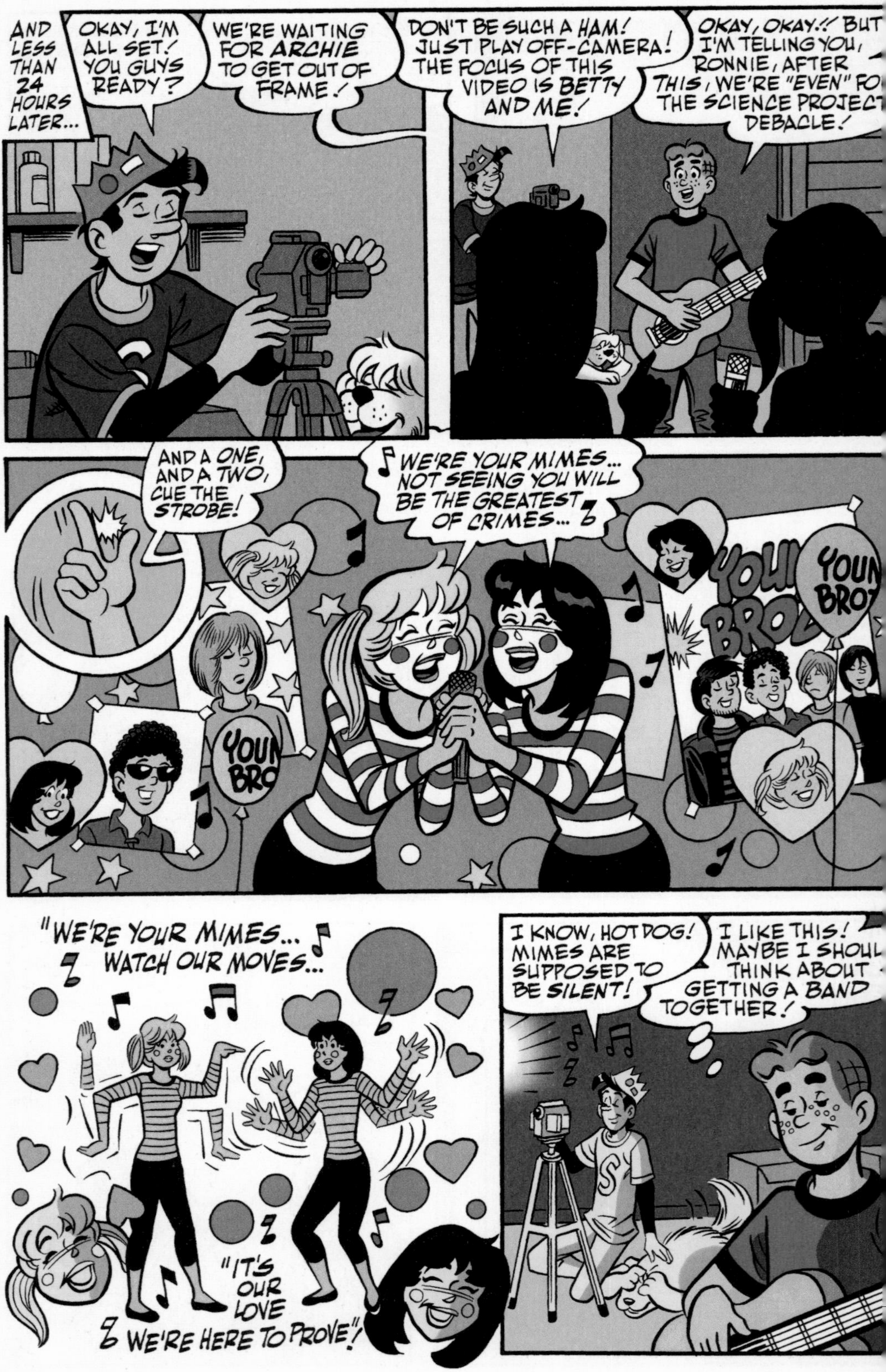
AND LESS THAN 24 HOURS LATER...
OKAY, I'M ALL SET! YOU GUYS READY?
WE'RE WAITING FOR ARCHIE TO GET OUT OF FRAME!
DON'T BE SUCH A HAM! JUST PLAY OFF-CAMERA! THE FOCUS OF THIS VIDEO IS BETTY AND ME!
OKAY, OKAY!! BUT I'M TELLING YOU, RONNIE, AFTER THIS, WE'RE "EVEN" FO THE SCIENCE PROJECT DEBACLE!
AND A ONE, AND A TWO, CUE THE STROBE!
WE'RE YOUR MIMES... NOT SEEING YOU WILL BE THE GREATEST OF CRIMES...
"WE'RE YOUR MIMES... WATCH OUR MOVES...
"IT'S OUR LOVE WE'RE HERE TO PROVE"!
I KNOW, HOT DOG! MIMES ARE SUPPOSED TO BE SILENT!
I LIKE THIS! MAYBE I SHOUL THINK ABOUT GETTING A BAND TOGETHER!

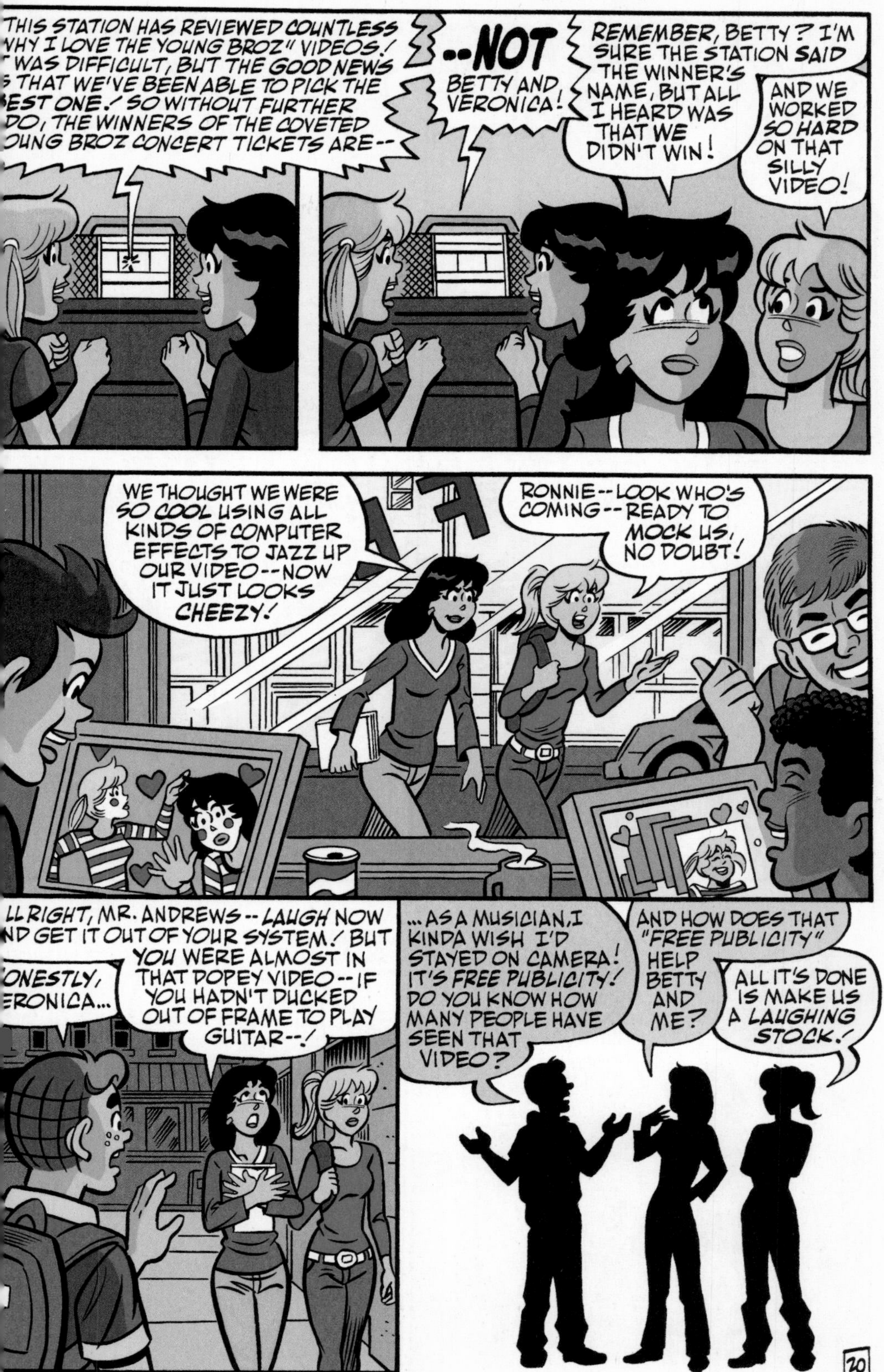
THIS STATION HAS REVIEWED COUNTLESS "WHY I LOVE THE YOUNG BROZ" VIDEOS! IT WAS DIFFICULT, BUT THE GOOD NEWS IS THAT WE'VE BEEN ABLE TO PICK THE BEST ONE! SO WITHOUT FURTHER ADO, THE WINNERS OF THE COVETED YOUNG BROZ CONCERT TICKETS ARE--
--NOT BETTY AND VERONICA!
REMEMBER, BETTY? I'M SURE THE STATION SAID THE WINNER'S NAME, BUT ALL I HEARD WAS THAT WE DIDN'T WIN!
AND WE WORKED SO HARD ON THAT SILLY VIDEO!
WE THOUGHT WE WERE SO COOL USING ALL KINDS OF COMPUTER EFFECTS TO JAZZ UP OUR VIDEO--NOW IT JUST LOOKS CHEEZY!
RONNIE--LOOK WHO'S COMING--READY TO MOCK US, NO DOUBT!
ALL RIGHT, MR. ANDREWS--LAUGH NOW AND GET IT OUT OF YOUR SYSTEM! BUT YOU WERE ALMOST IN THAT DOPEY VIDEO--IF YOU HADN'T DUCKED OUT OF FRAME TO PLAY GUITAR--!
HONESTLY, VERONICA...
...AS A MUSICIAN, I KINDA WISH I'D STAYED ON CAMERA! IT'S FREE PUBLICITY! DO YOU KNOW HOW MANY PEOPLE HAVE SEEN THAT VIDEO?
AND HOW DOES THAT "FREE PUBLICITY" HELP BETTY AND ME?
ALL IT'S DONE IS MAKE US A LAUGHING STOCK!
20

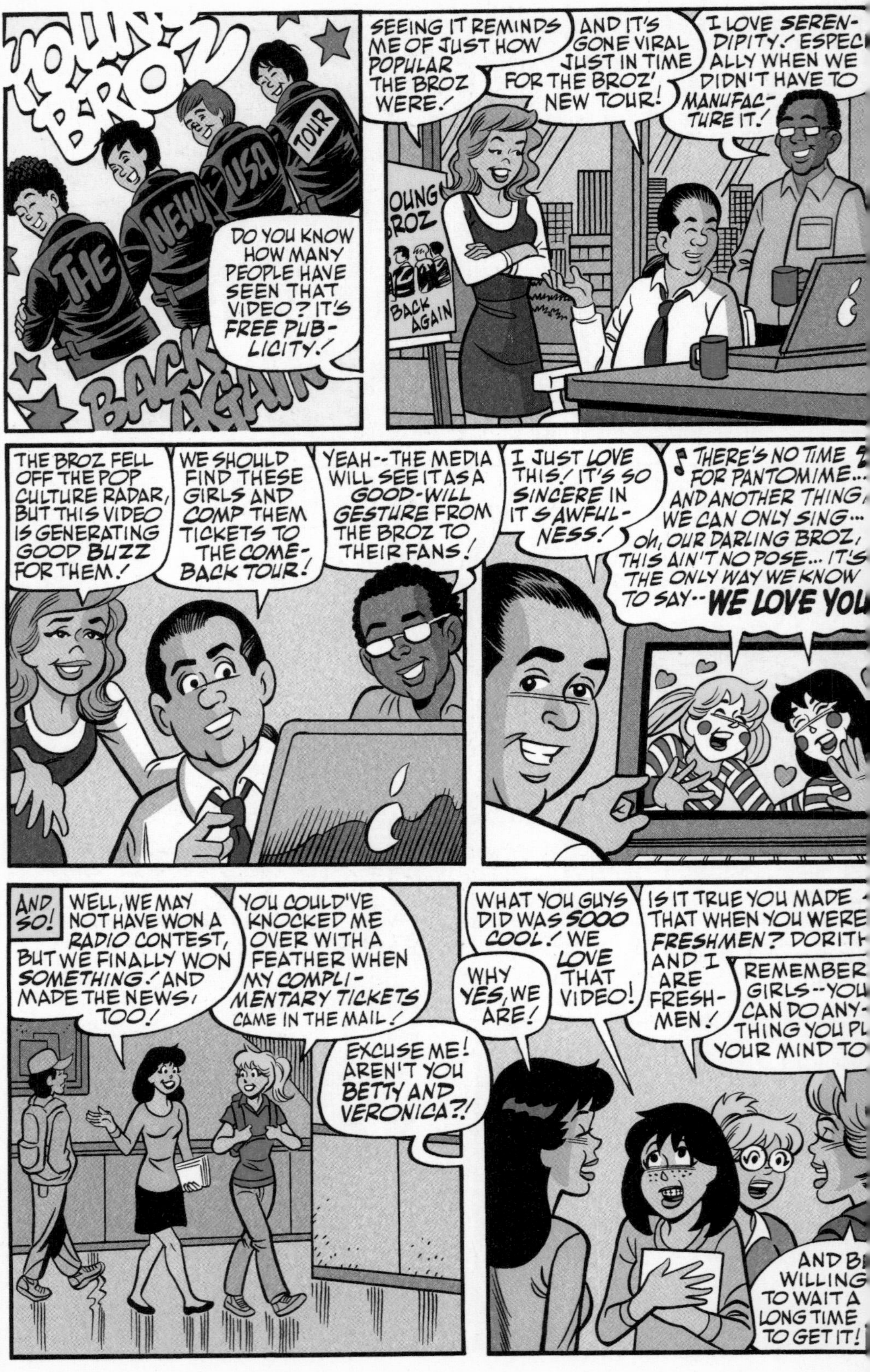

YOUNG BROZ
THE NEW USA TOUR
BACK AGAIN
DO YOU KNOW HOW MANY PEOPLE HAVE SEEN THAT VIDEO? IT'S FREE PUBLICITY!
SEEING IT REMINDS ME OF JUST HOW POPULAR THE BROZ WERE!
AND IT'S GONE VIRAL JUST IN TIME FOR THE BROZ' NEW TOUR!
I LOVE SERENDIPITY! ESPECI ALLY WHEN WE DIDN'T HAVE TO MANUFACTURE IT!
OUNG ROZ BACK AGAIN
THE BROZ FELL OFF THE POP CULTURE RADAR, BUT THIS VIDEO IS GENERATING GOOD BUZZ FOR THEM!
WE SHOULD FIND THESE GIRLS AND COMP THEM TICKETS TO THE COMEBACK TOUR!
YEAH--THE MEDIA WILL SEE IT AS A GOOD-WILL GESTURE FROM THE BROZ TO THEIR FANS!
I JUST LOVE THIS! IT'S SO SINCERE IN ITS AWFULNESS!
THERE'S NO TIME FOR PANTOMIME... AND ANOTHER THING, WE CAN ONLY SING... OH, OUR DARLING BROZ, THIS AIN'T NO POSE... IT'S THE ONLY WAY WE KNOW TO SAY--WE LOVE YOU
AND SO!
WELL, WE MAY NOT HAVE WON A RADIO CONTEST, BUT WE FINALLY WON SOMETHING! AND MADE THE NEWS, TOO!
YOU COULD'VE KNOCKED ME OVER WITH A FEATHER WHEN MY COMPLIMENTARY TICKETS CAME IN THE MAIL!
EXCUSE ME! AREN'T YOU BETTY AND VERONICA?!
WHY YES, WE ARE!
WHAT YOU GUYS DID WAS SOOO COOL! WE LOVE THAT VIDEO!
IS IT TRUE YOU MADE THAT WHEN YOU WERE FRESHMEN? DORITH AND I ARE FRESHMEN!
REMEMBER GIRLS--YOU CAN DO ANYTHING YOU PL YOUR MIND TO
AND BE WILLING TO WAIT A LONG TIME TO GET IT!

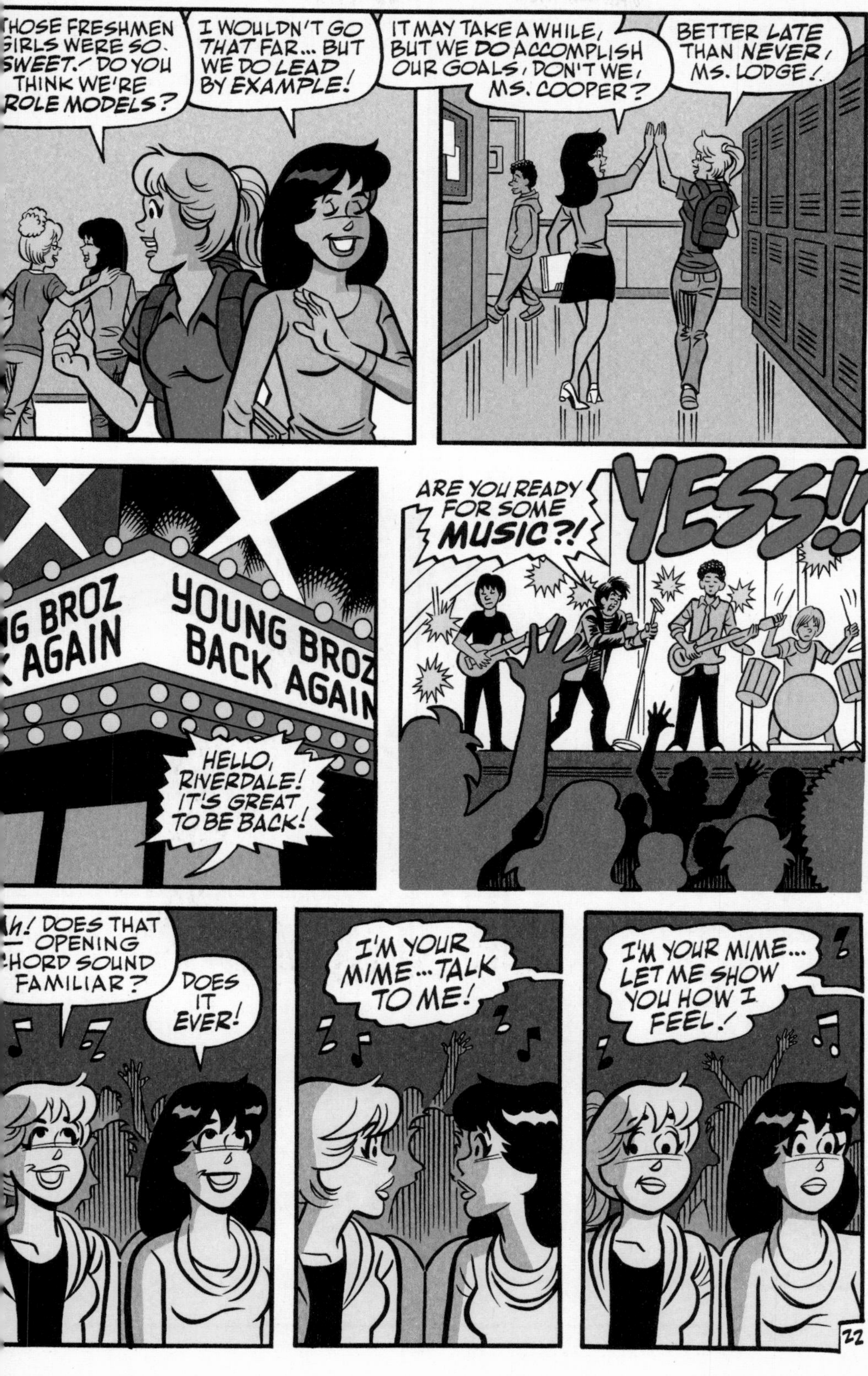
THOSE FRESHMEN GIRLS WERE SO SWEET! DO YOU THINK WE'RE ROLE MODELS?
I WOULDN'T GO THAT FAR... BUT WE DO LEAD BY EXAMPLE!
IT MAY TAKE A WHILE, BUT WE DO ACCOMPLISH OUR GOALS, DON'T WE, MS. COOPER?
BETTER LATE THAN NEVER, MS. LODGE!
G BROZ AGAIN
YOUNG BROZ BACK AGAIN
HELLO, RIVERDALE! IT'S GREAT TO BE BACK!
ARE YOU READY FOR SOME MUSIC?!
YESS!!
...h! DOES THAT OPENING CHORD SOUND FAMILIAR?
DOES IT EVER!
I'M YOUR MIME... TALK TO ME!
I'M YOUR MIME... LET ME SHOW YOU HOW I FEEL!

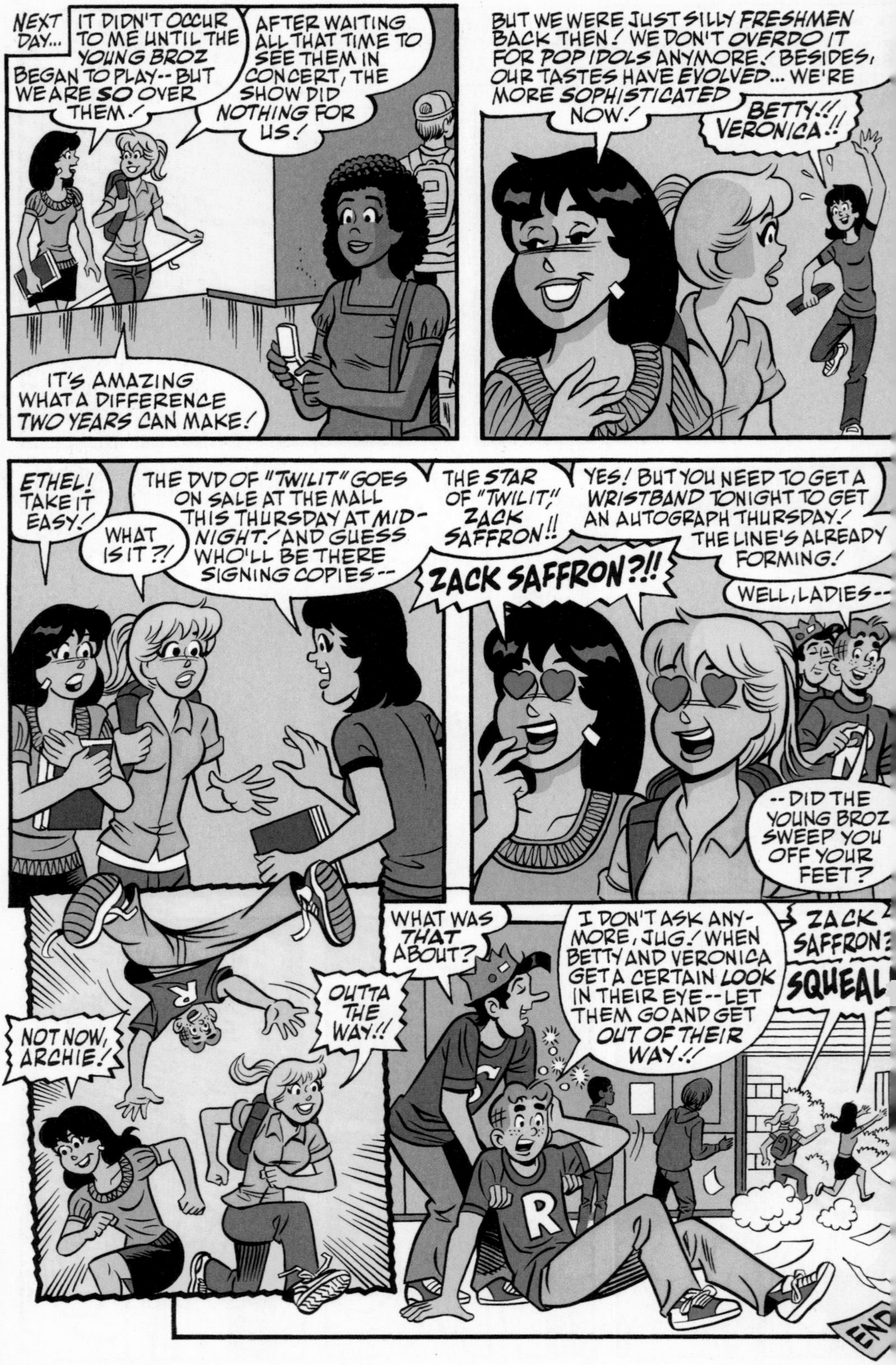
NEXT DAY...
IT DIDN'T OCCUR TO ME UNTIL THE YOUNG BROZ BEGAN TO PLAY-- BUT WE ARE SO OVER THEM.!
AFTER WAITING ALL THAT TIME TO SEE THEM IN CONCERT, THE SHOW DID NOTHING FOR US!
IT'S AMAZING WHAT A DIFFERENCE TWO YEARS CAN MAKE!
BUT WE WERE JUST SILLY FRESHMEN BACK THEN! WE DON'T OVERDO IT FOR POP IDOLS ANYMORE! BESIDES, OUR TASTES HAVE EVOLVED... WE'RE MORE SOPHISTICATED NOW!
BETTY!! VERONICA!!
ETHEL! TAKE IT EASY!
WHAT IS IT?!
THE DVD OF "TWILIT" GOES ON SALE AT THE MALL THIS THURSDAY AT MID-NIGHT! AND GUESS WHO'LL BE THERE SIGNING COPIES--
THE STAR OF "TWILIT," ZACK SAFFRON!!
YES! BUT YOU NEED TO GET A WRISTBAND TONIGHT TO GET AN AUTOGRAPH THURSDAY! THE LINE'S ALREADY FORMING!
ZACK SAFFRON?!!
WELL, LADIES--
--DID THE YOUNG BROZ SWEEP YOU OFF YOUR FEET?
OUTTA THE WAY!!
NOT NOW, ARCHIE!
WHAT WAS THAT ABOUT?
I DON'T ASK ANY-MORE, JUG! WHEN BETTY AND VERONICA GET A CERTAIN LOOK IN THEIR EYE--LET THEM GO AND GET OUT OF THEIR WAY!!
ZACK SAFFRON?
SQUEAL!
END

THE MISSING CHAPTERS: PART 3

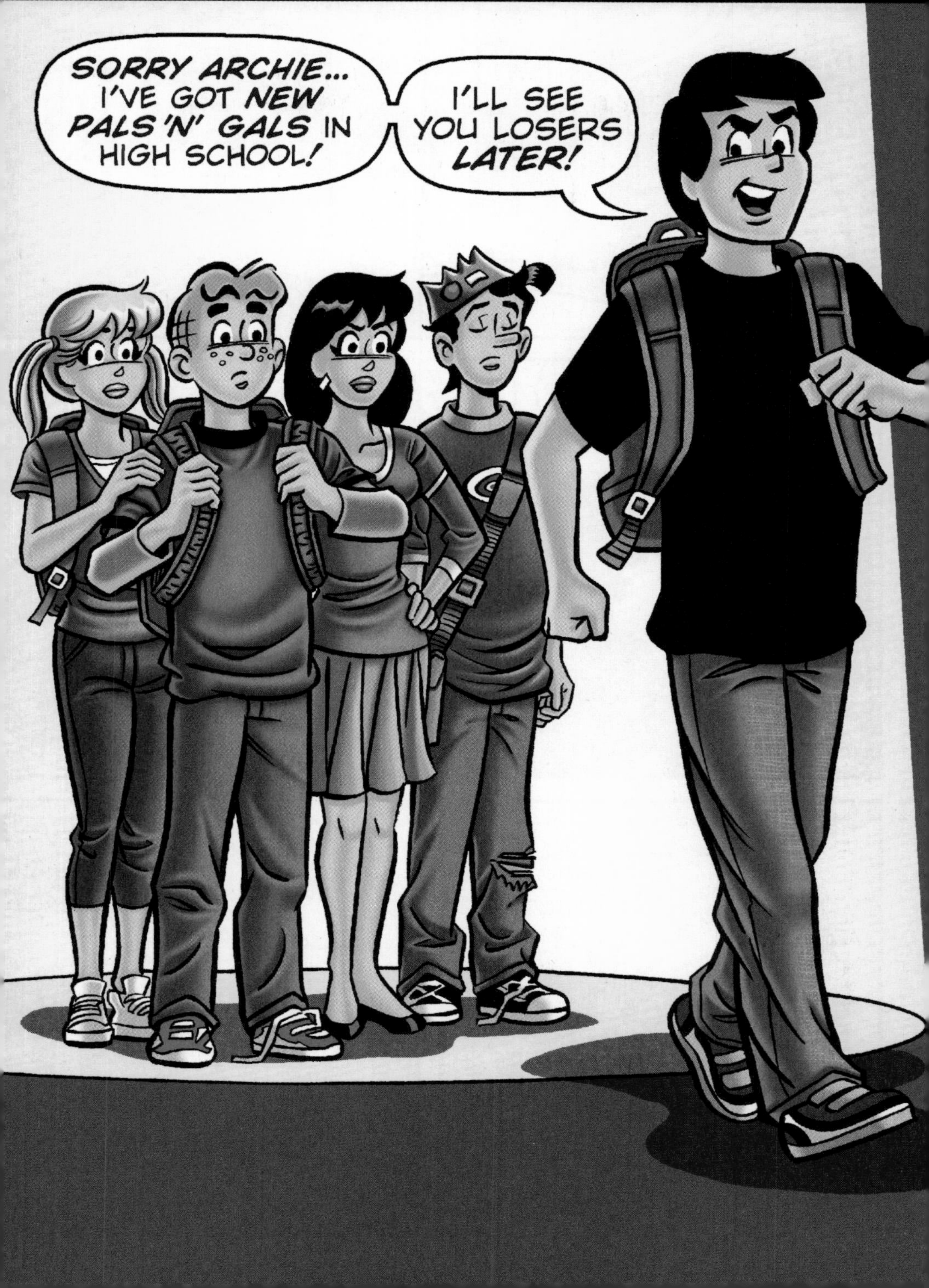
SORRY ARCHIE... I'VE GOT NEW PALS 'N' GALS IN HIGH SCHOOL!
I'LL SEE YOU LOSERS LATER!

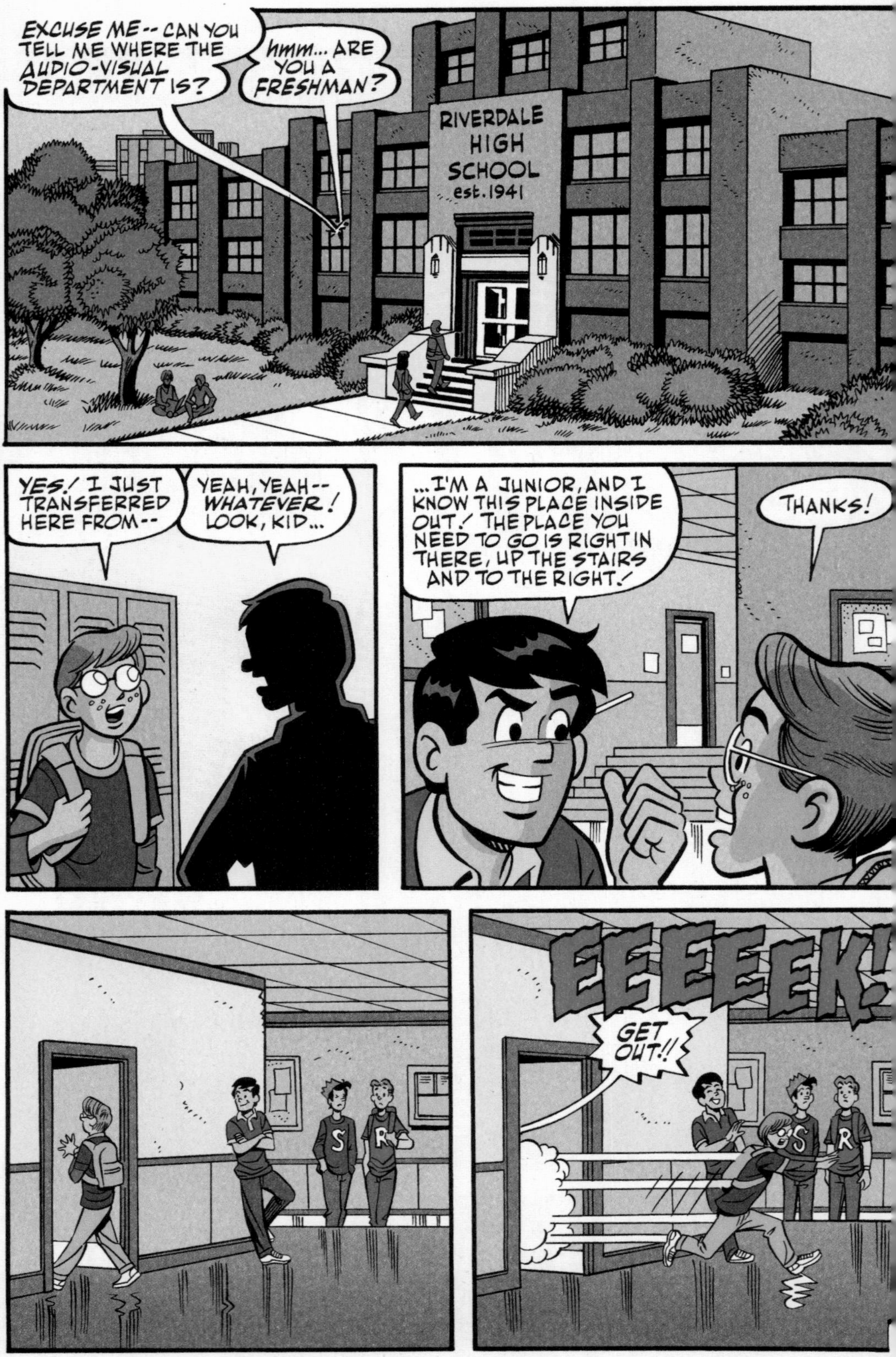
EXCUSE ME -- CAN YOU TELL ME WHERE THE AUDIO-VISUAL DEPARTMENT IS?
hmm... ARE YOU A FRESHMAN?
RIVERDALE HIGH SCHOOL est. 1941
YES! I JUST TRANSFERRED HERE FROM --
YEAH, YEAH -- WHATEVER! LOOK, KID...
...I'M A JUNIOR, AND I KNOW THIS PLACE INSIDE OUT! THE PLACE YOU NEED TO GO IS RIGHT IN THERE, UP THE STAIRS AND TO THE RIGHT!
THANKS!
EEEEEK!
GET OUT!!

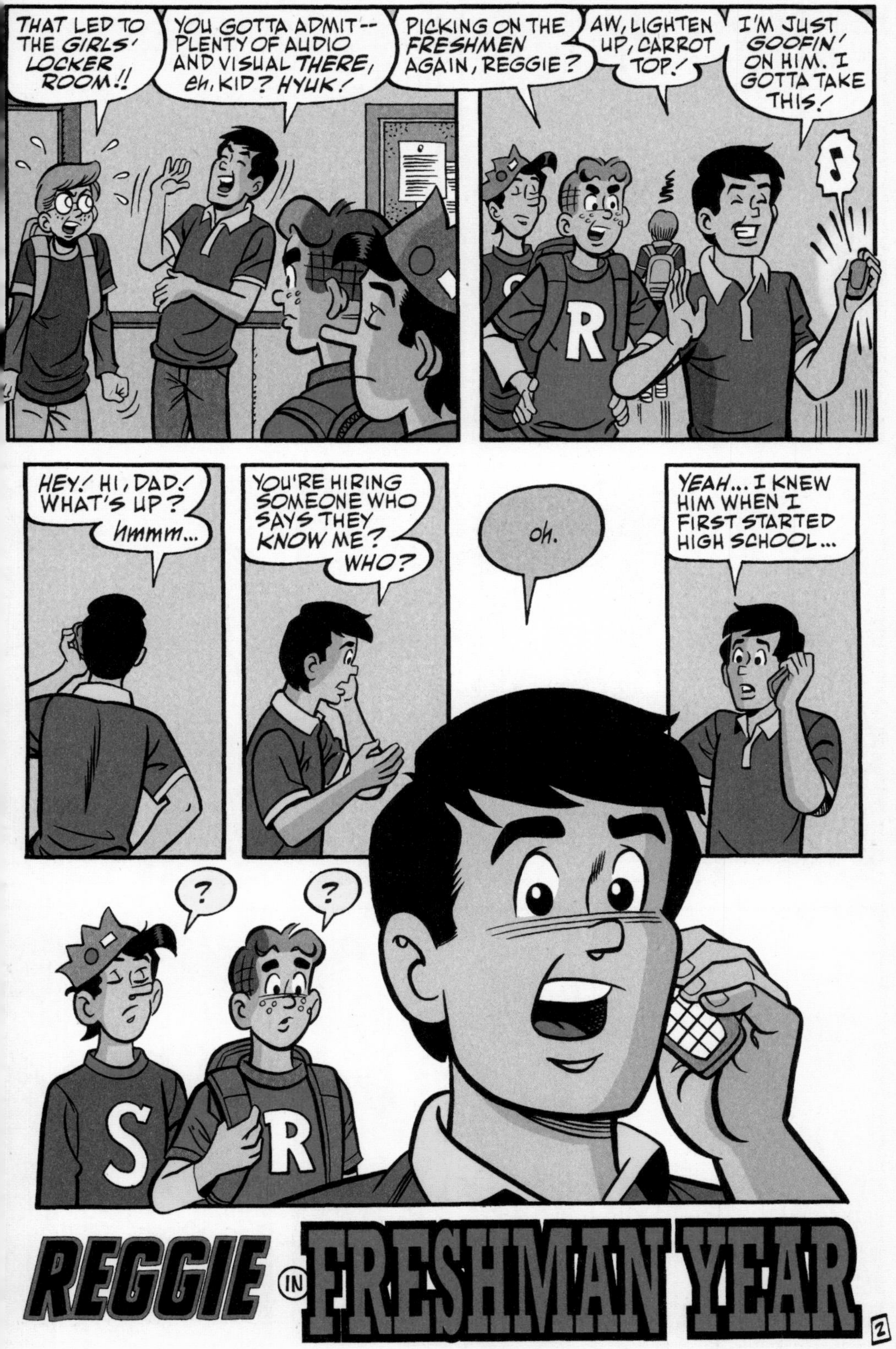
THAT LED TO THE GIRLS' LOCKER ROOM!!
YOU GOTTA ADMIT-- PLENTY OF AUDIO AND VISUAL THERE, eh, KID? HYUK!
PICKING ON THE FRESHMEN AGAIN, REGGIE?
AW, LIGHTEN UP, CARROT TOP!
I'M JUST GOOFIN' ON HIM. I GOTTA TAKE THIS!
R
HEY! HI, DAD! WHAT'S UP? hmmm...
YOU'RE HIRING SOMEONE WHO SAYS THEY KNOW ME? WHO?
oh.
YEAH... I KNEW HIM WHEN I FIRST STARTED HIGH SCHOOL...
?
?
S
R
REGGIE IN FRESHMAN YEAR

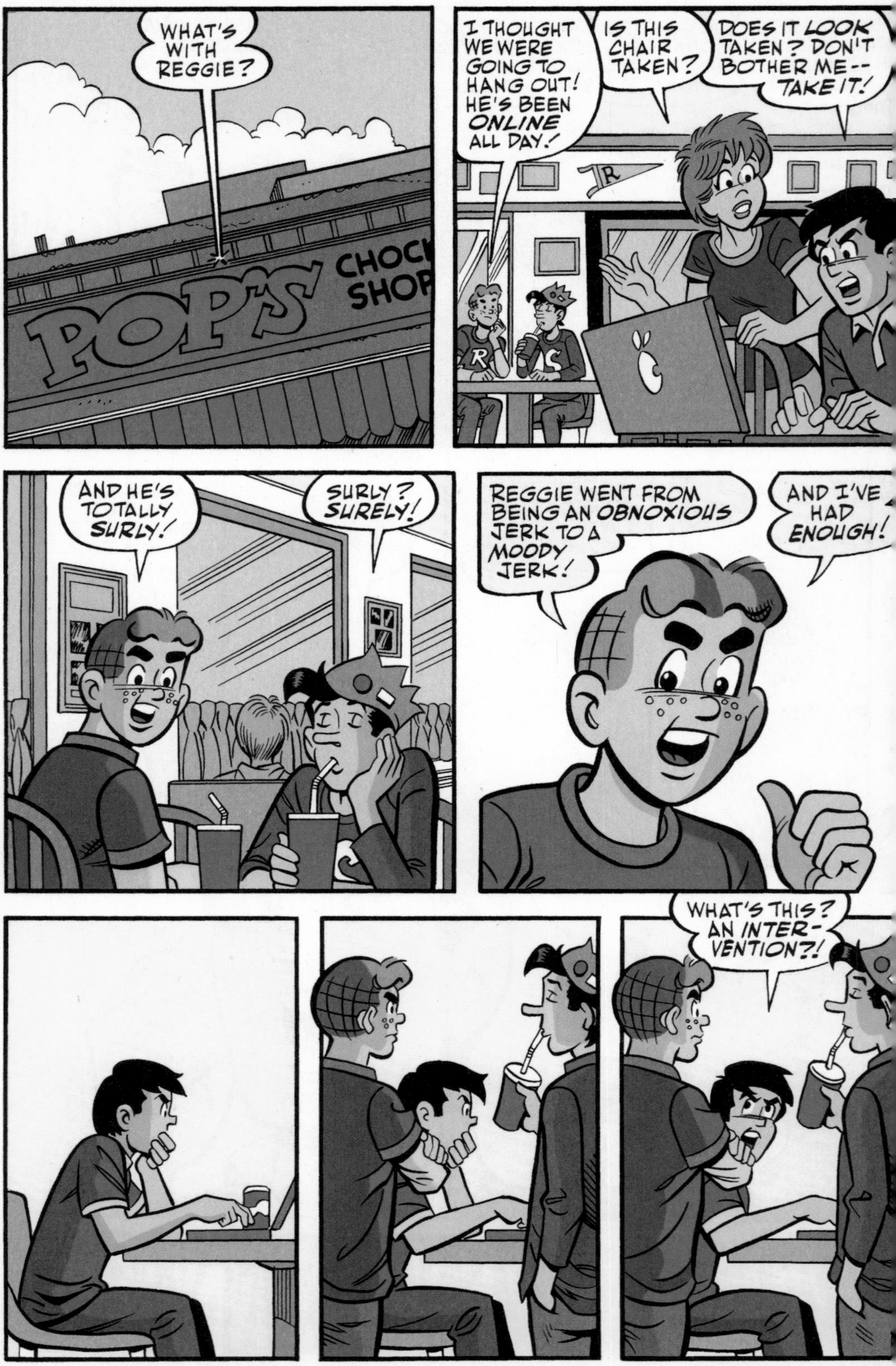
WHAT'S WITH REGGIE?
POP'S CHOC SHOP
I THOUGHT WE WERE GOING TO HANG OUT! HE'S BEEN ONLINE ALL DAY!
IS THIS CHAIR TAKEN?
DOES IT LOOK TAKEN? DON'T BOTHER ME-- TAKE IT!
AND HE'S TOTALLY SURLY!
SURLY? SURELY!
REGGIE WENT FROM BEING AN OBNOXIOUS JERK TO A MOODY JERK!
AND I'VE HAD ENOUGH!
WHAT'S THIS? AN INTER-VENTION?!

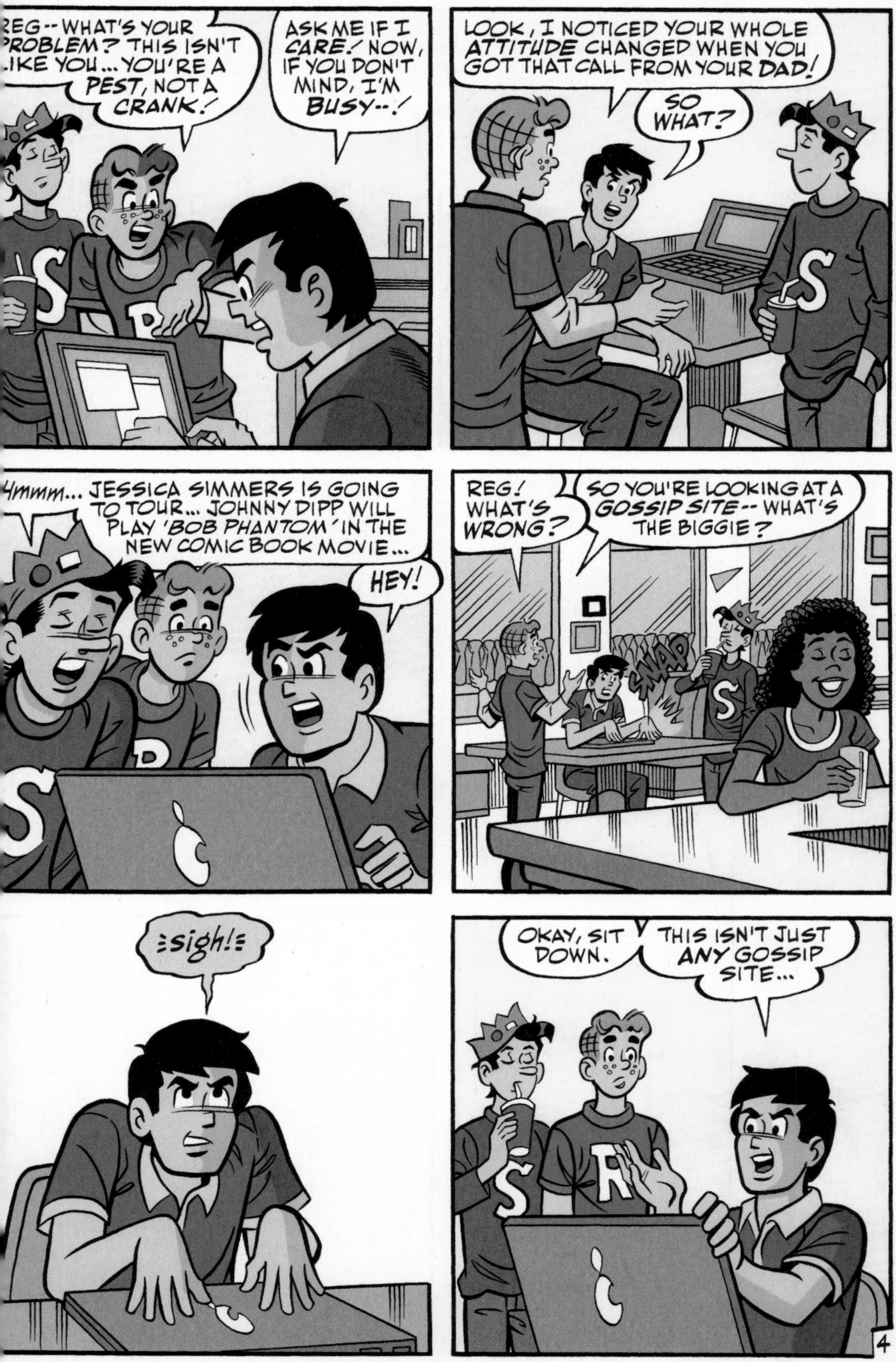
REG--WHAT'S YOUR PROBLEM? THIS ISN'T LIKE YOU...YOU'RE A PEST, NOT A CRANK!
ASK ME IF I CARE! NOW, IF YOU DON'T MIND, I'M BUSY--!
LOOK, I NOTICED YOUR WHOLE ATTITUDE CHANGED WHEN YOU GOT THAT CALL FROM YOUR DAD!
SO WHAT?
Hmmm... JESSICA SIMMERS IS GOING TO TOUR... JOHNNY DIPP WILL PLAY 'BOB PHANTOM' IN THE NEW COMIC BOOK MOVIE...
HEY!
REG! WHAT'S WRONG?
SO YOU'RE LOOKING AT A GOSSIP SITE--WHAT'S THE BIGGIE?
SNAP
sigh!
OKAY, SIT DOWN.
THIS ISN'T JUST ANY GOSSIP SITE...

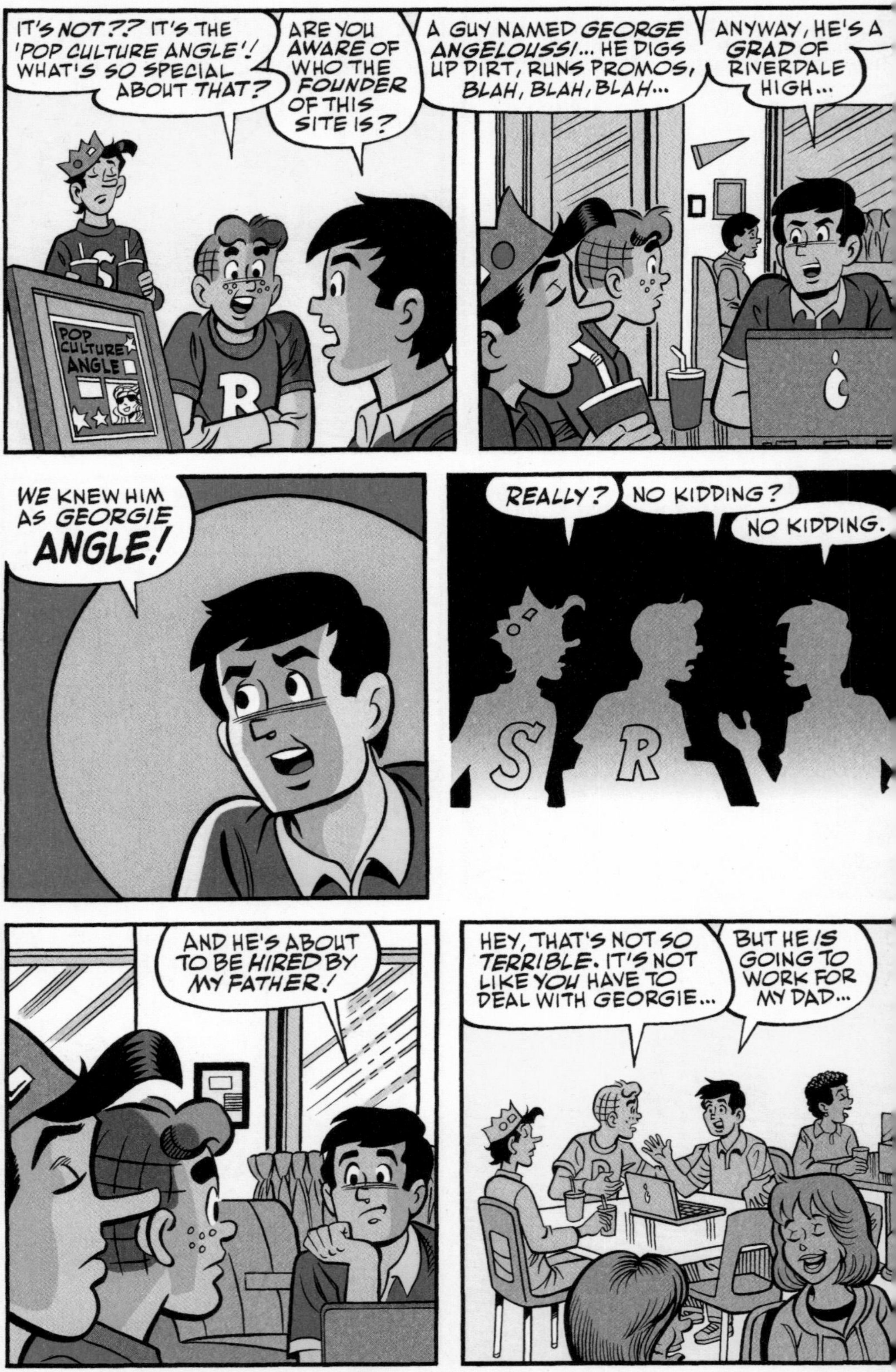
IT'S NOT?? IT'S THE 'POP CULTURE ANGLE'! WHAT'S SO SPECIAL ABOUT THAT?
ARE YOU AWARE OF WHO THE FOUNDER OF THIS SITE IS?
POP CULTURE ANGLE
A GUY NAMED GEORGE ANGELOUSSI... HE DIGS UP DIRT, RUNS PROMOS, BLAH, BLAH, BLAH...
ANYWAY, HE'S A GRAD OF RIVERDALE HIGH...
WE KNEW HIM AS GEORGIE ANGLE!
REALLY?
NO KIDDING?
NO KIDDING.
AND HE'S ABOUT TO BE HIRED BY MY FATHER!
HEY, THAT'S NOT SO TERRIBLE. IT'S NOT LIKE YOU HAVE TO DEAL WITH GEORGIE...
BUT HE IS GOING TO WORK FOR MY DAD...

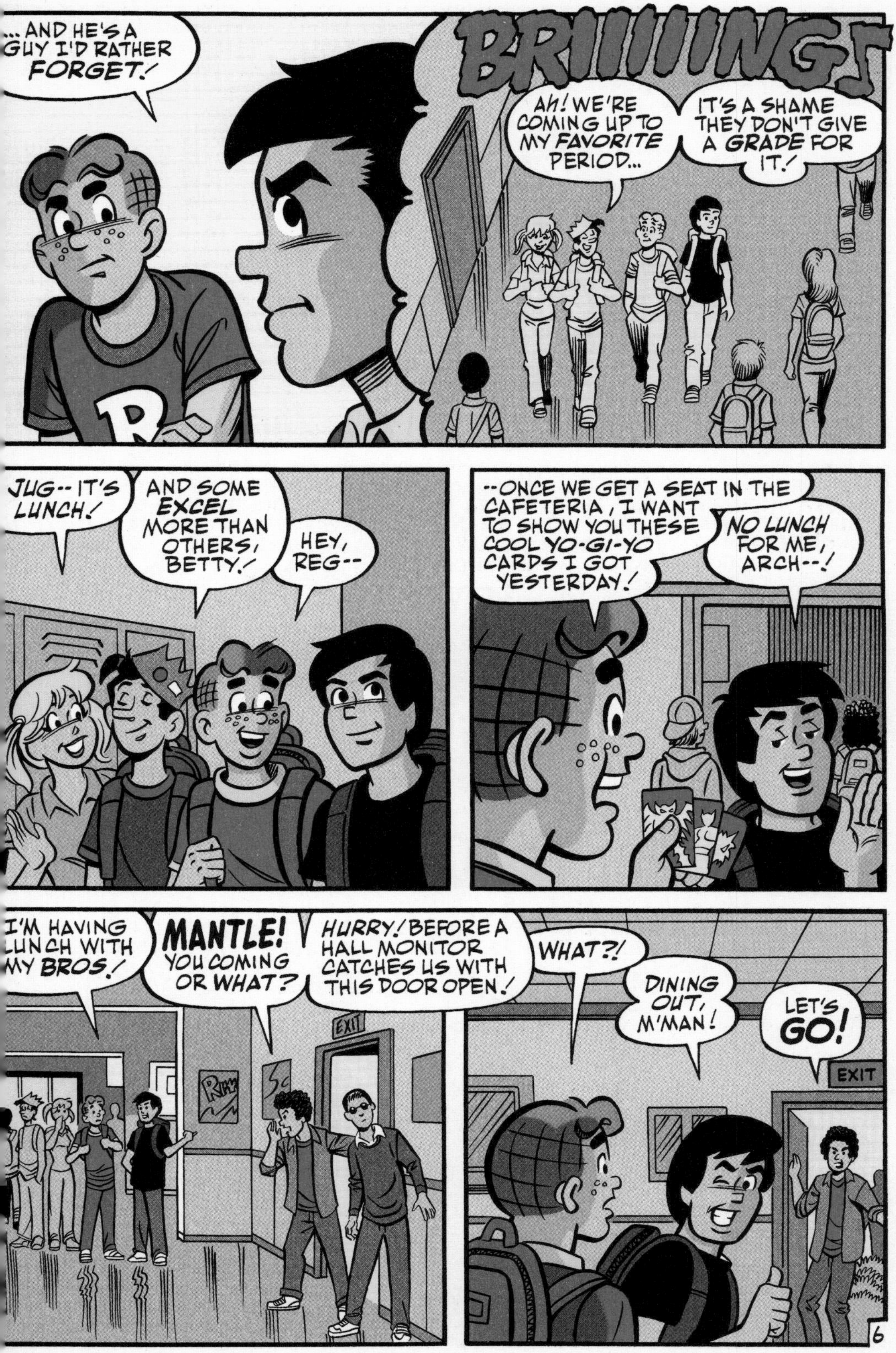
...AND HE'S A GUY I'D RATHER FORGET!
BRIIIIIING
AH! WE'RE COMING UP TO MY FAVORITE PERIOD...
IT'S A SHAME THEY DON'T GIVE A GRADE FOR IT!
JUG-- IT'S LUNCH!
AND SOME EXCEL MORE THAN OTHERS, BETTY!
HEY, REG--
--ONCE WE GET A SEAT IN THE CAFETERIA, I WANT TO SHOW YOU THESE COOL YO-GI-YO CARDS I GOT YESTERDAY!
NO LUNCH FOR ME, ARCH--!
I'M HAVING LUNCH WITH MY BROS!
MANTLE! YOU COMING OR WHAT?
HURRY! BEFORE A HALL MONITOR CATCHES US WITH THIS DOOR OPEN!
EXIT
WHAT?!
DINING OUT, M'MAN!
LET'S GO!
EXIT

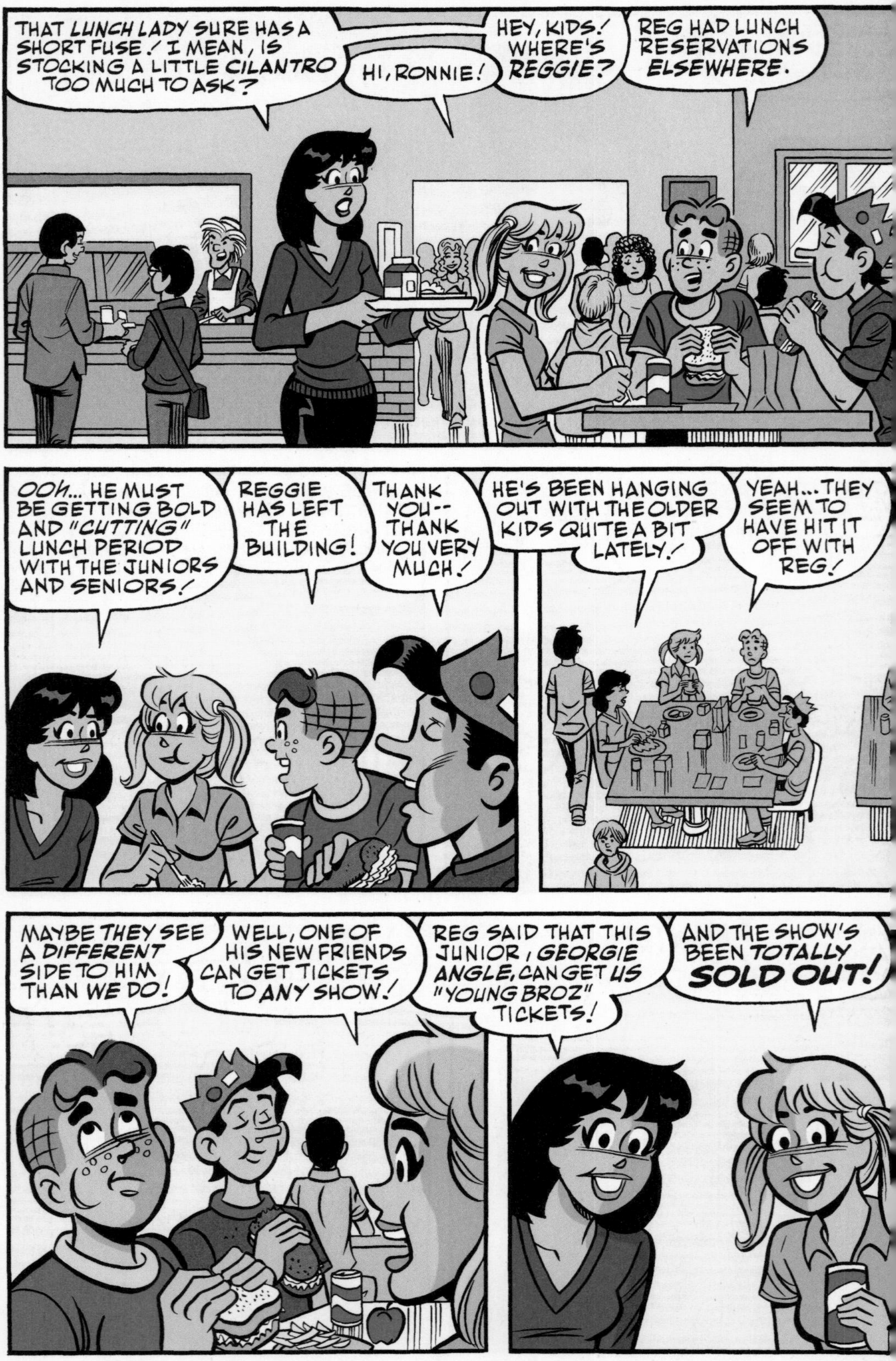
THAT LUNCH LADY SURE HAS A SHORT FUSE! I MEAN, IS STOCKING A LITTLE CILANTRO TOO MUCH TO ASK?
HI, RONNIE!
HEY, KIDS! WHERE'S REGGIE?
REG HAD LUNCH RESERVATIONS ELSEWHERE.
OOH... HE MUST BE GETTING BOLD AND "CUTTING" LUNCH PERIOD WITH THE JUNIORS AND SENIORS!
REGGIE HAS LEFT THE BUILDING!
THANK YOU-- THANK YOU VERY MUCH!
HE'S BEEN HANGING OUT WITH THE OLDER KIDS QUITE A BIT LATELY!
YEAH... THEY SEEM TO HAVE HIT IT OFF WITH REG!
MAYBE THEY SEE A DIFFERENT SIDE TO HIM THAN WE DO!
WELL, ONE OF HIS NEW FRIENDS CAN GET TICKETS TO ANY SHOW!
REG SAID THAT THIS JUNIOR, GEORGIE ANGLE, CAN GET US "YOUNG BROZ" TICKETS!
AND THE SHOW'S BEEN TOTALLY SOLD OUT!

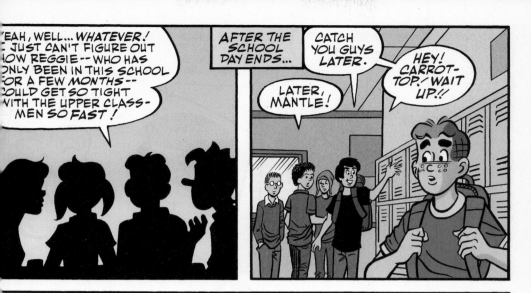

(top left panel): 'EAH, WELL... *WHATEVER!* I JUST CAN'T FIGURE OUT HOW REGGIE -- WHO HAS ONLY BEEN IN THIS SCHOOL FOR A FEW MONTHS -- COULD GET SO TIGHT WITH THE UPPER CLASSMEN SO FAST!

(top right panel): AFTER THE SCHOOL DAY ENDS...

CATCH YOU GUYS LATER.

LATER, MANTLE!

HEY! CARROT-TOP! WAIT UP!!

(middle left panel): 'OU *SURE* YOU 'VANT TO BE SEEN 'VITH A LOWLY FROSH, REG?

ARCH! HOW LONG HAVE WE KNOWN EACH OTHER?

(middle right panel): FOR *YOU*, I MAKE AN EXCEPTION! HEY, I NEED A FAVOR, BUDDY!

WHENEVER I HEAR *"FAVOR"* AND *"BUDDY"* IN THE SAME SENTENCE, *WATCH OUT!*

(bottom left panel): I'M GOING TO BE... UH... "AT LIBERTY" TOMORROW MORNING -- AND I WAS WONDERING IF YOU'D COVER FOR ME...

YOU MEAN YOU'RE CUTTING GRUNDY'S CLASS?!

(bottom right panel): I WOULDN'T ASK IF IT WASN'T IMPORTANT! GEORGIE ANGLE ASKED ME TO HELP HIM WITH SOMETHING!

BUT, REG...

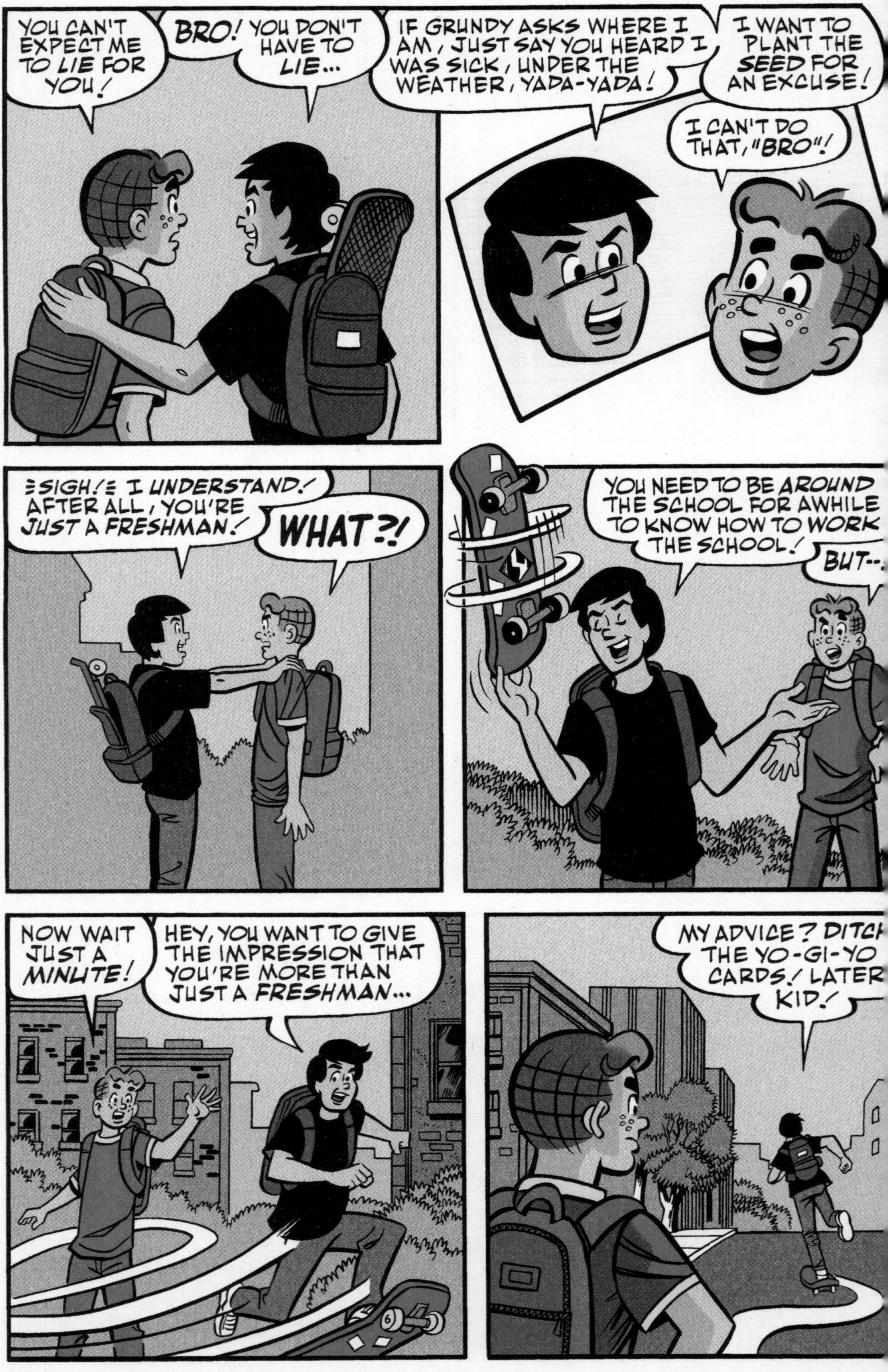
YOU CAN'T EXPECT ME TO LIE FOR YOU!
BRO! YOU DON'T HAVE TO LIE...
IF GRUNDY ASKS WHERE I AM, JUST SAY YOU HEARD I WAS SICK, UNDER THE WEATHER, YADA-YADA!
I WANT TO PLANT THE SEED FOR AN EXCUSE!
I CAN'T DO THAT, "BRO"!
SIGH! I UNDERSTAND! AFTER ALL, YOU'RE JUST A FRESHMAN!
WHAT?!
YOU NEED TO BE AROUND THE SCHOOL FOR AWHILE TO KNOW HOW TO WORK THE SCHOOL!
BUT--
NOW WAIT JUST A MINUTE!
HEY, YOU WANT TO GIVE THE IMPRESSION THAT YOU'RE MORE THAN JUST A FRESHMAN...
MY ADVICE? DITCH THE YO-GI-YO CARDS! LATER KID!

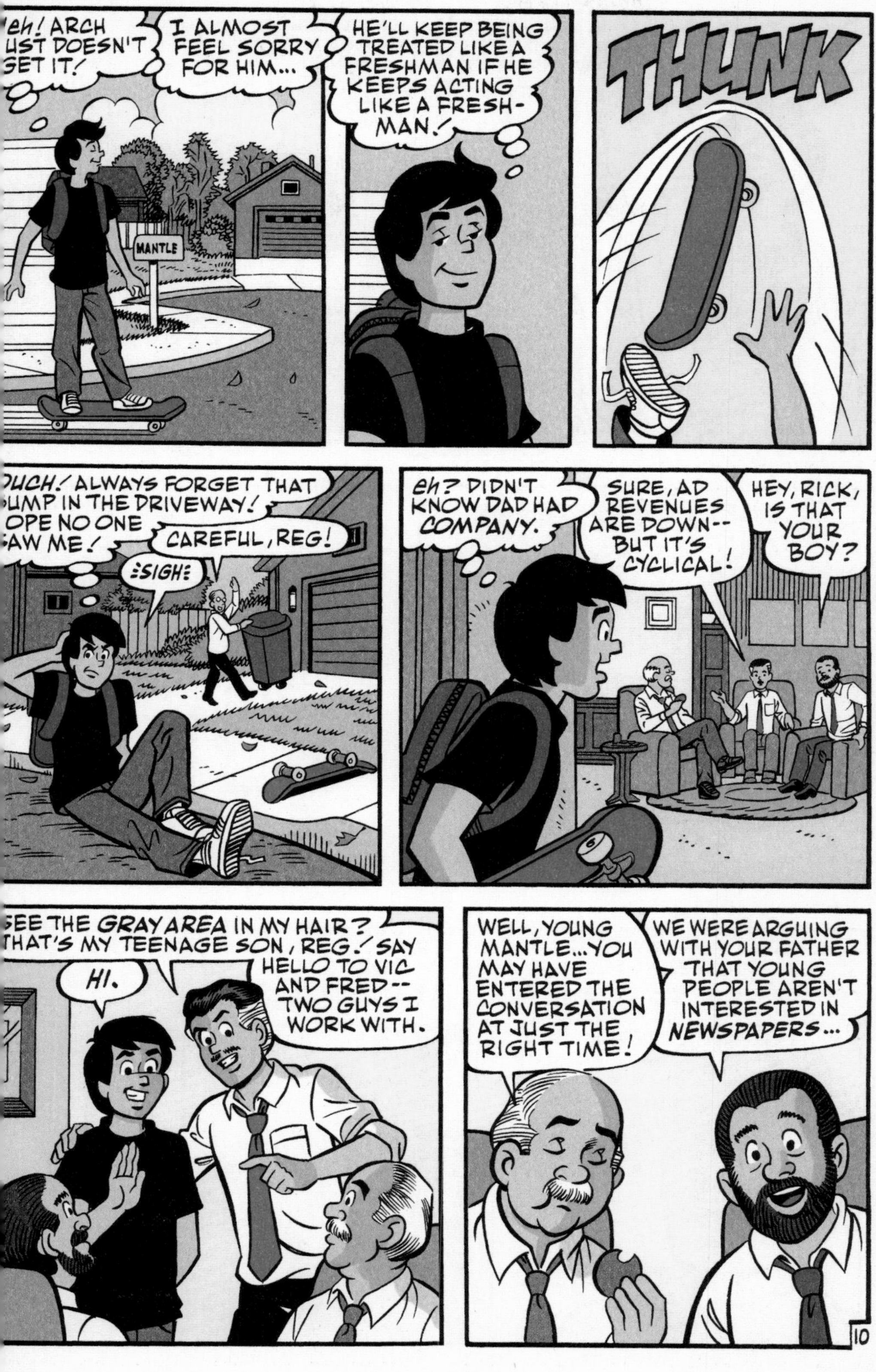

EH! ARCH JUST DOESN'T GET IT!
I ALMOST FEEL SORRY FOR HIM...
MANTLE
HE'LL KEEP BEING TREATED LIKE A FRESHMAN IF HE KEEPS ACTING LIKE A FRESH-MAN!
THUNK
OUCH! ALWAYS FORGET THAT BUMP IN THE DRIVEWAY! HOPE NO ONE SAW ME!
CAREFUL, REG!
SIGH
EH? DIDN'T KNOW DAD HAD COMPANY.
SURE, AD REVENUES ARE DOWN-- BUT IT'S CYCLICAL!
HEY, RICK, IS THAT YOUR BOY?
SEE THE GRAY AREA IN MY HAIR? THAT'S MY TEENAGE SON, REG! SAY HELLO TO VIC AND FRED-- TWO GUYS I WORK WITH.
HI.
WELL, YOUNG MANTLE...YOU MAY HAVE ENTERED THE CONVERSATION AT JUST THE RIGHT TIME!
WE WERE ARGUING WITH YOUR FATHER THAT YOUNG PEOPLE AREN'T INTERESTED IN NEWSPAPERS...
10

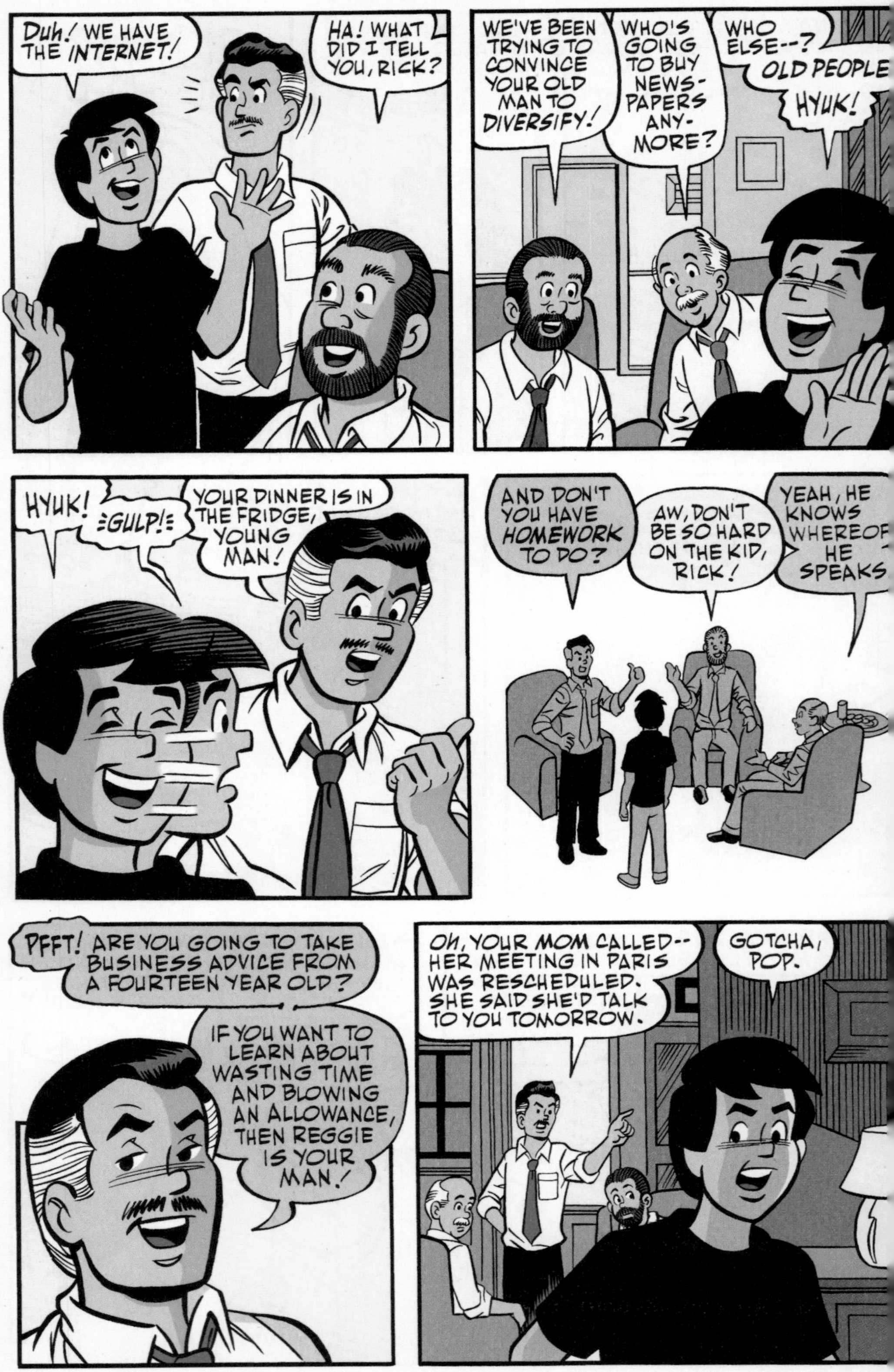
Duh! WE HAVE THE INTERNET!
HA! WHAT DID I TELL YOU, RICK?
WE'VE BEEN TRYING TO CONVINCE YOUR OLD MAN TO DIVERSIFY!
WHO'S GOING TO BUY NEWS-PAPERS ANY-MORE?
WHO ELSE--? OLD PEOPLE
HYUK!
HYUK!
GULP!
YOUR DINNER IS IN THE FRIDGE, YOUNG MAN!
AND DON'T YOU HAVE HOMEWORK TO DO?
AW, DON'T BE SO HARD ON THE KID, RICK!
YEAH, HE KNOWS WHEREOF HE SPEAKS
PFFT! ARE YOU GOING TO TAKE BUSINESS ADVICE FROM A FOURTEEN YEAR OLD?
IF YOU WANT TO LEARN ABOUT WASTING TIME AND BLOWING AN ALLOWANCE, THEN REGGIE IS YOUR MAN!
OH, YOUR MOM CALLED-- HER MEETING IN PARIS WAS RESCHEDULED. SHE SAID SHE'D TALK TO YOU TOMORROW.
GOTCHA, POP.

HEY, GEORGIE? YA THERE? IT'S REGGIE! PICK UP!

OOOKAY... CALL ME WHEN YOU GET THIS MESSAGE!

MY MOM'S OUT OF THE COUNTRY AND MY DAD'S BUSY... I THOUGHT I COULD COME OVER TO YOUR PLACE AND HANG OUT TONIGHT...

MAYBE WE CAN GRAB A PIZZA OR TACOS-- OR BOTH! YOU GOT MY NUMBER, BUDDY-- GET BACK TO ME!

THE NEXT DAY...

HEY... WHERE'S REGGIE?

RIVERDALE HIGH SCHOOL est. 1941

HE'S AH... AT LIBERTY!

HE'S BEEN CUTTING CLASS MORE AND MORE LATELY!

12

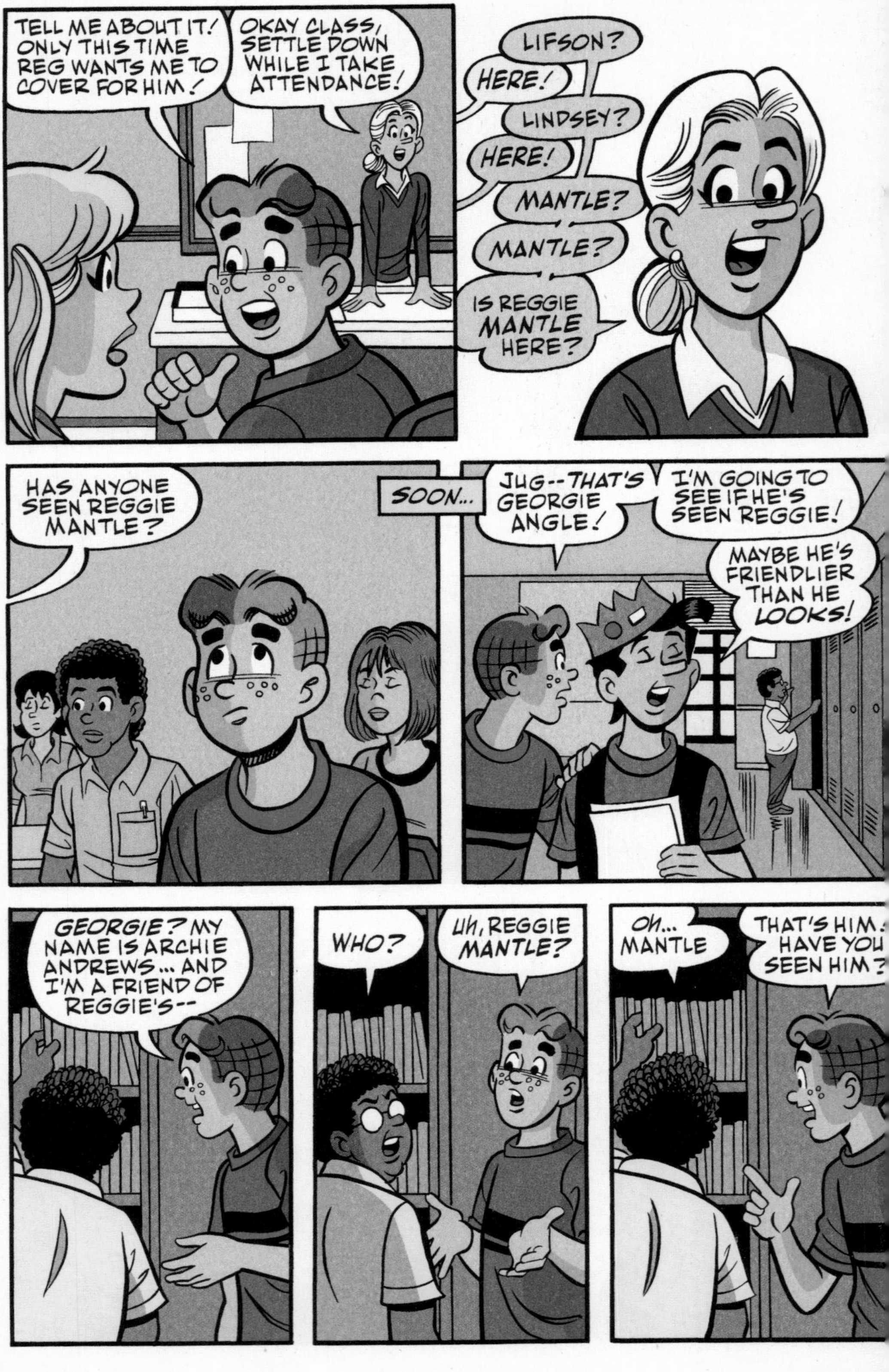
TELL ME ABOUT IT! ONLY THIS TIME REG WANTS ME TO COVER FOR HIM!
OKAY CLASS, SETTLE DOWN WHILE I TAKE ATTENDANCE!
LIFSON?
HERE!
LINDSEY?
HERE!
MANTLE?
MANTLE?
IS REGGIE MANTLE HERE?
HAS ANYONE SEEN REGGIE MANTLE?
SOON...
JUG--THAT'S GEORGIE ANGLE!
I'M GOING TO SEE IF HE'S SEEN REGGIE!
MAYBE HE'S FRIENDLIER THAN HE LOOKS!
GEORGIE? MY NAME IS ARCHIE ANDREWS... AND I'M A FRIEND OF REGGIE'S--
WHO?
UH, REGGIE MANTLE?
OH... MANTLE
THAT'S HIM! HAVE YOU SEEN HIM?

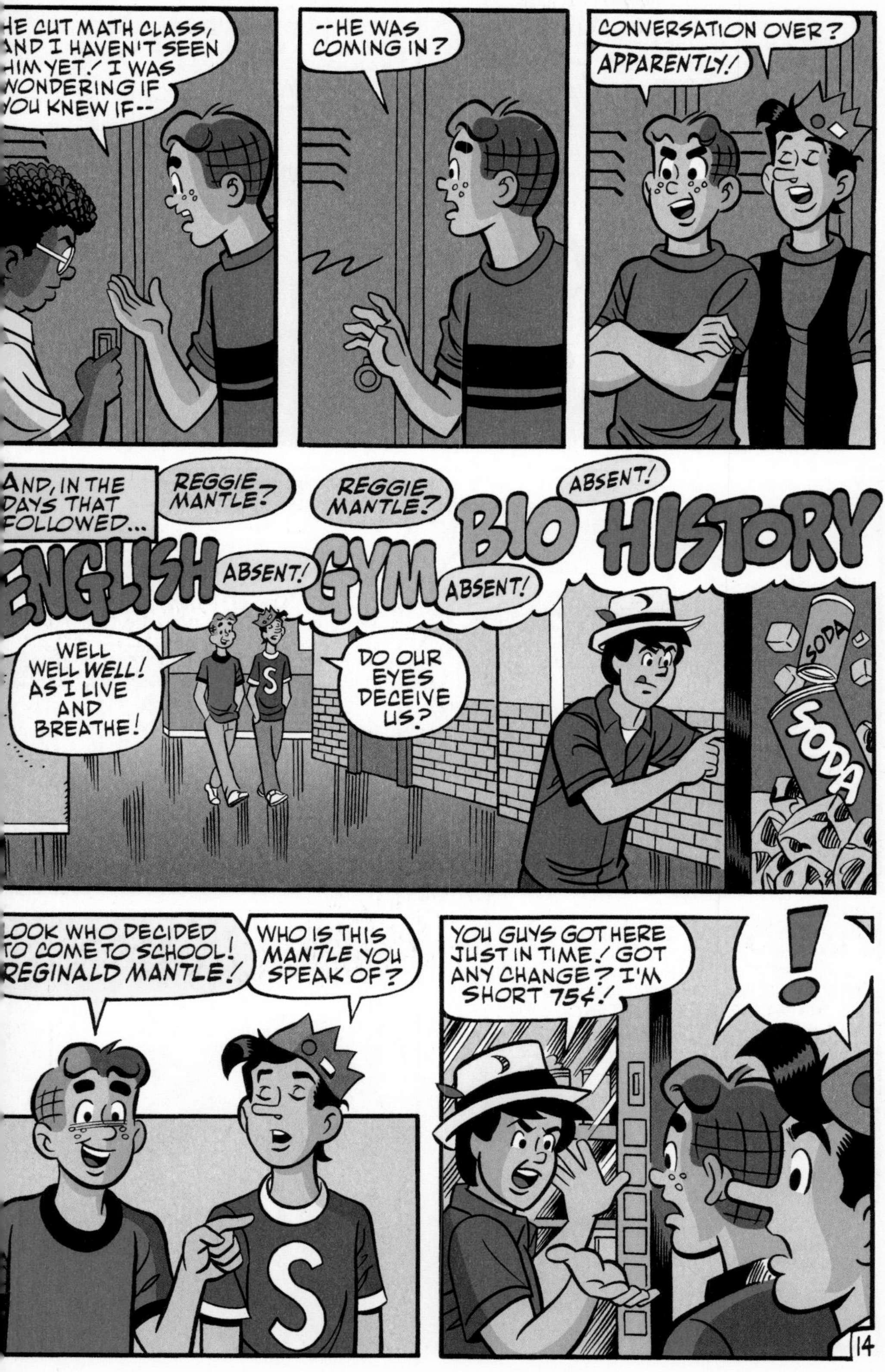
HE CUT MATH CLASS, AND I HAVEN'T SEEN HIM YET! I WAS WONDERING IF YOU KNEW IF--
--HE WAS COMING IN?
CONVERSATION OVER?
APPARENTLY!
AND, IN THE DAYS THAT FOLLOWED...
REGGIE MANTLE?
REGGIE MANTLE?
ABSENT!
ENGLISH
ABSENT!
GYM
ABSENT!
BIO
HISTORY
WELL WELL WELL! AS I LIVE AND BREATHE!
DO OUR EYES DECEIVE US?
SODA
SODA
LOOK WHO DECIDED TO COME TO SCHOOL! REGINALD MANTLE!
WHO IS THIS MANTLE YOU SPEAK OF?
YOU GUYS GOT HERE JUST IN TIME! GOT ANY CHANGE? I'M SHORT 75¢!
!

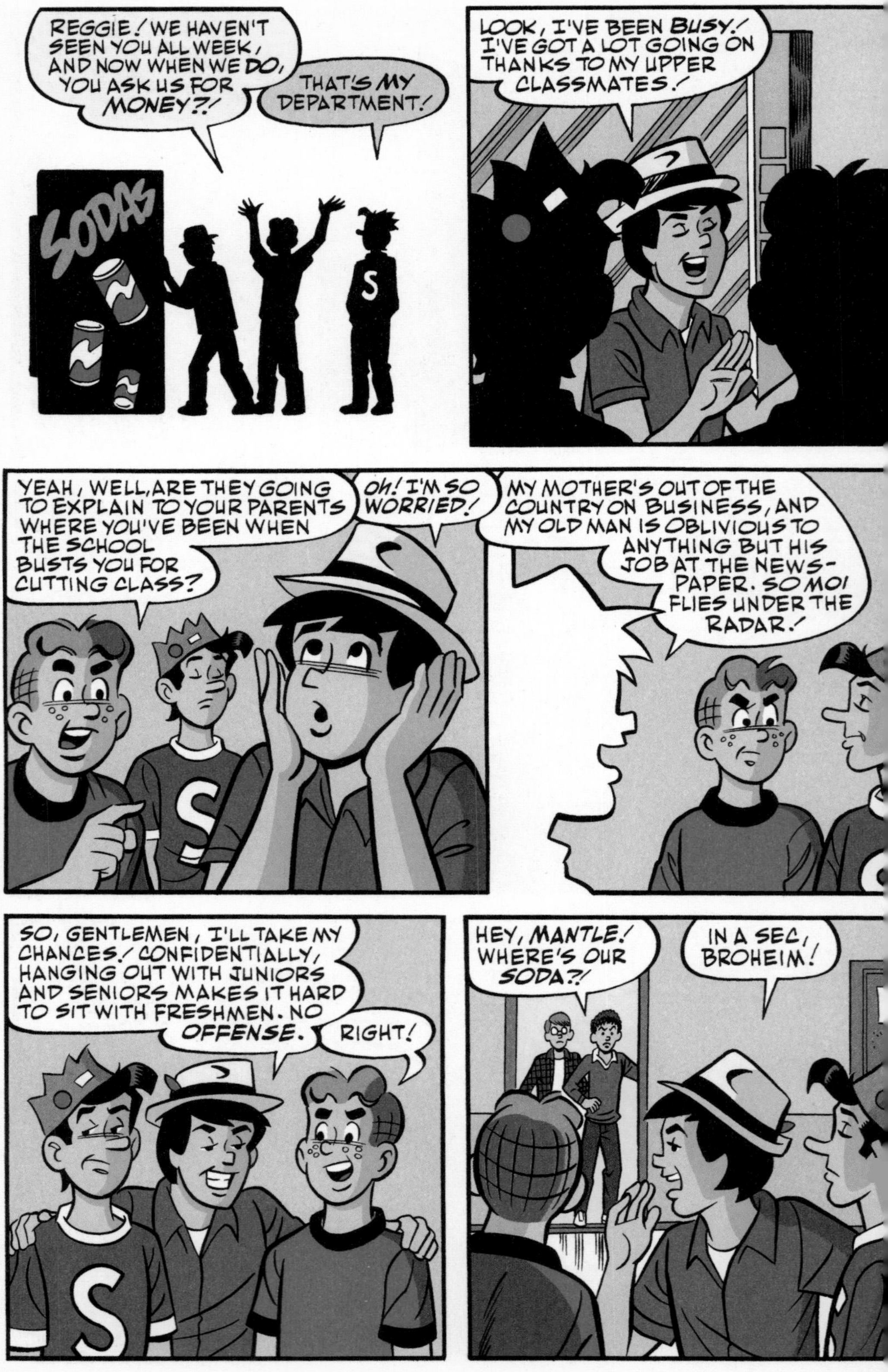
REGGIE! WE HAVEN'T SEEN YOU ALL WEEK, AND NOW WHEN WE DO, YOU ASK US FOR MONEY?!
THAT'S MY DEPARTMENT!
SODAS
LOOK, I'VE BEEN BUSY! I'VE GOT A LOT GOING ON THANKS TO MY UPPER CLASSMATES!
YEAH, WELL, ARE THEY GOING TO EXPLAIN TO YOUR PARENTS WHERE YOU'VE BEEN WHEN THE SCHOOL BUSTS YOU FOR CUTTING CLASS?
Oh! I'M SO WORRIED!
MY MOTHER'S OUT OF THE COUNTRY ON BUSINESS, AND MY OLD MAN IS OBLIVIOUS TO ANYTHING BUT HIS JOB AT THE NEWS-PAPER. SO MOI FLIES UNDER THE RADAR!
SO, GENTLEMEN, I'LL TAKE MY CHANCES! CONFIDENTIALLY, HANGING OUT WITH JUNIORS AND SENIORS MAKES IT HARD TO SIT WITH FRESHMEN. NO OFFENSE.
RIGHT!
HEY, MANTLE! WHERE'S OUR SODA?!
IN A SEC, BROHEIM!

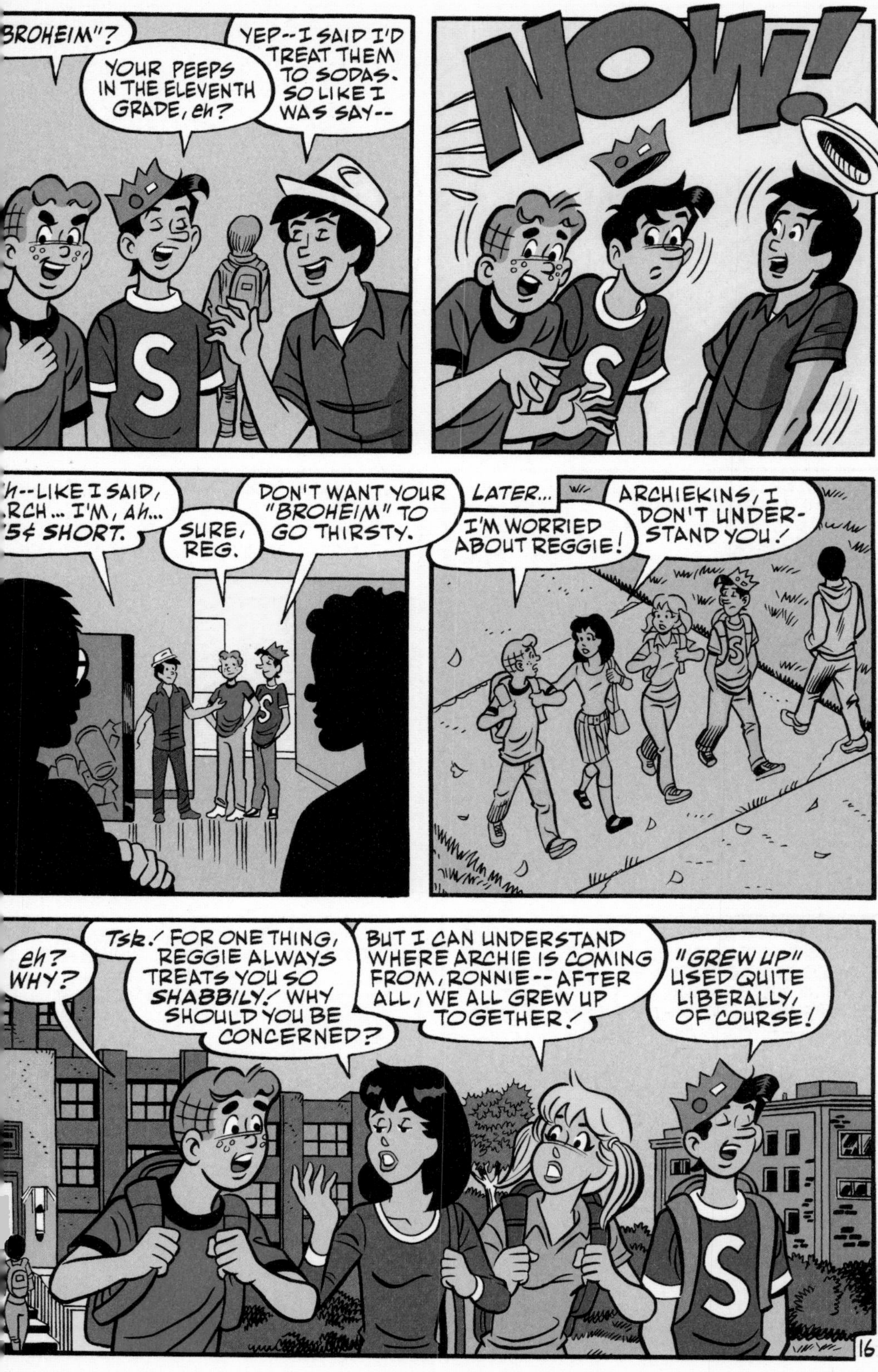
BROHEIM"?
YOUR PEEPS IN THE ELEVENTH GRADE, eh?
YEP--I SAID I'D TREAT THEM TO SODAS. SO LIKE I WAS SAY--
NOW!
h--LIKE I SAID, RCH ... I'M, ah... 5¢ SHORT.
SURE, REG.
DON'T WANT YOUR "BROHEIM" TO GO THIRSTY.
LATER...
I'M WORRIED ABOUT REGGIE!
ARCHIEKINS, I DON'T UNDERSTAND YOU!
eh? WHY?
Tsk! FOR ONE THING, REGGIE ALWAYS TREATS YOU SO SHABBILY! WHY SHOULD YOU BE CONCERNED?
BUT I CAN UNDERSTAND WHERE ARCHIE IS COMING FROM, RONNIE--AFTER ALL, WE ALL GREW UP TOGETHER!
"GREW UP" USED QUITE LIBERALLY, OF COURSE!
16

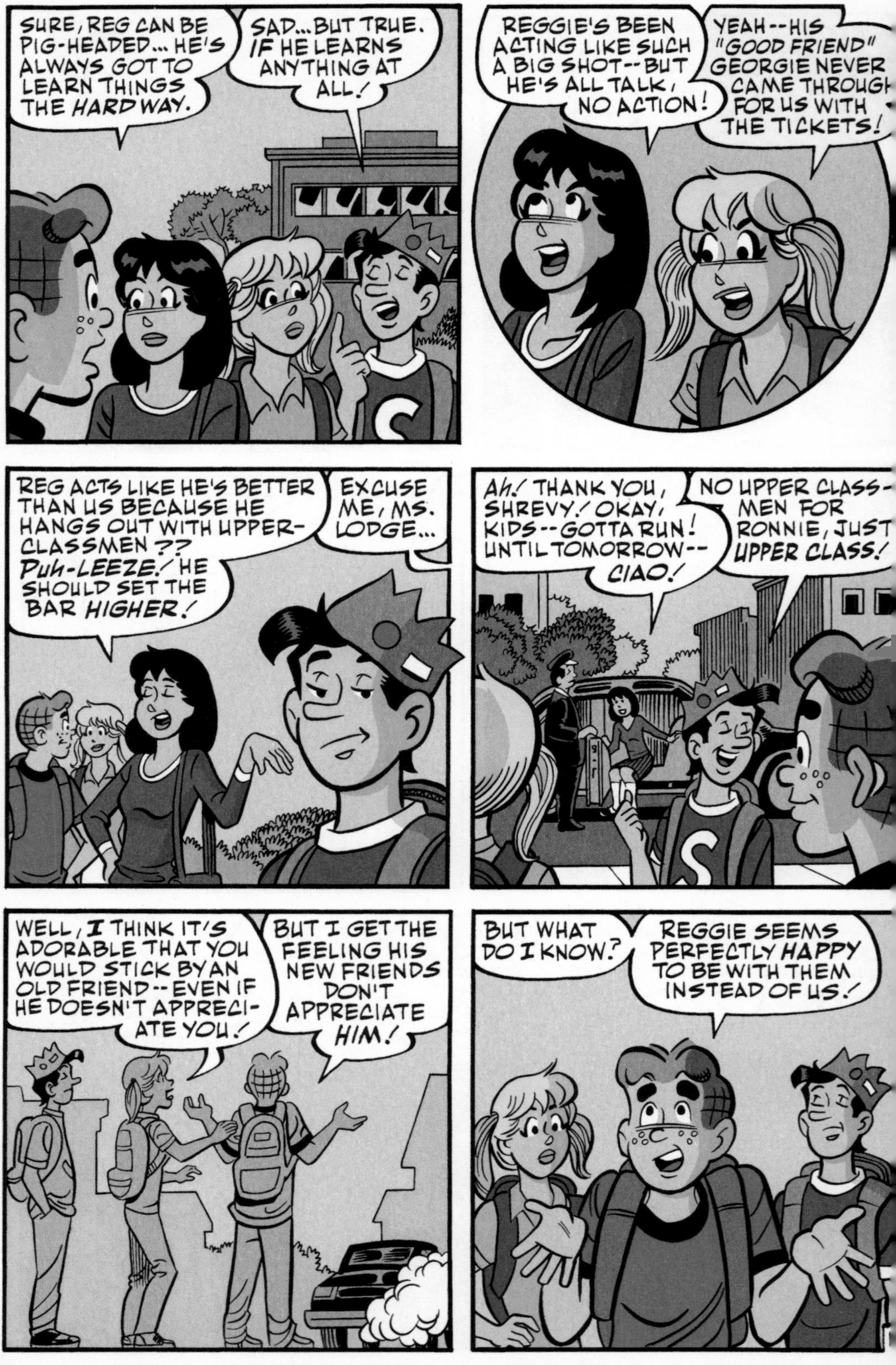
SURE, REG CAN BE PIG-HEADED... HE'S ALWAYS GOT TO LEARN THINGS THE HARD WAY.
SAD... BUT TRUE. IF HE LEARNS ANYTHING AT ALL!
REGGIE'S BEEN ACTING LIKE SUCH A BIG SHOT--BUT HE'S ALL TALK, NO ACTION!
YEAH--HIS "GOOD FRIEND" GEORGIE NEVER CAME THROUGH FOR US WITH THE TICKETS!
REG ACTS LIKE HE'S BETTER THAN US BECAUSE HE HANGS OUT WITH UPPER-CLASSMEN?? Puh-LEEZE! HE SHOULD SET THE BAR HIGHER!
EXCUSE ME, MS. LODGE...
Ah! THANK YOU, SHREVY! OKAY, KIDS--GOTTA RUN! UNTIL TOMORROW--CIAO!
NO UPPER CLASS-MEN FOR RONNIE, JUST UPPER CLASS!
WELL, I THINK IT'S ADORABLE THAT YOU WOULD STICK BY AN OLD FRIEND--EVEN IF HE DOESN'T APPRECI-ATE YOU!
BUT I GET THE FEELING HIS NEW FRIENDS DON'T APPRECIATE HIM!
BUT WHAT DO I KNOW?
REGGIE SEEMS PERFECTLY HAPPY TO BE WITH THEM INSTEAD OF US!

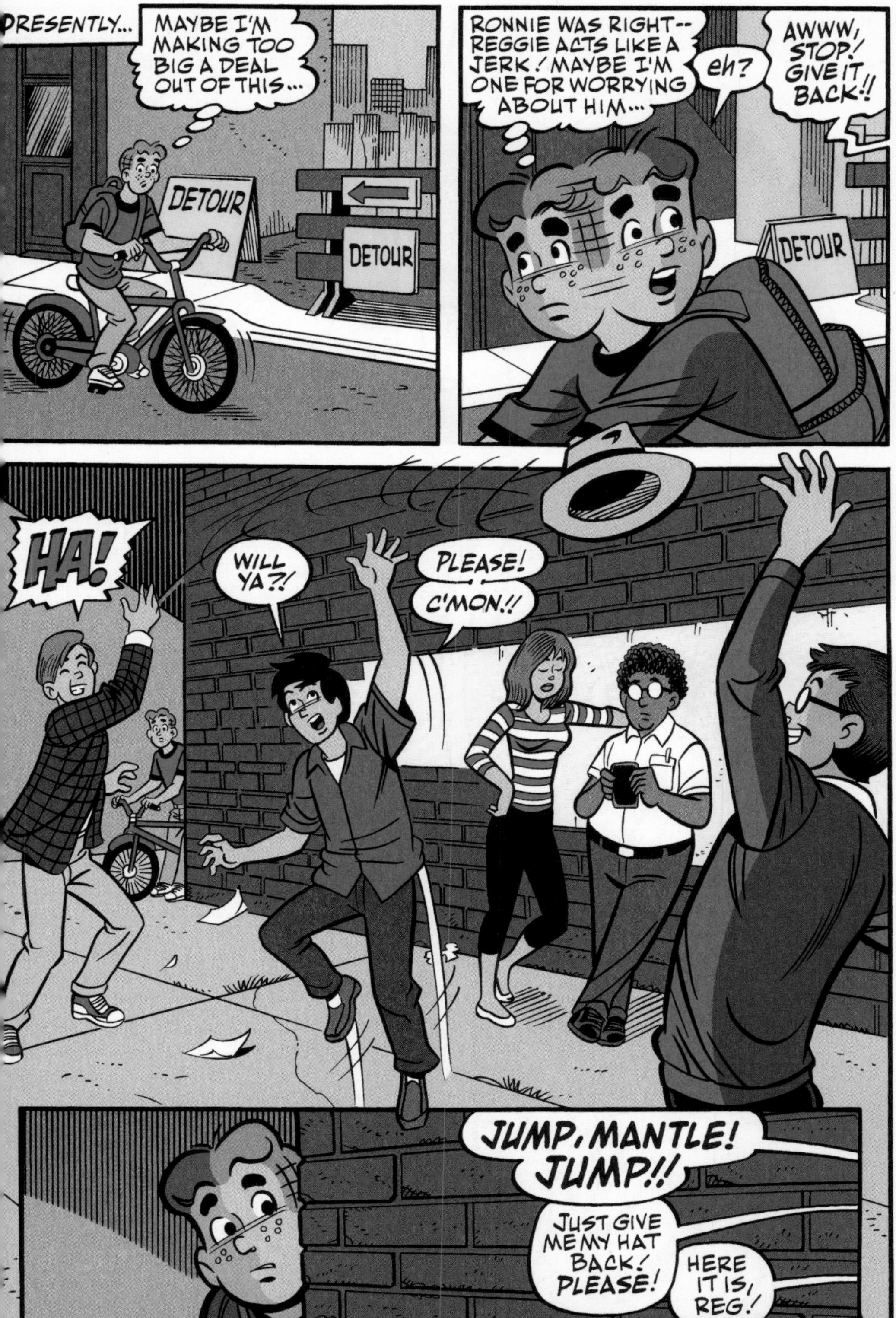
PRESENTLY...
MAYBE I'M MAKING TOO BIG A DEAL OUT OF THIS...
DETOUR
DETOUR
RONNIE WAS RIGHT-- REGGIE ACTS LIKE A JERK! MAYBE I'M ONE FOR WORRYING ABOUT HIM...
eh?
AWWW, STOP! GIVE IT BACK!!
DETOUR
HA!
WILL YA?!
PLEASE! C'MON!!
JUMP, MANTLE! JUMP!!
JUST GIVE ME MY HAT BACK! PLEASE!
HERE IT IS, REG!

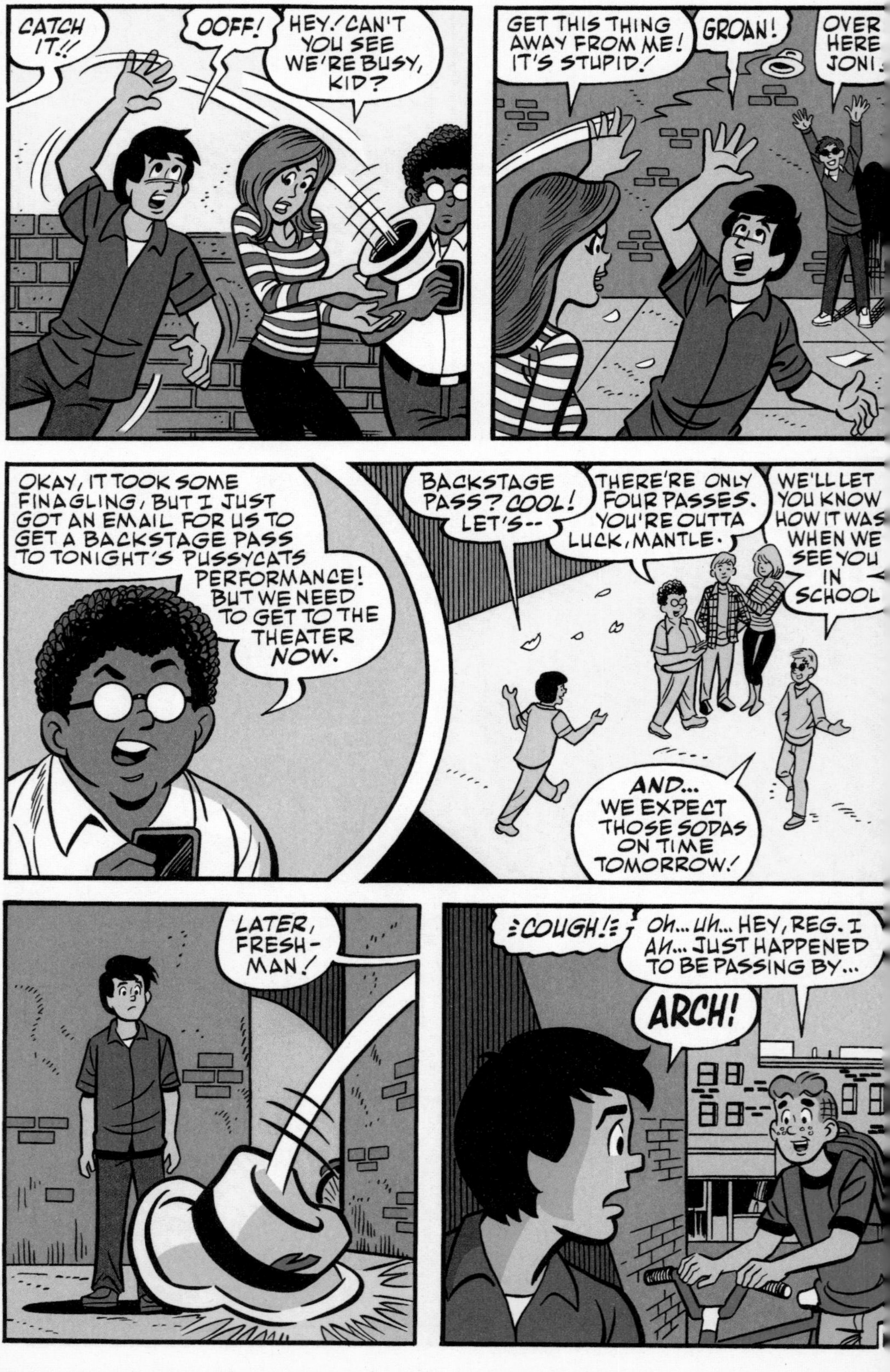

CATCH IT!!
OOFF!
HEY! CAN'T YOU SEE WE'RE BUSY, KID?
GET THIS THING AWAY FROM ME! IT'S STUPID!
GROAN!
OVER HERE JONI.
OKAY, IT TOOK SOME FINAGLING, BUT I JUST GOT AN EMAIL FOR US TO GET A BACKSTAGE PASS TO TONIGHT'S PUSSYCATS PERFORMANCE! BUT WE NEED TO GET TO THE THEATER NOW.
BACKSTAGE PASS? COOL! LET'S--
THERE'RE ONLY FOUR PASSES. YOU'RE OUTTA LUCK, MANTLE.
WE'LL LET YOU KNOW HOW IT WAS WHEN WE SEE YOU IN SCHOOL
AND... WE EXPECT THOSE SODAS ON TIME TOMORROW!
LATER, FRESH-MAN!
COUGH!
Oh... uh... HEY, REG. I Ah... JUST HAPPENED TO BE PASSING BY...
ARCH!

LOOK, ANDREWS, I DON'T KNOW WHAT YOU SAW, BUT MY FRIENDS ARE BUSY PEOPLE.! THEY'RE PRACTICALLY IN COLLEGE!

THEY DEPEND ON ME TO HELP THEM OUT-- I PICK UP STUFF FOR THEM, HELP THEM GET LUNCH, AND THINGS LIKE THAT!

IN OTHER WORDS, YOU'RE THEIR GO-FER!

YEAH...

WOULD YOU LIKE A RIDE HOME? IT'S EARLY ENOUGH TO GRAB A BURGER... WE CAN GIVE JUGHEAD A CALL... AND THE GIRLS, TOO!

THAT SURE SOUNDS GOOD...

HEY, ARCH-- MAYBE LATER WE CAN CHECK OUT THOSE YO-GI-YO CARDS OF YOURS.!

SURE, REG... SURE!

GEORGIE AND THOSE PUNKS USED ME!

I THOUGHT THEY WERE MY FRIENDS-- BUT THEY ONLY WANTED A GO-FER! "GO-FER THIS", AND "GO-FER THAT"! SHEESH.!

I'M SURPRISED YOU PUT UP WITH THAT, REG!

ME, TOO! I WAS YOUNG AND FOOLISH BACK THEN! I'VE LEARNED THAT I DON'T NEED TO BE PART OF AN ENTOURAGE... ...AN ENTOURAGE NEEDS TO BE PART OF ME!

20

LATER THAT EVENING...

YOUR FATHER TELLS ME YOU KNOW HIS NEW ASSISTANT, REGGIE...

The MANTLES

OH, YEAH, GEORGIE. HAS HE TRIED TO SCALP TICKETS TO DAD YET?

WHAT?

JUST KIDDING, MOM.

YOU KNOW...

IT'S A MIRACLE THE GAZETTE OKAYED MY HIRING OF GEORGE. THE PAPER'S BEEN DOWNSIZING IN RECENT YEARS!

YOUNG PEOPLE AREN'T INTERESTED IN NEWS-PAPERS. WE NEED TO DIVERSIFY!

MY JOB TAKES ME AROUND THE WORLD... I SEE IT'S THE INTERNET WHERE KIDS GET THEIR INFORMATION!

I'VE BEEN TELLING THAT TO YOUR FATHER, BUT DOES HE LISTEN? NO! HE HAS TO LEARN THINGS THE HARD WAY!

I GUESS THAT GEORGIE WILL BE AN ASSET TO THE GAZETTE, huh, DAD? HIS WEB-SITE IS PRETTY POPULAR.

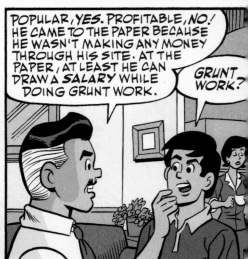

POPULAR, YES. PROFITABLE, NO! HE CAME TO THE PAPER BECAUSE HE WASN'T MAKING ANY MONEY THROUGH HIS SITE. AT THE PAPER, AT LEAST HE CAN DRAW A SALARY WHILE DOING GRUNT WORK.

GRUNT WORK?

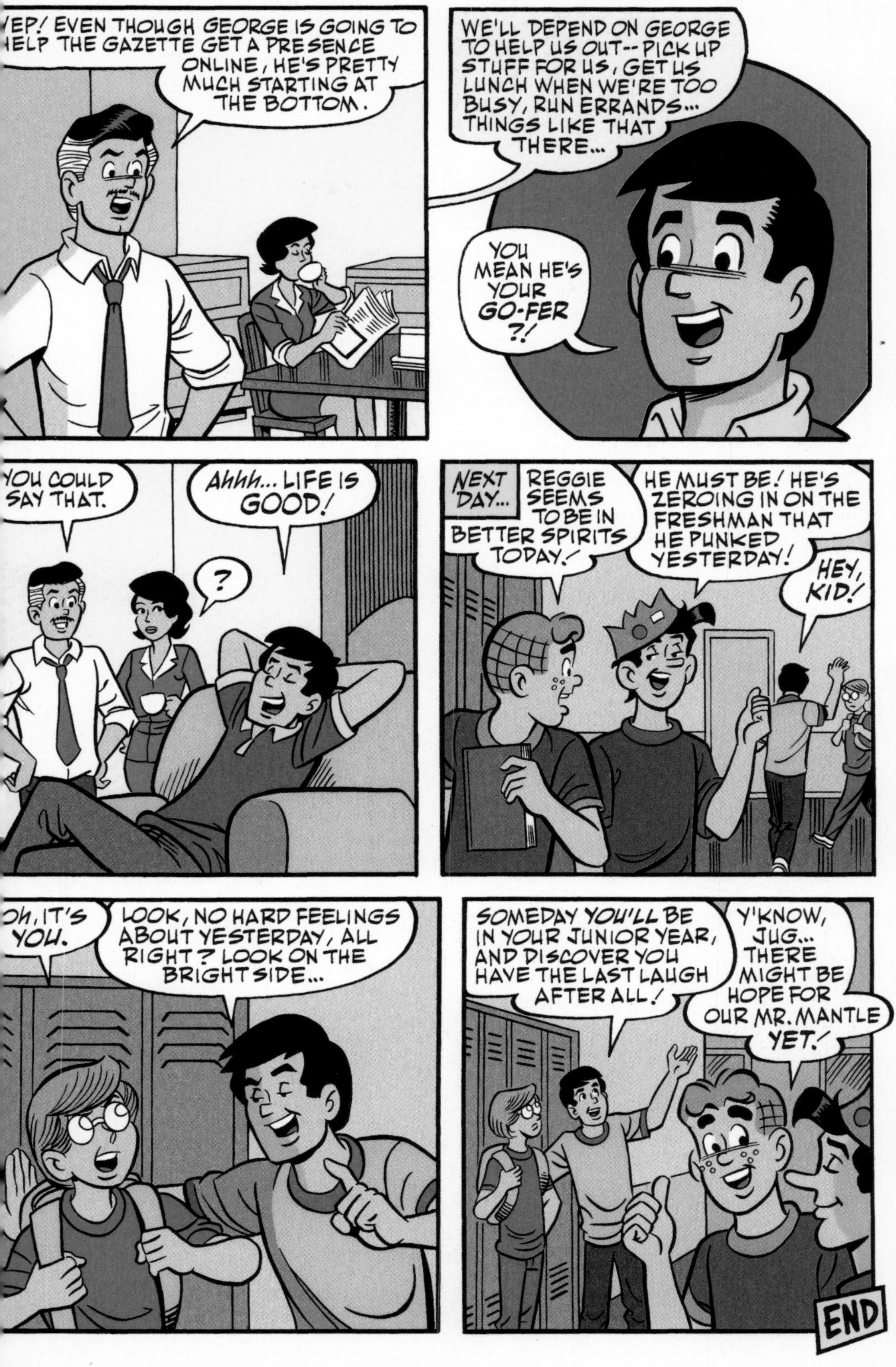
YEP! EVEN THOUGH GEORGE IS GOING TO HELP THE GAZETTE GET A PRESENCE ONLINE, HE'S PRETTY MUCH STARTING AT THE BOTTOM.
WE'LL DEPEND ON GEORGE TO HELP US OUT-- PICK UP STUFF FOR US, GET US LUNCH WHEN WE'RE TOO BUSY, RUN ERRANDS... THINGS LIKE THAT THERE...
YOU MEAN HE'S YOUR GO-FER ?!
YOU COULD SAY THAT.
Ahhh... LIFE IS GOOD!
?
NEXT DAY...
REGGIE SEEMS TO BE IN BETTER SPIRITS TODAY!
HE MUST BE! HE'S ZEROING IN ON THE FRESHMAN THAT HE PUNKED YESTERDAY!
HEY, KID!
Oh, IT'S YOU.
LOOK, NO HARD FEELINGS ABOUT YESTERDAY, ALL RIGHT? LOOK ON THE BRIGHT SIDE...
SOMEDAY YOU'LL BE IN YOUR JUNIOR YEAR, AND DISCOVER YOU HAVE THE LAST LAUGH AFTER ALL!
Y'KNOW, JUG... THERE MIGHT BE HOPE FOR OUR MR. MANTLE YET!
END

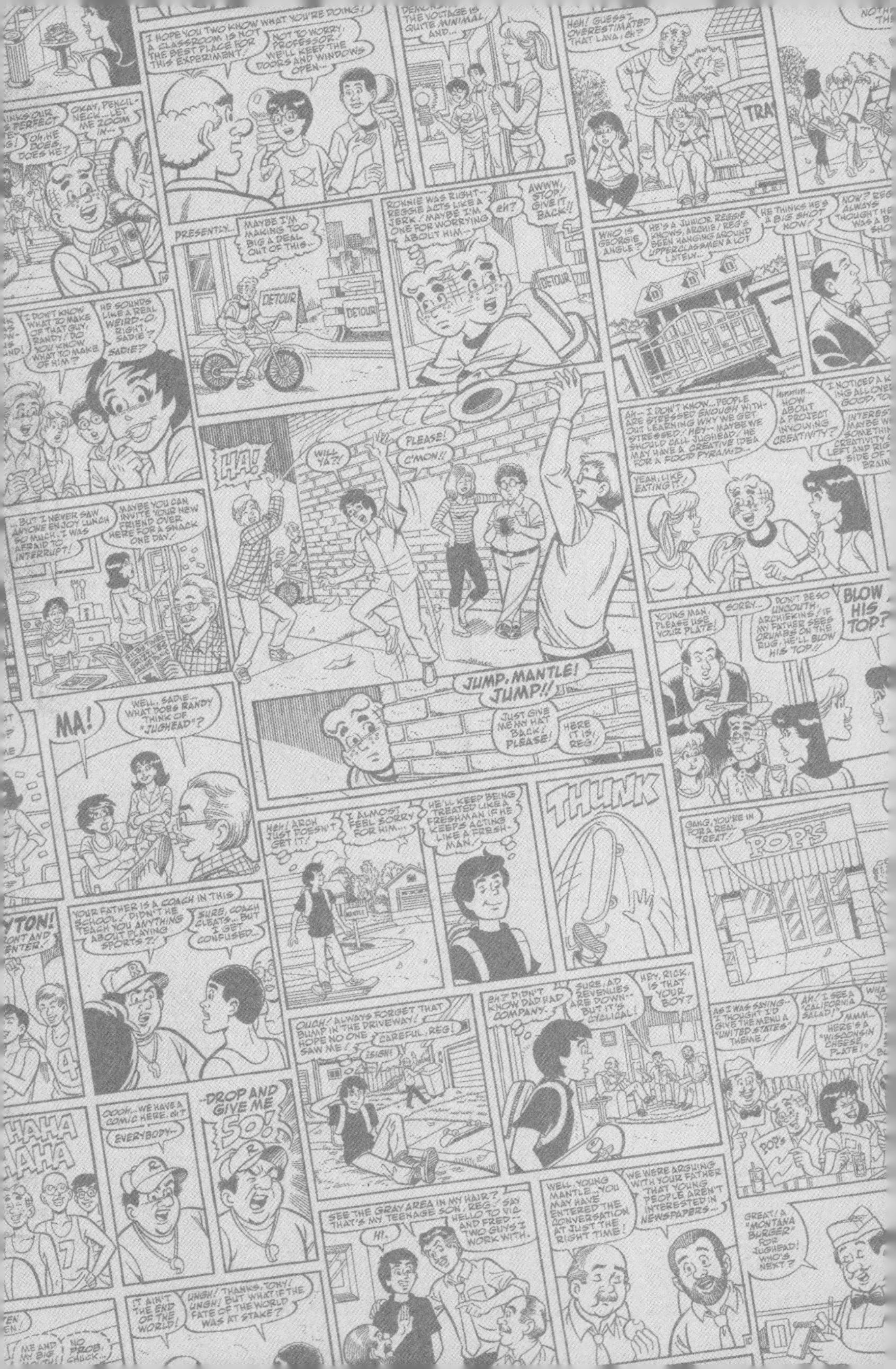

I HOPE YOU TWO KNOW WHAT YOU'RE DOING! A CLASSROOM IS NOT THE BEST PLACE FOR THIS EXPERIMENT!
NOT TO WORRY, PROFESSOR! WE'LL KEEP THE DOORS AND WINDOWS OPEN...
THE VOLTAGE IS QUITE MINIMAL, AND...
HEH! GUESS I OVERESTIMATED THAT LAVA, EH?
OKAY, PENCIL-NECK... LET ME ZOOM IN...
OH, HE DOES, DOES HE?
PRESENTLY...
MAYBE I'M MAKING TOO BIG A DEAL OUT OF THIS...
DETOUR
RONNIE WAS RIGHT-- REGGIE ACTS LIKE A JERK! MAYBE I'M ONE FOR WORRYING ABOUT HIM...
EH?
AWWW, STOP! GIVE IT BACK!!
WHO IS GEORGIE ANGLE?
HE'S A JUNIOR REGGIE KNOWS, ARCHIE! REG'S BEEN HANGING AROUND UPPERCLASSMEN A LOT LATELY...
HE THINKS HE'S A BIG SHOT NOW!
I DON'T KNOW WHAT TO MAKE OF THAT GUY, RANDY! DO YOU KNOW WHAT TO MAKE OF HIM?
HE SOUNDS LIKE A REAL WEIRD-O, RIGHT, SADIE?
SADIE?
HA!
WILL YA?!
PLEASE!
C'MON!!
AH... I DON'T KNOW... PEOPLE ARE STRESSED ENOUGH WITHOUT LEARNING WHY WE GET STRESSED! HEY-- MAYBE WE SHOULD CALL JUGHEAD! HE MAY HAVE A CREATIVE IDEA FOR A FOOD PYRAMID...
HMMM... HOW ABOUT A PROJECT INVOLVING CREATIVITY?
YEAH, LIKE EATING IT!
...BUT I NEVER SAW ANYONE ENJOY LUNCH SO MUCH. I WAS AFRAID TO INTERRUPT!
MAYBE YOU CAN INVITE YOUR NEW FRIEND OVER HERE FOR A SNACK ONE DAY!
YOUNG MAN, PLEASE USE YOUR PLATE!
SORRY...
DON'T BE SO UNCOUTH, ARCHIEKINS! IF MY FATHER SEES CRUMBS ON THE RUG, HE'LL BLOW HIS TOP!!
BLOW HIS TOP?
MA!
WELL, SADIE... WHAT DOES RANDY THINK OF "JUGHEAD"?
JUMP, MANTLE! JUMP!!
JUST GIVE ME MY HAT BACK! PLEASE!
HERE IT IS, REG!
HEH! ARCH JUST DOESN'T GET IT!
I ALMOST FEEL SORRY FOR HIM...
HE'LL KEEP BEING TREATED LIKE A FRESHMAN IF HE KEEPS ACTING LIKE A FRESHMAN.
THUNK
GANG, YOU'RE IN FOR A REAL TREAT!
POP'S
YOUR FATHER IS A COACH IN THIS SCHOOL! DIDN'T HE TEACH YOU ANYTHING ABOUT PLAYING SPORTS?!
SURE, COACH CLEATS... BUT I GET CONFUSED...
OUCH! ALWAYS FORGET THAT BUMP IN THE DRIVEWAY! HOPE NO ONE SAW ME!
CAREFUL, REG!
SIGH
EH? DIDN'T KNOW DAD HAD COMPANY.
SURE, AD REVENUES ARE DOWN-- BUT IT'S CYCLICAL!
HEY, RICK, IS THAT YOUR BOY?
AS I WAS SAYING-- I THOUGHT I'D GIVE THE MENU A "UNITED STATES" THEME!
AH! I SEE A "CALIFORNIA SALAD"!
MMM... HERE'S A "WISCONSIN CHEESE PLATE"!
HAHAHA
OOOH... WE HAVE A COMIC HERE, EH?
EVERYBODY--
--DROP AND GIVE ME 50!
SEE THE GRAY AREA IN MY HAIR? THAT'S MY TEENAGE SON, REG!
SAY HELLO TO VIC AND FRED-- TWO GUYS I WORK WITH.
HI.
WELL, YOUNG MANTLE... YOU MAY HAVE ENTERED THE CONVERSATION AT JUST THE RIGHT TIME!
WE WERE ARGUING WITH YOUR FATHER THAT YOUNG PEOPLE AREN'T INTERESTED IN NEWSPAPERS...
GREAT! A "MONTANA BURGER" FOR JUGHEAD! WHO'S NEXT?
IT AIN'T THE END OF THE WORLD!
UNGH! THANKS, TONY! UNGH! BUT WHAT IF THE FATE OF THE WORLD WAS AT STAKE?
ME AND MY BIG MOUTH!
NO PROB, CHUCK...

THE MISSING CHAPTERS: PART 4

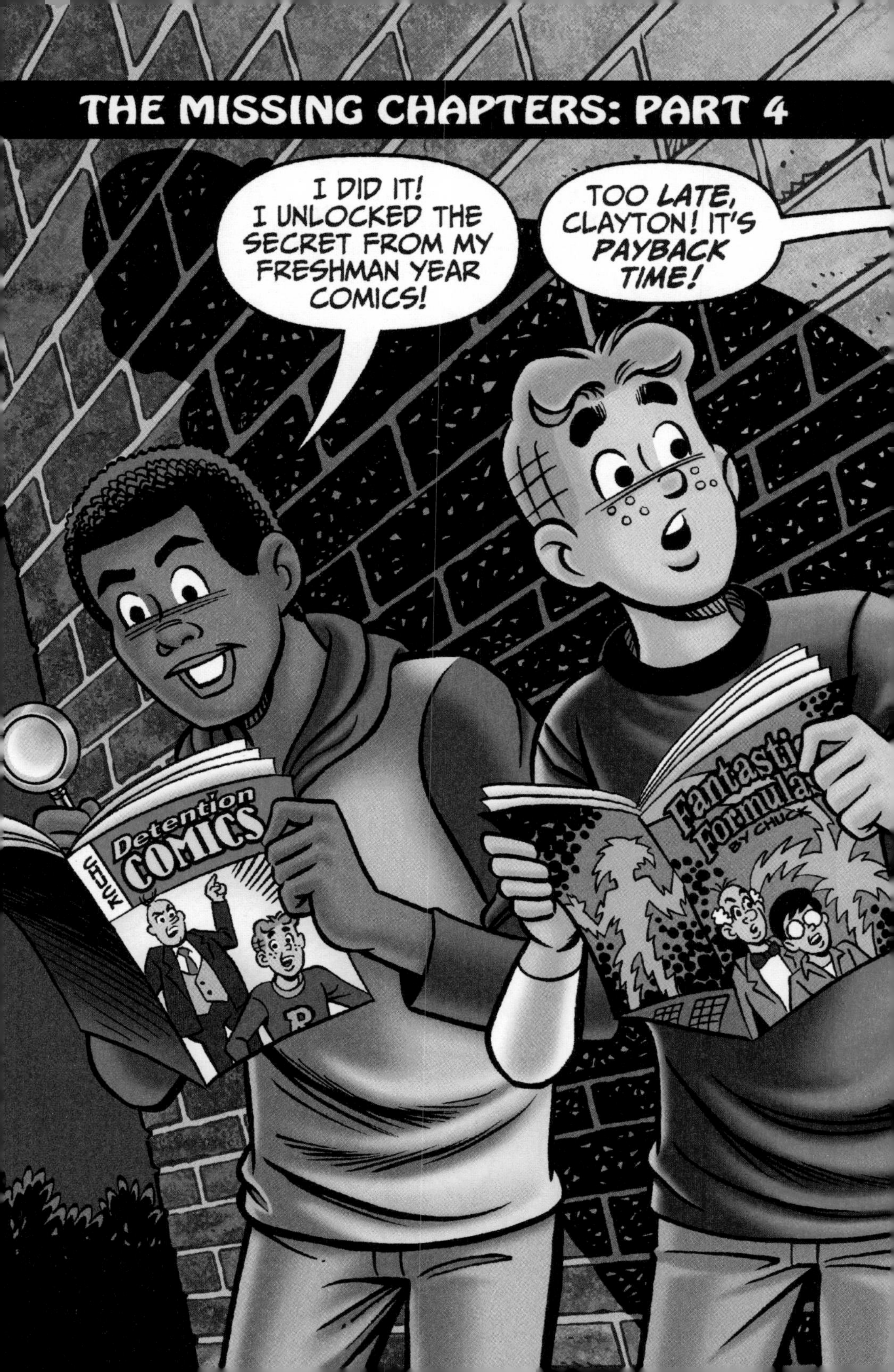
I DID IT! I UNLOCKED THE SECRET FROM MY FRESHMAN YEAR COMICS!
TOO LATE, CLAYTON! IT'S PAYBACK TIME!
Detention COMICS
CHUCK
BY CHUCK

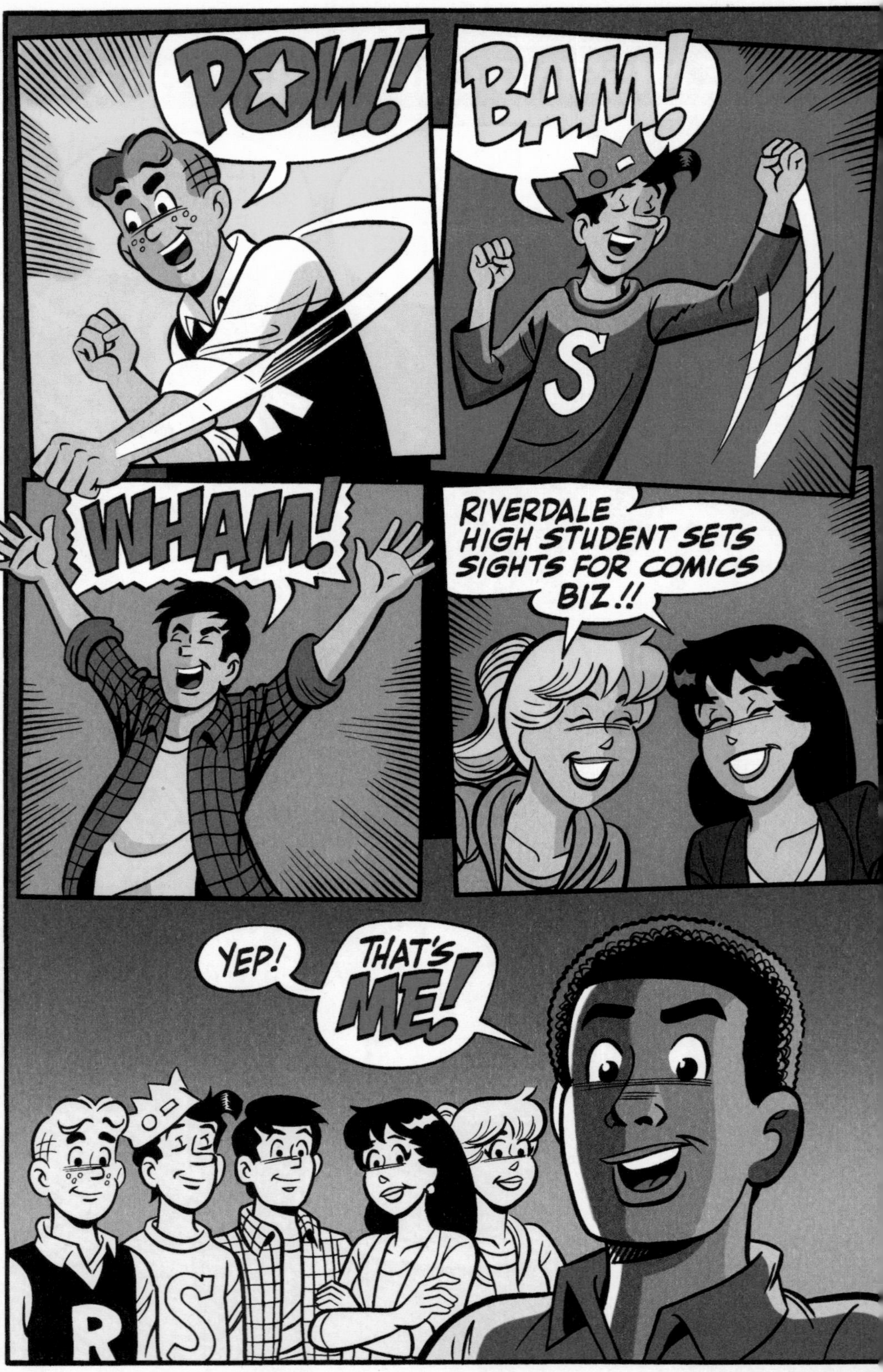
POW!
BAM!
WHAM!
RIVERDALE HIGH STUDENT SETS SIGHTS FOR COMICS BIZ!!
YEP!
THAT'S ME!

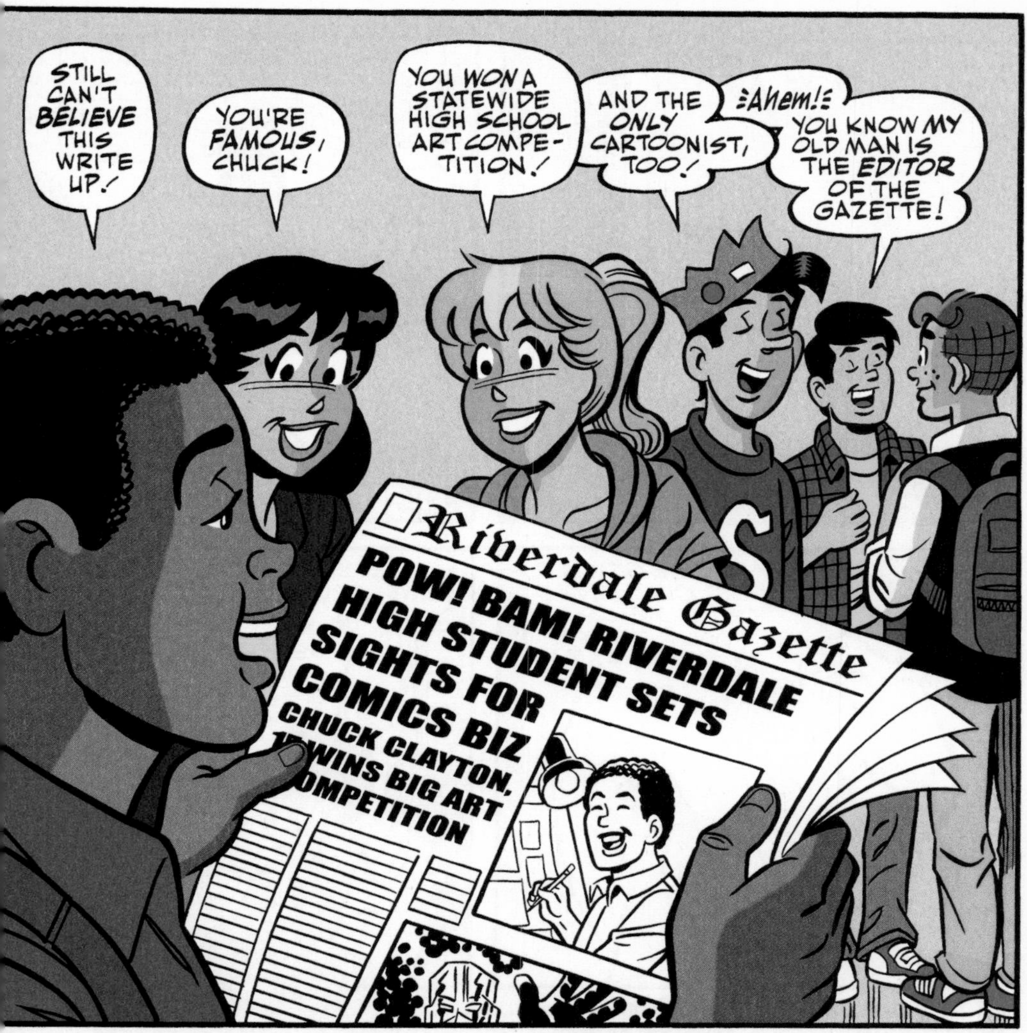
STILL CAN'T BELIEVE THIS WRITE UP!
YOU'RE FAMOUS, CHUCK!
YOU WON A STATEWIDE HIGH SCHOOL ART COMPETITION!
AND THE ONLY CARTOONIST, TOO!
Ahem!
YOU KNOW MY OLD MAN IS THE EDITOR OF THE GAZETTE!
Riverdale Gazette
POW! BAM! RIVERDALE HIGH STUDENT SETS SIGHTS FOR COMICS BIZ
CHUCK CLAYTON,
WINS BIG ART
OMPETITION

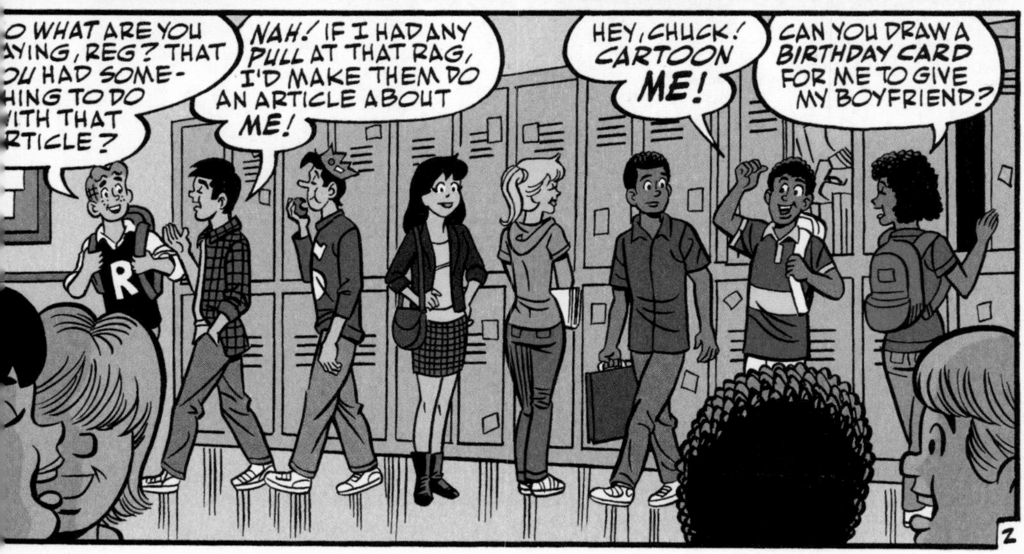
O WHAT ARE YOU AYING, REG? THAT OU HAD SOME-HING TO DO VITH THAT RTICLE?
NAH! IF I HAD ANY PULL AT THAT RAG, I'D MAKE THEM DO AN ARTICLE ABOUT ME!
HEY, CHUCK! CARTOON ME!
CAN YOU DRAW A BIRTHDAY CARD FOR ME TO GIVE MY BOYFRIEND?

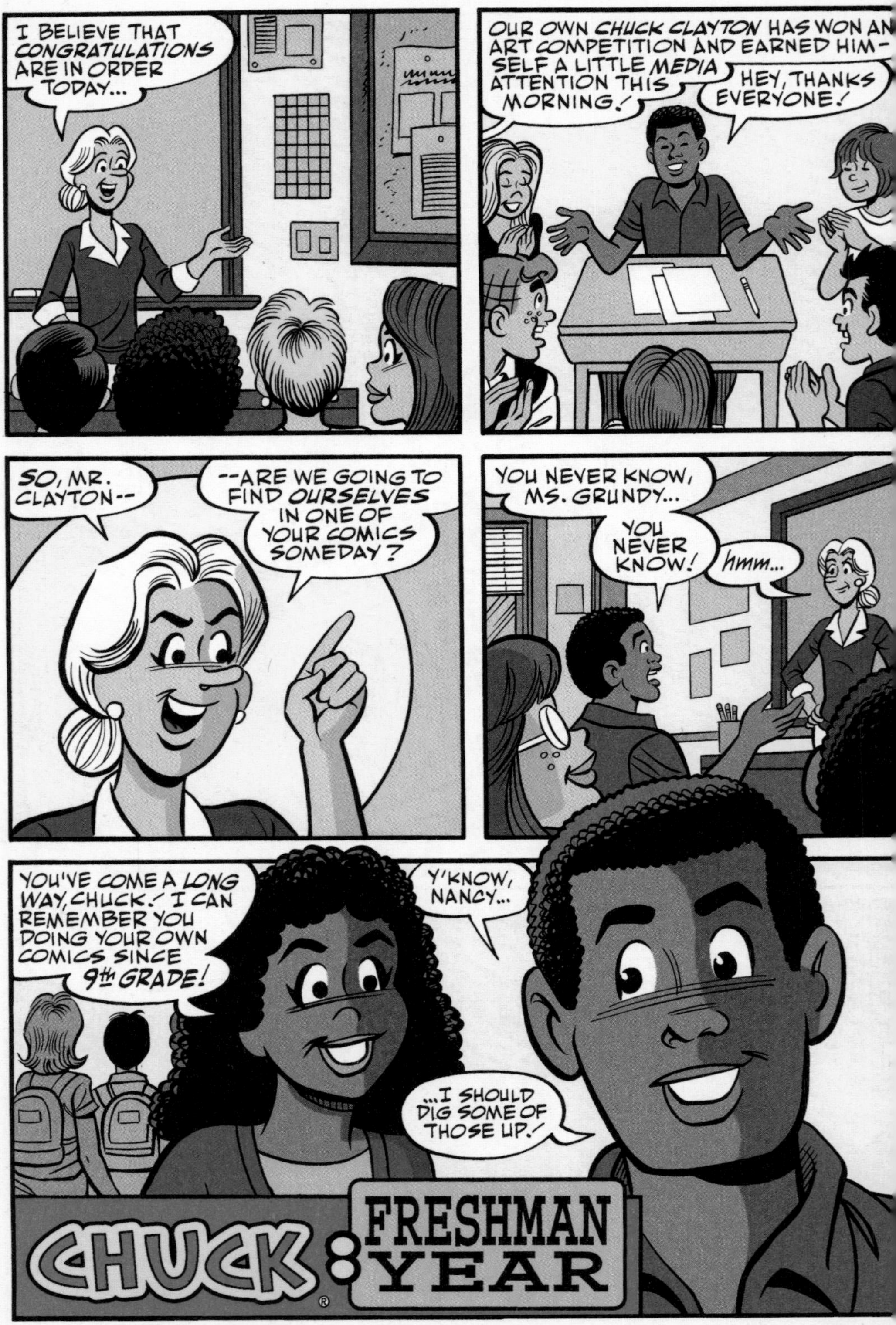
I BELIEVE THAT CONGRATULATIONS ARE IN ORDER TODAY...
OUR OWN CHUCK CLAYTON HAS WON AN ART COMPETITION AND EARNED HIMSELF A LITTLE MEDIA ATTENTION THIS MORNING!
HEY, THANKS EVERYONE!
SO, MR. CLAYTON--
--ARE WE GOING TO FIND OURSELVES IN ONE OF YOUR COMICS SOMEDAY?
YOU NEVER KNOW, MS. GRUNDY...
YOU NEVER KNOW!
hmm...
YOU'VE COME A LONG WAY, CHUCK! I CAN REMEMBER YOU DOING YOUR OWN COMICS SINCE 9th GRADE!
Y'KNOW, NANCY...
...I SHOULD DIG SOME OF THOSE UP!
CHUCK®: FRESHMAN YEAR

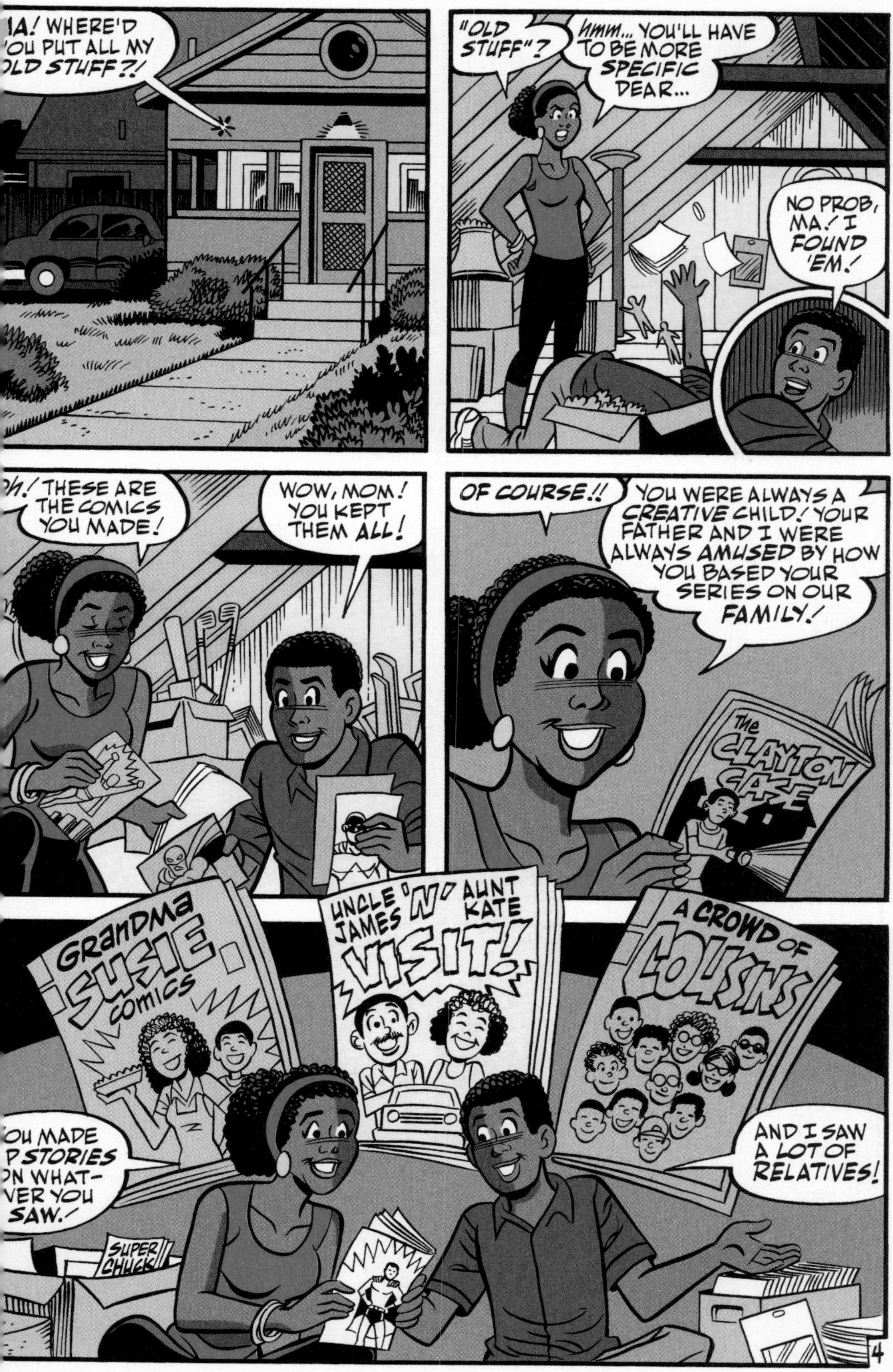
MA! WHERE'D
OU PUT ALL MY
OLD STUFF?!
"OLD STUFF"?
HMM... YOU'LL HAVE TO BE MORE SPECIFIC DEAR...
NO PROB, MA! I FOUND 'EM!
h! THESE ARE THE COMICS YOU MADE!
WOW, MOM! YOU KEPT THEM ALL!
OF COURSE!!
YOU WERE ALWAYS A CREATIVE CHILD! YOUR FATHER AND I WERE ALWAYS AMUSED BY HOW YOU BASED YOUR SERIES ON OUR FAMILY!
The CLAYTON CASE
GRANDMA SUSIE COMICS
UNCLE JAMES 'N' AUNT KATE VISIT!
A CROWD OF COUSINS
OU MADE
P STORIES
ON WHAT-
VER YOU
SAW.
SUPER CHUCK
AND I SAW A LOT OF RELATIVES!

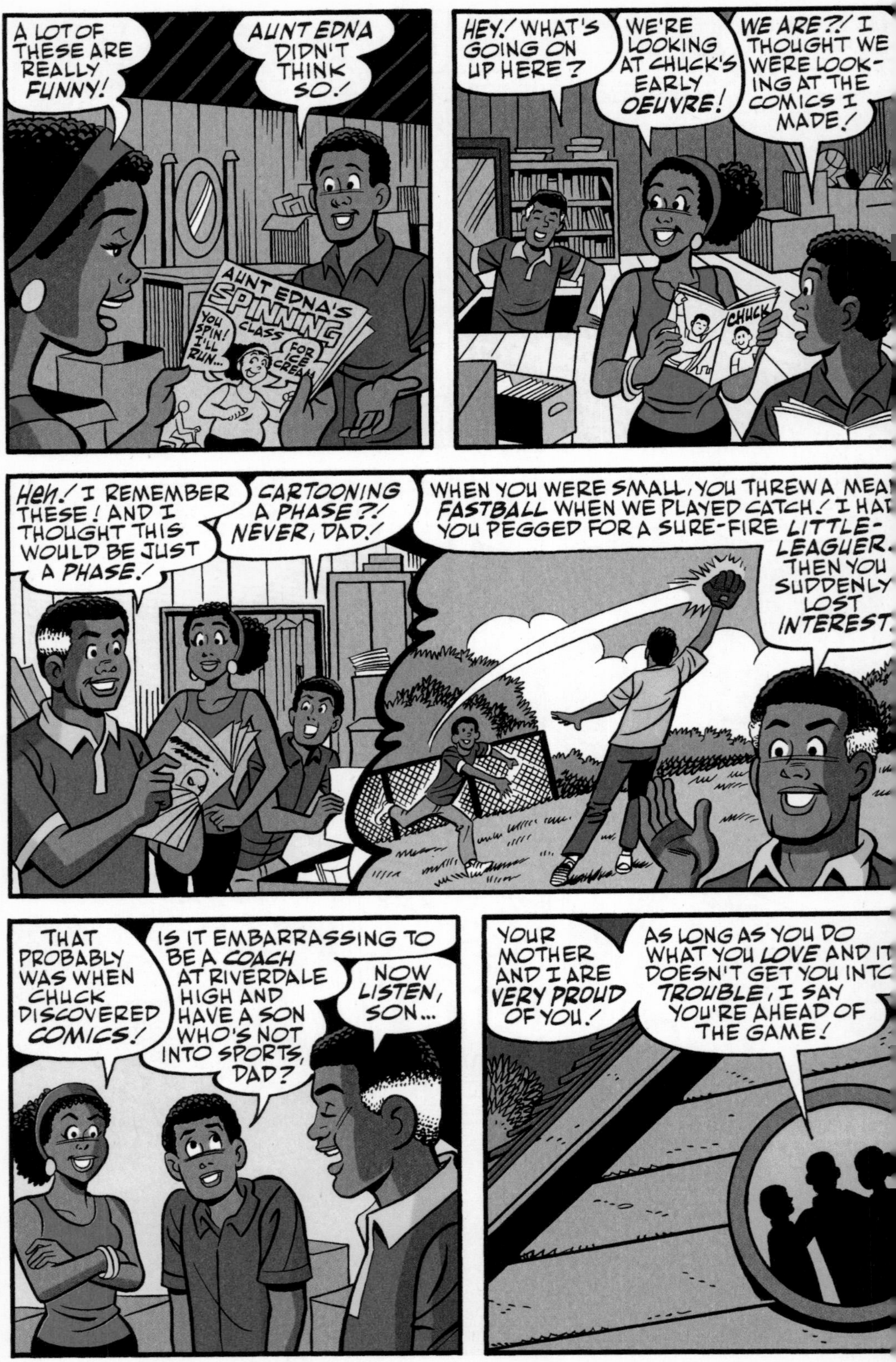

A LOT OF THESE ARE REALLY FUNNY!
AUNT EDNA DIDN'T THINK SO!
AUNT EDNA'S SPINNING CLASS
YOU SPIN! I'LL RUN...
FOR ICE CREAM
HEY! WHAT'S GOING ON UP HERE?
WE'RE LOOKING AT CHUCK'S EARLY OEUVRE!
WE ARE?! I THOUGHT WE WERE LOOKING AT THE COMICS I MADE!
CHUCK
Heh! I REMEMBER THESE! AND I THOUGHT THIS WOULD BE JUST A PHASE!
CARTOONING A PHASE?! NEVER, DAD!
WHEN YOU WERE SMALL, YOU THREW A MEA FASTBALL WHEN WE PLAYED CATCH! I HA YOU PEGGED FOR A SURE-FIRE LITTLE-LEAGUER. THEN YOU SUDDENLY LOST INTEREST.
THAT PROBABLY WAS WHEN CHUCK DISCOVERED COMICS!
IS IT EMBARRASSING TO BE A COACH AT RIVERDALE HIGH AND HAVE A SON WHO'S NOT INTO SPORTS, DAD?
NOW LISTEN, SON...
YOUR MOTHER AND I ARE VERY PROUD OF YOU!
AS LONG AS YOU DO WHAT YOU LOVE AND IT DOESN'T GET YOU INTO TROUBLE, I SAY YOU'RE AHEAD OF THE GAME!

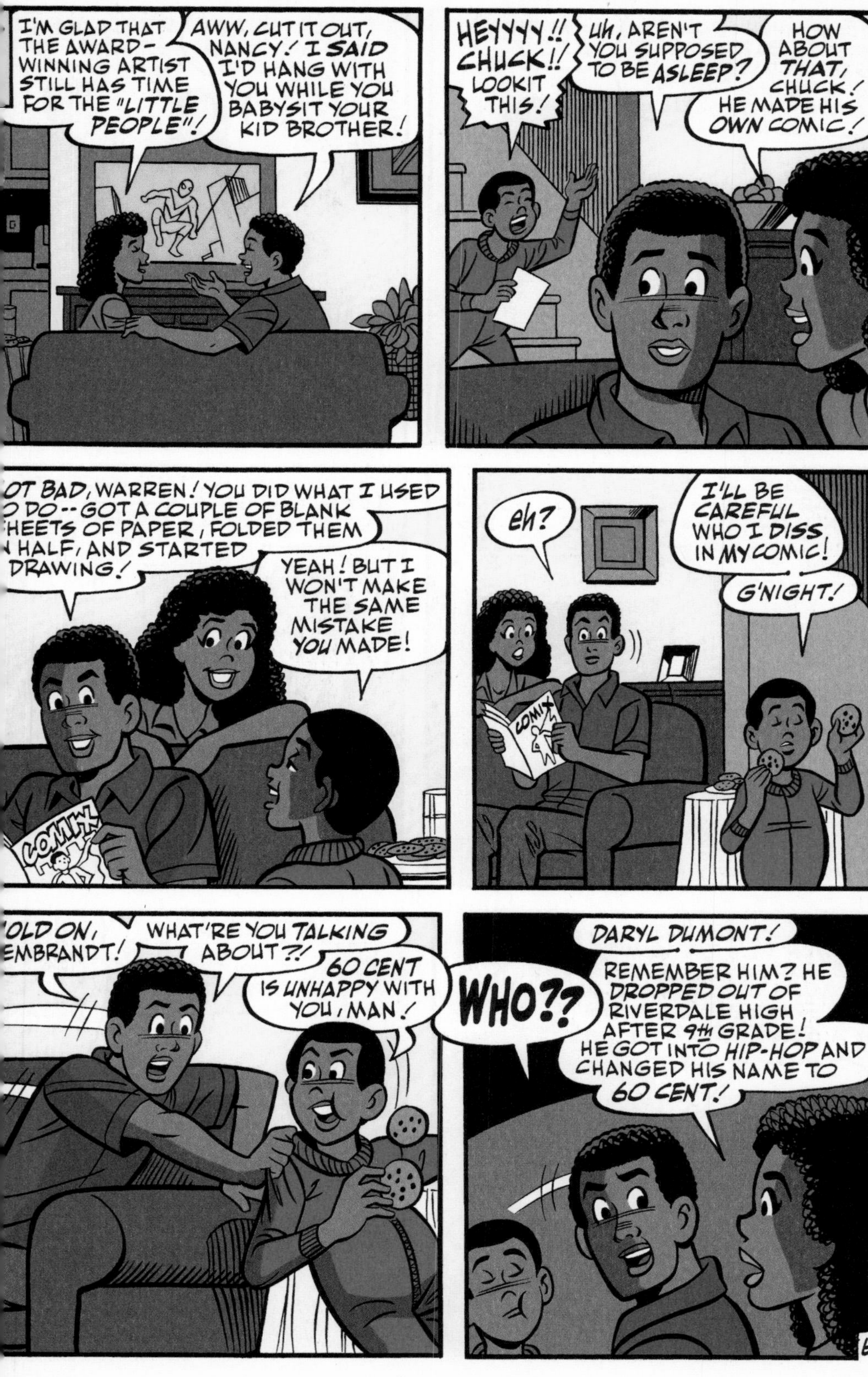

I'M GLAD THAT THE AWARD-WINNING ARTIST STILL HAS TIME FOR THE "LITTLE PEOPLE"!
AWW, CUT IT OUT, NANCY! I SAID I'D HANG WITH YOU WHILE YOU BABYSIT YOUR KID BROTHER!
HEYYYY!! CHUCK!! LOOKIT THIS!
uh, AREN'T YOU SUPPOSED TO BE ASLEEP?
HOW ABOUT THAT, CHUCK! HE MADE HIS OWN COMIC!
OT BAD, WARREN! YOU DID WHAT I USED O DO-- GOT A COUPLE OF BLANK HEETS OF PAPER, FOLDED THEM N HALF, AND STARTED DRAWING!
YEAH! BUT I WON'T MAKE THE SAME MISTAKE YOU MADE!
COMIX
eh?
I'LL BE CAREFUL WHO I DISS IN MY COMIC!
G'NIGHT!
OLD ON, EMBRANDT!
WHAT'RE YOU TALKING ABOUT?!
60 CENT IS UNHAPPY WITH YOU, MAN!
WHO??
DARYL DUMONT!
REMEMBER HIM? HE DROPPED OUT OF RIVERDALE HIGH AFTER 9th GRADE! HE GOT INTO HIP-HOP AND CHANGED HIS NAME TO 60 CENT!

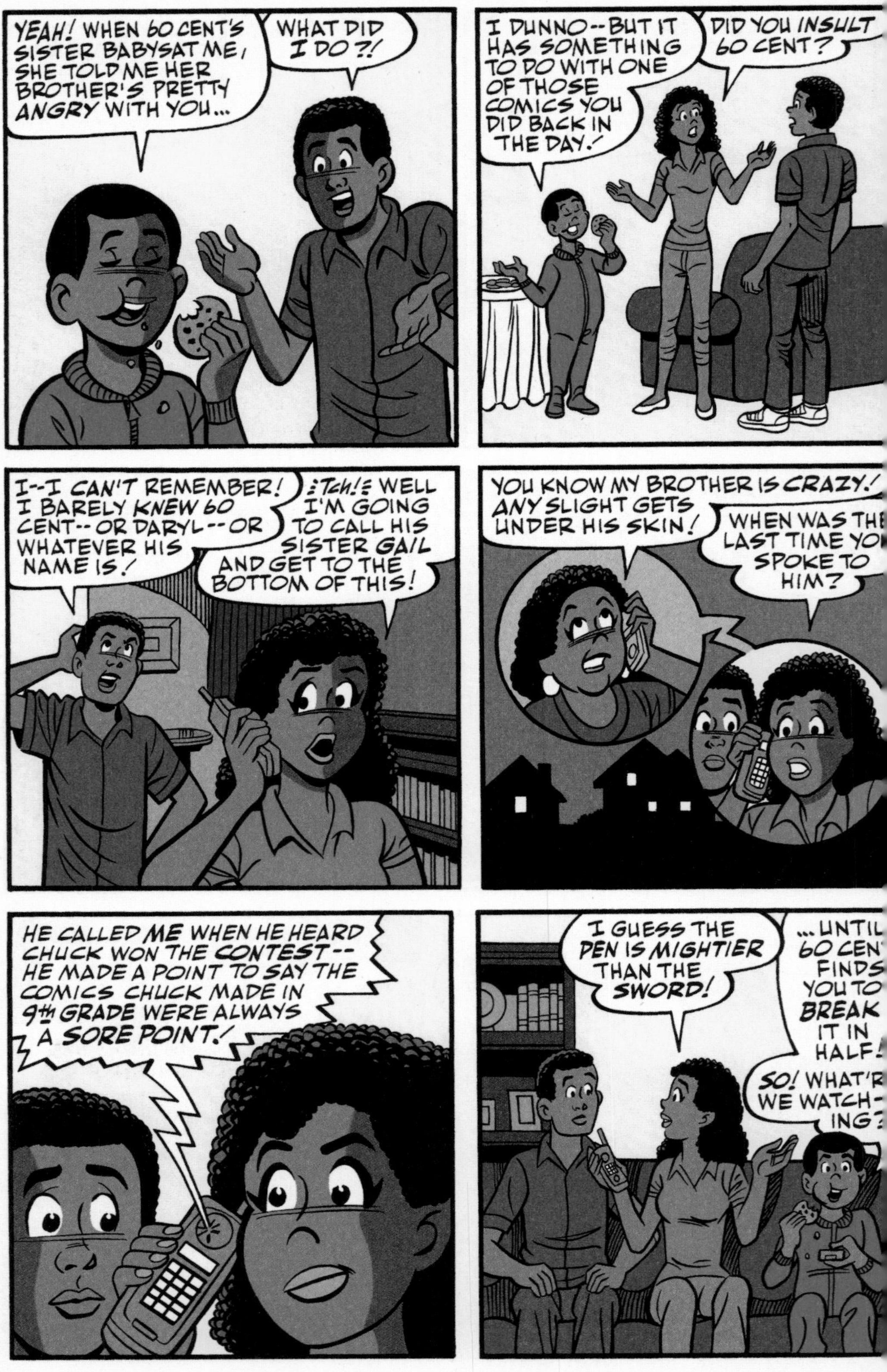
YEAH! WHEN 60 CENT'S SISTER BABYSAT ME, SHE TOLD ME HER BROTHER'S PRETTY ANGRY WITH YOU...
WHAT DID I DO?!
I DUNNO--BUT IT HAS SOMETHING TO DO WITH ONE OF THOSE COMICS YOU DID BACK IN THE DAY!
DID YOU INSULT 60 CENT?
I--I CAN'T REMEMBER! I BARELY KNEW 60 CENT--OR DARYL--OR WHATEVER HIS NAME IS!
TCH! WELL I'M GOING TO CALL HIS SISTER GAIL AND GET TO THE BOTTOM OF THIS!
YOU KNOW MY BROTHER IS CRAZY! ANY SLIGHT GETS UNDER HIS SKIN!
WHEN WAS THE LAST TIME YO SPOKE TO HIM?
HE CALLED ME WHEN HE HEARD CHUCK WON THE CONTEST--HE MADE A POINT TO SAY THE COMICS CHUCK MADE IN 9th GRADE WERE ALWAYS A SORE POINT!
I GUESS THE PEN IS MIGHTIER THAN THE SWORD!
...UNTIL 60 CEN FINDS YOU TO BREAK IT IN HALF!
SO! WHAT'R WE WATCH-ING?

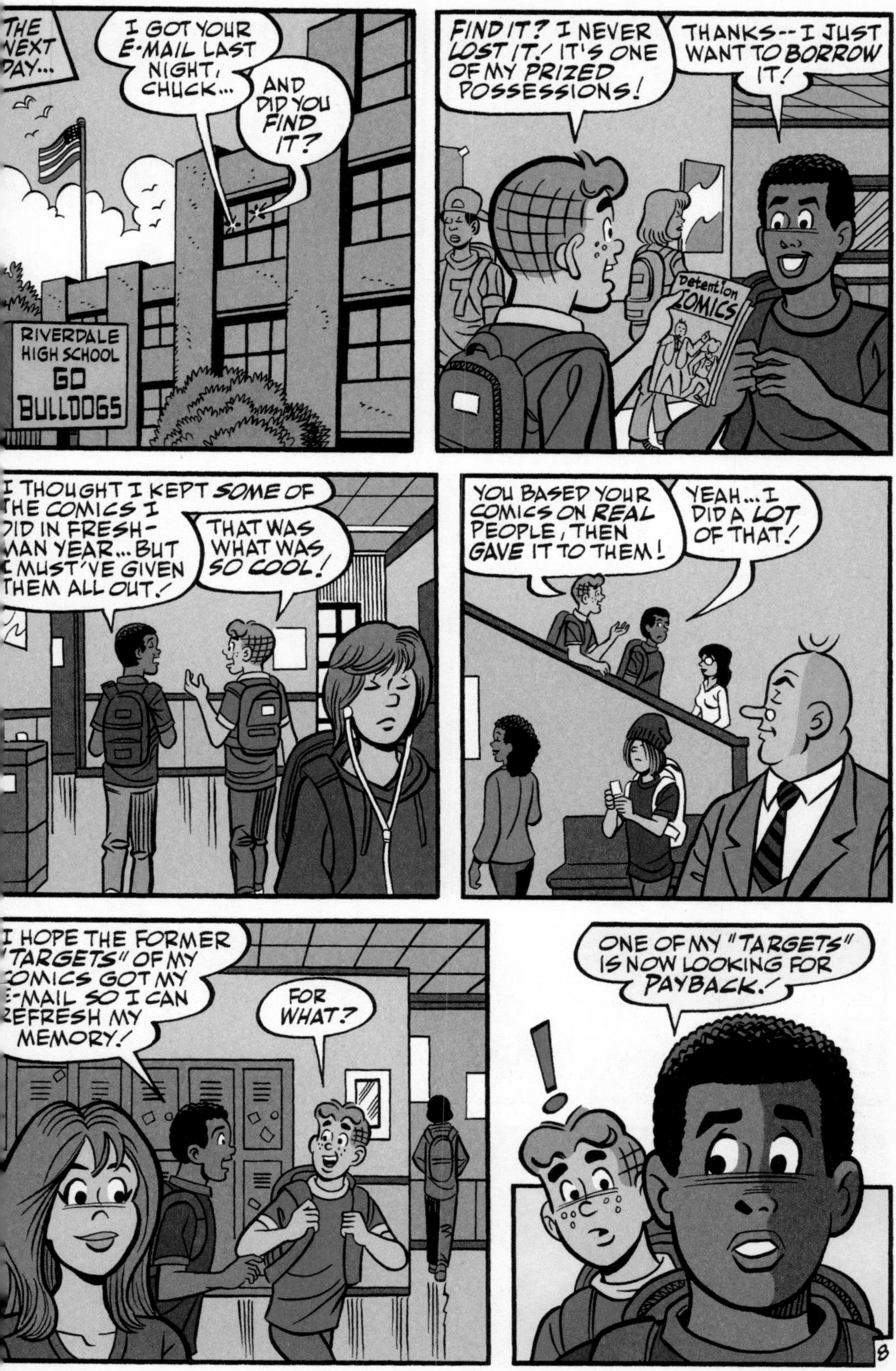
THE NEXT DAY...
I GOT YOUR E-MAIL LAST NIGHT, CHUCK...
AND DID YOU FIND IT?
FIND IT? I NEVER LOST IT! IT'S ONE OF MY PRIZED POSSESSIONS!
THANKS-- I JUST WANT TO BORROW IT!
RIVERDALE HIGH SCHOOL GO BULLDOGS
Detention COMICS
I THOUGHT I KEPT SOME OF THE COMICS I DID IN FRESH-MAN YEAR... BUT I MUST'VE GIVEN THEM ALL OUT!
THAT WAS WHAT WAS SO COOL!
YOU BASED YOUR COMICS ON REAL PEOPLE, THEN GAVE IT TO THEM!
YEAH... I DID A LOT OF THAT!
I HOPE THE FORMER "TARGETS" OF MY COMICS GOT MY E-MAIL SO I CAN REFRESH MY MEMORY!
FOR WHAT?
ONE OF MY "TARGETS" IS NOW LOOKING FOR PAYBACK!
!

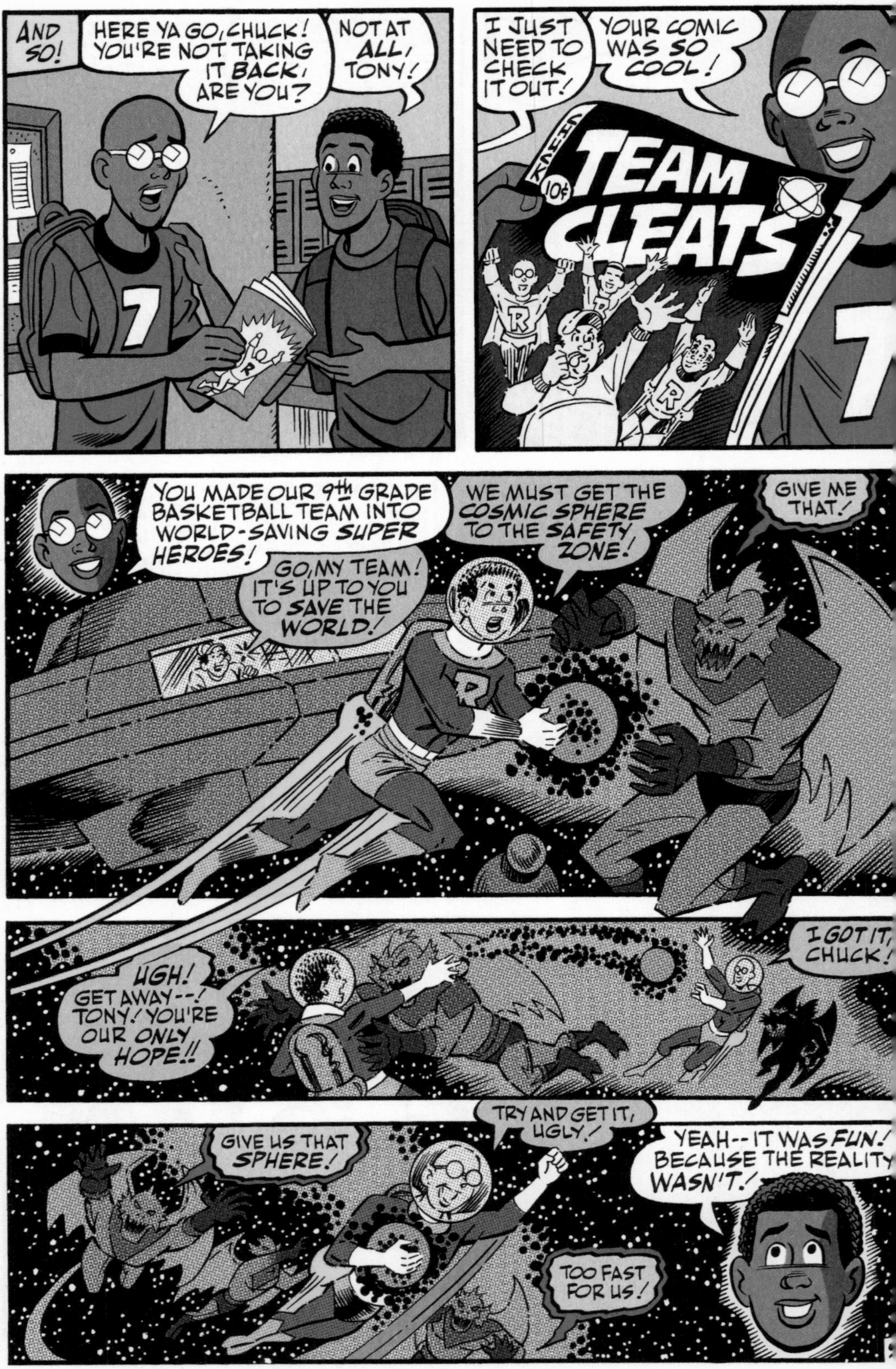
AND SO!
HERE YA GO, CHUCK! YOU'RE NOT TAKING IT BACK, ARE YOU?
NOT AT ALL, TONY!
I JUST NEED TO CHECK IT OUT!
YOUR COMIC WAS SO COOL!
TEAM CLEATS
10¢
YOU MADE OUR 9th GRADE BASKETBALL TEAM INTO WORLD-SAVING SUPER HEROES!
GO, MY TEAM! IT'S UP TO YOU TO SAVE THE WORLD!
WE MUST GET THE COSMIC SPHERE TO THE SAFETY ZONE!
GIVE ME THAT!
UGH! GET AWAY--! TONY! YOU'RE OUR ONLY HOPE!!
I GOT IT, CHUCK!
GIVE US THAT SPHERE!
TRY AND GET IT, UGLY!
TOO FAST FOR US!
YEAH--IT WAS FUN! BECAUSE THE REALITY WASN'T!

WELL, THAT GAME WAS *PATHETIC!* THAT TEAM MOPPED THE FLOOR WITH YOU GUYS...

CLAYTON! FRONT AND CENTER!

HOME 10 VISITOR 40

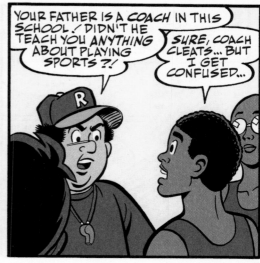

YOUR FATHER IS A *COACH* IN THIS SCHOOL! DIDN'T HE TEACH YOU ANYTHING ABOUT PLAYING SPORTS?!

SURE, COACH CLEATS... BUT I GET CONFUSED...

I THOUGHT THIS WAS THE ONE WITH NINE INNINGS!

HAHA HAHA

OOOh... WE HAVE A *COMIC* HERE, eh? EVERYBODY--

--DROP AND GIVE ME 50!

...38...39...40...! TEN MORE, GENTLEMEN!

ME AND MY *BIG MOUTH!*

NO PROB, CHUCK...

IT AIN'T THE *END OF THE WORLD!*

UNGH! THANKS, TONY! UNGH! BUT WHAT IF THE FATE OF THE WORLD WAS AT STAKE?

10

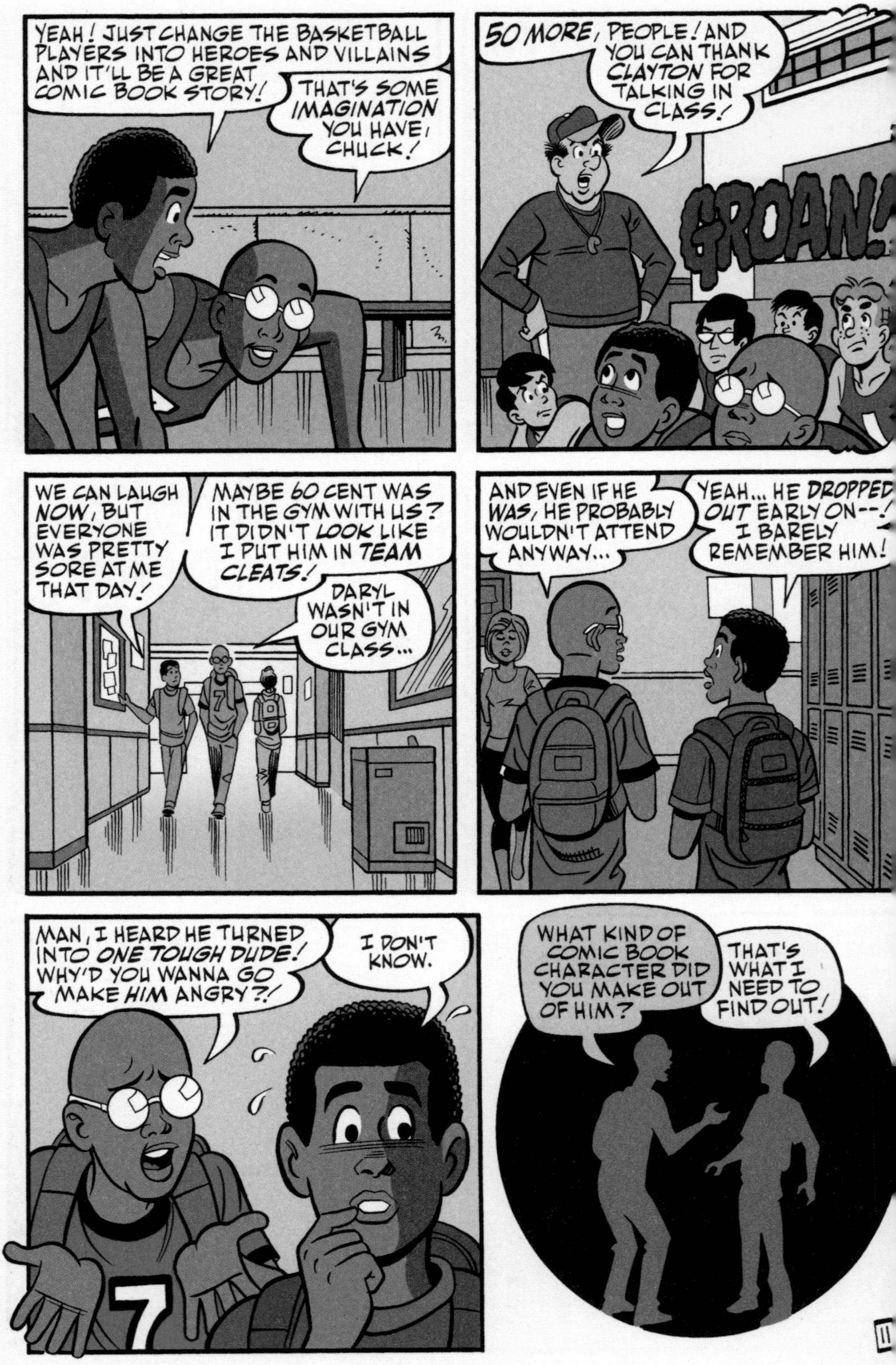
YEAH! JUST CHANGE THE BASKETBALL PLAYERS INTO HEROES AND VILLAINS AND IT'LL BE A GREAT COMIC BOOK STORY!
THAT'S SOME IMAGINATION YOU HAVE, CHUCK!
50 MORE, PEOPLE! AND YOU CAN THANK CLAYTON FOR TALKING IN CLASS!
GROAN!
WE CAN LAUGH NOW, BUT EVERYONE WAS PRETTY SORE AT ME THAT DAY!
MAYBE 60 CENT WAS IN THE GYM WITH US? IT DIDN'T LOOK LIKE I PUT HIM IN TEAM CLEATS!
DARYL WASN'T IN OUR GYM CLASS...
AND EVEN IF HE WAS, HE PROBABLY WOULDN'T ATTEND ANYWAY...
YEAH... HE DROPPED OUT EARLY ON--! I BARELY REMEMBER HIM!
MAN, I HEARD HE TURNED INTO ONE TOUGH DUDE! WHY'D YOU WANNA GO MAKE HIM ANGRY?!
I DON'T KNOW.
WHAT KIND OF COMIC BOOK CHARACTER DID YOU MAKE OUT OF HIM?
THAT'S WHAT I NEED TO FIND OUT!

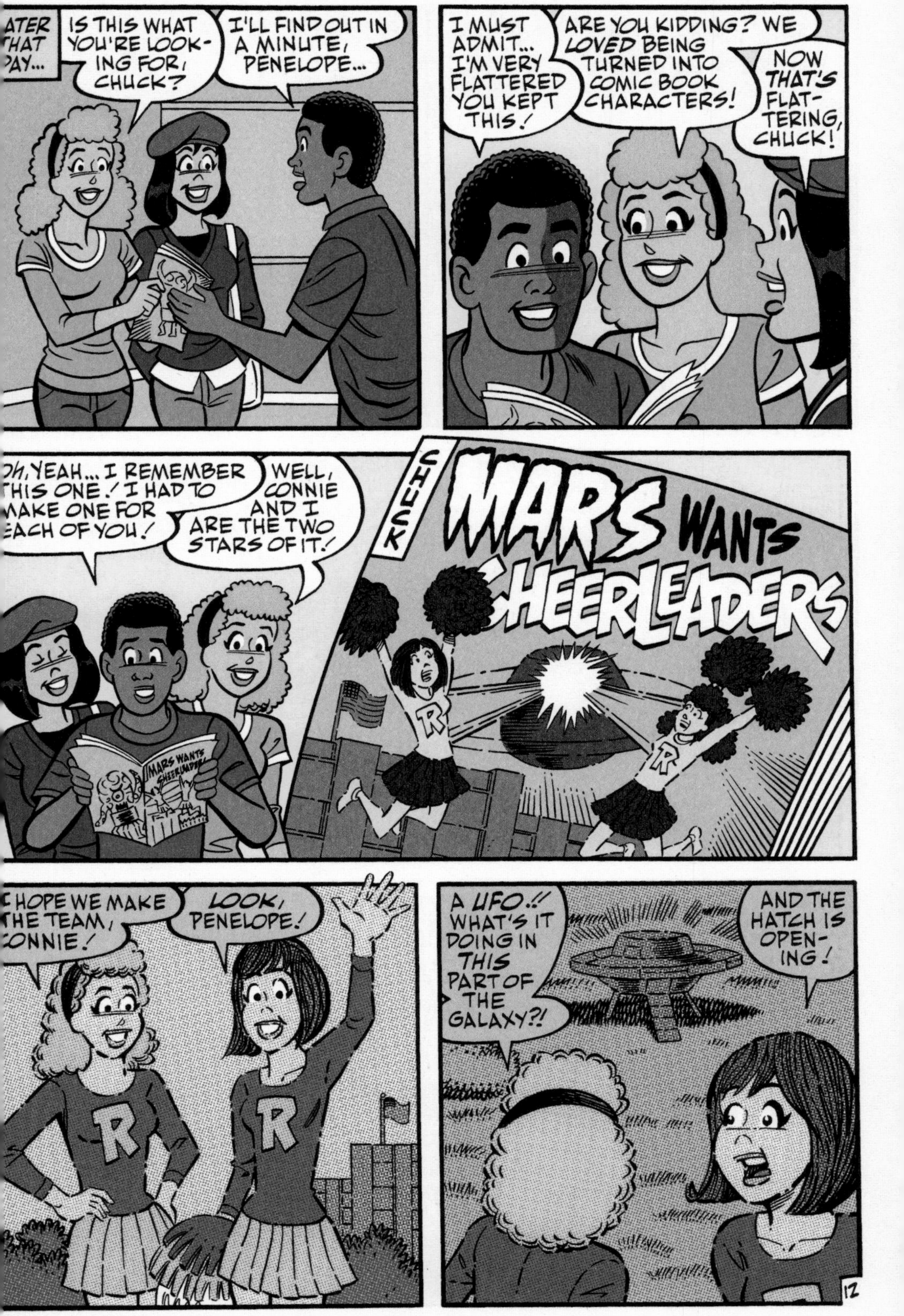
ATER THAT PAY...
IS THIS WHAT YOU'RE LOOK-ING FOR, CHUCK?
I'LL FIND OUT IN A MINUTE, PENELOPE...
I MUST ADMIT... I'M VERY FLATTERED YOU KEPT THIS!
ARE YOU KIDDING? WE LOVED BEING TURNED INTO COMIC BOOK CHARACTERS!
NOW THAT'S FLAT-TERING, CHUCK!
OH, YEAH... I REMEMBER THIS ONE! I HAD TO MAKE ONE FOR EACH OF YOU!
WELL, CONNIE AND I ARE THE TWO STARS OF IT!
CHUCK
MARS WANTS CHEERLEADERS
I HOPE WE MAKE THE TEAM, CONNIE!
LOOK, PENELOPE!
A UFO!! WHAT'S IT DOING IN THIS PART OF THE GALAXY?!
AND THE HATCH IS OPEN-ING!
12

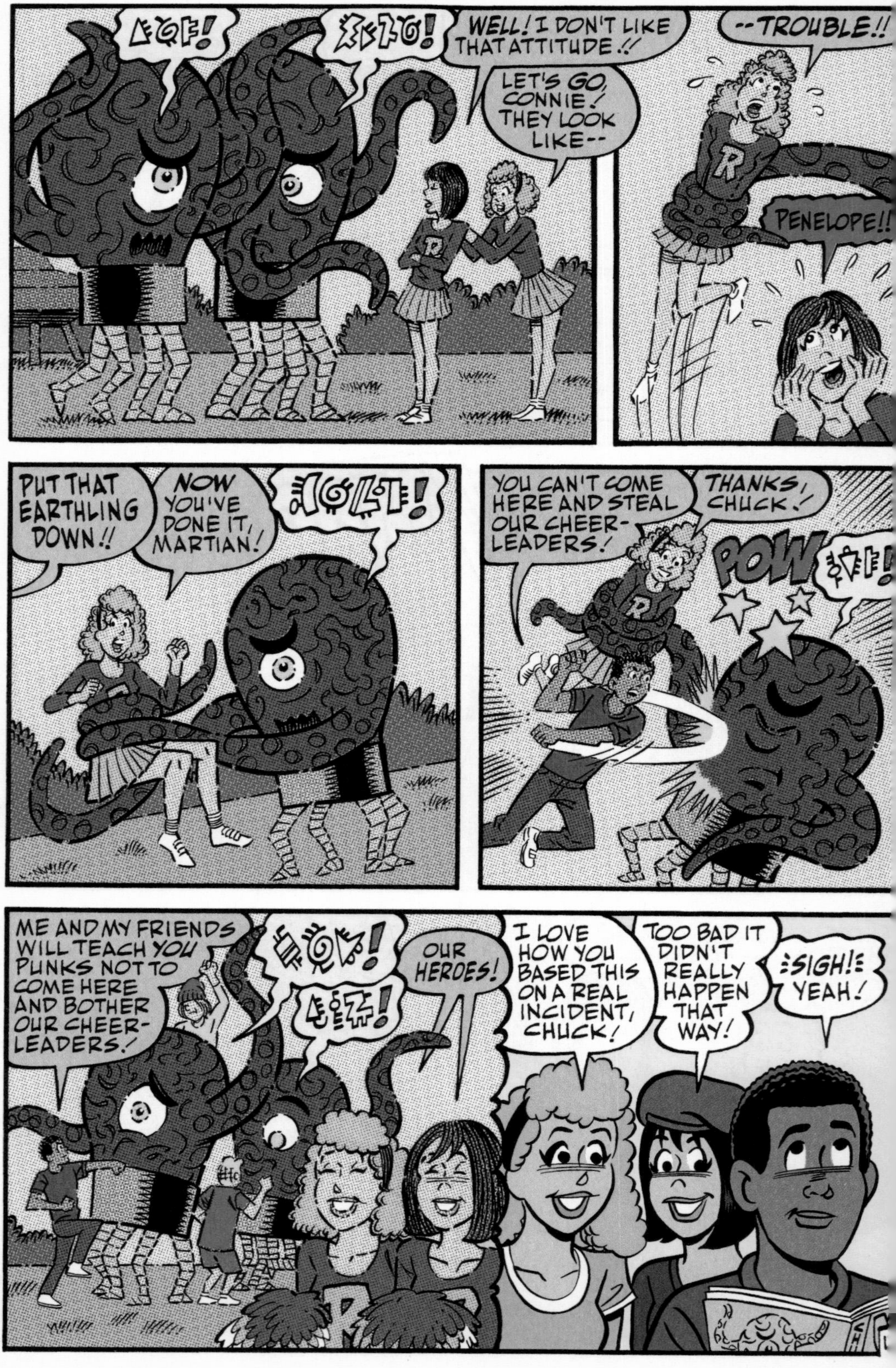
WELL! I DON'T LIKE THAT ATTITUDE.!!
LET'S GO, CONNIE! THEY LOOK LIKE--
--TROUBLE!!
PENELOPE!!
PUT THAT EARTHLING DOWN!!
NOW YOU'VE DONE IT, MARTIAN!
YOU CAN'T COME HERE AND STEAL OUR CHEER-LEADERS!
THANKS, CHUCK!
POW
ME AND MY FRIENDS WILL TEACH YOU PUNKS NOT TO COME HERE AND BOTHER OUR CHEER-LEADERS!
OUR HEROES!
I LOVE HOW YOU BASED THIS ON A REAL INCIDENT, CHUCK!
TOO BAD IT DIDN'T REALLY HAPPEN THAT WAY!
SIGH! YEAH!

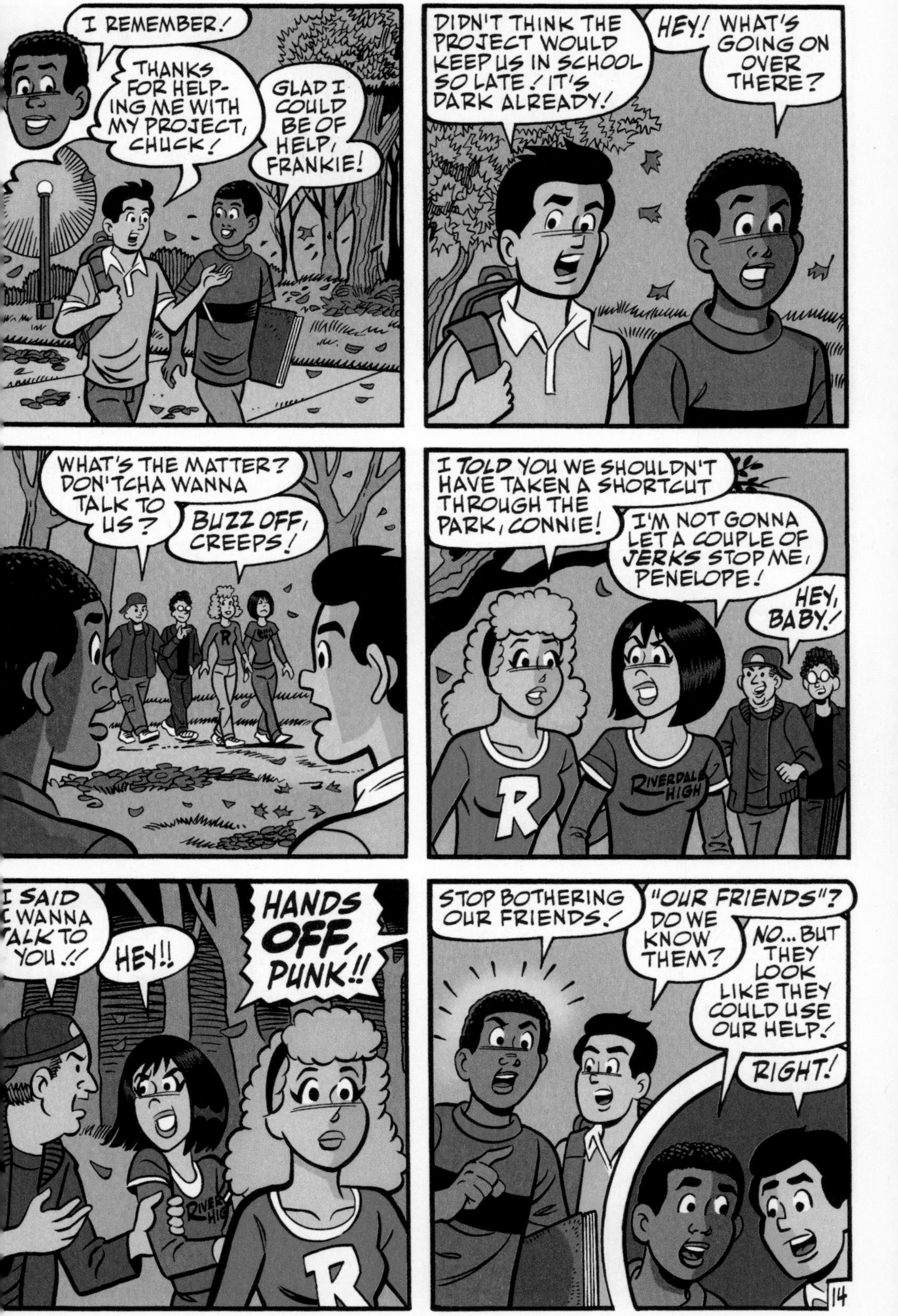
I REMEMBER!
THANKS FOR HELPING ME WITH MY PROJECT, CHUCK!
GLAD I COULD BE OF HELP, FRANKIE!
DIDN'T THINK THE PROJECT WOULD KEEP US IN SCHOOL SO LATE! IT'S DARK ALREADY!
HEY! WHAT'S GOING ON OVER THERE?
WHAT'S THE MATTER? DON'TCHA WANNA TALK TO US?
BUZZ OFF, CREEPS!
I TOLD YOU WE SHOULDN'T HAVE TAKEN A SHORTCUT THROUGH THE PARK, CONNIE!
I'M NOT GONNA LET A COUPLE OF JERKS STOP ME, PENELOPE!
HEY, BABY!
I SAID I WANNA TALK TO YOU!!
HEY!!
HANDS OFF, PUNK!!
STOP BOTHERING OUR FRIENDS!
"OUR FRIENDS"? DO WE KNOW THEM?
NO... BUT THEY LOOK LIKE THEY COULD USE OUR HELP!
RIGHT!
14

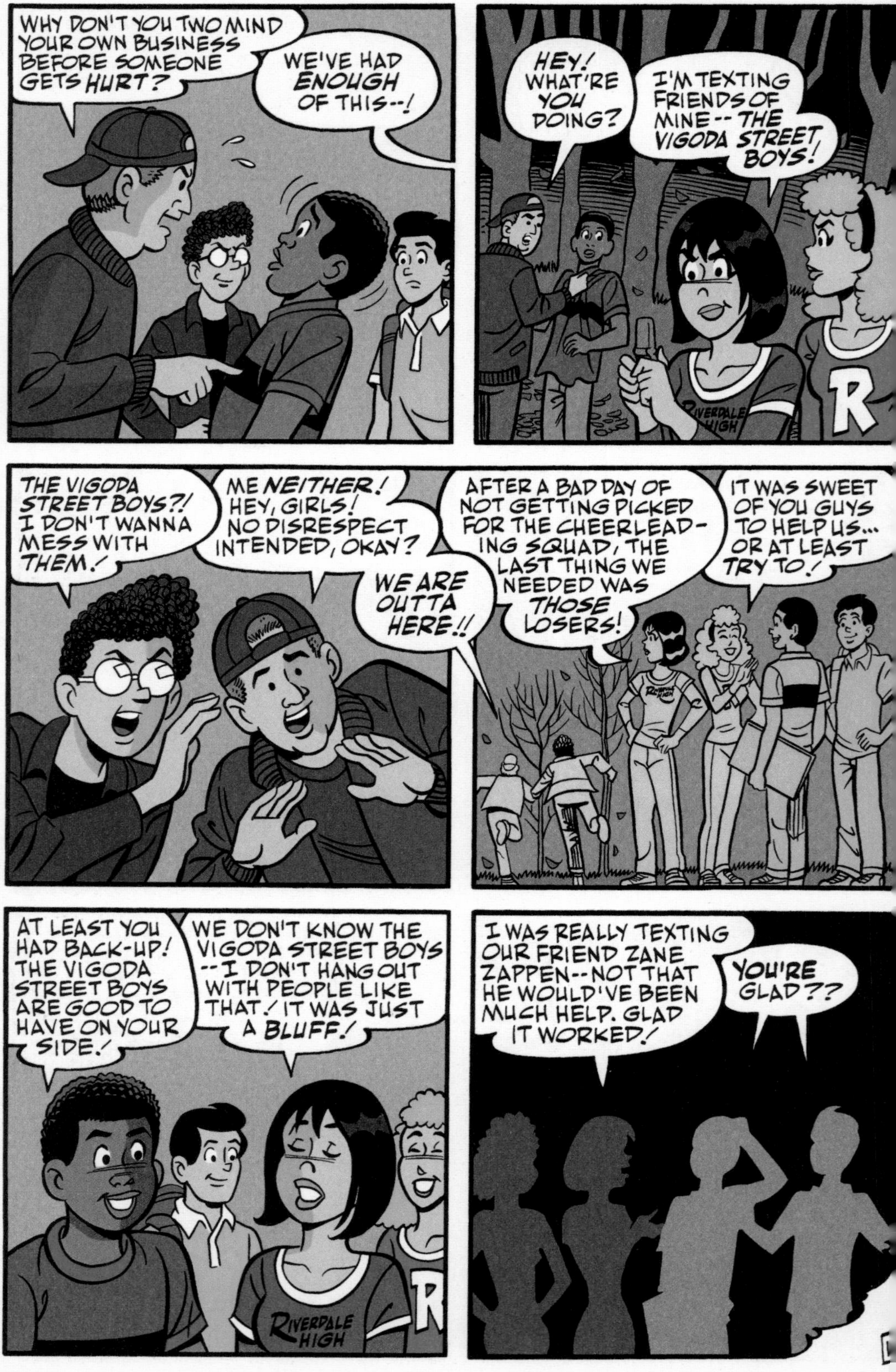
WHY DON'T YOU TWO MIND YOUR OWN BUSINESS BEFORE SOMEONE GETS HURT?
WE'VE HAD ENOUGH OF THIS--!
HEY! WHAT'RE YOU DOING?
I'M TEXTING FRIENDS OF MINE -- THE VIGODA STREET BOYS!
RIVERDALE HIGH
R
THE VIGODA STREET BOYS?! I DON'T WANNA MESS WITH THEM.!
ME NEITHER! HEY, GIRLS! NO DISRESPECT INTENDED, OKAY?
WE ARE OUTTA HERE!!
AFTER A BAD DAY OF NOT GETTING PICKED FOR THE CHEERLEAD-ING SQUAD, THE LAST THING WE NEEDED WAS THOSE LOSERS!
IT WAS SWEET OF YOU GUYS TO HELP US... OR AT LEAST TRY TO!
AT LEAST YOU HAD BACK-UP! THE VIGODA STREET BOYS ARE GOOD TO HAVE ON YOUR SIDE!
WE DON'T KNOW THE VIGODA STREET BOYS -- I DON'T HANG OUT WITH PEOPLE LIKE THAT! IT WAS JUST A BLUFF!
R
RIVERDALE HIGH
I WAS REALLY TEXTING OUR FRIEND ZANE ZAPPEN--NOT THAT HE WOULD'VE BEEN MUCH HELP. GLAD IT WORKED!
YOU'RE GLAD??

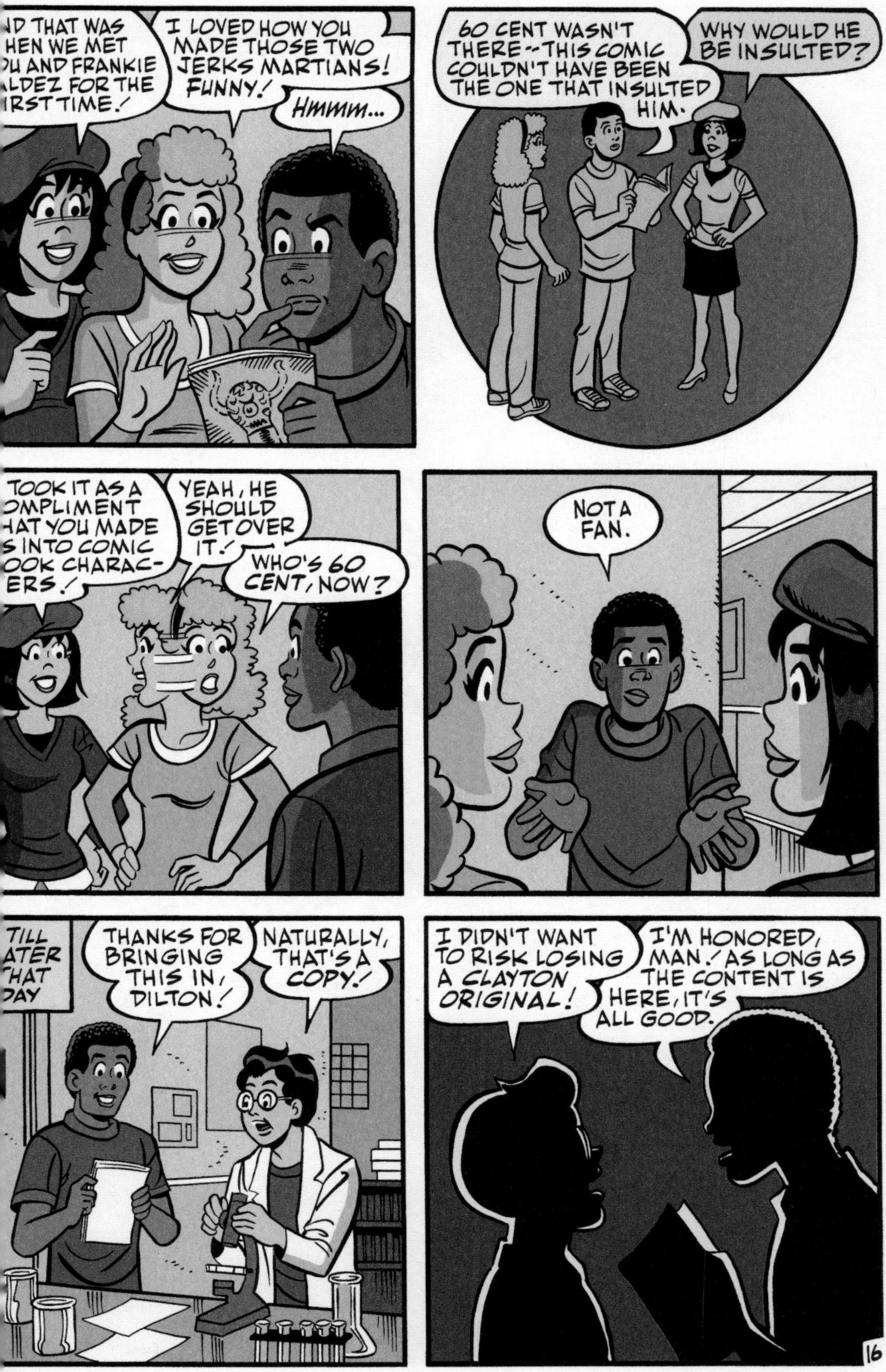

ND THAT WAS HEN WE MET OU AND FRANKIE ALDEZ FOR THE IRST TIME!
I LOVED HOW YOU MADE THOSE TWO JERKS MARTIANS! FUNNY!
HMMM...
60 CENT WASN'T THERE -- THIS COMIC COULDN'T HAVE BEEN THE ONE THAT INSULTED HIM.
WHY WOULD HE BE INSULTED?
TOOK IT AS A OMPLIMENT HAT YOU MADE S INTO COMIC OOK CHARAC- ERS!
YEAH, HE SHOULD GET OVER IT!
WHO'S 60 CENT, NOW?
NOT A FAN.
TILL ATER HAT DAY
THANKS FOR BRINGING THIS IN, DILTON!
NATURALLY, THAT'S A COPY!
I DIDN'T WANT TO RISK LOSING A CLAYTON ORIGINAL!
I'M HONORED, MAN! AS LONG AS THE CONTENT IS HERE, IT'S ALL GOOD.

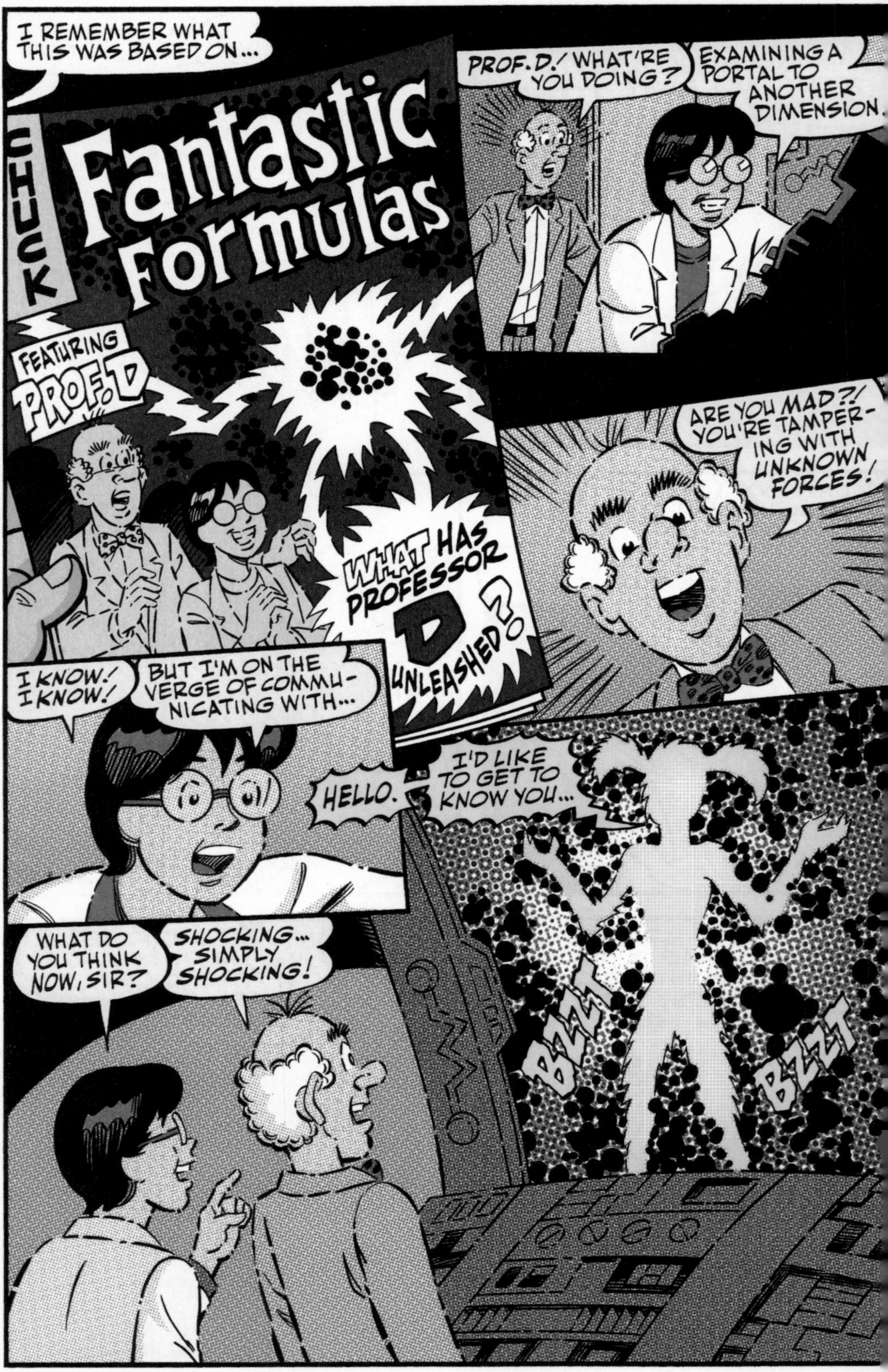
I REMEMBER WHAT THIS WAS BASED ON...
SHUCK
Fantastic Formulas
FEATURING PROF. D
WHAT HAS PROFESSOR D UNLEASHED?
PROF. D.! WHAT'RE YOU DOING?
EXAMINING A PORTAL TO ANOTHER DIMENSION.
ARE YOU MAD?! YOU'RE TAMPERING WITH UNKNOWN FORCES!
I KNOW! I KNOW!
BUT I'M ON THE VERGE OF COMMUNICATING WITH...
HELLO.
I'D LIKE TO GET TO KNOW YOU...
BZZT
BZZT
WHAT DO YOU THINK NOW, SIR?
SHOCKING... SIMPLY SHOCKING!

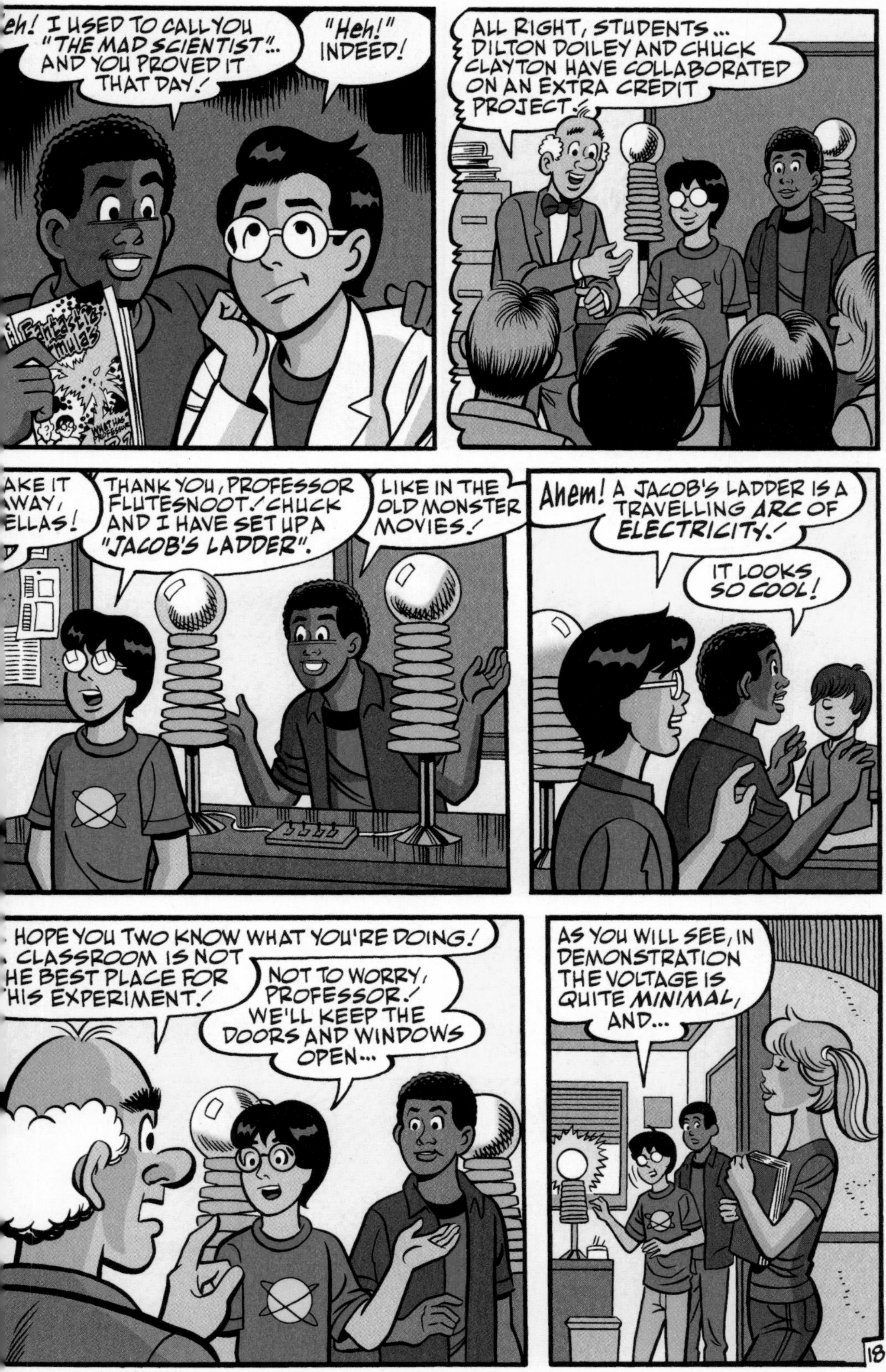
eh! I USED TO CALL YOU "THE MAD SCIENTIST"!... AND YOU PROVED IT THAT DAY!
"Heh!" INDEED!
ALL RIGHT, STUDENTS... DILTON DOILEY AND CHUCK CLAYTON HAVE COLLABORATED ON AN EXTRA CREDIT PROJECT!
AKE IT WAY, ELLAS!
THANK YOU, PROFESSOR FLUTESNOOT! CHUCK AND I HAVE SET UP A "JACOB'S LADDER".
LIKE IN THE OLD MONSTER MOVIES!
Ahem! A JACOB'S LADDER IS A TRAVELLING ARC OF ELECTRICITY!
IT LOOKS SO COOL!
HOPE YOU TWO KNOW WHAT YOU'RE DOING! CLASSROOM IS NOT HE BEST PLACE FOR HIS EXPERIMENT!
NOT TO WORRY, PROFESSOR! WE'LL KEEP THE DOORS AND WINDOWS OPEN...
AS YOU WILL SEE, IN DEMONSTRATION THE VOLTAGE IS QUITE MINIMAL, AND...

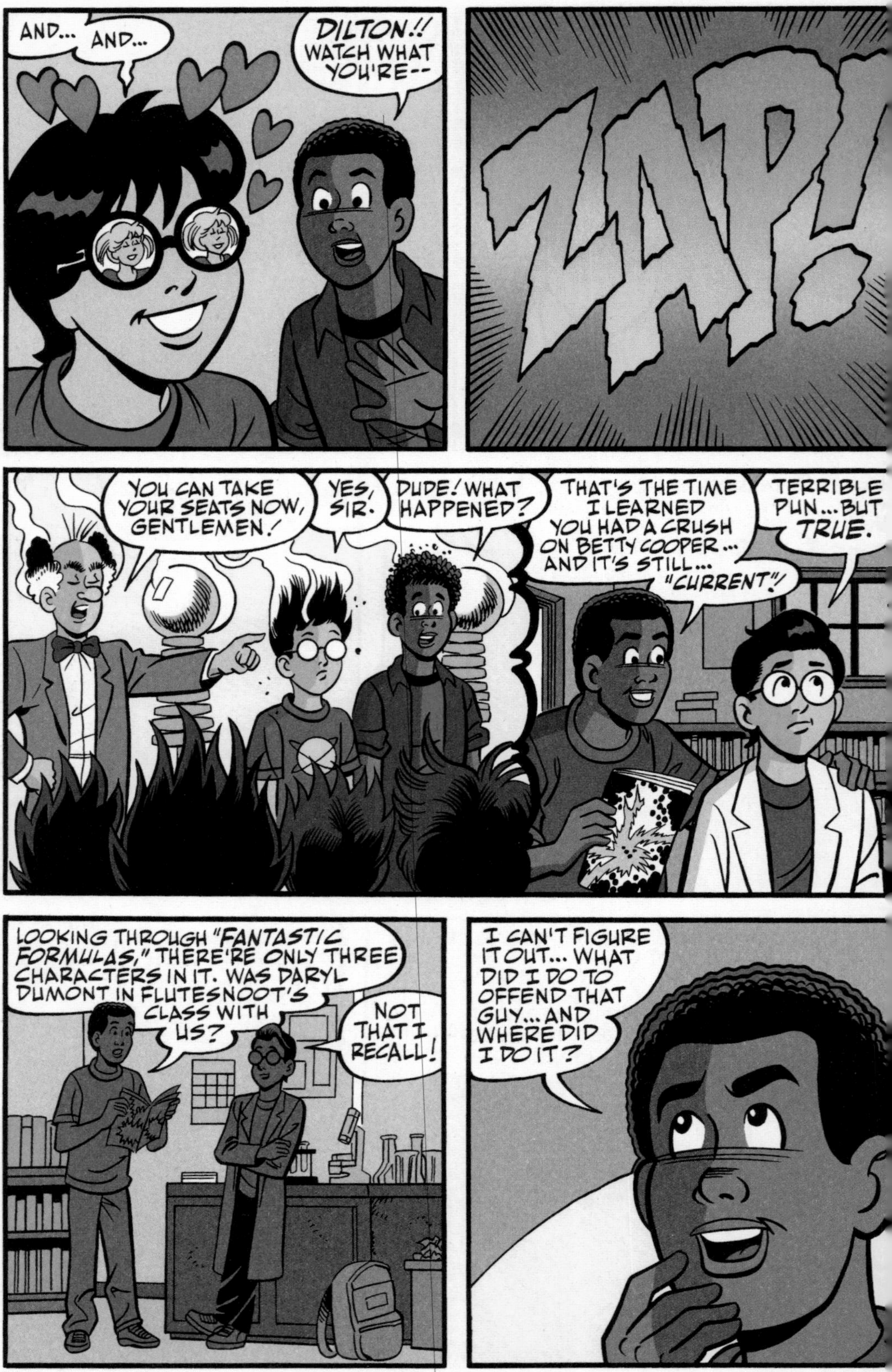
AND... AND...
DILTON!! WATCH WHAT YOU'RE--
ZAP!
YOU CAN TAKE YOUR SEATS NOW, GENTLEMEN!
YES, SIR.
DUDE! WHAT HAPPENED?
THAT'S THE TIME I LEARNED YOU HAD A CRUSH ON BETTY COOPER... AND IT'S STILL... "CURRENT"!
TERRIBLE PUN... BUT TRUE.
LOOKING THROUGH "FANTASTIC FORMULAS," THERE'RE ONLY THREE CHARACTERS IN IT. WAS DARYL DUMONT IN FLUTESNOOT'S CLASS WITH US?
NOT THAT I RECALL!
I CAN'T FIGURE IT OUT... WHAT DID I DO TO OFFEND THAT GUY... AND WHERE DID I DO IT?

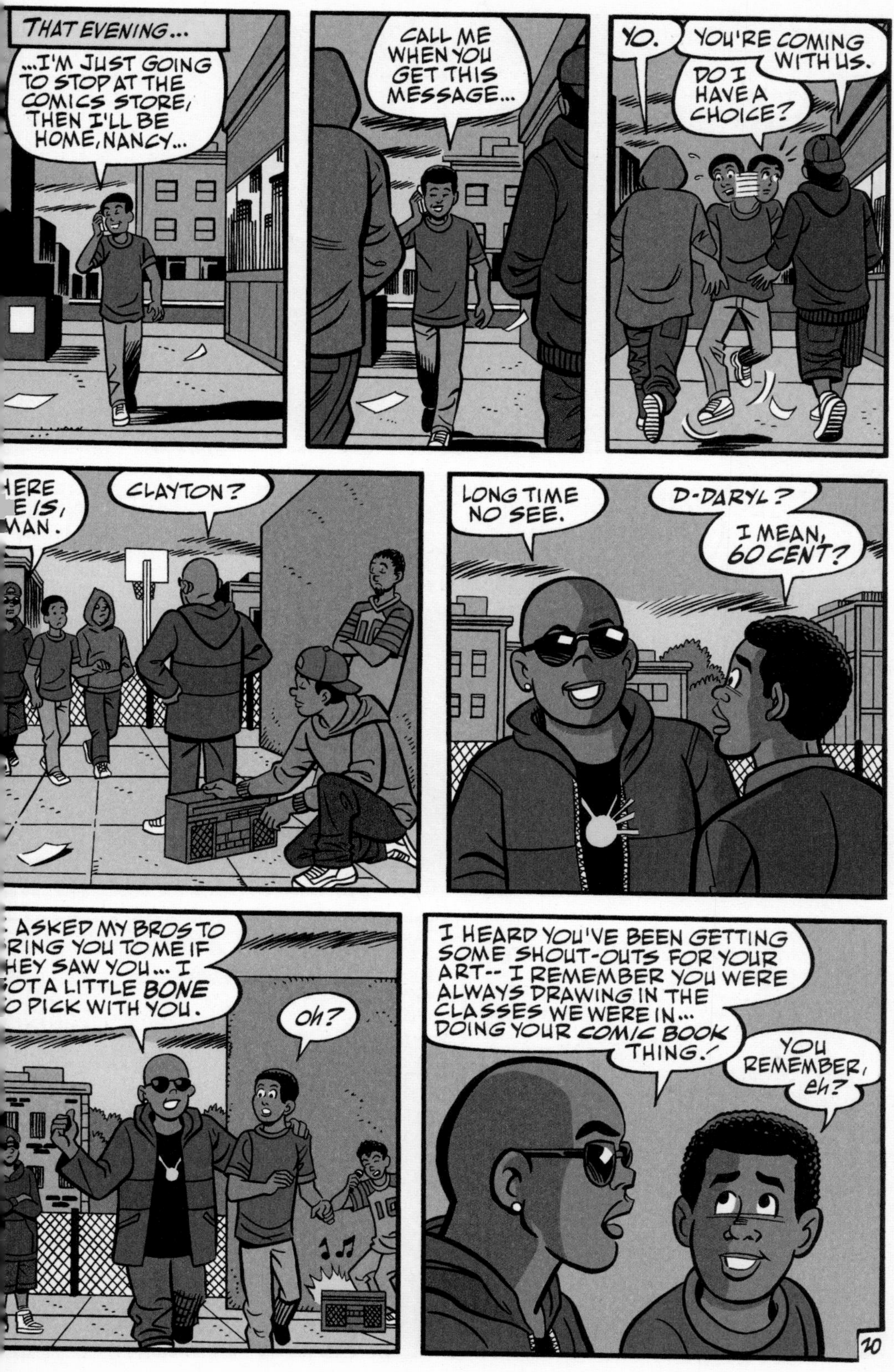
THAT EVENING...
...I'M JUST GOING TO STOP AT THE COMICS STORE, THEN I'LL BE HOME, NANCY...
CALL ME WHEN YOU GET THIS MESSAGE...
YO.
YOU'RE COMING WITH US.
DO I HAVE A CHOICE?
HERE E IS, MAN.
CLAYTON?
LONG TIME NO SEE.
D-DARYL?
I MEAN, 60 CENT?
ASKED MY BROS TO RING YOU TO ME IF HEY SAW YOU... I OT A LITTLE BONE O PICK WITH YOU.
oh?
I HEARD YOU'VE BEEN GETTING SOME SHOUT-OUTS FOR YOUR ART-- I REMEMBER YOU WERE ALWAYS DRAWING IN THE CLASSES WE WERE IN... DOING YOUR COMIC BOOK THING.
YOU REMEMBER, eh?
20

I SAW SOME OF THOSE COMICS YOU DID-- YOU USED PEOPLE IN OUR CLASSROOM...

WAS THERE A, ER... PROBLEM WITH THAT?

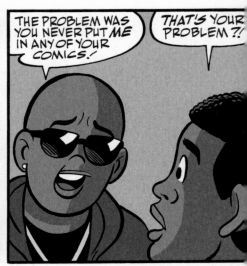

THE PROBLEM WAS YOU NEVER PUT *ME* IN ANY OF YOUR COMICS!

THAT'S YOUR PROBLEM?!

OH, YEAH! COMICS ARE OFF THE CHARTS!

WHO WOULDN'T WANNA BE DRAWN BY A FAMOUS ARTIST?

WELLLL... NOT *THAT* FAMOUS!

YOU KNOW, YOU DROPPED OUT OF SCHOOL BEFORE I GOT TO KNOW YOU...

...I CERTAINLY WOULD'VE PUT YOU IN ONE OF MY COMICS!

I SHOULDA STAYED IN SCHOOL...

MAN, YOU'RE LUCKY! I WISH I COULD DRAW!

WHAT ABOUT HIP-HOP? YOU'RE PASSIONATE ABOUT THAT, AREN'T YOU?

YOU KNOW IT! MY BROS AND I HAVE OUR FIRST GIG IN A COUPLE OF WEEKS!

REALLY?

hmm... 60 CENT, I HAVE AN IDEA...

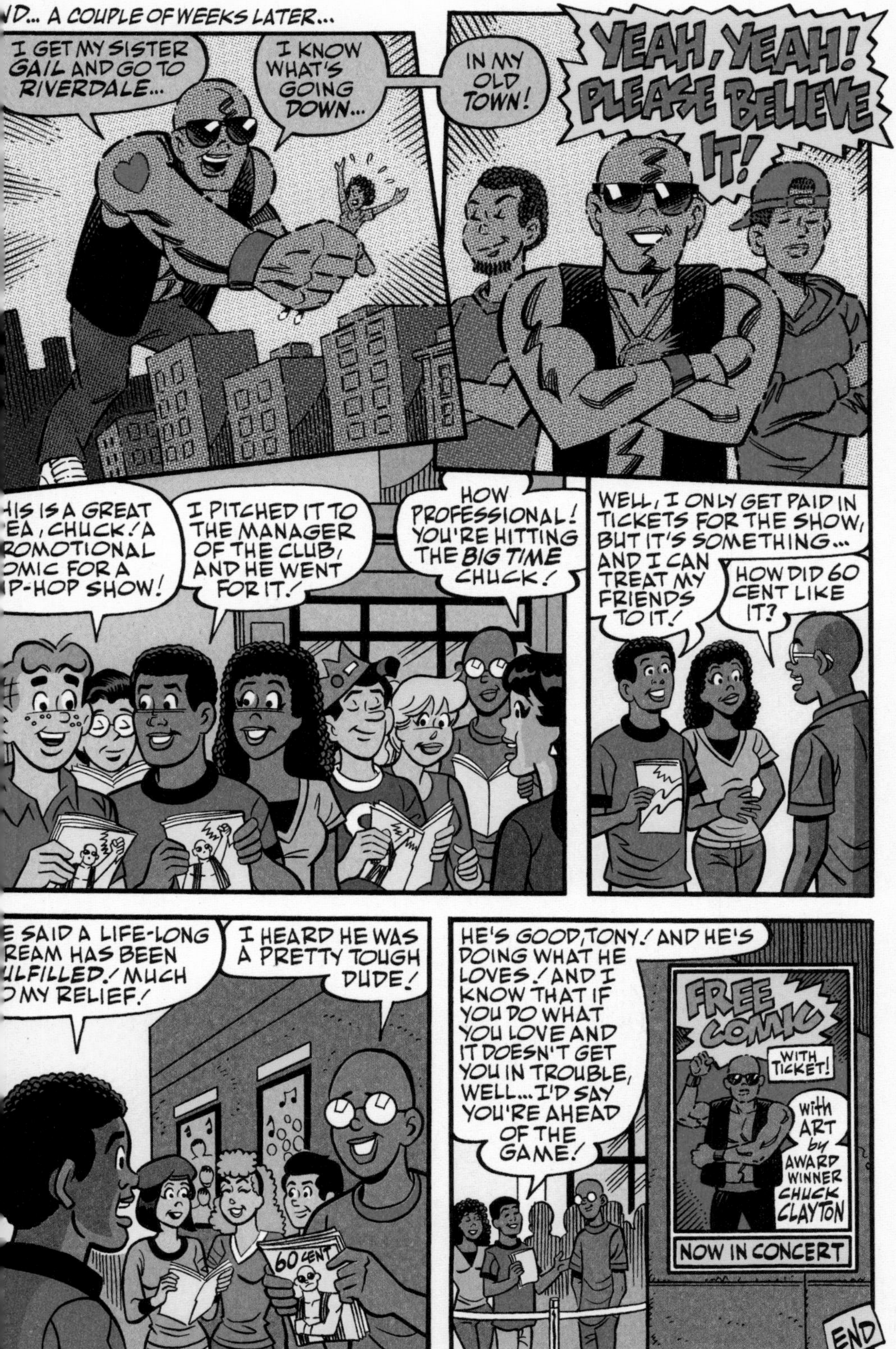
ND... A COUPLE OF WEEKS LATER...
I GET MY SISTER GAIL AND GO TO RIVERDALE...
I KNOW WHAT'S GOING DOWN...
IN MY OLD TOWN!
YEAH, YEAH! PLEASE BELIEVE IT!
HIS IS A GREAT EA, CHUCK! A ROMOTIONAL OMIC FOR A IP-HOP SHOW!
I PITCHED IT TO THE MANAGER OF THE CLUB, AND HE WENT FOR IT!
HOW PROFESSIONAL! YOU'RE HITTING THE BIG TIME CHUCK!
WELL, I ONLY GET PAID IN TICKETS FOR THE SHOW, BUT IT'S SOMETHING... AND I CAN TREAT MY FRIENDS TO IT!
HOW DID 60 CENT LIKE IT?
E SAID A LIFE-LONG REAM HAS BEEN ULFILLED! MUCH O MY RELIEF!
I HEARD HE WAS A PRETTY TOUGH DUDE!
60 CENT
HE'S GOOD, TONY! AND HE'S DOING WHAT HE LOVES! AND I KNOW THAT IF YOU DO WHAT YOU LOVE AND IT DOESN'T GET YOU IN TROUBLE, WELL... I'D SAY YOU'RE AHEAD OF THE GAME!
FREE COMIC
WITH TICKET!
with ART by AWARD WINNER CHUCK CLAYTON
NOW IN CONCERT
END

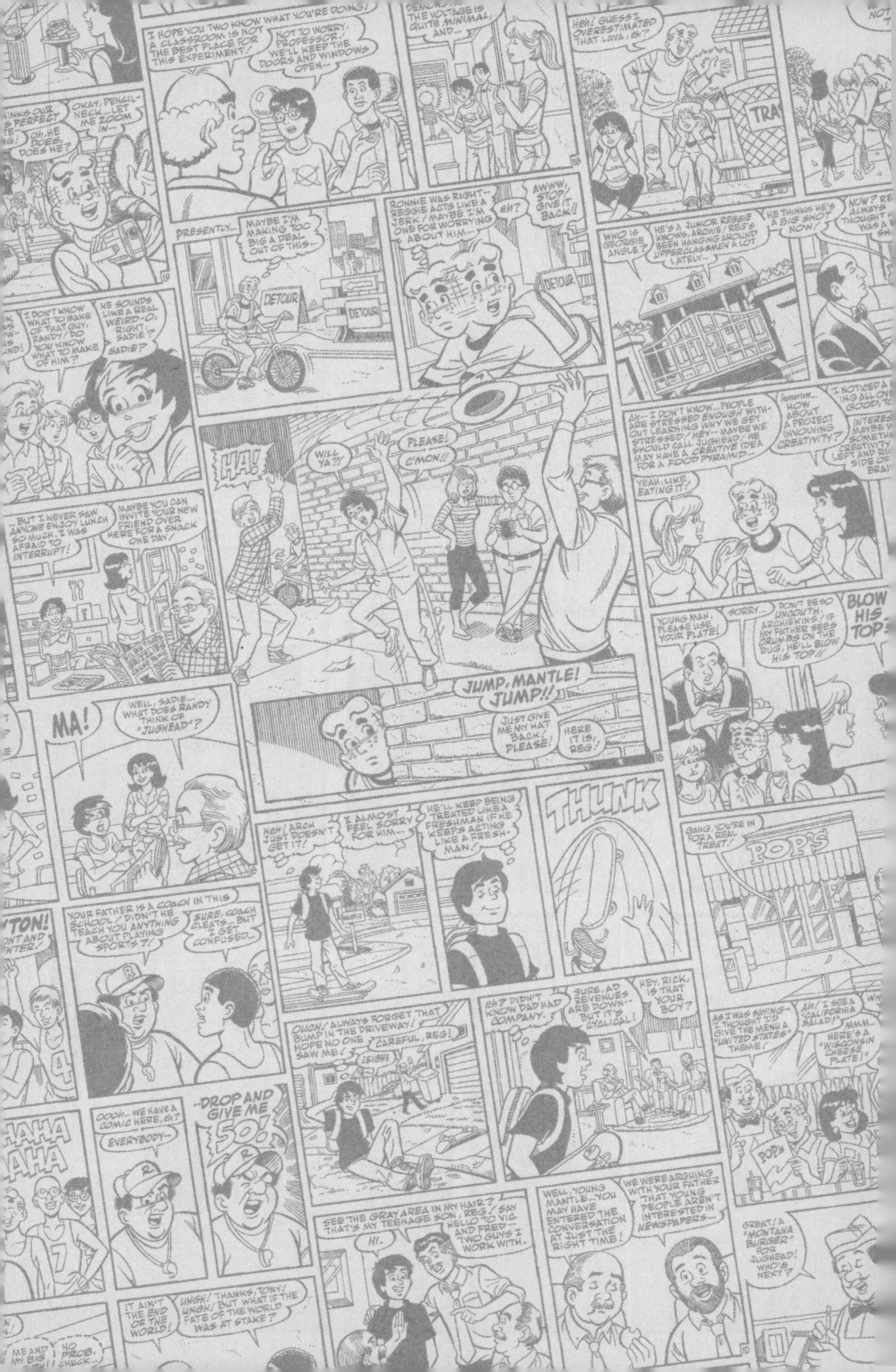
I HOPE YOU TWO KNOW WHAT YOU'RE DOING! A CLASSROOM IS NOT THE BEST PLACE FOR THIS EXPERIMENT!
NOT TO WORRY, PROFESSOR! WE'LL KEEP THE DOORS AND WINDOWS OPEN...
THE VOLTAGE IS QUITE MINIMAL, AND...
HEH! GUESS I OVERESTIMATED THAT LAVA, EH?
OKAY, PENCIL-NECK... LET ME ZOOM IN...
OH, HE DOES, DOES HE?
PRESENTLY...
MAYBE I'M MAKING TOO BIG A DEAL OUT OF THIS...
DETOUR
DETOUR
RONNIE WAS RIGHT-- REGGIE ACTS LIKE A JERK! MAYBE I'M ONE FOR WORRYING ABOUT HIM...
EH?
AWWW, STOP, GIVE IT BACK!!
DETOUR
WHO IS GEORGIE ANGLE?
HE'S A JUNIOR REGGIE KNOWS, ARCHIE! REG'S BEEN HANGING AROUND UPPERCLASSMEN A LOT LATELY...
HE THINKS HE'S A BIG SHOT NOW!
I DON'T KNOW WHAT TO MAKE OF THAT GUY, RANDY! DO YOU KNOW WHAT TO MAKE OF HIM?
HE SOUNDS LIKE A REAL WEIRD-O, RIGHT, SADIE? SADIE?
HA!
WILL YA?!
PLEASE!
C'MON!!
AH-- I DON'T KNOW... PEOPLE ARE STRESSED ENOUGH WITH-OUT LEARNING WHY WE GET STRESSED! HEY-- MAYBE WE SHOULD CALL JUGHEAD! HE MAY HAVE A CREATIVE IDEA FOR A FOOD PYRAMID...
HMMM... HOW ABOUT A PROJECT INVOLVING CREATIVITY?
YEAH, LIKE EATING IT?
...BUT I NEVER SAW ANYONE ENJOY LUNCH SO MUCH, I WAS AFRAID TO INTERRUPT!
MAYBE YOU CAN INVITE YOUR NEW FRIEND OVER HERE FOR A SNACK ONE DAY!
YOUNG MAN, PLEASE USE YOUR PLATE!
SORRY...
DON'T BE SO UNCOUTH, ARCHIEKINS! IF MY FATHER SEES CRUMBS ON THE RUG, HE'LL BLOW HIS TOP!!
MA!
WELL, SADIE... WHAT DOES RANDY THINK OF "JUGHEAD"?
JUMP, MANTLE! JUMP!!
JUST GIVE ME MY HAT BACK! PLEASE!
HERE IT IS, REG!
THUNK
HEH! ARCH JUST DOESN'T GET IT!
I ALMOST FEEL SORRY FOR HIM...
HE'LL KEEP BEING TREATED LIKE A FRESHMAN IF HE KEEPS ACTING LIKE A FRESH-MAN!
GANG, YOU'RE IN FOR A REAL TREAT!
POP'S
YOUR FATHER IS A COACH IN THIS SCHOOL! DIDN'T HE TEACH YOU ANYTHING ABOUT PLAYING SPORTS?!
SURE, COACH CLEATS... BUT I GET CONFUSED...
OUCH! ALWAYS FORGET THAT BUMP IN THE DRIVEWAY! HOPE NO ONE SAW ME!
CAREFUL, REG!
SIGH
EH? DIDN'T KNOW DAD HAD COMPANY.
SURE, AD REVENUES ARE DOWN-- BUT IT'S CYCLICAL!
HEY, RICK, IS THAT YOUR BOY?
AS I WAS SAYING-- I THOUGHT I'D GIVE THE MENU A "UNITED STATES" THEME!
AH! I SEE A "CALIFORNIA SALAD!"
MMM... HERE'S A "WISCONSIN CHEESE PLATE!"
HAHA
HAHA
OOOH... WE HAVE A COMIC HERE, EH?
EVERYBODY...
--DROP AND GIVE ME 50!
SEE THE GRAY AREA IN MY HAIR? THAT'S MY TEENAGE SON, REG!
SAY HELLO TO VIC AND FRED-- TWO GUYS I WORK WITH.
HI.
WELL, YOUNG MANTLE... YOU MAY HAVE ENTERED THE CONVERSATION AT JUST THE RIGHT TIME!
WE WERE ARGUING WITH YOUR FATHER THAT YOUNG PEOPLE AREN'T INTERESTED IN NEWSPAPERS...
GREAT! A "MONTANA BURGER" FOR JUGHEAD! WHO'S NEXT?
POP'S
IT AIN'T THE END OF THE WORLD!
UNGH! THANKS, TONY! UNGH! BUT WHAT IF THE FATE OF THE WORLD WAS AT STAKE?
NO PROB, CHUCK...

THE MISSING CHAPTERS: PART 5

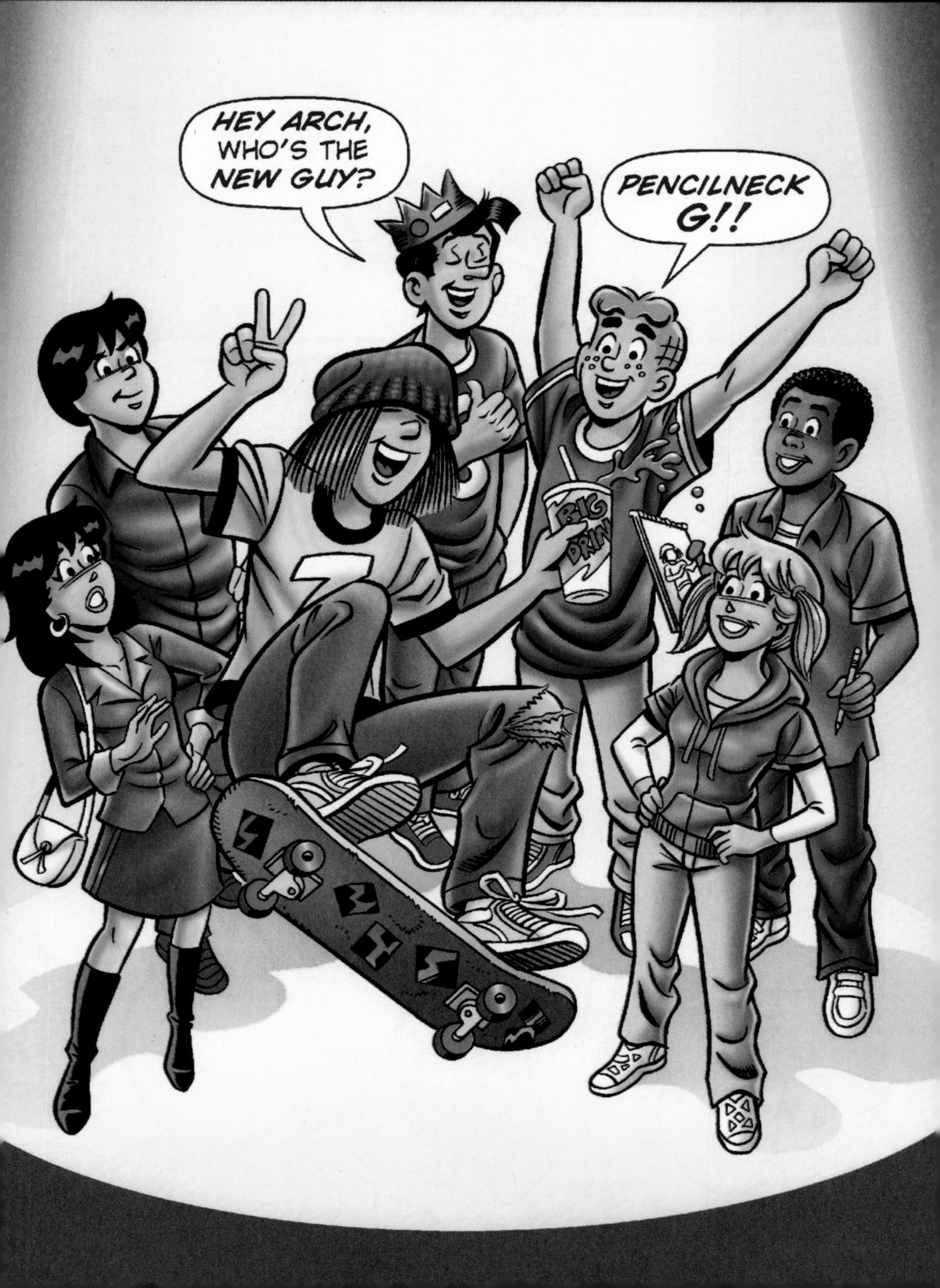
HEY ARCH, WHO'S THE NEW GUY?
PENCILNECK G!!
BIG DRINK

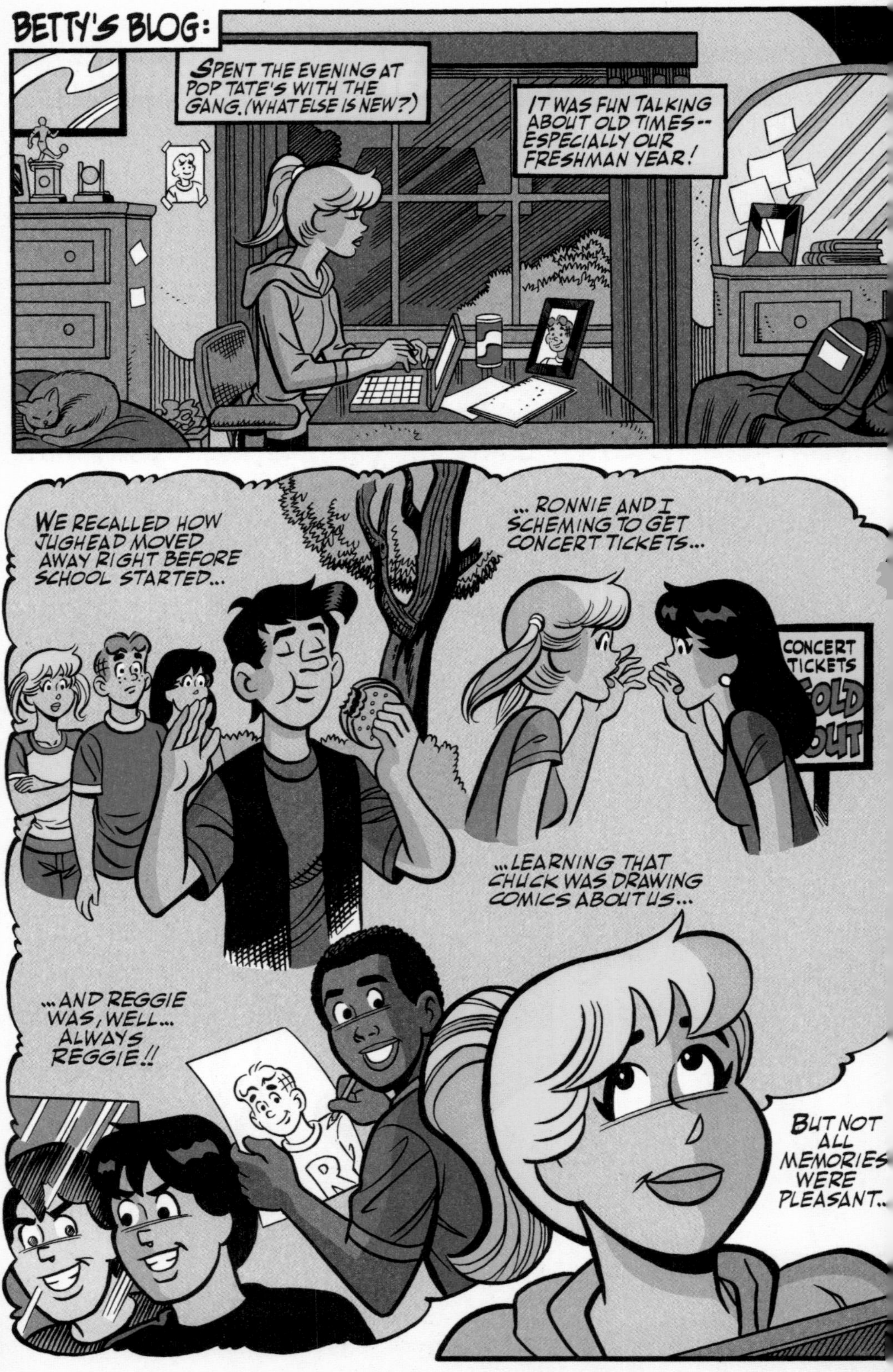
BETTY'S BLOG:
SPENT THE EVENING AT POP TATE'S WITH THE GANG. (WHAT ELSE IS NEW?)
IT WAS FUN TALKING ABOUT OLD TIMES-- ESPECIALLY OUR FRESHMAN YEAR!
WE RECALLED HOW JUGHEAD MOVED AWAY RIGHT BEFORE SCHOOL STARTED...
... RONNIE AND I SCHEMING TO GET CONCERT TICKETS...
CONCERT TICKETS
...LEARNING THAT CHUCK WAS DRAWING COMICS ABOUT US...
...AND REGGIE WAS, WELL... ALWAYS REGGIE!!
BUT NOT ALL MEMORIES WERE PLEASANT..

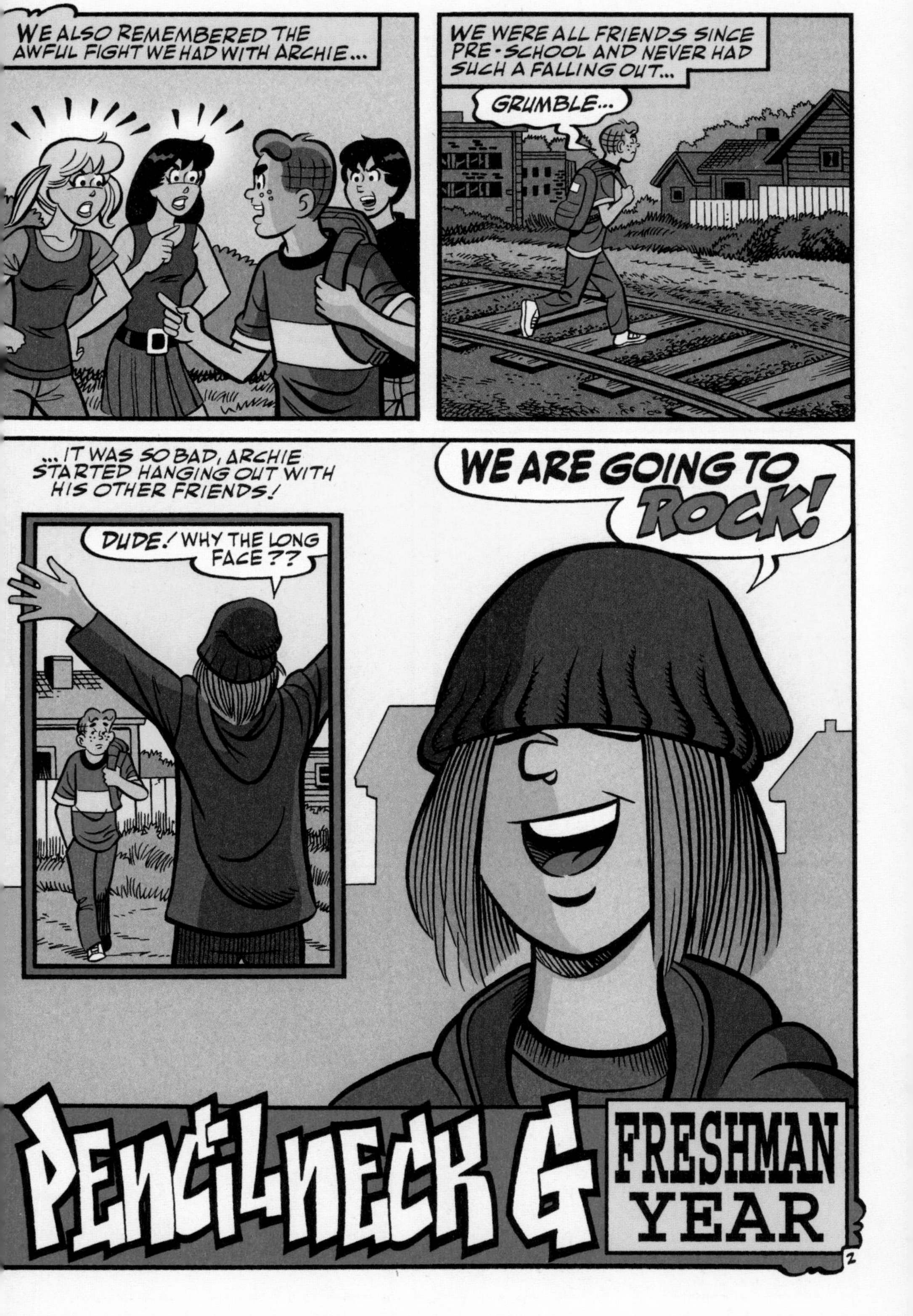
WE ALSO REMEMBERED THE AWFUL FIGHT WE HAD WITH ARCHIE...
WE WERE ALL FRIENDS SINCE PRE-SCHOOL AND NEVER HAD SUCH A FALLING OUT...
GRUMBLE...
...IT WAS SO BAD, ARCHIE STARTED HANGING OUT WITH HIS OTHER FRIENDS!
DUDE! WHY THE LONG FACE??
WE ARE GOING TO ROCK!
PENCILNECK G
FRESHMAN YEAR
2

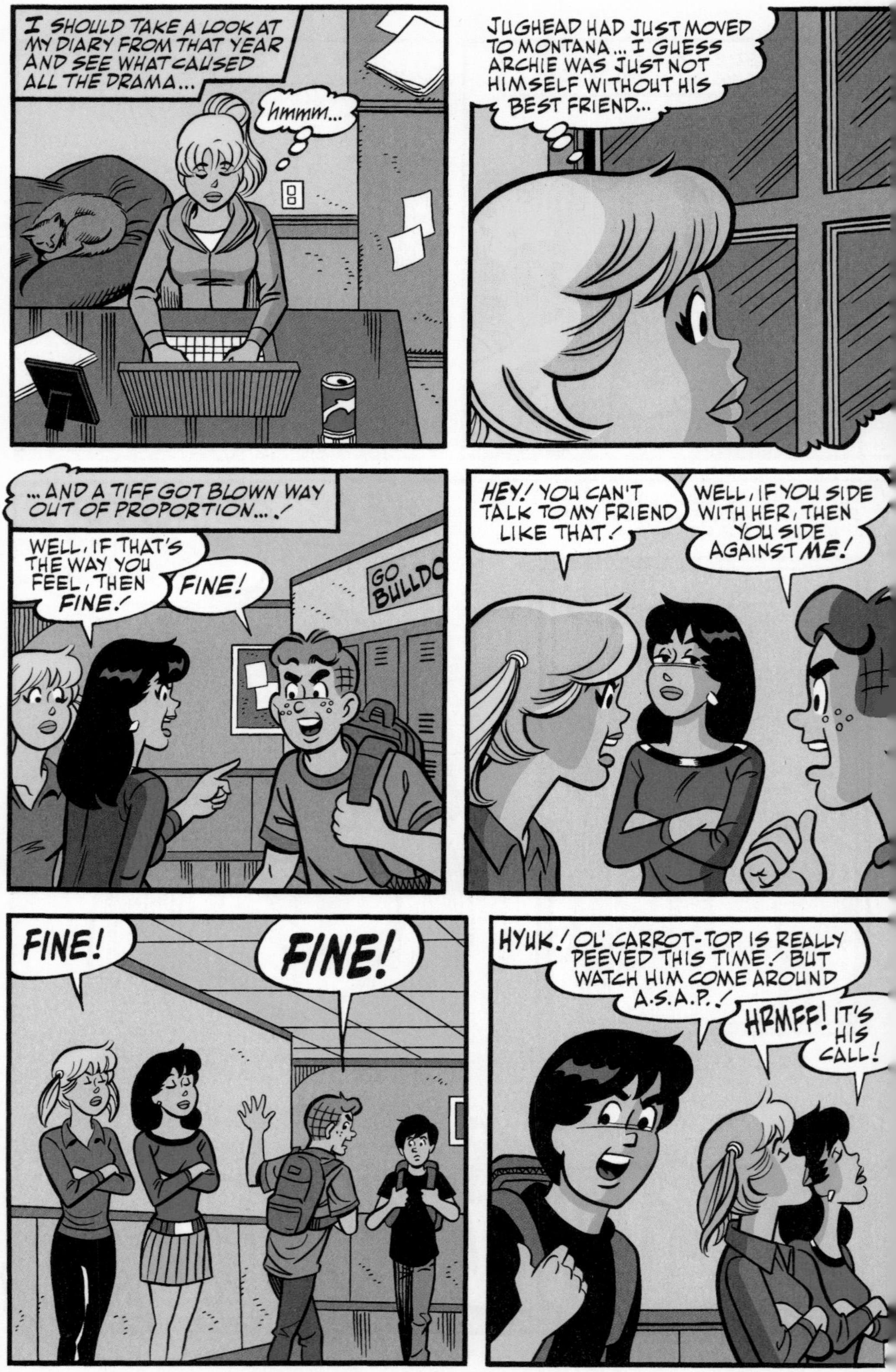
I SHOULD TAKE A LOOK AT MY DIARY FROM THAT YEAR AND SEE WHAT CAUSED ALL THE DRAMA...
hmmm...
JUGHEAD HAD JUST MOVED TO MONTANA... I GUESS ARCHIE WAS JUST NOT HIMSELF WITHOUT HIS BEST FRIEND...
...AND A TIFF GOT BLOWN WAY OUT OF PROPORTION...!
WELL, IF THAT'S THE WAY YOU FEEL, THEN FINE!
FINE!
GO BULLDO
HEY! YOU CAN'T TALK TO MY FRIEND LIKE THAT!
WELL, IF YOU SIDE WITH HER, THEN YOU SIDE AGAINST ME!
FINE!
FINE!
HYUK! OL' CARROT-TOP IS REALLY PEEVED THIS TIME! BUT WATCH HIM COME AROUND A.S.A.P.!
HRMFF! IT'S HIS CALL!

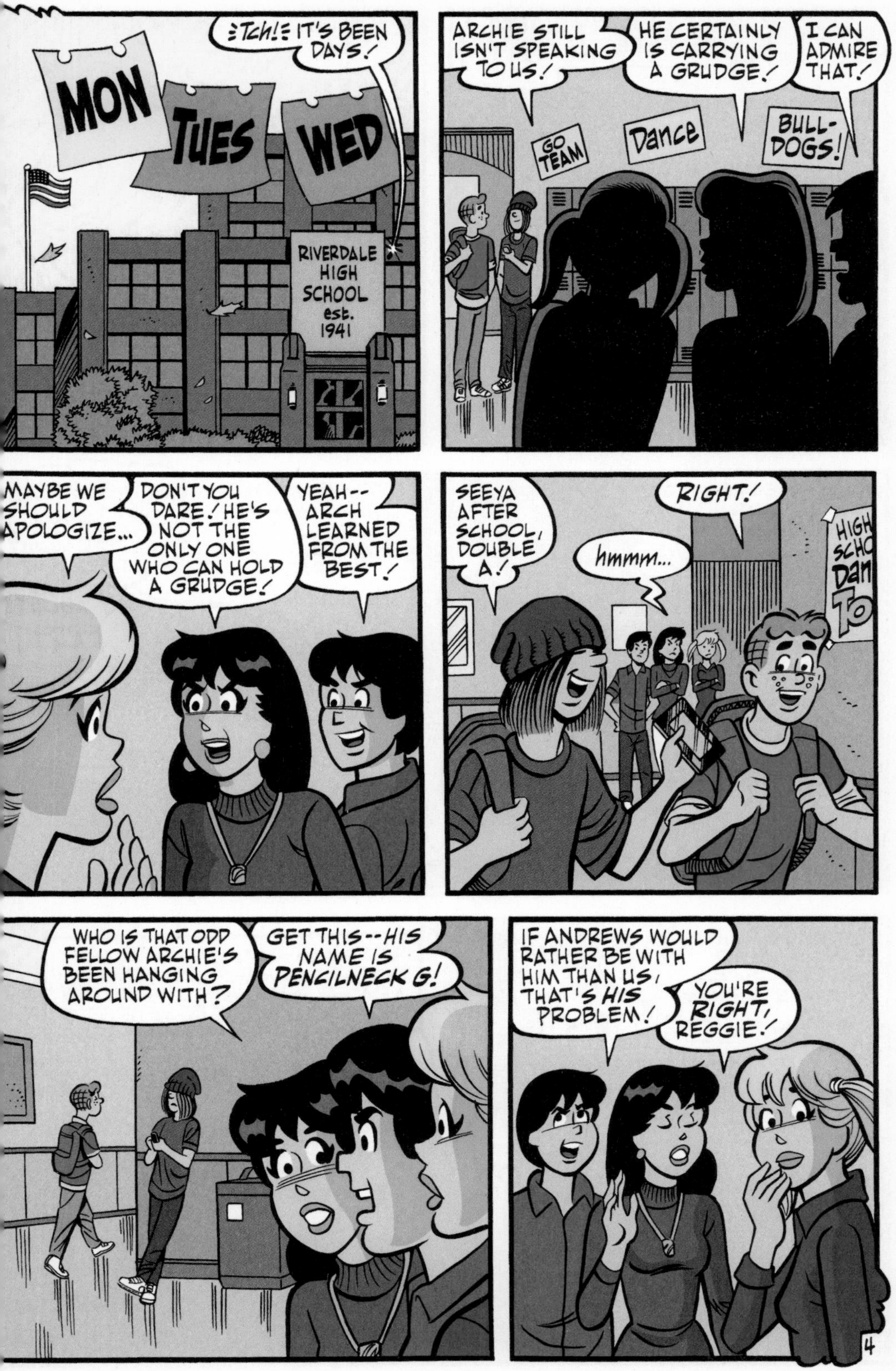

MON
TUES
WED
RIVERDALE HIGH SCHOOL est. 1941
=Tch!= IT'S BEEN DAYS!
ARCHIE STILL ISN'T SPEAKING TO US!
HE CERTAINLY IS CARRYING A GRUDGE!
I CAN ADMIRE THAT!
GO TEAM
Dance
BULL-DOGS!
MAYBE WE SHOULD APOLOGIZE...
DON'T YOU DARE! HE'S NOT THE ONLY ONE WHO CAN HOLD A GRUDGE!
YEAH-- ARCH LEARNED FROM THE BEST!
SEEYA AFTER SCHOOL, DOUBLE A!
RIGHT!
hmmm...
WHO IS THAT ODD FELLOW ARCHIE'S BEEN HANGING AROUND WITH?
GET THIS--HIS NAME IS PENCILNECK G!
IF ANDREWS WOULD RATHER BE WITH HIM THAN US, THAT'S HIS PROBLEM!
YOU'RE RIGHT, REGGIE!

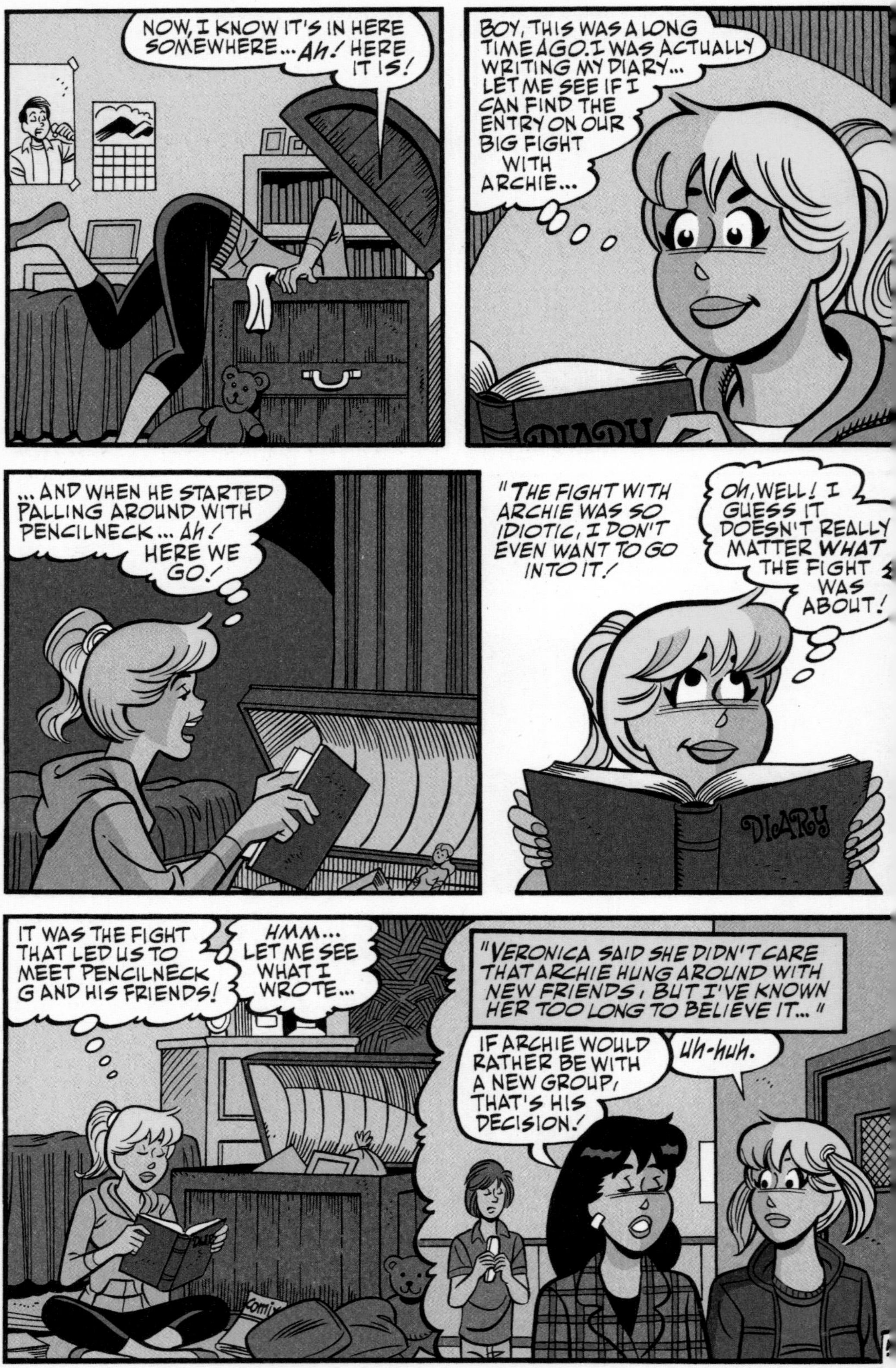
NOW, I KNOW IT'S IN HERE SOMEWHERE... Ah! HERE IT IS!
BOY, THIS WAS A LONG TIME AGO. I WAS ACTUALLY WRITING MY DIARY... LET ME SEE IF I CAN FIND THE ENTRY ON OUR BIG FIGHT WITH ARCHIE...
...AND WHEN HE STARTED PALLING AROUND WITH PENCILNECK... Ah! HERE WE GO!
"THE FIGHT WITH ARCHIE WAS SO IDIOTIC, I DON'T EVEN WANT TO GO INTO IT!
Oh, WELL! I GUESS IT DOESN'T REALLY MATTER WHAT THE FIGHT WAS ABOUT!
DIARY
IT WAS THE FIGHT THAT LED US TO MEET PENCILNECK G AND HIS FRIENDS!
HMM... LET ME SEE WHAT I WROTE...
"VERONICA SAID SHE DIDN'T CARE THAT ARCHIE HUNG AROUND WITH NEW FRIENDS, BUT I'VE KNOWN HER TOO LONG TO BELIEVE IT..."
IF ARCHIE WOULD RATHER BE WITH A NEW GROUP, THAT'S HIS DECISION!
uh-huh.

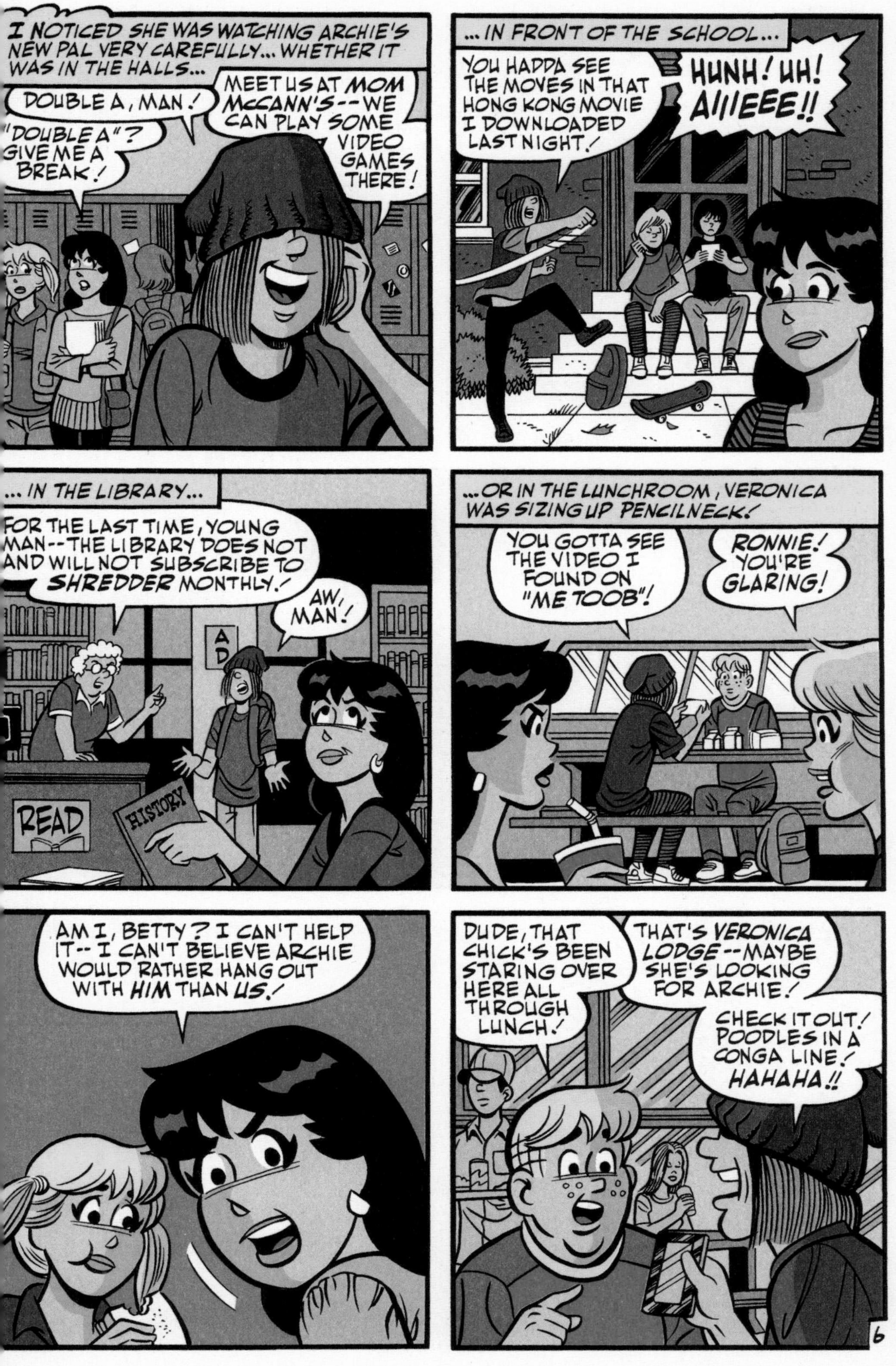

I NOTICED SHE WAS WATCHING ARCHIE'S NEW PAL VERY CAREFULLY... WHETHER IT WAS IN THE HALLS...
DOUBLE A, MAN!
"DOUBLE A"? GIVE ME A BREAK!
MEET US AT MOM McCANN'S--WE CAN PLAY SOME VIDEO GAMES THERE!
... IN FRONT OF THE SCHOOL...
YOU HADDA SEE THE MOVES IN THAT HONG KONG MOVIE I DOWNLOADED LAST NIGHT!
HUNH! UH! AIIIEEE!!
... IN THE LIBRARY...
FOR THE LAST TIME, YOUNG MAN--THE LIBRARY DOES NOT AND WILL NOT SUBSCRIBE TO SHREDDER MONTHLY!
AW, MAN!
AD
READ
HISTORY
...OR IN THE LUNCHROOM, VERONICA WAS SIZING UP PENCILNECK!
YOU GOTTA SEE THE VIDEO I FOUND ON "ME TOOB"!
RONNIE! YOU'RE GLARING!
AM I, BETTY? I CAN'T HELP IT-- I CAN'T BELIEVE ARCHIE WOULD RATHER HANG OUT WITH HIM THAN US!
DUDE, THAT CHICK'S BEEN STARING OVER HERE ALL THROUGH LUNCH!
THAT'S VERONICA LODGE--MAYBE SHE'S LOOKING FOR ARCHIE!
CHECK IT OUT! POODLES IN A CONGA LINE! HAHAHA!!

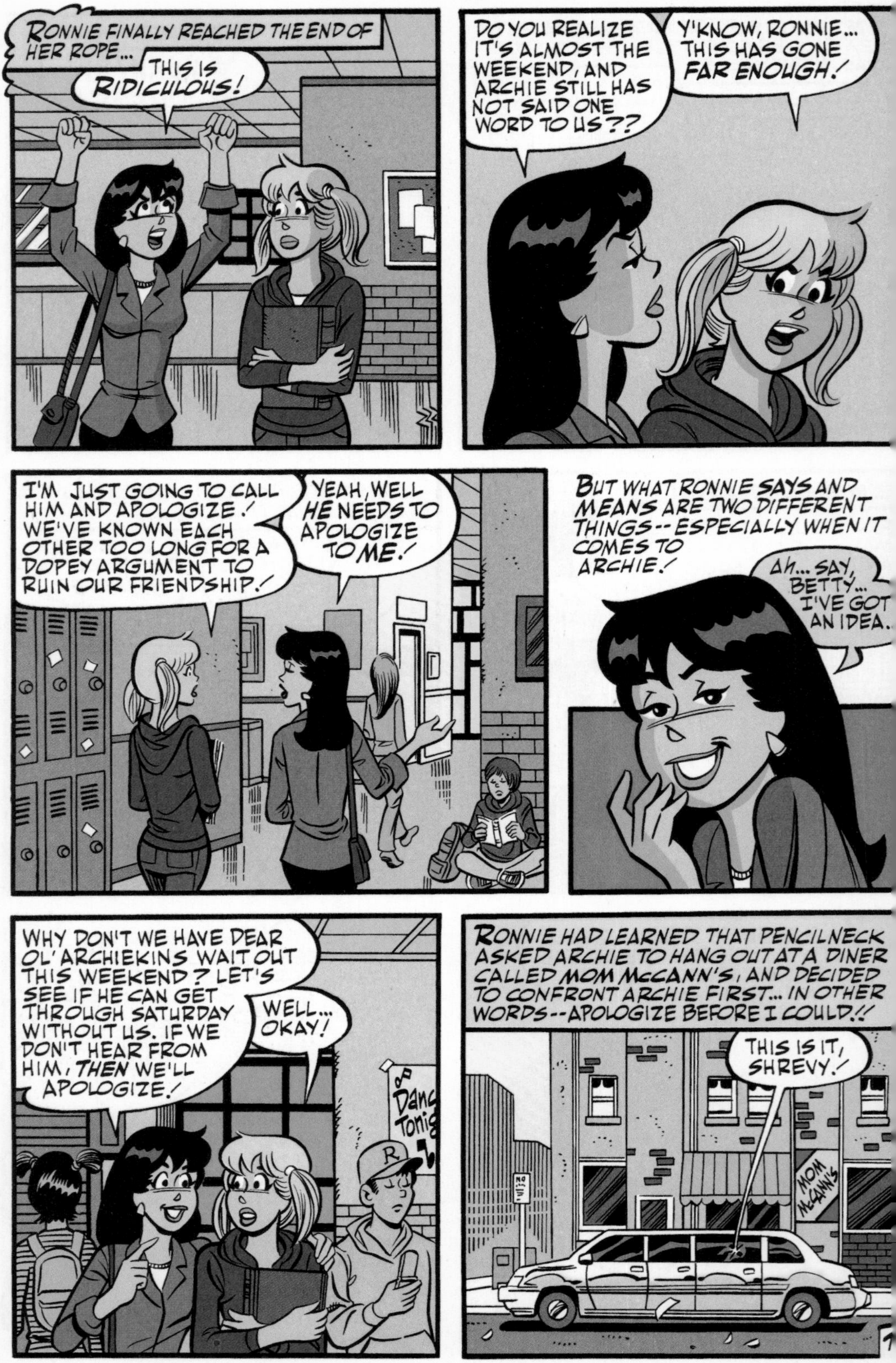
RONNIE FINALLY REACHED THE END OF HER ROPE...
THIS IS RIDICULOUS!
DO YOU REALIZE IT'S ALMOST THE WEEKEND, AND ARCHIE STILL HAS NOT SAID ONE WORD TO US??
Y'KNOW, RONNIE... THIS HAS GONE FAR ENOUGH!
I'M JUST GOING TO CALL HIM AND APOLOGIZE! WE'VE KNOWN EACH OTHER TOO LONG FOR A DOPEY ARGUMENT TO RUIN OUR FRIENDSHIP!
YEAH, WELL HE NEEDS TO APOLOGIZE TO ME!
BUT WHAT RONNIE SAYS AND MEANS ARE TWO DIFFERENT THINGS--ESPECIALLY WHEN IT COMES TO ARCHIE!
AH... SAY, BETTY... I'VE GOT AN IDEA...
WHY DON'T WE HAVE DEAR OL' ARCHIEKINS WAIT OUT THIS WEEKEND? LET'S SEE IF HE CAN GET THROUGH SATURDAY WITHOUT US. IF WE DON'T HEAR FROM HIM, THEN WE'LL APOLOGIZE!
WELL... OKAY!
RONNIE HAD LEARNED THAT PENCILNECK ASKED ARCHIE TO HANG OUT AT A DINER CALLED MOM McCANN'S, AND DECIDED TO CONFRONT ARCHIE FIRST... IN OTHER WORDS--APOLOGIZE BEFORE I COULD!!
THIS IS IT, SHREVY!
MOM McCANN'S

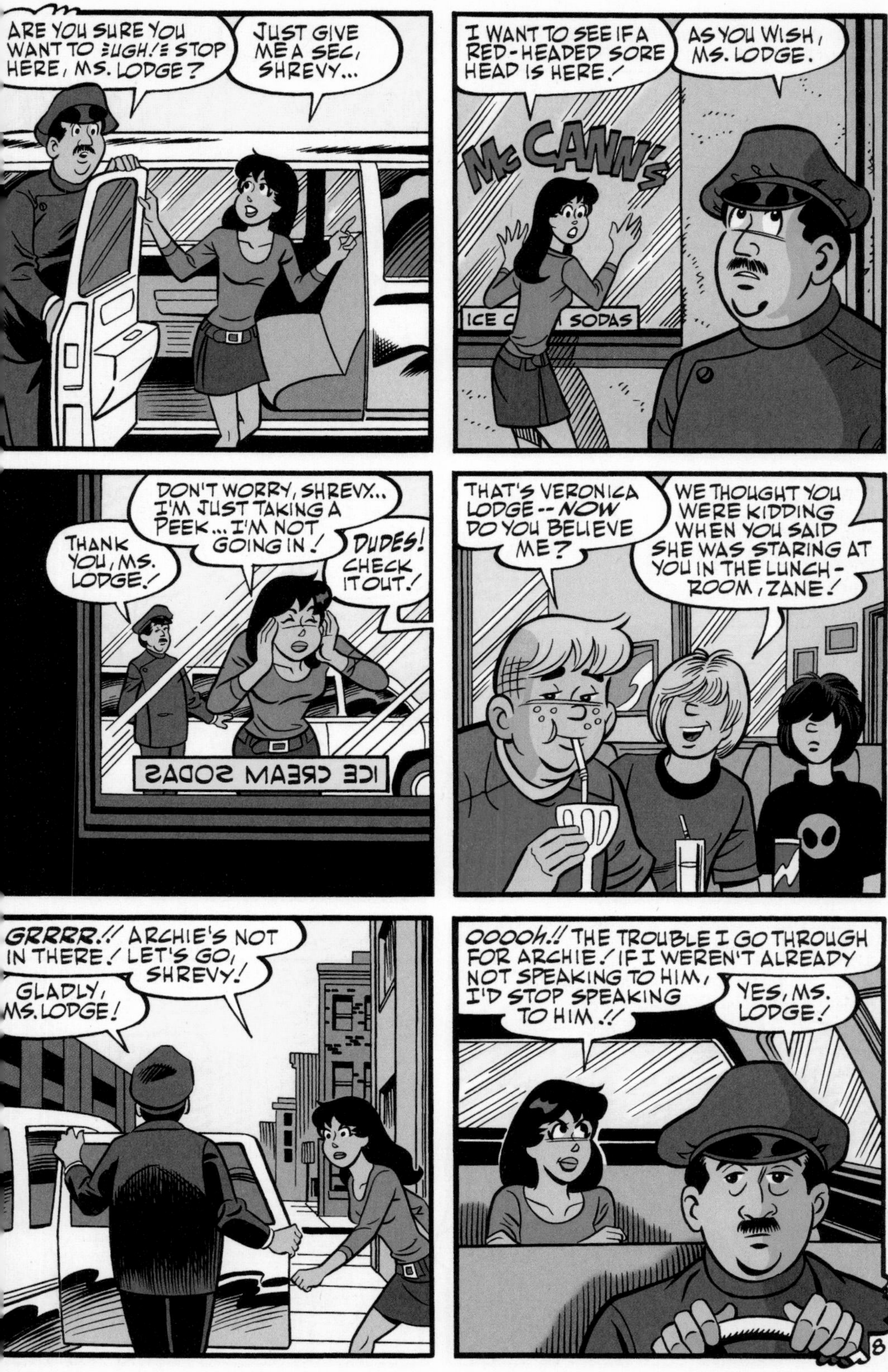

ARE YOU SURE YOU WANT TO =UGH!= STOP HERE, MS. LODGE?
JUST GIVE ME A SEC, SHREVY...
I WANT TO SEE IF A RED-HEADED SORE HEAD IS HERE!
AS YOU WISH, MS. LODGE.
McCANN's
ICE C SODAS
DON'T WORRY, SHREVY... I'M JUST TAKING A PEEK... I'M NOT GOING IN!
THANK YOU, MS. LODGE!
DUDES! CHECK IT OUT!
ICE CREAM SODAS
THAT'S VERONICA LODGE -- NOW DO YOU BELIEVE ME?
WE THOUGHT YOU WERE KIDDING WHEN YOU SAID SHE WAS STARING AT YOU IN THE LUNCH-ROOM, ZANE!
GRRRR.!! ARCHIE'S NOT IN THERE! LET'S GO, SHREVY!
GLADLY, MS. LODGE!
OOOOH.!! THE TROUBLE I GO THROUGH FOR ARCHIE! IF I WEREN'T ALREADY NOT SPEAKING TO HIM, I'D STOP SPEAKING TO HIM.!!
YES, MS. LODGE!

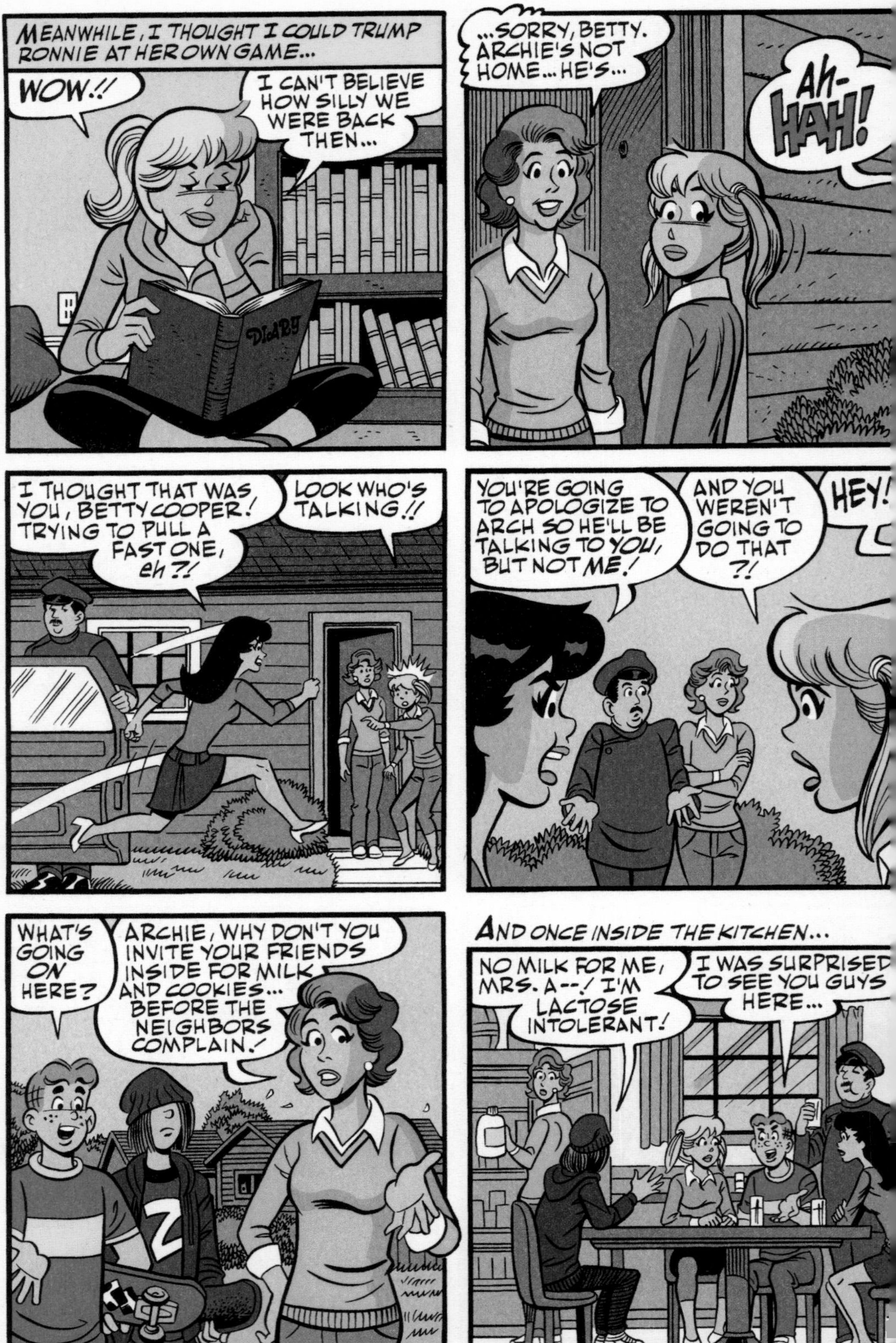
MEANWHILE, I THOUGHT I COULD TRUMP RONNIE AT HER OWN GAME...
WOW!!
I CAN'T BELIEVE HOW SILLY WE WERE BACK THEN...
DIARY
...SORRY, BETTY. ARCHIE'S NOT HOME... HE'S...
AH-HAH!
I THOUGHT THAT WAS YOU, BETTY COOPER! TRYING TO PULL A FAST ONE, eh?!
LOOK WHO'S TALKING!!
YOU'RE GOING TO APOLOGIZE TO ARCH SO HE'LL BE TALKING TO YOU, BUT NOT ME!
AND YOU WEREN'T GOING TO DO THAT?!
HEY!
WHAT'S GOING ON HERE?
ARCHIE, WHY DON'T YOU INVITE YOUR FRIENDS INSIDE FOR MILK AND COOKIES... BEFORE THE NEIGHBORS COMPLAIN!
AND ONCE INSIDE THE KITCHEN...
NO MILK FOR ME, MRS. A--! I'M LACTOSE INTOLERANT!
I WAS SURPRISED TO SEE YOU GUYS HERE...

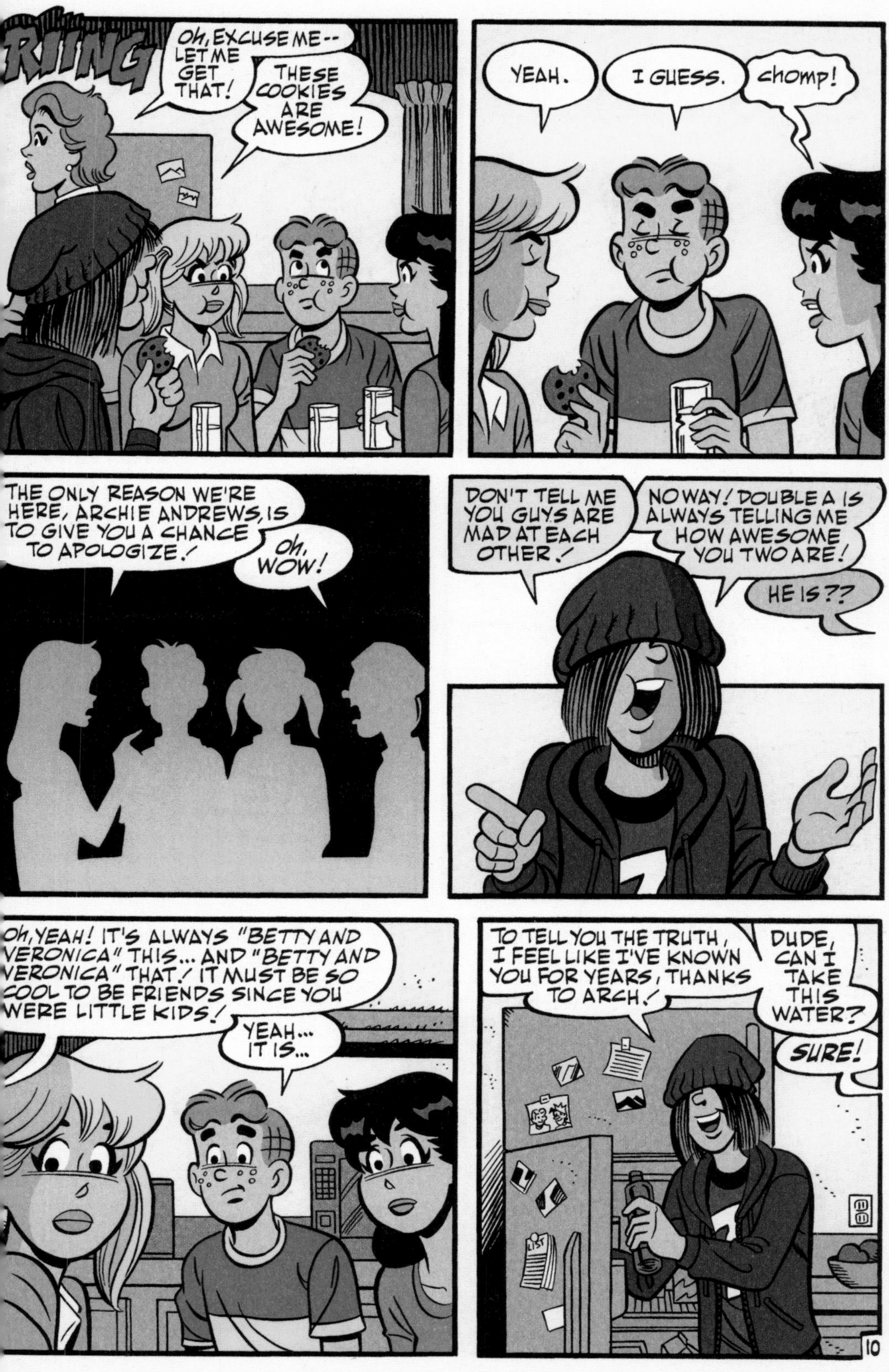
RIING
Oh, EXCUSE ME -- LET ME GET THAT!
THESE COOKIES ARE AWESOME!
YEAH.
I GUESS.
chomp!
THE ONLY REASON WE'RE HERE, ARCHIE ANDREWS, IS TO GIVE YOU A CHANCE TO APOLOGIZE!
Oh, WOW!
DON'T TELL ME YOU GUYS ARE MAD AT EACH OTHER!
NO WAY! DOUBLE A IS ALWAYS TELLING ME HOW AWESOME YOU TWO ARE!
HE IS??
Oh, YEAH! IT'S ALWAYS "BETTY AND VERONICA" THIS... AND "BETTY AND VERONICA" THAT! IT MUST BE SO COOL TO BE FRIENDS SINCE YOU WERE LITTLE KIDS!
YEAH... IT IS...
TO TELL YOU THE TRUTH, I FEEL LIKE I'VE KNOWN YOU FOR YEARS, THANKS TO ARCH!
DUDE, CAN I TAKE THIS WATER?
SURE!

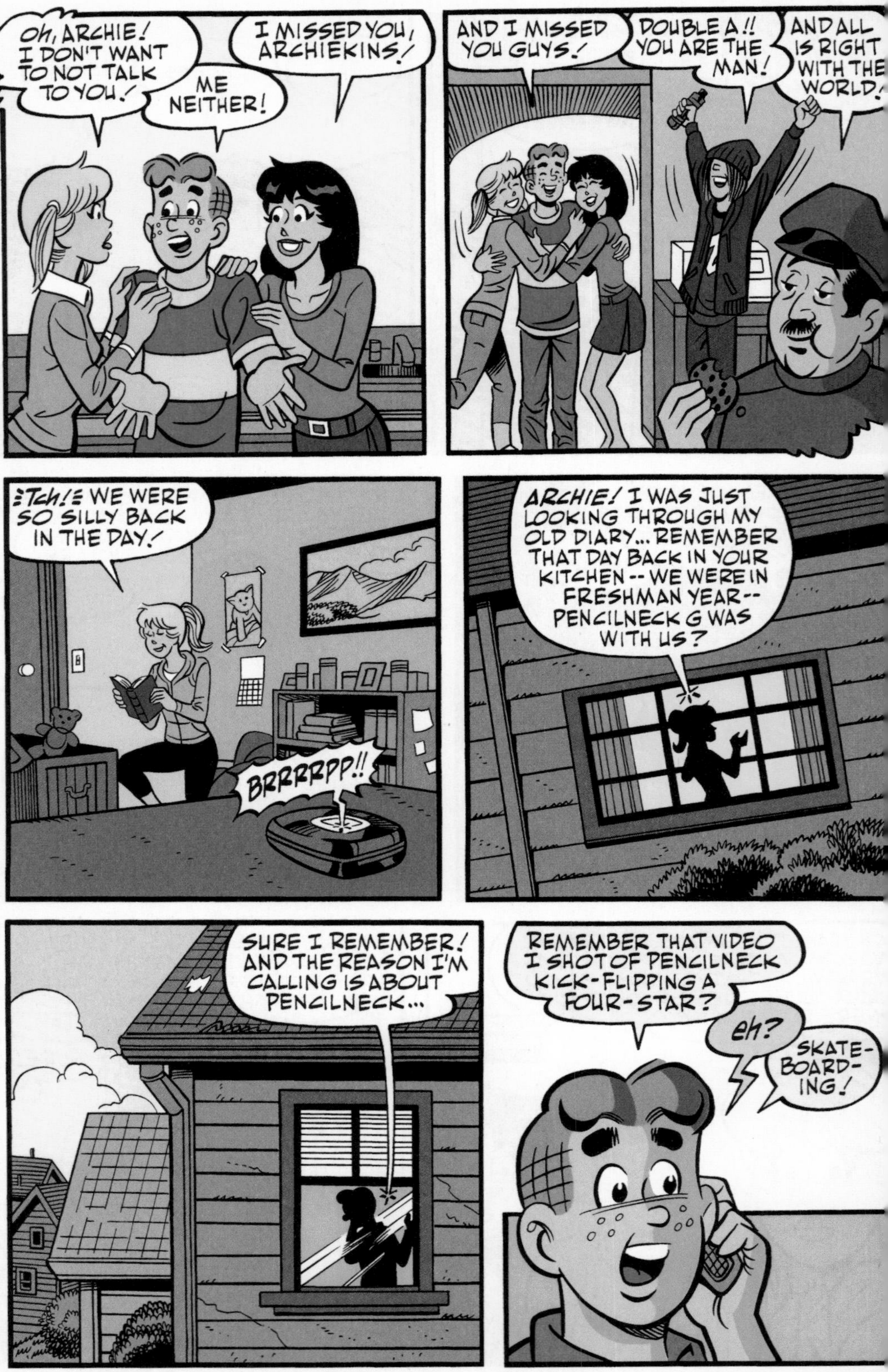

Oh, ARCHIE! I DON'T WANT TO NOT TALK TO YOU!
ME NEITHER!
I MISSED YOU, ARCHIEKINS!
AND I MISSED YOU GUYS!
DOUBLE A!! YOU ARE THE MAN!
AND ALL IS RIGHT WITH THE WORLD!
Tch! WE WERE SO SILLY BACK IN THE DAY!
BRRRRPP!!
ARCHIE! I WAS JUST LOOKING THROUGH MY OLD DIARY... REMEMBER THAT DAY BACK IN YOUR KITCHEN -- WE WERE IN FRESHMAN YEAR -- PENCILNECK G WAS WITH US?
SURE I REMEMBER! AND THE REASON I'M CALLING IS ABOUT PENCILNECK...
REMEMBER THAT VIDEO I SHOT OF PENCILNECK KICK-FLIPPING A FOUR-STAR?
eh?
SKATE-BOARD-ING!

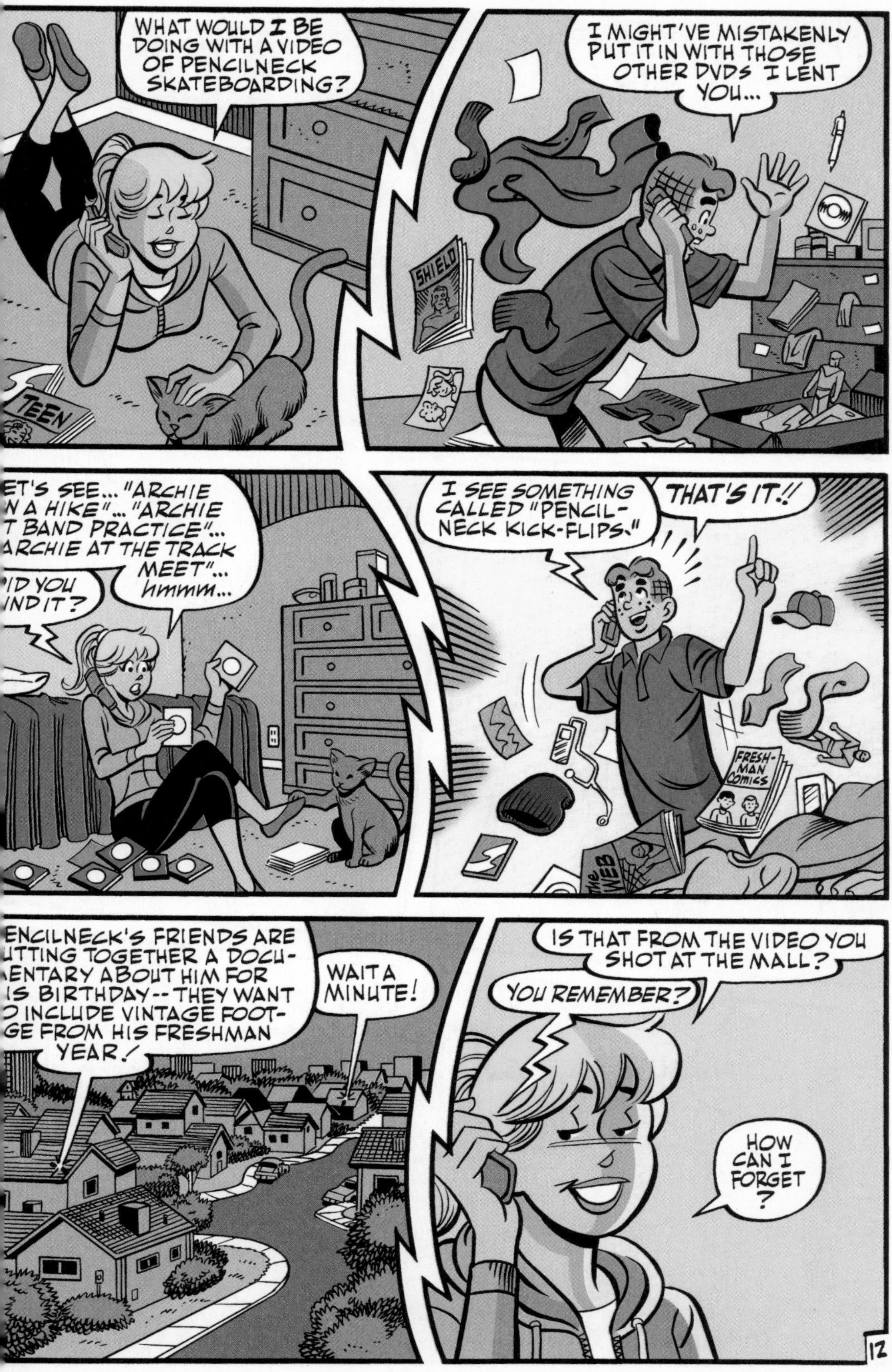
WHAT WOULD I BE DOING WITH A VIDEO OF PENCILNECK SKATEBOARDING?
I MIGHT'VE MISTAKENLY PUT IT IN WITH THOSE OTHER DVDS I LENT YOU...
SHIELD
TEEN
ET'S SEE... "ARCHIE N A HIKE"... "ARCHIE T BAND PRACTICE"... ARCHIE AT THE TRACK MEET"... HMMM...
ID YOU IND IT?
I SEE SOMETHING CALLED "PENCIL-NECK KICK-FLIPS."
THAT'S IT!!
FRESH-MAN COMICS
WEB
ENCILNECK'S FRIENDS ARE UTTING TOGETHER A DOCU-ENTARY ABOUT HIM FOR IS BIRTHDAY-- THEY WANT O INCLUDE VINTAGE FOOT-GE FROM HIS FRESHMAN YEAR!
WAIT A MINUTE!
IS THAT FROM THE VIDEO YOU SHOT AT THE MALL?
YOU REMEMBER?
HOW CAN I FORGET?

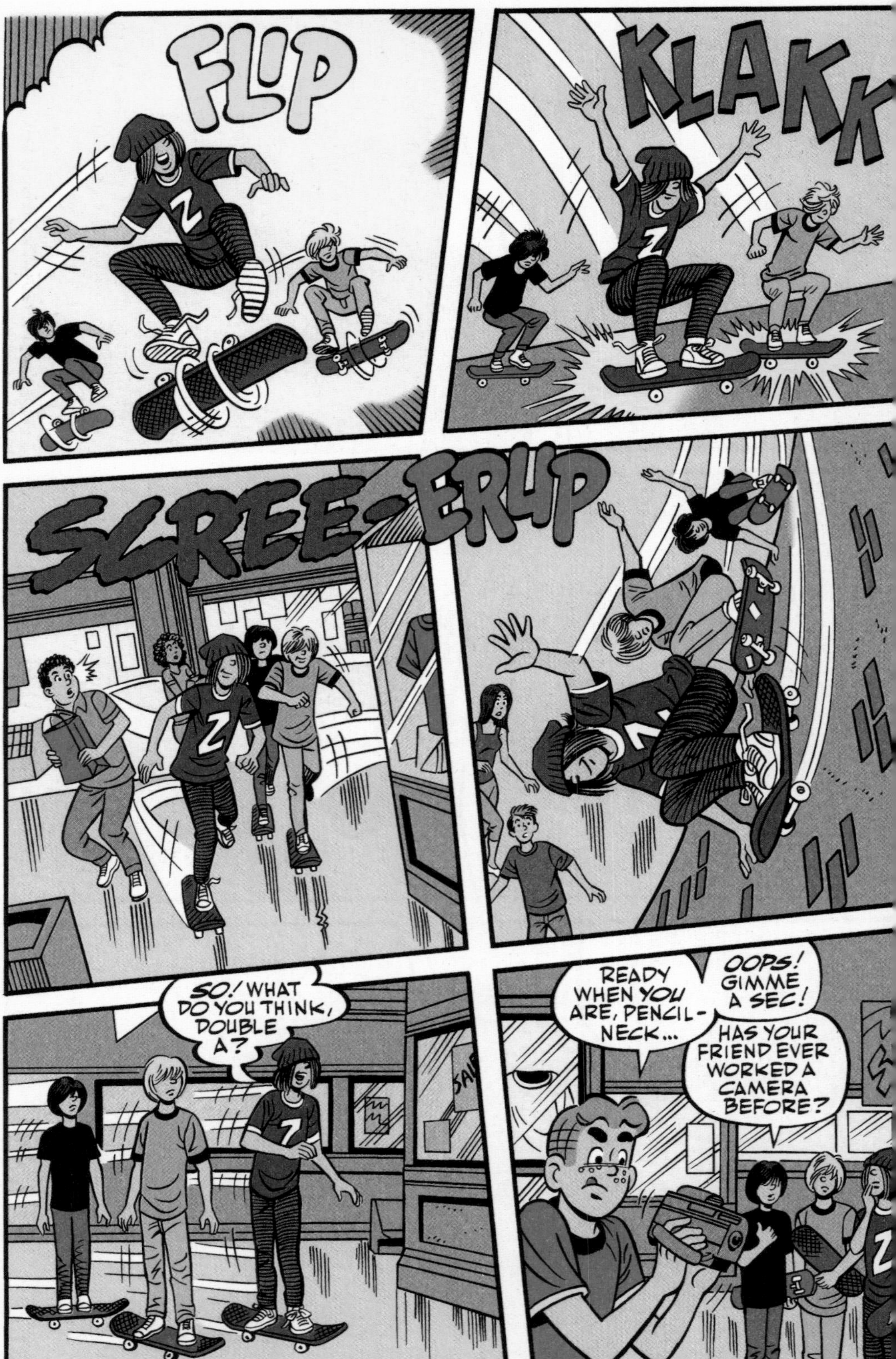

FLIP
KLAKK
SCREE-ERUP
SO! WHAT DO YOU THINK, DOUBLE A?
READY WHEN YOU ARE, PENCIL-NECK...
OOPS! GIMME A SEC!
HAS YOUR FRIEND EVER WORKED A CAMERA BEFORE?

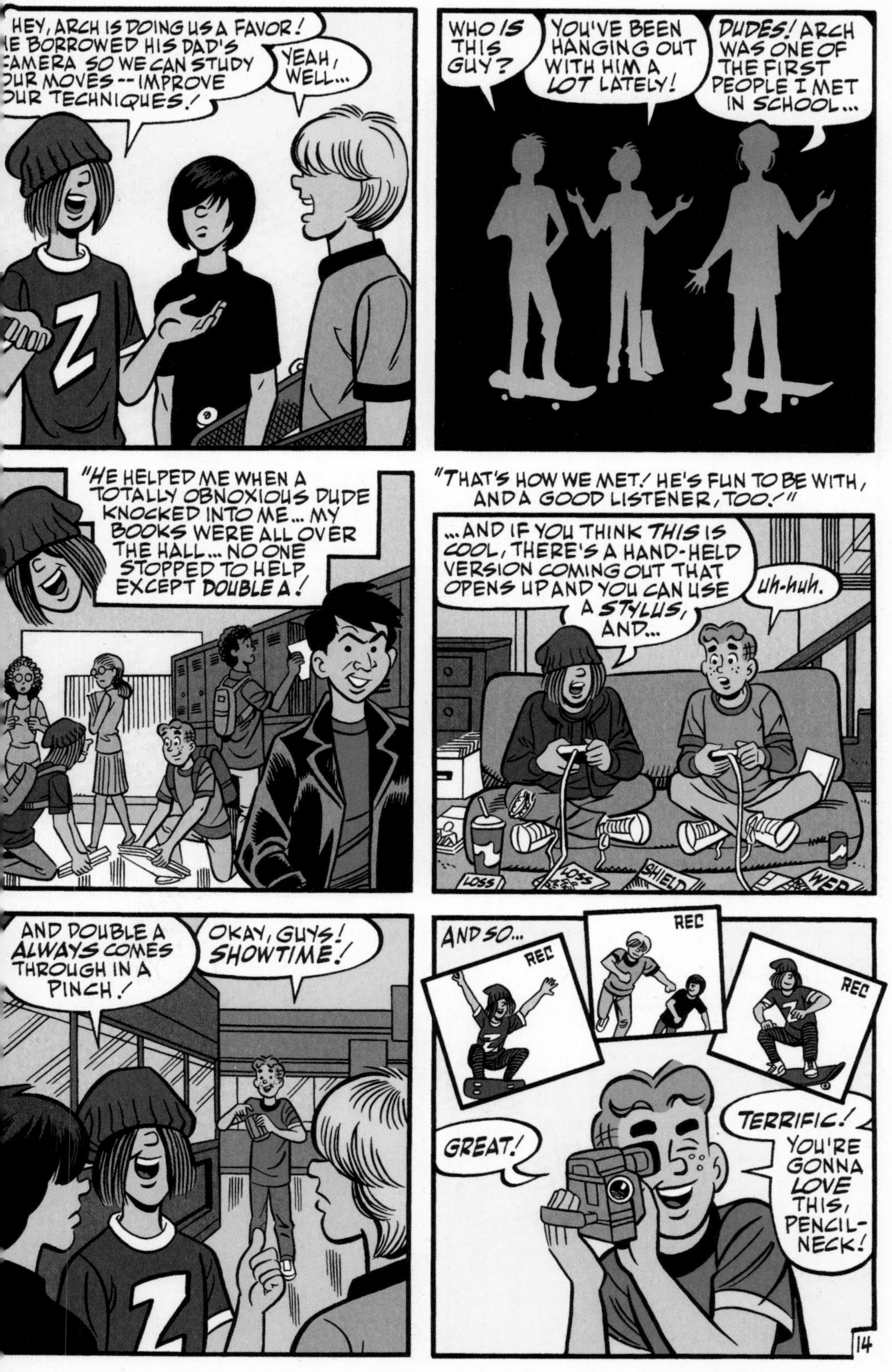
HEY, ARCH IS DOING US A FAVOR! HE BORROWED HIS DAD'S CAMERA SO WE CAN STUDY OUR MOVES -- IMPROVE OUR TECHNIQUES!
YEAH, WELL...
WHO IS THIS GUY?
YOU'VE BEEN HANGING OUT WITH HIM A LOT LATELY!
DUDES! ARCH WAS ONE OF THE FIRST PEOPLE I MET IN SCHOOL...
"HE HELPED ME WHEN A TOTALLY OBNOXIOUS DUDE KNOCKED INTO ME... MY BOOKS WERE ALL OVER THE HALL... NO ONE STOPPED TO HELP EXCEPT DOUBLE A!
"THAT'S HOW WE MET! HE'S FUN TO BE WITH, AND A GOOD LISTENER, TOO!"
...AND IF YOU THINK THIS IS COOL, THERE'S A HAND-HELD VERSION COMING OUT THAT OPENS UP AND YOU CAN USE A STYLUS, AND...
UH-HUH.
LOSS
LOSS
SHIELD
WEB
AND DOUBLE A ALWAYS COMES THROUGH IN A PINCH!
OKAY, GUYS! SHOWTIME!
AND SO...
REC
REC
REC
GREAT!
TERRIFIC!
YOU'RE GONNA LOVE THIS, PENCIL-NECK!

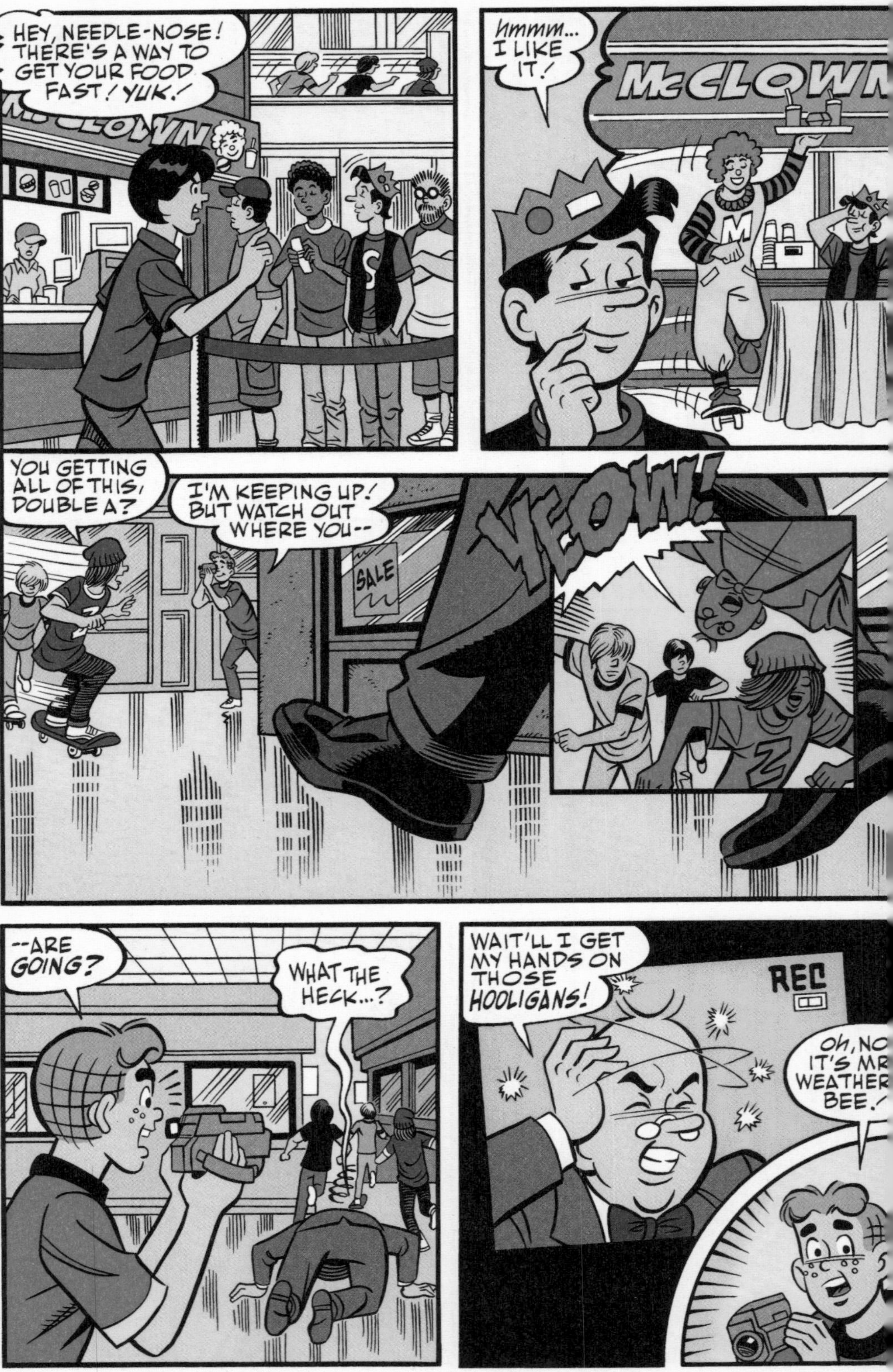
HEY, NEEDLE-NOSE! THERE'S A WAY TO GET YOUR FOOD FAST! YUK!
McCLOWN
hmmm... I LIKE IT!
McCLOWN
YOU GETTING ALL OF THIS, DOUBLE A?
I'M KEEPING UP! BUT WATCH OUT WHERE YOU--
SALE
YEOW!
--ARE GOING?
WHAT THE HECK...?
WAIT'LL I GET MY HANDS ON THOSE HOOLIGANS!
REC
Oh, NO IT'S MR WEATHER BEE!

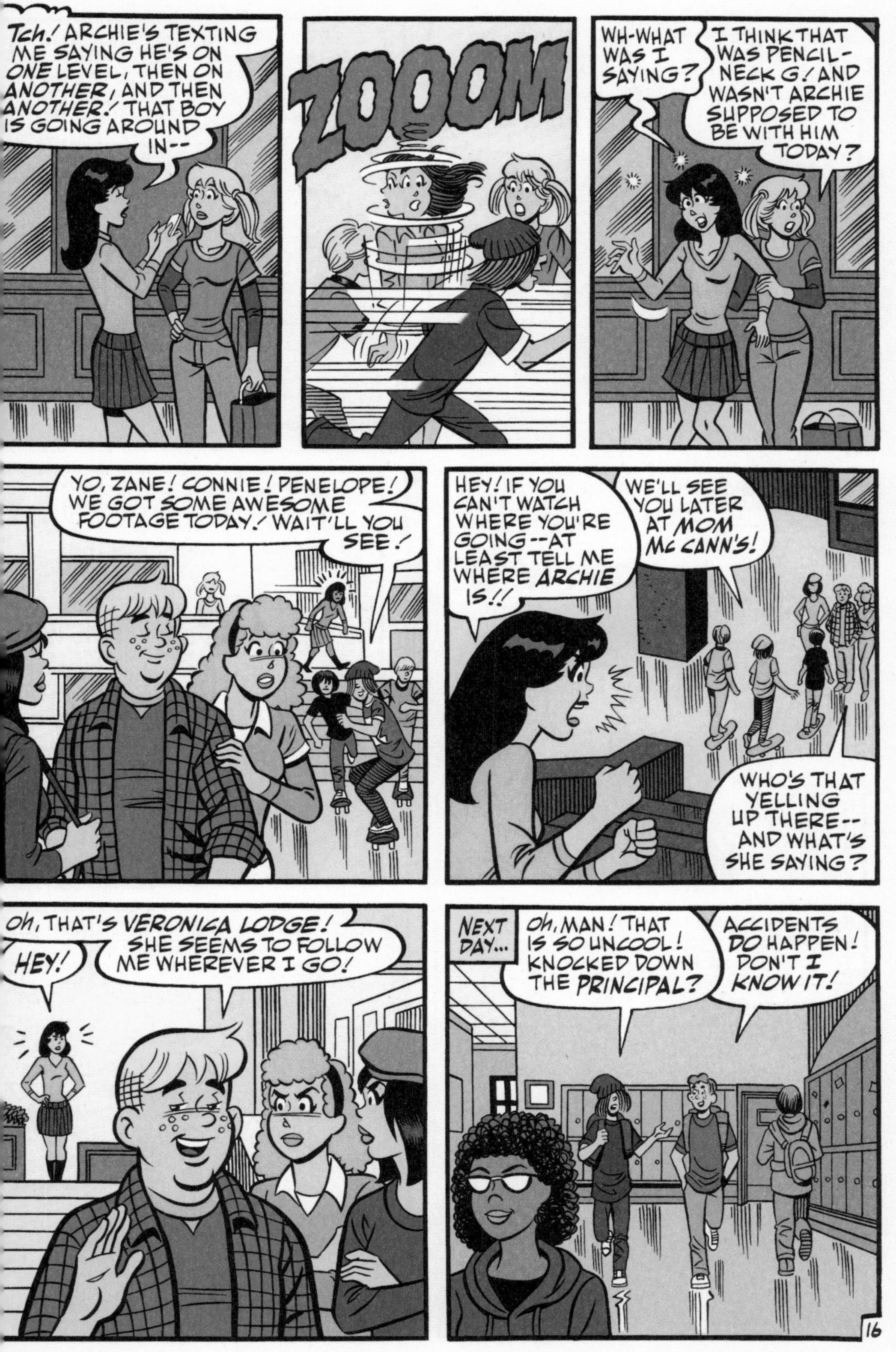
Tch! ARCHIE'S TEXTING ME SAYING HE'S ON ONE LEVEL, THEN ON ANOTHER, AND THEN ANOTHER! THAT BOY IS GOING AROUND IN--
ZOOOM
WH-WHAT WAS I SAYING?
I THINK THAT WAS PENCIL-NECK G! AND WASN'T ARCHIE SUPPOSED TO BE WITH HIM TODAY?
YO, ZANE! CONNIE! PENELOPE! WE GOT SOME AWESOME FOOTAGE TODAY! WAIT'LL YOU SEE!
HEY! IF YOU CAN'T WATCH WHERE YOU'RE GOING--AT LEAST TELL ME WHERE ARCHIE IS!!
WE'LL SEE YOU LATER AT MOM McCANN'S!
WHO'S THAT YELLING UP THERE--AND WHAT'S SHE SAYING?
Oh, THAT'S VERONICA LODGE! SHE SEEMS TO FOLLOW ME WHEREVER I GO!
HEY!
NEXT DAY...
Oh, MAN! THAT IS SO UNCOOL! KNOCKED DOWN THE PRINCIPAL?
ACCIDENTS DO HAPPEN! DON'T I KNOW IT!

WHAT DO YOU THINK, DOUBLE A? AM I GONNA GET DETENTION -- OR ≈GULP!≈ WORSE?

ALL OF THIS COULD HAVE BEEN AVOIDED IF ONLY RIVER-DALE HAD A SKATEPARK!

IF I GET EXPELLED, MY MOM'S GONNA BE SO BUMMED! I JUST STARTED HIGH SCHOOL!

NO ONE SAID ANYTHING ABOUT BEING EXPELLED, PENCILNECK!

LOOK, I'VE GOT TO TAKE SOME OF THE RESPONSIBILITY-- I HAD THE CAMERA! WE'LL BOTH TALK TO MR. WEATHER-BEE AND EXPLAIN WHAT HAPPENED!

SOOOOO... I HEAR YOU HAVE THE HOTS FOR ZANE ZAPPEN!

WHO?

I GUESS THE BEE WILL GO EASY ON YOU SINCE HE'S KNOWN YOU SINCE GRAMMAR SCHOOL!

UH... I WOULDN'T COUNT ON THAT BEING AN ASSET! SHHH! LISTEN...

PRINCIPAL'S OFFICE

EVEN THE MALL'S NOT SAFE, GRUNDY!

I WAS BOWLED OVER BY A GANG OF SKATE BOARDERS! I WAS LUCKY I DIDN'T BREAK MY NECK IN THE FALL!

DID YOU SEE WHO THEY WERE?

NO! BY THE TIME I REGAINED MY COMPOSURE, THEY WERE GONE! PENCILNECK! DO YOU KNOW WHAT THIS MEANS?

THAT WE HAVE TO SHOW HIM THE TAPE?

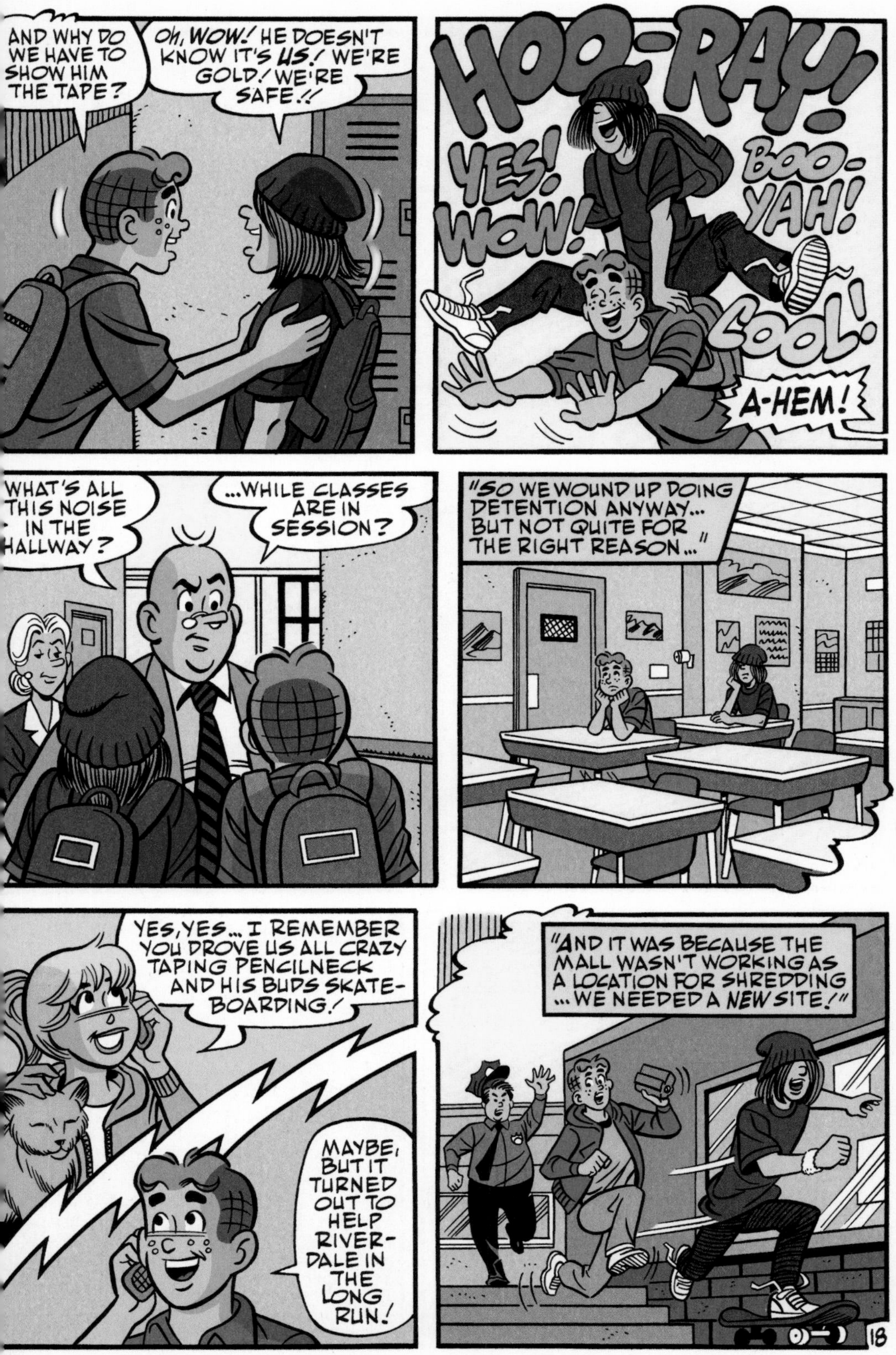
AND WHY DO WE HAVE TO SHOW HIM THE TAPE?
OH, WOW! HE DOESN'T KNOW IT'S US! WE'RE GOLD! WE'RE SAFE!!
HOO-RAY!
YES! WOW!
BOO-YAH!
COOL!
A-HEM!
WHAT'S ALL THIS NOISE IN THE HALLWAY?
...WHILE CLASSES ARE IN SESSION?
"SO WE WOUND UP DOING DETENTION ANYWAY... BUT NOT QUITE FOR THE RIGHT REASON..."
YES, YES... I REMEMBER YOU DROVE US ALL CRAZY TAPING PENCILNECK AND HIS BUDS SKATE-BOARDING!
MAYBE, BUT IT TURNED OUT TO HELP RIVER-DALE IN THE LONG RUN!
"AND IT WAS BECAUSE THE MALL WASN'T WORKING AS A LOCATION FOR SHREDDING ... WE NEEDED A NEW SITE!"
18

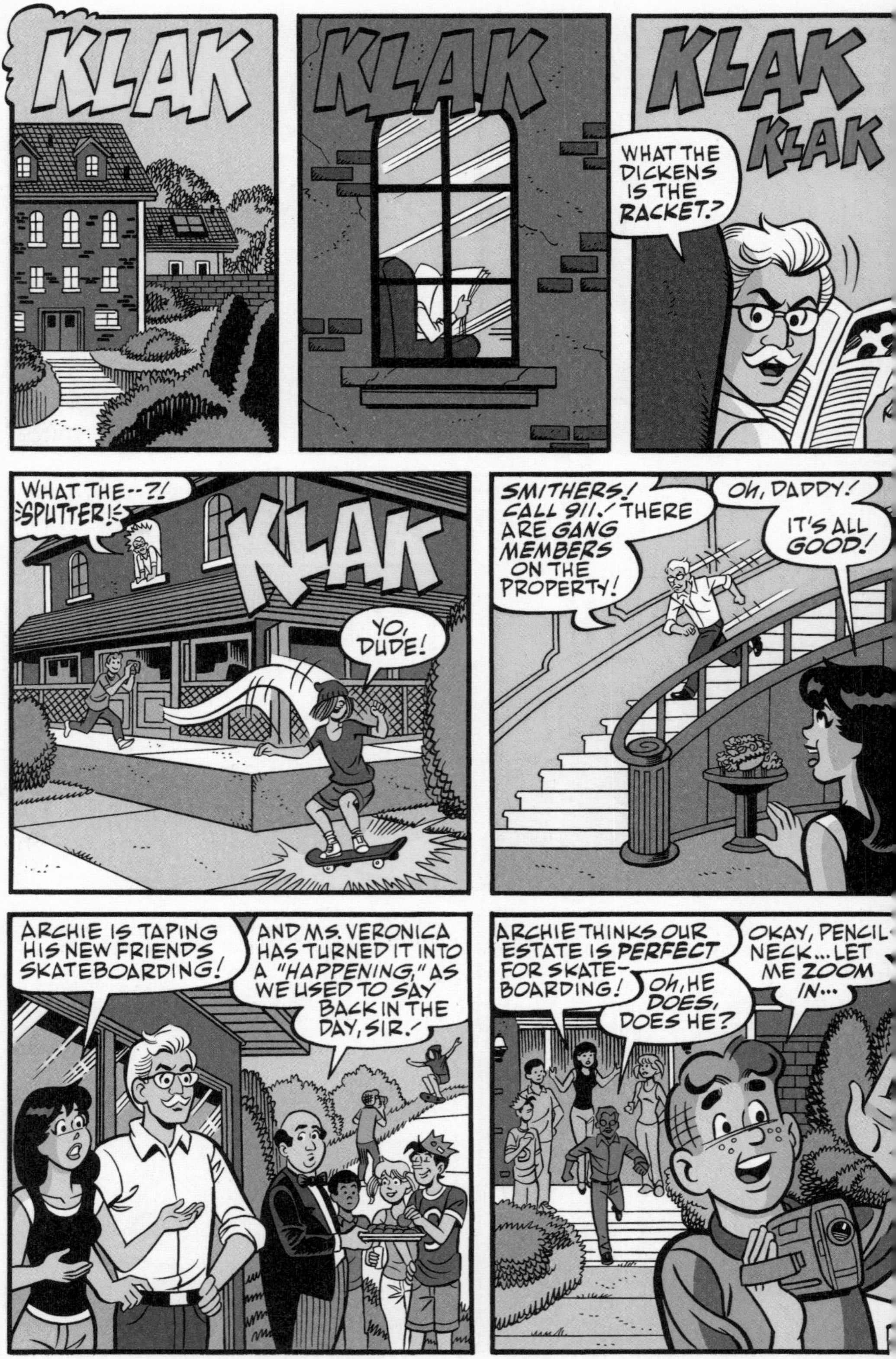
KLAK
KLAK
KLAK
KLAK
WHAT THE DICKENS IS THE RACKET?
WHAT THE--?! SPUTTER!
KLAK
YO, DUDE!
SMITHERS! CALL 911! THERE ARE GANG MEMBERS ON THE PROPERTY!
Oh, DADDY!
IT'S ALL GOOD!
ARCHIE IS TAPING HIS NEW FRIENDS SKATEBOARDING!
AND MS. VERONICA HAS TURNED IT INTO A "HAPPENING," AS WE USED TO SAY BACK IN THE DAY, SIR!
ARCHIE THINKS OUR ESTATE IS PERFECT FOR SKATE-BOARDING!
Oh, HE DOES, DOES HE?
OKAY, PENCIL-NECK... LET ME ZOOM IN...

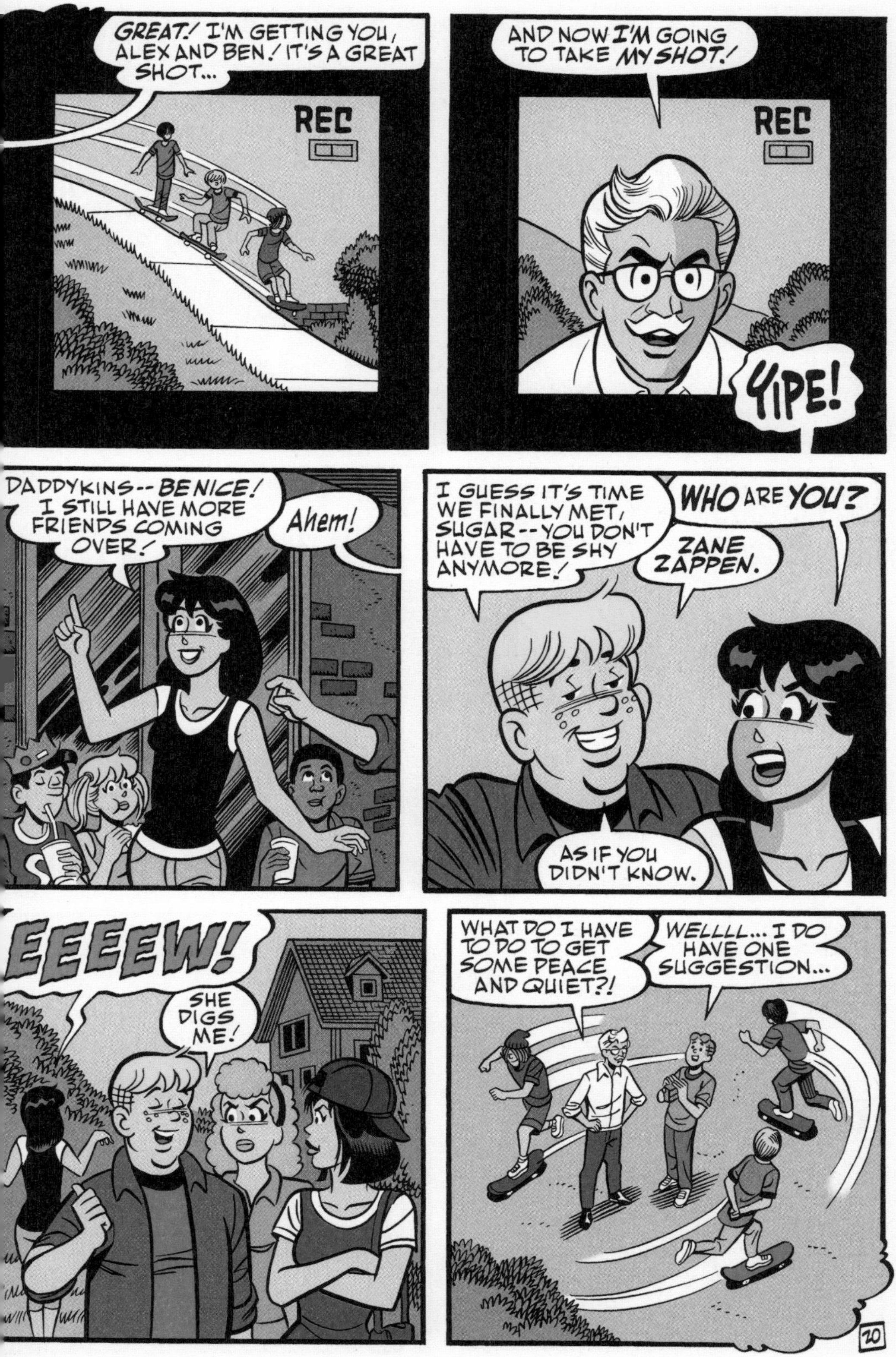

GREAT! I'M GETTING YOU, ALEX AND BEN! IT'S A GREAT SHOT...
REC
AND NOW I'M GOING TO TAKE MY SHOT!
REC
YIPE!
DADDYKINS-- BE NICE! I STILL HAVE MORE FRIENDS COMING OVER!
Ahem!
I GUESS IT'S TIME WE FINALLY MET, SUGAR-- YOU DON'T HAVE TO BE SHY ANYMORE!
WHO ARE YOU?
ZANE ZAPPEN.
AS IF YOU DIDN'T KNOW.
EEEEW!
SHE DIGS ME!
WHAT DO I HAVE TO DO TO GET SOME PEACE AND QUIET?!
WELLLL... I DO HAVE ONE SUGGESTION...
20

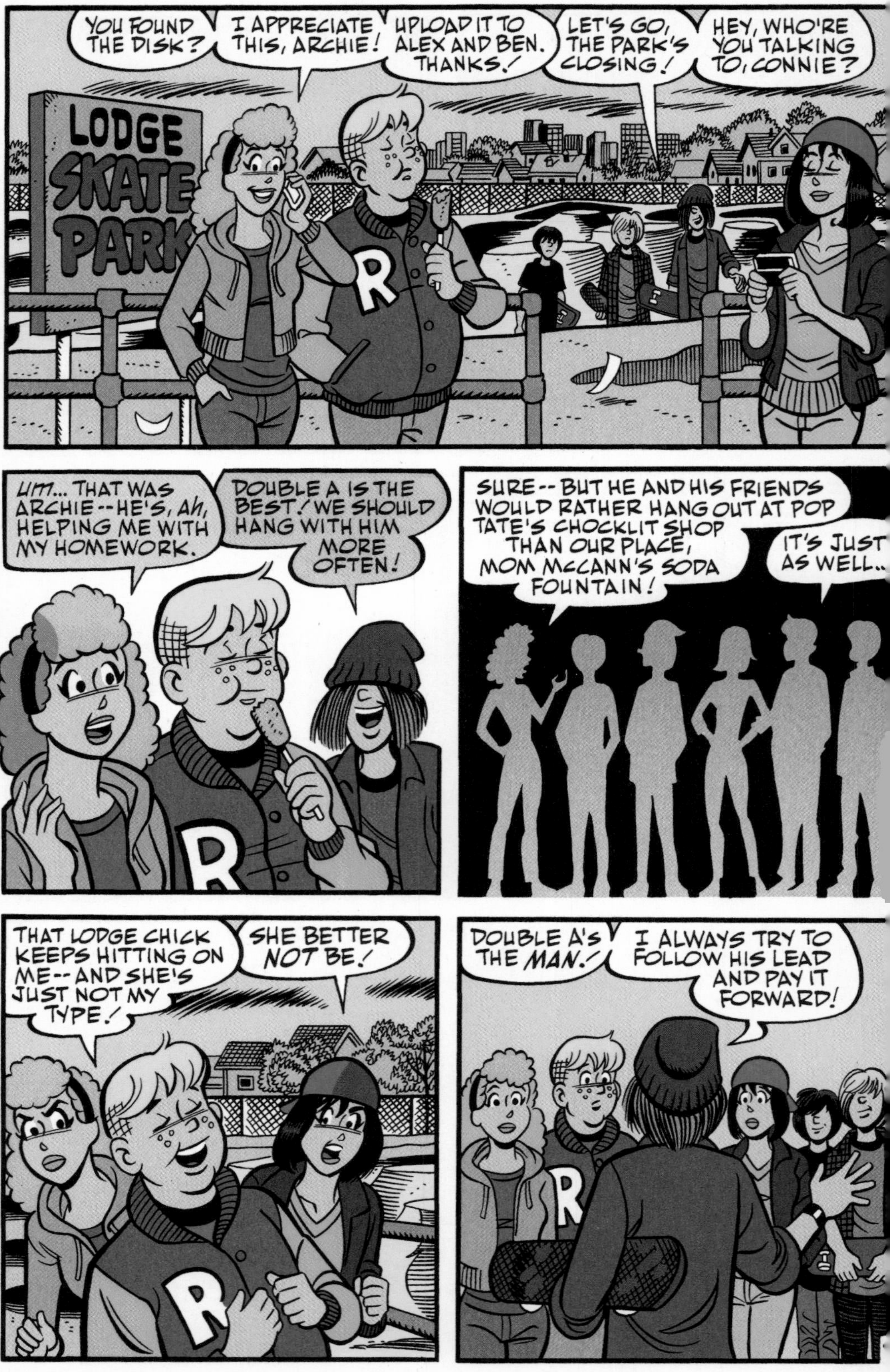
YOU FOUND THE DISK?
I APPRECIATE THIS, ARCHIE!
UPLOAD IT TO ALEX AND BEN. THANKS!
LET'S GO, THE PARK'S CLOSING!
HEY, WHO'RE YOU TALKING TO, CONNIE?
LODGE SKATE PARK
UM... THAT WAS ARCHIE -- HE'S, AH, HELPING ME WITH MY HOMEWORK.
DOUBLE A IS THE BEST! WE SHOULD HANG WITH HIM MORE OFTEN!
SURE -- BUT HE AND HIS FRIENDS WOULD RATHER HANG OUT AT POP TATE'S CHOCKLIT SHOP THAN OUR PLACE, MOM McCANN'S SODA FOUNTAIN!
IT'S JUST AS WELL...
THAT LODGE CHICK KEEPS HITTING ON ME -- AND SHE'S JUST NOT MY TYPE!
SHE BETTER NOT BE!
DOUBLE A'S THE MAN!
I ALWAYS TRY TO FOLLOW HIS LEAD AND PAY IT FORWARD!

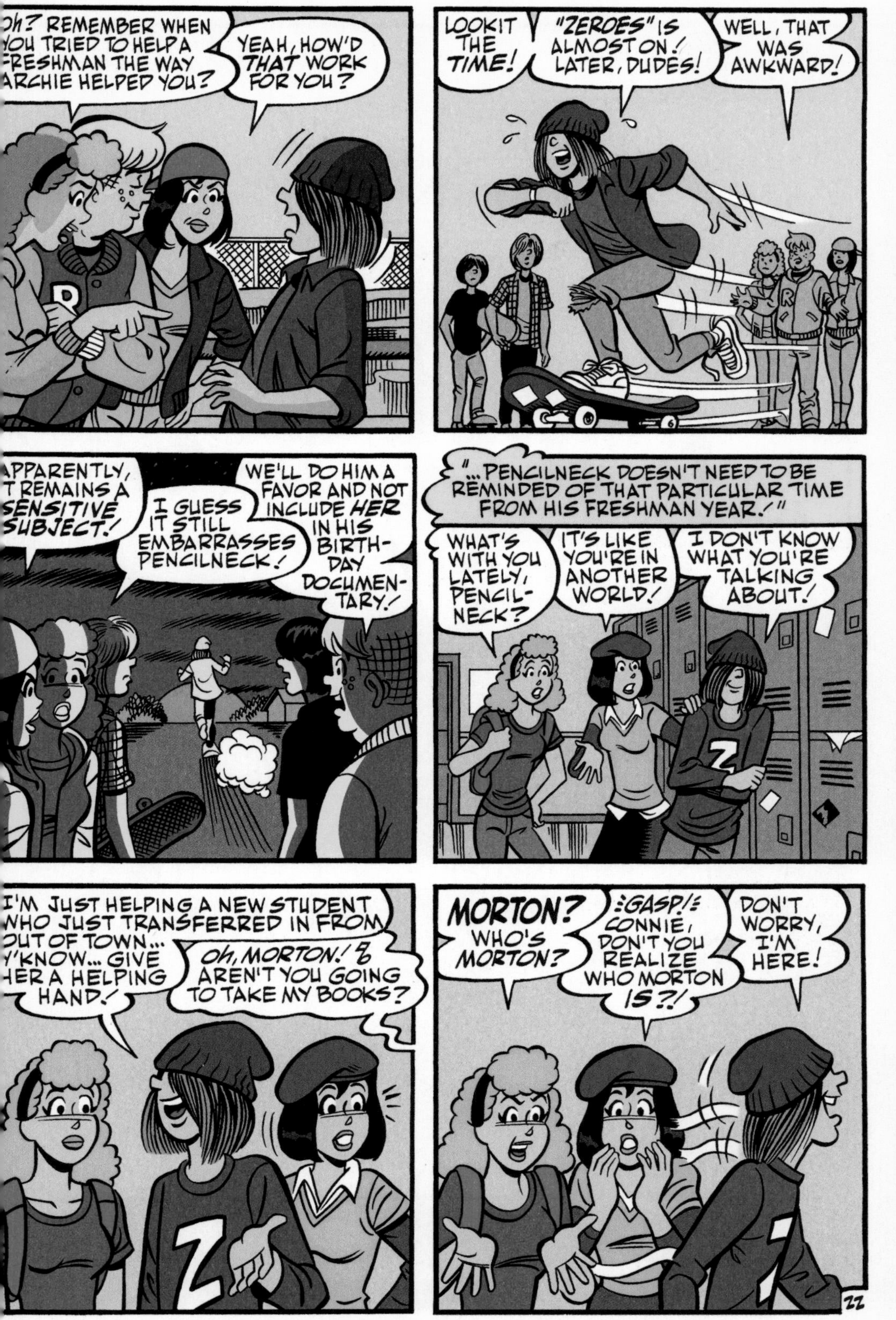
OH? REMEMBER WHEN YOU TRIED TO HELP A FRESHMAN THE WAY ARCHIE HELPED YOU?
YEAH, HOW'D THAT WORK FOR YOU?
LOOKIT THE TIME!
"ZEROES" IS ALMOST ON! LATER, DUDES!
WELL, THAT WAS AWKWARD!
APPARENTLY, IT REMAINS A SENSITIVE SUBJECT!
I GUESS IT STILL EMBARRASSES PENCILNECK!
WE'LL DO HIM A FAVOR AND NOT INCLUDE HER IN HIS BIRTH-DAY DOCUMEN-TARY!
"...PENCILNECK DOESN'T NEED TO BE REMINDED OF THAT PARTICULAR TIME FROM HIS FRESHMAN YEAR!"
WHAT'S WITH YOU LATELY, PENCIL-NECK?
IT'S LIKE YOU'RE IN ANOTHER WORLD!
I DON'T KNOW WHAT YOU'RE TALKING ABOUT!
I'M JUST HELPING A NEW STUDENT WHO JUST TRANSFERRED IN FROM OUT OF TOWN... Y'KNOW... GIVE HER A HELPING HAND!
OH, MORTON! AREN'T YOU GOING TO TAKE MY BOOKS?
MORTON? WHO'S MORTON?
GASP! CONNIE, DON'T YOU REALIZE WHO MORTON IS?!
DON'T WORRY, I'M HERE!
22

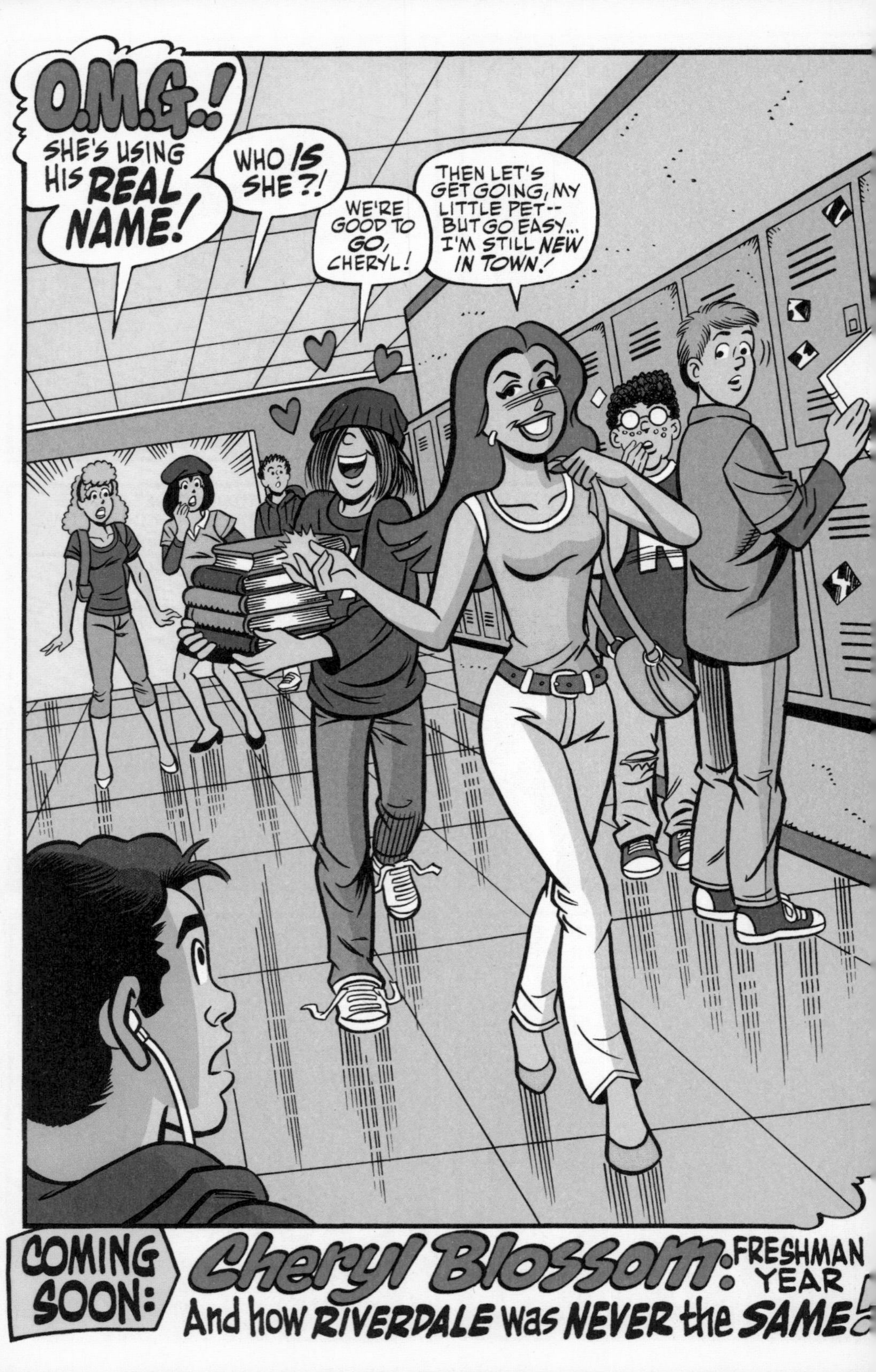
O.M.G..! SHE'S USING HIS REAL NAME!
WHO IS SHE?!
WE'RE GOOD TO GO, CHERYL!
THEN LET'S GET GOING, MY LITTLE PET-- BUT GO EASY... I'M STILL NEW IN TOWN!
COMING SOON:
Cheryl Blossom: FRESHMAN YEAR
And how RIVERDALE was NEVER the SAME!

Archie

FRESHMAN YEAR
BOOK TWO

NEW STUDENT FILES

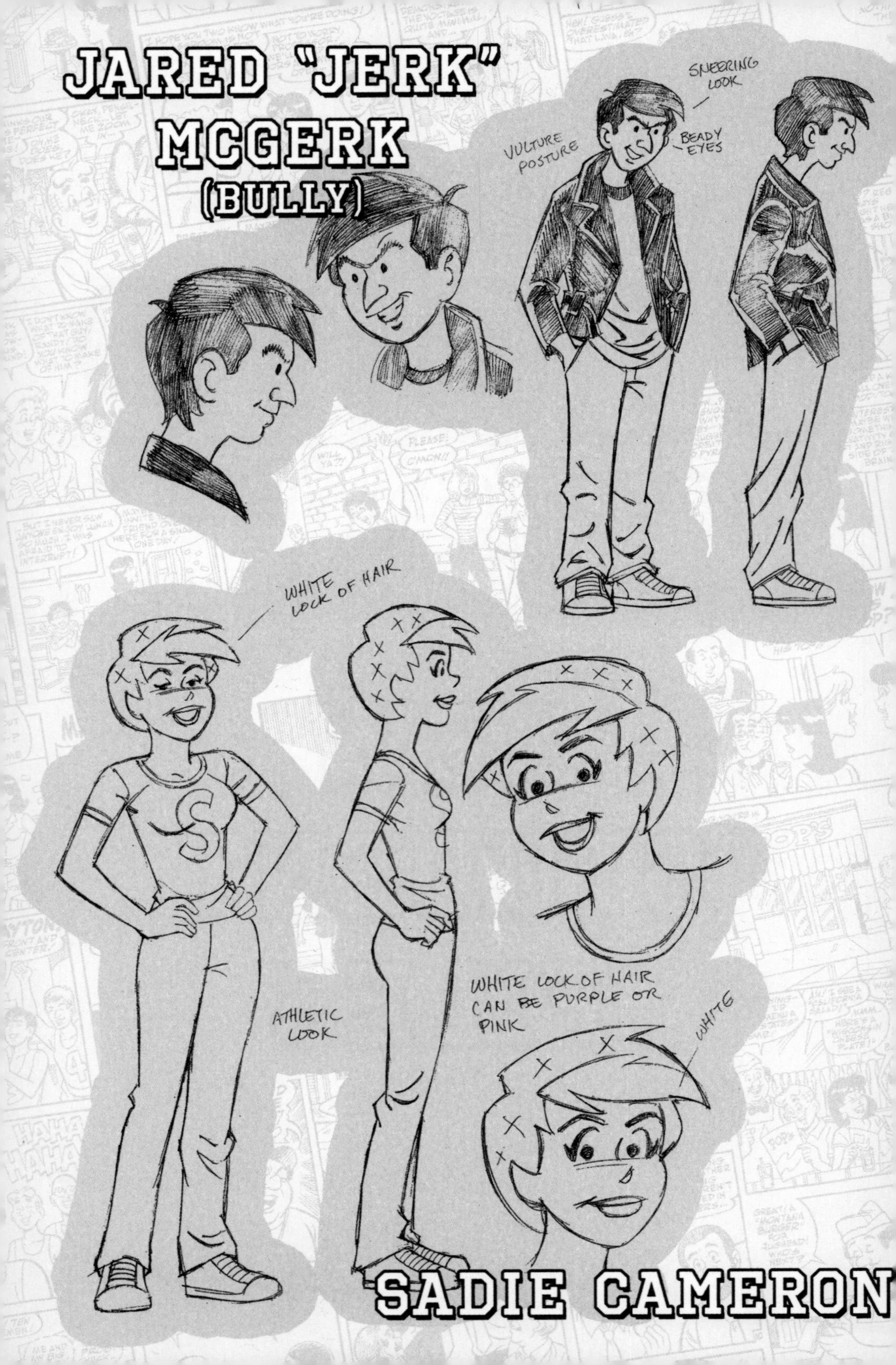
JARED "JERK" MCGERK
(BULLY)
SNEERING LOOK
VULTURE POSTURE
BEADY EYES
WHITE LOCK OF HAIR
ATHLETIC LOOK
WHITE LOCK OF HAIR CAN BE PURPLE OR PINK
WHITE
SADIE CAMERON

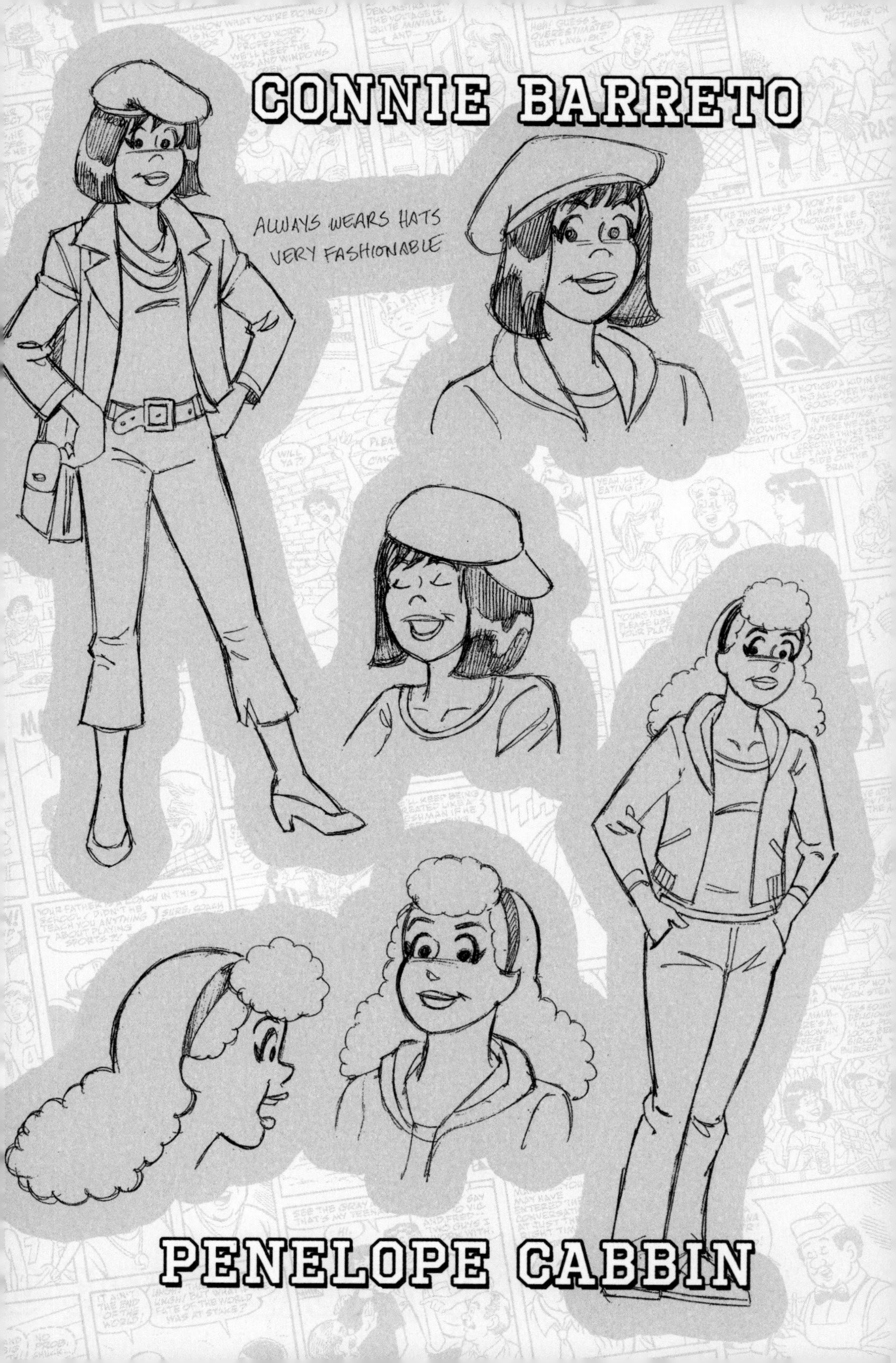
CONNIE BARRETO
ALWAYS WEARS HATS
VERY FASHIONABLE
PENELOPE CABBIN

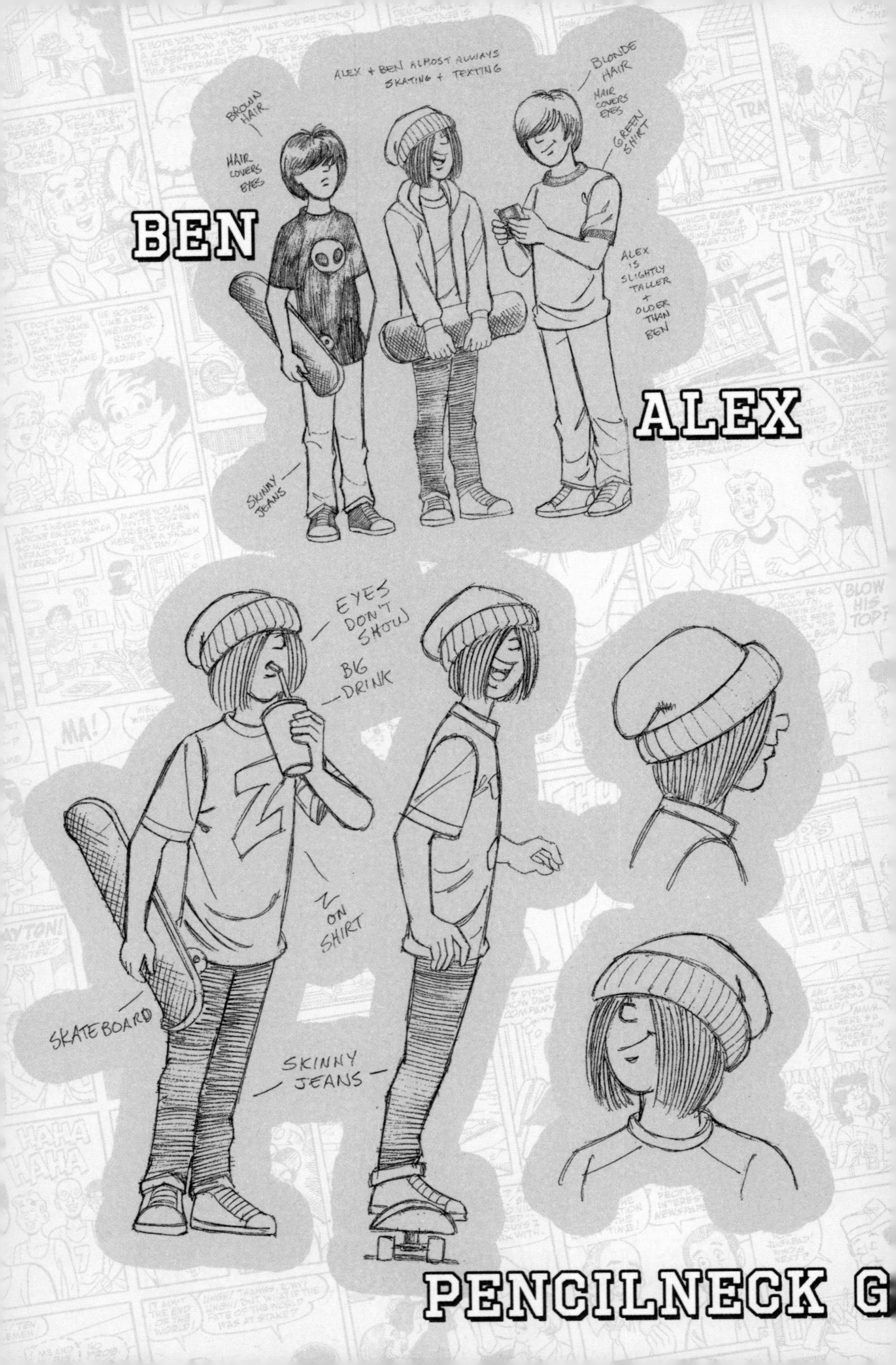
ALEX + BEN ALMOST ALWAYS SKATING + TEXTING
BROWN HAIR
HAIR COVERS EYES
BLONDE HAIR
HAIR COVERS EYES
GREEN SHIRT
BEN
ALEX IS SLIGHTLY TALLER + OLDER THAN BEN
ALEX
SKINNY JEANS
EYES DON'T SHOW
BIG DRINK
Z ON SHIRT
SKATEBOARD
SKINNY JEANS
PENCILNECK G